D1500031

THE ST. AUGUSTINE TRILOGY: BOOK TWO

Stepping Off a Cliff
Doug Dillon

Old St. Augustine Publications
Altamonte Springs, Florida

Published by

Old St. Augustine Publications
Altamonte Springs, Florida
www.oldstaugustinepublications.com

The contents of this book are a work of fiction. Although some of the events and details described are from the historical record, the majority of this work springs from the author's imagination.

Library of Congress Control Number 2011936691

ISBN 978-0-983364-3-4

Edition: November 2013

*To all those adults who guide young people
when they need help the most.*

Contents

Prologue   1

PART ONE
Awareness

1. **After the Funeral**   9
2. **Speechless and Forgetting to Breathe**   16
3. **Crime Scene Tape**   25
4. **Frozen Time**   31
5. **Predictions and Warnings**   46
6. **Seloy**   54

PART TWO
Discovery

7. **The Living Past**   65
8. **The Search**   79
9. **Gasping for Air**   87
10. **Maria Sanchez Creek**   91
11. **Proud Warriors**   100
12. **Eruptions**   109
13. **Attracted to Humans**   120

PART THREE
Exploration

14. **It's Back!**   135
15. **Flagler College**   140
16. **The Caryatids**   147
17. **A Flower for Henry**   152
18. **A Thin Stream of Drool**   155
19. **Infested**   160
20. **Damaged Forever**   165

PART FOUR
Fishing

21. **The St. Augustine Monster**   173
22. **The Slab**   176
23. **Bait**   187
24. **Setting Traps**   191
25. **Spanish Night Watch**   197
26. **The Swarm**   205
27. **Downpour**   211

PART FIVE
Information

28. **Blue Glow**   221
29. **The Creature Down Deep**   229
30. **Glittery Snakes**   238
31. **Lobo's World**   245
32. **Life Forms**   254
33. **Particle People**   267
34. **She's Waiting for You.**   275

PART SIX
Decisions

35. **What Went on in There?**   287
36. **Strategy**   295
37. **Quiet Before the Storm**   302
38. **No Long Goodbyes**   311

PART SEVEN
War

39. **Lunch Date**   319
40. **The Fight**   328
41. **Butt First**   336
42. **The Traveling Bag**   345
43. **Blessing of the Fleet**   352

Epilogue   364

Author's Notes   377

Acknowledgments   381

About the Author   384

Prologue

St. Augustine, Florida
May 15

I'm sure you probably saw some of the news reports about what happened in our city back in mid-March, right? I mean you would have to be a hermit living in a cave to miss all that media coverage.

March and parts of April around here were pretty wild and crazy, to say the least. Actually, to be honest about it, things haven't completely settled down. Government types, scientists and reporters are still looking for answers they'll never find.

Even if I told all those investigators exactly what went on, they would never believe me. Not that I intend to tell them, but I've been thinking about it—what would happen if I tried. Having firsthand knowledge about something so important and yet not being able to say anything is really hard.

So what do I do? Well, I look in the mirror and say, "Jeff Golden, you just keep your mouth shut about all that stuff. Go back to good old St. Augustine High, study hard like mom wanted you to and try to forget it ever happened."

Easier said than done.

Have you ever tried to *not* think about something? At times, the slightly overweight, blond kid in the mirror laughs at me and says, "Yeah, right."

I guess way too many really strange things have gone on in my life since I met Carla and Lobo for me to mentally put a lid on them.

Why am I talking to you about all this?

Both Lobo and Carla would raise hell with me if they knew, but I think going over it one more time with somebody who wasn't directly involved, and not in any kind of official capacity, will help me sort things out a little more. So you're elected, if you're willing. All I ask is that you keep it between the two of us. Then again, if you do tell someone, nobody would believe you any more than they would me.

Those news reports about what went on here, back in March? They only tell the final results of something that happened almost two days before all that disruption. Nobody knows about it except the four of us who were involved—me, my girlfriend Carla Rodriguez, and two other friends, old guys named Lobo and Lyle. In a way, I suppose you could say it was us who caused all that chaos in St. Augustine.

Maybe those words sound like an admission of guilt, but it isn't.

Oh man, this is so hard to explain. Look, maybe I had better start from the beginning. The thing is though, that beginning is really painful for me to talk about or even remember. But I guess you need to hear as many of the details as I can remember if you're going to get the full picture.

You see, about a week before the big event that put our city in the headlines, my mom ... died. No. She was murdered. By her boyfriend. Shot three times at point blank range. And I … I'm the one who found her.

That night before she got killed, I had dinner with Carla, Lobo and Carla's grandmother. I came home a little late because after eating, we watched an old Star Trek movie from Carla's collection.

It isn't a long walk to my place because I don't live very far away. But when I got there, I saw mom's boyfriend's truck parked in front of the house and almost turned around and went somewhere else—anywhere. Besides not being able to stand the guy, mom's relationship with him made me want to gag.

But I was really tired. So I figured I would just head straight to my room, hop into bed, wrap my pillow around my head and go to sleep. Never happened. In fact, I didn't sleep at all that night.

Right as I got the front door all the way open, Eddie, the boyfriend, smashed into me with his shoulder.

He must have taken a running start because the next thing I knew, I was on the floor, writhing in pain, trying desperately to get my breath back and hearing a truck squeal away.

The force of Eddie's body had knocked me hard against the doorjamb and back out onto the porch. I'm pretty big for fifteen, but Eddie outweighs me by at least sixty pounds. It was no contest any way you look at it.

Dazed, but finally breathing again, I picked myself up and staggered back into the house.

It was all dark in there. No wonder I hadn't seen the guy coming. By the time I got partway inside, the only light visible, besides the glowing green of both the stove clock and the fire alarm, was a thin sliver of brightness down the hallway under my mom's door.

"Mom?" I shouted, but there wasn't any answer.

Sometimes my mom, she, well, used to drink too much. On that night though, after Eddie pretty much ran over me, I had this sick feeling in the pit of my stomach that alcohol wasn't the only problem. "Mom?" I yelled even louder when I got to her door and banged on it with my fist.

In the thickening silence, I listened, hoping for an answer I was scared wouldn't arrive.

Crazy with worry, I opened the door and immediately wished I hadn't.

A silly wish, I know, but one I still make sometimes, even today. Guess it's the little kid part of me that thinks if I hadn't opened her door, maybe somehow I could have magically changed what I saw that night and what actually happened.

Yeah, a crazy kind of reaction, but welcome to what goes on inside my head.

To be honest, my mom and I weren't real close. Oh, we had some good times together, but especially after my dad's suicide a few years back, we really drifted apart. She lived her life, and I lived mine.

But still, for me to see her like that, sprawled out on her bed, face up, eyes staring at the ceiling and covered with blood, it, well, just ripped through me and I screamed.

OK. Enough of that depressing stuff. To make a really long, nasty story a lot shorter, the cops caught Eddie. He's in jail, and his trial comes up in August.

I'll be a witness, but they say the case is a slam-dunk even without my testimony. Eddie will be going away for a very long time. Knowing that has made me feel a little better, but it won't bring Mom back.

With both my parents gone, and no other close relatives to take me in, I almost ended up in foster care. Almost, but not quite. I don't know how she did it, but Carla's grandma, with Lobo's help, convinced the authorities to grant her temporary custody.

We must have made quite a sight talking to all those officials. I have to smile when I think about it.

There we were in an old southern town where some pretty nasty civil rights battles were fought back in the 1960s, and here's this blond-headed, blue-eyed white kid joining an African-American family. And arguing in our favor just like an attorney would, was Lobo, a great big Native American guy I know. He lives right next door to Carla on a little oak-shaded peninsula sticking out into Matanzas Bay.

As I said, we must have been quite a sight.

What a sweet deal the final ruling was for me though. After mom died, I thought for sure my life had ended, and I would never see Carla again. A great turnaround, huh? How cool is that being able to live with your girlfriend?

In a way though, Carla's grandma and Lobo had sort of unofficially adopted me before mom's death, so it was a very natural kind of thing when it happened. Mom used to say that I ate more meals at their houses than I ever did at home, which was probably true.

OK, there you have it, where things stood just before, well, before everything got really crazy. My mom's murder was like a lighted fuse igniting dynamite.

As much as I hoped to settle into my new life and take a deep breath, no such luck. I had lived through some really weird times with Carla and Lobo back in December, but my education in strangeness was about to take some radical new twists and turns.

Yeah, I know. It's time for me to stop dancing around this story and jump in with both feet, so here goes.

Part One

Awareness

1

After the Funeral

It felt good sitting there fishing on Lobo's dock with Carla in the quiet warmth of that late Friday afternoon in the middle of March, the day after Mom's funeral.

The horror of finding her body like I did still haunted me, but the comfort of feeling Carla's arm around my shoulders sure helped me stay balanced. Without that girl being by my side back then, I'm sure I wouldn't have made it to today in one piece—especially when I think about what was yet to come.

I glanced over at her and smiled at how great she looked, even dressed in an old blue work shirt, a pair of brown cutoffs and sandals. That type of outfit she calls her fish-hunting uniform.

Before meeting Carla and Lobo, I had never even held a fishing rod, and there I was making an accurate cast off the tip of the old guy's little peninsula out into Matanzas Bay.

In the distance though, things didn't look the way they were supposed to for some reason—not to me anyway. On the waterfront, just past our neighborhood, the grey coquina walls of the old fort—the Castillo de San Marcos—made me think of a jail for some odd reason.

Jail? Really? The thing was built by the Spanish over 100 years before the American Revolution to defend St. Augustine. It had nothing to do with jails.

And when I glanced at the Bridge of Lions beyond the Castillo, I had this feeling there shouldn't be a bridge over to Anastasia Island. That reaction made me wonder more since the original bridge was built in the 1920s. And Carla tells me a wooden one, close to the same spot, existed further back in time.

I figured all that strange stuff going through my head must be from all the stress I had been under in the last week.

"Not bad for an amateur." Carla's comment was aimed at my casting skills. "But can you catch any fish today?"

At that point, she had pulled in two sheepsheads and a seatrout to my one blue crab. By stirring up a little competition, she seemed intent on keeping my mind busy and not thinking about my mom and Eddie.

"Why work that hard when I can let you do it all?" I replied, faking a yawn.

To be honest, I was just happy sitting there with her and not having to attend school. Carla's grandma knew there was no way for me to function in my classes yet, so she let both of us stay home. St. Augustine High, she figured, could survive another twenty-four hours minus our involvement. And with the weekend coming up, she said, that would give me some more time to pull myself together.

That morning, Grandma had fixed us a big breakfast, which was wonderful as always. Can she ever cook, and no matter what, I'm always ready to eat. Those pecan pancakes and homemade sausages of hers are really something else. Carla just watched me stuff my face and shook her head. That's because besides eating like a bird, she's also a vegetarian.

Just as we were about to wash the dishes, Grandma got a disturbing phone call from a hospital in Jacksonville. Turned out her sister broke a hip.

Normally, Grandma would have been on the road in minutes, but now I figured into the picture. Yeah, me. Only a few days before, I had joined her family under the temporary custody arrangement, and that presented a problem.

Grandma was not about to take a chance the authorities in America's oldest city would take me away because she let me roam free without adult supervision.

Just as importantly, she didn't intend to allow Carla and me to stay by ourselves overnight for who knew how long. Even when we promised she could trust us, Grandma said, "That's simply not going to happen in my house." No discussion. End of story.

Grandma is a very sweet and kind lady, but she can turn very firm in the blink of an eye. I see where Carla gets it from.

The solution to both problems came when Lobo volunteered to let me stay at his place until Grandma returned. The idea of actually living with Lobo, even for a short amount of time, wasn't very appealing, especially without Carla. Of course, Grandma didn't give me a choice.

Lobo and I get along OK, but he's the kind of person I can only takes in small doses. The man can be a very tough, abrupt, controlling, and critical kind of character. In fact, when I first met the guy, we clashed, and I mean a lot. He was tough on me at the time, and I mean *really* tough. But in the end, he helped save my life and that's no small thing.

Since then, we've gotten along better than I ever thought possible.

So, yeah, I moved in with Lobo just before Grandma left for Jacksonville on that Friday afternoon. And as soon as she was on the road, Carla came over and joined me out on Lobo's dock where we fished and talked. The old guy sat in one of the three rocking chairs on the front porch of his house behind us, reading a newspaper.

With the tide on the way out, the shallower water made for increasingly poor fishing but it really didn't matter. Just being with Carla and petting her black lab, Spock, continued to make life bearable. Spock licked my hand as he often does when he senses someone is sick, upset or hurting in some way.

The hint of saltwater in the air coming from the bay and the Atlantic beyond mixed with the more putrid smell of newly exposed mud flats. My overly sensitive nose picks it all up, both the good and the bad. At times, I really wish I could turn down the volume on what I smell.

Overhead, the hazy sky was slowly giving way to heavy, dark colored clouds coming in from the west. According to the weather report, rain, wind and cooler temperatures were heading towards us. Out on Matanzas Bay, a flock of seagulls screeched, dived and fought over some kind of food people on a large boat kept tossing up in the air.

Watching the seagulls made me think of Lobo's crazy pet crow, Edgar. On his single leg, he kept jumping around on the dock near our feet hoping we would send a piece of bait his way.

Even though that bird has a nasty habit of dive-bombing my head, since the fish weren't biting, I figured he might as well enjoy himself.

To make that happen, I hoisted the bait bucket out of the water, pulled a big squirming shrimp out of the chilly water and chucked it in his direction.

Bam! Edgar flapped up into the air, caught the shrimp before it hit the dock and winged his way over to Lobo's porch.

Both Carla and I had to turn around on our bench to see where he went. As we watched, old Edgar dropped his tasty little morsel near Lobo's feet where he proceeded to alternately pick at it and flip it into the air, over and over again.

"Oooo," Carla said, her eyes flashing. She sang the rest of her words like little kids will do, while pointing at Edgar, the shrimp and Lobo. "You're gonna get in trouble." Stifling a laugh behind a cupped hand, but also giving me the gift of one of her dazzling, wide smiles, she sang it to me again. "You're gonna get in trouble."

The thing is, I got lost in her smile. So instead of responding, or really even hearing what she said, I just stood there with what I'm sure must have been a silly grin on my face as I stared at her.

"What?" she asked, arching a slender eyebrow and catching me in my hypnotic-like trance. In one of the huge oak trees around Lobo's house, a dove cooed softly.

That girl has the most expressive eyebrows. Seriously. I swear they have a whole language of their own with a whole bunch of meanings I can't always interpret. But this time those eyebrows just reflected simple curiosity.

"I was just, uh, admiring you as usual," I replied, really meaning it. But what I really wanted to say was that I still didn't believe I could be so lucky as to have such a tight connection with such a beautiful and fantastic girl. Maybe I would say it to her someday but not right then.

Physically, we make such an unlikely couple. Truly. Tall, bulky me, and slender, curvaceous Carla. I'm right at six feet and she's five-four. Her flawless cocoa skin makes my pale white surface look like the color of a dead fish you might find on the beach. And the short, shaggy blond mop that covers my head is quite a contrast to Carla's long, dark brown hair. Yeah, we are quite a pair.

"Oh puleeease," she shot back at me scrunching up her face like she didn't believe what I had said about admiring her, but down deep, I know it pleased her.

You see, that's one of the things I really like about Carla. So many good-looking girls know it and show it, if you catch my meaning. They kind of expect to be admired because they're hot and it's all they care about.

Well, that sure isn't Carla. I really don't think she understands how gorgeous she is. The best thing though is, even if she did, she wouldn't let it go to her head. Never.

"Jeff!" Lobo's bellow shook me out of my thoughts. He had folded his newspaper and put it in his lap.

When I looked up, I saw him staring in disgust at Edgar as the stupid bird continued to flip and peck what was left of his shrimp. "Stop feeding your bait to Edgar!" he shouted. "He's getting it all over the porch, and it's going to stink eventually."

As I opened my mouth to offer Lobo an apology, something stirred in the air between him and me. What, I didn't know, but it made me think of rippling water. Right after that, I had the weirdest feeling. I couldn't explain it to myself except it definitely seemed familiar somehow.

That's when I realized both Carla and Lobo were sensing something as well. I felt Carla grab my hand, and I watched as Lobo's head slowly swiveled as he scanned his front yard.

Almost in that same instant, Edgar the crow let out a squawk and flapped himself wildly up into the air until I lost sight of him somewhere in the branches of Lobo's oak trees. As Edgar vanished, Spock jumped to his feet, stared intently at where Lobo's dock met the tip of the peninsula and let out the most eerie howl you have ever heard a dog make.

With Spock continuing to howl, Lobo slowly stood up, letting his newspaper fall to the porch floor.

2

Speechless and Forgetting to Breathe

O h, dear God," Carla whispered next to me as her hand squeezed mine in an iron grip.

"What?" I asked, looking at her, but she didn't respond. Instead, she stared wide-eyed at where the dock began.

Quickly, I turned my head to see what everyone else was seeing. Still, no luck.

Feeling really left out, I let go of Carla's hand and stood up trying to find what was so interesting.

Thinking my vision must be failing me, I blinked rapidly for a couple of seconds, and then on the third blink, I saw her.

I'm telling you, as my eyes opened back up that last time, there she stood, right on the first few boards of the dock—my mom—looking just as alive as you and me but younger, slimmer and prettier than I remembered. She was dressed in her dark blue suit and heels, exactly like she was about to go to work. I watched as a slight breeze coming off the bay ruffled her long, straight blond hair. Speechless and forgetting to breathe, all I could do was stare along with everybody else.

Somehow, I knew I was seeing her the way she looked before my dad's suicide and alcohol had taken their toll. As that realization flowed through my mind, she stared right at me with tears streaming down her face, but that's also when she smiled.

It wasn't much of a smile, really, but it was enough of one for it to somehow fill me with a warmth I hadn't felt for her in a very long time.

From concentrating on me, Mom shifted her gaze out over the bay with the breeze still playing with her hair. Slowly, the smile vanished and when it did, her head whipped back around causing us to lock eyes once more. My body actually jumped with the suddenness of the movement.

Mom's eyes widened and her face contorted in what seemed like pure terror.

And as if she was being forced to face something she didn't want to see, she turned her head and pointed to the end of the dock where Carla and I sat. But just as she did that, Mom's body disintegrated into tiny sparkling pieces.

Those incredibly small specks hung there for a few seconds in a human-shaped cloud before firing straight up and finally disappearing at a height of about fifteen feet or so. It reminded me of the shower of sparks coming out of one of those firework cones or cylinders you light on the Fourth of July.

Stunned, I stood there for I don't know how long, gaping at the empty air that had just been occupied by what looked like my mom's solid form.

"Jeff?" Carla wrapped both her hands around my arm. "You all right?" Her voice was a little shaky. She had never met my mom, but she recognized her from a picture I once showed her.

I never used to believe in anything paranormal, super-natural, psychic or whatever you want to call it. Until I met Lobo, life for me consisted of the physical world as we all know it and when you died, that was it. End of story. When you're gone from this earth, you're gone for good.

Well, tell you what. My outlook changed completely in less than twenty-four hours last December when an ancestor of mine who lost his life in 1835 came looking for me. Back then, I experienced things that, especially when Carla was with me, still boggle my mind.

If old Lobo hadn't been around, I can't imagine what I would have done.

So you see, such events were anything but new to both Carla and me. I'm telling you all this because, up until I saw my mom out there on the dock, I didn't think seeing someone appear after their death could ever truly shock me, or Carla, again.

Was I ever wrong—on both counts.

Looking at Mom and watching her break into those little specs like that shook me up pretty badly. And when I turned to look at Carla after she asked me if I was OK, I saw in her eyes some of the same awe and confusion swimming through my own mind.

Did I answer Carla after she asked how I was doing? No. My mind was just so overloaded that I didn't know what to say.

Not until Lobo came up and put a big old hand on my shoulder was I able to better focus. As soon as he touched me, his familiar soothing energy rushed through that side of my body. And at the same time, Carla's healing force flowed up through my arm that she held with both hands.

I'm sure none of what I just said makes any sense, but you need to know that old Lobo is ... well ... he's a shaman. An honest to God, Native American shaman with knowledge and power you wouldn't believe—power I still don't really understand. His energy thing is wild, but it works, and it's something Carla is also learning to do.

Those energy infusions from the both of them on that day I saw my mom helped me from going off the deep end. Even after they did their thing with me though, I guess I ended up still pretty mentally numb for a while.

"Sit back down," Lobo ordered. When I say *ordered*, I mean exactly that. The old guy likes to be in control, sometimes for good reasons and sometimes not. Right at that moment though, I still felt shaky enough to follow instructions without an argument.

Right as I took my seat, Edgar the crow flew out to join us. Using his only leg, he perched on the table behind me, close to the fire pit opening. Spock wagged his tail, happy it seemed to have everyone together.

Lobo crossed his big, bare arms over his broad chest while he studied me with those piercing eyes of his. I knew what he was doing and I can sometimes block him like Carla taught me, but not that day. I just didn't have the ability to focus.

You see, old Lobo can sort of read your mind—at least to some degree. I didn't believe it at first, but I've had it proved to me over and over again. Talk about lack of privacy and being embarrassed at times.

For a man in his sixties, Lobo is in pretty good shape. The guy is big, probably around six-four or so and solid muscle. Most of his shirts have no sleeves because he rips them off. He's a woodcarver by trade and says that sleeves, even short ones, get in his way. I think his arms are just too big.

On that day, he wore a white tee shirt with different colored stick figures across the front along with the words YMCA Kids Day. Where he got that thing I have no idea. The guy doesn't have a lot of use for kids and doesn't associate much with adults either, so I knew he didn't get the shirt as a YMCA volunteer.

For all kinds of reasons, Carla and I are the only young people he seems to be able to tolerate.

Deep under shaggy, steel grey eyebrows, the man's dark, glittering and unblinking eyes seemed to drill their way right into me as they always did.

And, when I use the word "unblinking," I really mean it. I swear, I have never seen Lobo blink or even close his eyes on windy days with grit flying everywhere. Not natural, of course, but as you'll see, that's simply part of Lobo's unending strangeness.

While I looked at him, the breeze coming off Matanzas Bay sort of twirled his long hair as it had my mother's.

That afternoon, Lobo wore his hair loose, creating a steel grey frame around his slightly dark and sharp facial features, that include a prominent, but thin nose. Usually he pulls his hair together at the base of his neck with a leather strip.

As he shoved his hands into the pockets of his faded blue jeans, the man's intense gaze jumped to the air all around me.

The old guy does that sometimes. Staring so intently. It's one of the ways he picks up information about people. I don't think I understand it enough to explain it to you, but it seems to have something to do with the aura of energy around your body.

Lobo did his staring thing for the longest time, his full lips puckering more than usual. This told me he was in full analysis mode, and I felt like a patient waiting for a doctor to give me the result of some kind of lab test.

Finally, he shifted his gaze to Carla and crooked a finger at her. When she got to him, he took her down to the foot of the dock where we had seen my mom appear. Spock went with them. There, with his back turned towards me, Lobo talked to Carla, his voice unusually low so I wouldn't hear.

Their quiet chat made me nervous, especially when Carla looked back at me and then wrapped her arms around herself as if she was cold. She seemed even more worried than before.

After another minute or so, the conversation ended with the only words I was able to hear. "OK?" Lobo asked Carla.

Looking back at me once more and shrugging her shoulders she said, "I suppose, but I need to talk to him before you two go anywhere." After speaking, she sent Spock to go sit on Lobo's porch.

Before you two go anywhere?

Whatever his plan, Carla intended to add her own twist to it, and she wanted me to know that by speaking loudly. She likes Lobo a lot and really respects him, but she doesn't let the guy boss her around. Actually, she doesn't let anybody boss her around.

Without waiting for a response, she walked back up the dock towards me. In Lobo's yard behind her, a sudden gust of wind out of nowhere whipped sand, leaves and grit into a dust devil. It rotated like a miniature tornado up to about ten feet tall in not much more than a few seconds before blowing itself apart as Lobo stood there watching, as always, without blinking.

Part of me wondered if the old guy created that little weather disturbance in order to remind us both how we needed to do things his way. I didn't know if he had that kind of power, but from what I had already seen, I knew it was definitely possible.

"Whew!" Carla said as she got to me, looking back at where the dust devil had lived its short life. "That was time-ly. You're doing?" she called to Lobo in a challenging voice as he turned around to face us.

With his mostly expressionless face, the man just stood there, looking at us without saying a word. To me, that confirmed the suspicion both Carla and I had about the dust devil's origin, whether Lobo admitted it or not.

Ignoring the man's lack of response, Carla bent forward, kissed my forehead and then sat back down next to me.

"You sure know how to make a guy forget his troubles," I said with a weak smile, still feeling the warmth of her lips on my skin.

"Don't I wish," she muttered. Written all over her face was deep concern for me and shock at having seen my mother. At least that's how she looked to me.

"You do, really, help me keep my balance," I protested, taking one of her hands in both of mine. "It's just that I get a little extra worried when Lobo wants to take me off somewhere. I heard that part of what you said to him. What's going on?"

"Well, all I know is that he wants to talk with you alone for a while."

"Oh great." I groaned. A little personal talk with old Lobo, I knew, couldn't be good news.

"Mmm hmm." Carla nodded, sensing the agitation in my reaction. "You two are going to have a chat while he takes you for a walk. "

"A walk?" I said it a little too loudly. Lobo had to have heard me, but he didn't growl something back like I thought he might. "You gotta be kidding," I continued almost in a whisper this time. "A walk?" That sure didn't sound like Lobo.

"I know, it seems a little strange." Her light brown eyes were all soft with worry. "But he's concerned about you. Me too. So before you go, I want to know how you're doing after … after seeing your mom and all? I asked you before but you didn't answer. It was an incredibly weird experience for me, but it had to have been a really tough thing for you to go through." As she spoke, she put a hand on my shoulder and I melted as I always do at her touch.

"I'm, uh, not sure, really," I told her honestly. "But Carla, it was like Mom wanted to tell me something."

"I don't think there's any question about that," she said gently. "But I've got to go now. He's firing the old evil eye in my direction because he wants me to leave you two alone." Without giving me time to reply, she quickly stood, stroked my cheek with her fingertips and walked back down the dock.

As she edged her way around Lobo, he looked at me rather than her. Even from that distance, his laser-like eyes seemed to nail me to the bench. Seconds later, he crooked a finger in my direction exactly as he had done with Carla.

It was time for our walking and talking session.

"Oh man," I grumbled under my breath as I stood up and stretched. "Here we go."

3

Crime Scene Tape

On most of our walk through the neighborhood, Lobo never said a word. So much for the "chatting" part our little journey Carla mentioned. But in that silence I realized I had a lot of questions to ask Lobo about my mom's appearance. The thing is, I didn't want to be the one to speak first. Our little outing was his project, not mine. I wanted to see what he had to say first.

But when we got to Osceola Street and Lobo jerked a thumb to the right, I stopped walking. "Why do you want to go down there?" I asked, getting the chills just thinking about turning that corner.

"Why not? Lobo fired back, his rough voice full of challenge.

"You wanted to talk, so let's talk." I had no patience for any of his little word games. Not that day.

"Afraid of seeing your old house, are you?"

"Come on, Lobo, it's just too soon that's all. There's no reason to go there now."

"On the contrary. We have every reason. Your mother's warning a short time ago tells me we have no time to waste."

"A warning about what?" My irritation showed in my voice. The nervousness about going back to my house so soon was really getting to me. But Lobo's use of the word "warning" definitely caught my attention.

I expected the guy to growl some more, but he didn't. In fact, surprisingly, his voice softened a little and he said, "For several days now, I've sensed the possibility something might happen involving you and Carla, something that could get very complex and difficult, dangerous even. Your mom's visit confirmed my suspicions."

"Carla?" My mind swirled. I had almost gotten her killed back in December and the thought of her being in danger once more was just too much. "What do you mean, 'something might happen?'"

"This could involve Carla and even more people besides her. As to what could occur, I have some ideas, but I can't really be sure. What I do know for certain is that the more prepared you and she are, the better off you'll both be."

"OK, now wait." I needed to fully understand what I'd just been told. "So what is it you think is going to happen?"

Lobo shook his head. "I'm not going to tell you. If I'm wrong, you would both worry needlessly over nothing and then maybe get blindsided by what turns out to be the actual event. The most I can do is to offer you help in getting prepared for any eventuality."

"And so what does my old house have to do with all this?"

"Your mind still clings to the horror of your mother's murder as well as the surprise of seeing her spirit today. As natural as those reactions are, we need to soften them in order for your emotions to become agile enough to handle whatever develops. We are here to do just that."

"Oh," was all I could say. The man sort of made sense and I really had learned to trust his understanding of such things. Besides, if doing it his way could protect Carla in some way, I wasn't about to argue.

So that's how we ended up at 4347 Osceola Street.

Yellow crime scene tape still crisscrossed the front door as well as the four-by-fours holding up the roof covering our tiny front porch. No. Correction. My tiny porch. It was my house now with Mom gone.

I thought sure the cops would have finished their poking around inside by then, but who knew? Maybe, I figured, they just forgot to take the stupid tape down.

Mom's car sat parked in the street where she left it just before she died. In some strange way, it seemed like that terrible night happened long ago, even though I knew better. Had it only been a week?

Slowly and deliberately, I scanned the tiny yard, the cement blocks holding the little place up off the ground, the tin roof, and the faded paint job—sky blue with white trim.

Memories of Eddie and Mom flashed through my brain. Look at something specific and focus on it, I kept telling myself, but whatever you do, don't let your mind wander. Problem was, a hard knot in my stomach kept sending me other messages and I could feel my hands tighten into fists.

"Relax," Lobo ordered. "Close your eyes. Breathe deeply. Focus only on the in and outflows of those breaths. And above all, don't fight the problem."

Not since late last December, when Lobo's instructions saved my sanity and my life, had he told me to use my breathing to help calm my chaotic thoughts and emotions.

At the time, he also pounded into my head the fact that I tend to mentally fight things I don't like, as if I was wrestling an alligator or simply running away—my two methods of handling problems. Instead of accepting whatever issue came up in my life as a reality, and effectively dealing with my reactions to it, he said, I only made things a lot worse in the end.

It took me a while, but once I found I really did have little mental switches in my head that allowed me to adjust my emotional reactions, like he said, it made all the difference in the world.

No, I hadn't forgotten those lessons from the past while standing there, but as I heard his words tell me again what to do, I knew I needed the extra reminder.

Just as Lobo had taught me, I shut my eyes, breathed deeply, focused on my breath and told myself over and over to relax and not fight the problem. Believe it or not, in seconds I could feel muscles in my neck, shoulders and stomach begin to loosen.

"Now," Lobo continued, "with your eyes still closed, reach out and move your hand around until you find a strip of the crime scene tape. After that, all you have to do is just hold onto it."

Going along with the old guy's instructions, I extended my right arm and moved my hand up and down until I finally touched the tape. As I grabbed it, the stuff felt super thin and very slick, almost unreal somehow.

Right as I had that thought, I found myself walking up to the house at night, exactly as I did the night mom died. A few seconds later, I became another Jeff watching as the first Jeff went through all the pain and horror of getting hit by

Eddie, stumbling around in the darkness and finally finding Mom.

All the time I watched the first Jeff, I felt so sorry for him, knowing what was going to happen, what he was going to find. I wanted so much to help that poor guy, make it better for him, stop the pain and horror before it became real, but it all happened too fast.

I only got to him as he opened Mom's bedroom door and together we stared at her blood covered body.

As bad as that scene was for me to view all over again, I knew it had to be infinitely worse for the other Jeff. As he began to scream, without even thinking, I reached out and put my hand on his shoulder.

Now, you might think what I just said was the weirdest thing you have ever heard but it isn't so strange to me. You see, before that day with Lobo at my old house, I had experienced seeing myself on several different occasions and I'm not talking about using mirrors.

Once was right after having an accident on my bike when I seemed to leave my body and look down on it. In fact, that was the day I first met Carla and her grandmother.

Another time was when Lobo and Carla were trying to help me deal with the ghost of my ancestor. That's when I saw another Jeff right outside the Athena restaurant on the sidewalk in downtown St. Augustine. Yeah, it freaked me out, but I got freaked out even more right after that when I ran into two actual physical doubles of Lobo.

Being around that old guy definitely exposes you to the weird and strange. But up until those events, I would have labeled anybody who told me such stories as crazy. Maybe you think I'm crazy, and if you do, I understand. That just means you haven't been there—yet.

Lobo says all people can have doubles given the right circumstances. Some you can see, some you can't. Some you can touch, and others, your hand goes right through them.

Can you understand now, why, when I was with the other Jeff in my, our, house, I wasn't really surprised?

Right after I touched the first Jeff and he screamed, I found myself standing again outside my old house with my eyes open holding the crime scene tape.

Feeling a hand on my shoulder, for a split second, I thought the hand was from even another Jeff. And that seemed comforting for some reason, like a huge weight rapidly lifting off my body, allowing me to breathe more deeply.

Slowly, my fingers release the tape, and the knot in my stomach just ... went away. At the same time, a single tear ran down my face. Seeing mom's body again and watching myself scream in horror had taken its toll.

Yes, weird, but that's what happened.

It took me until that moment though, to recognize the hand on my shoulder was Lobo's. Only when he saw that recognition did he let loose of my shoulder.

He stared into my eyes for a few seconds, his good old unblinking, fiery gaze. Nodding slightly, he said, "Good. Now you're ready." Telling me nothing more than that, he turned around and walked away, waving me to join him.

4

Frozen Time

After our visit to my old house, I hoped we would head back to be with Carla, but no such luck. Where we were going next, I didn't know and Lobo wouldn't say. In fact, again, he wouldn't speak at all no matter how much I tried talking to him.

Of course with Mom's appearance, and what Lobo had to say about it, my mind kept running away with itself. The old guy's words about some kind of danger had me imagining all kinds of possibilities until we arrived at San Marco Avenue.

When we got there, he directed me to sit with him on some concrete and wood benches facing the street right in front of the Firestone tire place.

The single lane of cars on San Marco heading into downtown St. Augustine was a lot heavier than the traffic in the lane flowing the opposite way. The sounds of all those engines and whispering tires washed over me like noisy, irritating waves.

More tourists than usual strolled around on nearby sidewalks, checking out the little antique shops and other stores lining the street. Extra people in town and lots more cars than usual, I figured, probably meant another weekend full of special events coming up in America's oldest city.

So there we sat, me and big old Lobo in his sleeveless YMCA shirt.

Seconds later, the traffic rushing towards downtown slowed and came to a complete stop. Soon, the flow in the opposite direction dwindled and quickly dried up as well. It looked like an accident or something closer to downtown had caused the interruption both ways.

Finally, Lobo decided to say something. "OK, Jeff, what do you see?" He looked straight ahead towards the other side of the street.

"What do I see?" I wondered what exactly he meant and where the conversation was going.

Without moving his head, he replied with the usual Lobo sharpness to his voice, "You heard me! What do you see in front of you?"

Heaving a big sigh, I listed for him everything in my line of sight: cars; people; street; sidewalks; stores; signs; and trees.

"You missed something. Living creatures other than humans. Look closer."

Living creatures? It took a little more concentration, but I eventually I found them. Dragonflies. Lots of them. With bright green bodies. Probably forty or fifty. Right over the stalled traffic in front of us. Some were hovering and others zipped here and there. They reminded me of the dragonflies on two of Lobo's old-fashioned Tiffany stained glass lamps back at his house.

"Some people call dragonflies Mosquito Hawks." Lobo realized I had found what he wanted me to see. "They are one of the finest predators on earth and eat hundreds of mosquitoes a day. Those little creatures haven't changed much in their basic structure during the 300 million years or so they've been around. They didn't need to. Their particular type of wings allow them to fly in all directions, even backwards. And their multifaceted eye structure allows them to see in all directions."

"And I need to know all this, why?" The last thing I wanted was a National Geographic lecture.

As if I hadn't spoken, Lobo continued. "Dragonflies are swarming creatures, like bees, and they tend to migrate in huge numbers. Observers estimate one such vast grouping near here at Crescent Beach in 1993 contained about 200,000 individuals. Very intelligent little beings, they are endlessly curious about people. Watch them."

OK, humor him, I told myself. Just go along with what the guy wants you to do even though it's silly. The sooner we get this over with, the sooner I get back to Carla.

I didn't see anything unusual right away, just hovering dragonflies that occasionally raced all around so fast it was hard to follow them for long.

But as I watched, I noticed some of the things swoop down, stay in place over certain cars or trucks, and shift again only to hover right in front of windshields headfirst. It almost looked like they were trying to see inside. Some even circled cars, while others followed people walking on the sidewalks or window-shopping.

"See what I mean about curiosity?" As Lobo spoke, something happened to the dragonflies. Every one of them lifted straight up into the air just above the line of traffic and quickly came together in a dense group that looked to be maybe ten feet in diameter.

For a few seconds, the weird looking ball of green bodies and fluttering wings hung there like some sort of giant living thing. But as I watched, one after the other, individual dragonflies exploded from the swarm and rocketed right at Lobo and me.

At first, I put up my hands, certain they were going to hit me square in the face, but that didn't happen. Instead, each of the insects sheared off at the last second and ended up creating a new flight path, this one, a tight oval going completely around the benches where we sat. In seconds, all of the dragonflies were orbiting Lobo and me, their bodies flashing an iridescent green and the sound of all those wings a constant dry rustle.

My head spun, trying to look in all directions at once, but through it all, old Lobo never moved a muscle. Next to me, he stared straight ahead just as he had been doing since we sat down. "Don't worry," he said, "they don't bite."

As soon as Lobo spoke the word, "bite," the entire swarm sort of unwrapped itself from flying around us, and in a long fluttering stream, flew high over San Marco and its stalled traffic towards downtown until they disappeared.

I know I sat there for a while with my mouth hanging open, wondering what had just happened. As I glanced at the idling cars in front of us, I also wondered if anyone else had seen the actions of those dragonflies.

Several drivers I saw were staring in our direction. And one guy, whose window was open, kept shaking his head as if he couldn't believe his eyes. I knew exactly how he felt. Behind him, horns started honking because whatever caused the traffic back-up into downtown had gone away and his car was the only one left blocking all the rest.

Suddenly realizing he needed to pull forward, the confused man put his car in gear, squealed his tires and raced down the street. The flow of traffic on both sides of San Marco went back to where it was when we first sat down.

"You did all that with the dragonflies, didn't you?" I asked Lobo. "That was anything but natural."

"You give me too much credit." He still stared straight ahead. "Besides being intelligent and curious, dragonflies are at times drawn to heightened psychic energy just like we're giving off right now. They see it as we would see heat waves rising from the distant surface of a street on a hot day and they feel it as a slight tingling in their nervous systems."

Part of me wanted to ask him how he could possibly know any of that, but a bigger part just accepted what the man had said. There were times, I knew, not to question Lobo's ability to see way beyond normal human awareness.

"Some Native American lore says the appearance of many dragonflies is a sign of coming change and enlightenment." Lobo turned to look right at me with his eyes flashing. "You've already had a lot of change in your life since Carla introduced us in my workshop, haven't you?"

"No kidding." Was that ever an understatement. "At the time, you said I had problems buzzing around me like yellow jackets."

"And so you did, but you had the courage to face what you must, head-on."

Wow, I thought, a rare compliment from Lobo. "Yeah, and almost got Carla and myself trapped in my ancestor's self-created spiritual hell or even killed." Thinking back on that time though, I had no doubt that Lobo's guidance helped us to survive.

Through all of those experiences, I came to believe in the existence of worlds beyond the one most people know and abilities all people have right beneath the surface of their awareness whether they ever learn to use them or not.

"But survive you both did," Lobo replied to my unspoken thoughts. "And you were changed in the process. You and Carla have continued to mature at a much faster rate than most teenagers do, whether you know it or not. This has to do with changes in body chemistry and brain configuration that I won't even begin to explain."

Mature? Me? I couldn't believe what I was hearing.

"True, Carla was way ahead of you when you first met her, but your multiple and intense interactions with other realities has made a tremendous difference in you specifically. It isn't just me who sees this change. Carla and her grandmother remark on it all the time. Your self-control, your ability to think more clearly and your better decision making are quite evident."

The man's words continued to be so different from the critical way he treated me when we first met that I didn't know what to think.

"This increased maturity also comes out in both your verbal and written communications.

"As you know, I've read a few of the reports you've done in school as well as some of your essays. It isn't any wonder you're getting excellent grades where you were failing before. Like Carla, you already had superior intelligence, but it is increasing at a rapid pace.

"The one thing that strikes me above all others, however, is that you now read everything you can get your hands on from novels to nonfiction subjects that interest you. When we first met, you rarely read anything."

STEPPING OFF A CLIFF 37

I had to admit he was right about my reading. But as I thought about it, I realized how I was no longer the same mixed up kid who moved to St. Augustine back in November. My head was definitely screwed on a little tighter than it had been before.

"Um, OK, thanks for the kind words," I said, needing to respond to the man's comments somehow. "But to be honest, Lobo, it isn't like you to give me compliments. What's this all leading up to? Back at my old house you talked about something that may happen and now you're talking about progress in school?"

Lobo gave me one of his grunts and swung his head to look back at the passing traffic before replying. "If something does happen involving you and Carla, as I think it might, it will be unlike anything you have ever seen in your lives. Whatever you have experienced with me, so far, will pale in comparison. For both of you, it will be like stepping off a cliff."

Cliff? His words stirred my fear of heights to life. In his eyes, I saw the clear attempt to get me to focus. A sinking feeling in my stomach told me he had done a very good job.

"Now that I know you're really listening, look at the flow of vehicles in front of you and tell me what you see." Lobo had gone back into his active teaching mode.

Oh great! I wasn't really in the mood to have him quiz me again like he did with the dragonflies, but his positive comments on my growth forced me to play along with him. So I shifted my gaze back to San Marco Avenue as directed and I told him what I observed. "There are cars and some trucks." A bearded guy without a helmet rumbled by on a big old Harley. "And a motorcycle or two."

"Uh huh. Look again."

This time, the traffic changed midstream into ... I don't know, I guess you would call it a fast moving parade of weirdness. That's the only way I can describe it.

On top of a huge flatbed truck coming our way, there was a large commercial barbeque grill with a guy holding up a plate full of food in one hand and pointing towards it with the other. As that odd sight roared by, the delicious scent of cooking meat slid up my nose.

Going in the opposite direction, a shiny new convertible passed by with Carla at the wheel and she waved. *Carla?* "What the hell?" I asked of no one in particular, but the parade was just beginning.

Right after I spoke, another flatbed truck went by and this one had my old house on top of it with all the crime tape fluttering.

Mom drove a Harley past us, looking extremely scared. *My Mom!*

And not giving me time to recover from that appearance, my dad drove by going the opposite direction in a cab with this vacant look on his face. I hadn't seen him since just before his suicide.

"Lobo," I said, "how can all this be happening?" None of what I was seeing could be possible, I knew, but it looked so real.

Lobo didn't answer, but I hardly noticed as an RV went past us with Carla's grandma sitting on its roof in one of her kitchen chairs. In her hands, she held a flagpole with a flapping flag attached that said, "Grandma's Soups."

Another Lobo rode a horse that made sharp, clattering sounds as its hooves hit the street.

On and on it went with scenes of people, places and crazy things from right out of my life's history and then they repeated, over and over again. I sat there hypnotized, my eyes shifting rapidly back and forth until Lobo finally said something.

"Jeff?"

"Um, yeah?" I replied, still too fascinated to take much of an interest in what Lobo wanted by that time. I was certain he had to be creating what I was seeing somehow, but I couldn't stop staring.

Lobo spoke to me again, his voice a very distant rumble against the traffic noise. Although the man sat right next to me, he seemed very far away, and frankly I didn't care. I was having too much fun. "What?" I asked, not really trying to hear or understand.

"Do you see the convenience store on the other side of the street?" he said, louder this time.

Oh, I knew it was there, but it took a lot of will power to tear my gaze away from the wild parade going by in front of me. "Sure," I said, sneaking a peek to watch Carla again rush past in her convertible. I seemed to be lost in a strange waking dream.

"OK," Lobo said, "now read me what that big sign in the window to the left of the door says."

Nodding my agreement, I stole a quick glance at the store through a space between two cars, but once again that flatbed truck with the barbeque rumbled by, and it smelled so good. "I can't read the words," I said, but I hadn't tried very hard. Not really.

"Jeff, listen to me. What you are seeing are repeated fragments of your thinking I am making visible to you. That's all they are. No matter whether they are good or bad thoughts, none of them are real. They are just that— thoughts—things you *create* in your brain.

"You don't ever have to be captured by what flows through your mind ever again like you are right now. You are not a slave to your thinking and emotions unless you allow it. You know this because of what you experienced with your ancestor back in December. Just focus on that sign in the store beyond the traffic and you'll see what I mean."

When Lobo mentioned being a slave to what my mind creates, I didn't like that. No way, I told myself. Even though I knew he had to be creating those weird images in my mind somehow, it was hard to tear my attention away from the weirdness rolling by in front of me.

After trying and failing three or four times to read that sign, I got very frustrated and wished strongly I could just stop the flow of traffic so I could do as Lobo asked.

Right as I had that thought, the wording Lobo wanted me to concentrate on in the store window across the street finally snapped into focus. And instantly, the parade of strangeness passing in front of me evaporated, bringing back the usual cars, trucks and motorcycles.

And as I recognized each letter on that sign, the traffic in front of me slowed more and more. A few seconds later, I was able to read the words to Lobo. "Lottery Tickets inside!"

As soon as those three words came out of my mouth, the flow of cars and trucks stopped dead. I mean it didn't continue slowing down. No, it instantaneously ceased moving and so did all sound.

There was no movement anywhere except Lobo sitting there, looking at me and nodding slowly. Not a leaf moved on any of the trees. Even the clouds seemed pinned to the sky. Two crows no longer flew directly overhead. They stayed where they were in mid-flap of their wings as if hung up there by strings. Tourists on the sidewalks held whatever position they were in when I said, "Lottery Tickets Inside."

The air around us felt heavy, syrupy like and very familiar.

"Well done," Lobo said, shattering the total silence as he got up from the bench.

His voice filled the air all around us like a thunderclap. Even his footsteps, as he walked the short distance over to the curb, sounded super loud.

After surveying the inactivity on San Marco, Lobo continued talking almost as if nothing had happened. "Frozen Time. It's an interesting phenomena isn't it? Not that you haven't seen it before."

"This is your doing too, just like the dragonflies," I replied, startling myself with my own voice. Thing is though, he was right. I had seen it before.

Turning to me, he said, "When it happened to you the first time on the battlefield in your ancestor's dream world, you were astounded. And when it happened to you in my truck once, you found it interesting. Now, it's almost like an old friend, isn't it?"

After looking around again for a few seconds, I realized I couldn't disagree with the guy. "Frozen Time," as Lobo had just called it, was weird, but I had definitely seen it before.

"Come here," he ordered, as he stepped out onto San Marco Avenue and walked over to stand right between both lanes of stilled traffic.

I didn't like the idea of walking out in the middle of where cars and trucks had just been whizzing by, but I did it anyway. And when I got to Lobo, he directed me to look all up and down San Marco. In both directions as far as I could see, nothing moved. Nothing.

"You did this," Lobo said to me, "not me. Your talent is raw and unrefined but you're getting there."

"Aw come on," I protested, "you can't be serious."

"On the contrary, your experiences with Frozen Time up to now, including this one, were all caused by you. Up until now, only a deeper part of you controlled it on an unconscious basis, but that has just changed. With what might be coming your way, you needed to be fully aware of this ability. That's why I staged this little demonstration."

"But how did I—"

"How did you get such an ability?"

"You opened yourself up to such development by having that little bike accident a while back. That event shook up your brain in ways that allowed you to start perceiving many things that the average person can't.

"Then when you add to that all those intense connections you had with your deceased ancestor in December, as well as your association with both Carla and me, you get this." When he said the word "this," he swung his arm outward in an openhanded, flowing motion that included all of San Marco Avenue in its cocoon of unmoving silence.

"As I've told you before, every human being has unlimited potential in many such areas but they're seldom released. You're looking at an example of it right now."

Standing there in the middle of the street, I found it incredibly hard to believe I was the cause of everything and everyone around me looking like a stop-action segment in a TV football game.

"How far does this Frozen Time thing extend?" I asked in awe.

"There's no clear-cut answer I can give you on that. It's much too complex to explain. What you need to know, however, are the basics of controlling this ability. It might make a real difference to you, and soon.

"First of all, never let your thoughts and emotions dazzle you like they did as you watched that wild parade go by. If you do, you'll never be able to use Frozen Time effectively.

"Remember to start by focusing on your breathing and of course, don't fight the problem. Then do just as you did today, concentrate intently on making everything stop.

"This does get easier every time you do it. Keep in mind though that Frozen Time only lasts for short periods—shorter when you're new at it. Now, to undo what you have created here, you just concentrate on the reverse and think about everything moving again. Very simple, really."

As Lobo spoke, I bent over and stared at two people in a grey and black Mini Cooper about ten feet behind me—a man and a woman, probably in their thirties.

"OK, I understand, but what if we touched any of these people?" I asked, fascinated by the possibilities of what I was seeing. "Would they feel it?"

"No. During periods of Frozen Time, all living things around you become solidified in a manner that makes it impossible for them to be impacted in any way. You could take a hammer to a leaf from any of the trees around here, for example, and do no damage.

"But if you wanted to speak with those two people in the car and you concentrated hard enough, they would awaken.

"That, however, is something you don't want to do just now. They're not prepared in any way to deal with what we're experiencing. You might give them heart attacks or mental breakdowns."

"Oh," I replied, becoming increasingly aware of the incredible responsibility I now possessed in addition to having such a powerful ability. The more I thought about it, the more I wondered if I would know how to use it properly. Reading my thoughts, Lobo said, "You wouldn't have gotten this far if you didn't possess that capacity. It's sort like a built-in fail-safe mechanism. It comes with the territory."

"Really?" I asked in wonder, especially after all the hard times Lobo had given me since I first met him. Before replying, he motioned me to follow him as he walked off the street and back to the benches.

Once we were seated again, he growled a response to the one word question I had just asked, "Don't get the big head. I didn't say you were perfect," Now, that was the old Lobo I remembered.

"One other thing," he continued. "At the exact moment you create Frozen Time, you also create a bubble around yourself of about six feet in diameter. Anyone within that bubble, just as I was, is automatically excluded from the phenomena, after a short lag time of a few seconds. That is unless you wish it to be otherwise. Eventually, you will be able to include or exclude anyone within that bubble by simply intending it to happen."

Looking at the timeless world all around me, and listening to old Lobo talk, really made my mind spin. As I tried to make sense of it all though, one question kept coming up so I had to ask it. "OK, there's still one thing I still don't understand. Just … exactly how and when would I use this ability?"

From looking out at the motionless traffic on San Marco, Lobo turned his head and fixed me with one of his most intense and fiery stares. "You'll know when the time comes," he said. "You'll know."

5

Predictions and Warnings

Traffic noise came rushing back on San Marco as soon as I focused my mind and concentrated intently on everything moving again—exactly as Lobo instructed me to do.

Like the man said, it wasn't hard, but when action returned to the world, all those sounds really startled me and I don't just mean the cars, trucks and motorcycles. Suddenly things I hear every day and take for granted sort of, well, gently exploded inside my head as if I had never experienced them before.

Leaves rustled loudly in the trees.

Those two crows above Lobo and me called their buddies up the street and they answered.

Church bells rang in the distance.

A small plane droned lazily high overhead.

A train on the other side of nearby U.S. 1 rumbled through the city going opposite the direction of the flying crows, its horn blasting.

It felt so weird, all of it—the Frozen Time stuff and right after it happened, that eruption of everyday sounds. I wanted to just sit there for a while and think about those experiences. And part of me wanted to take the time to fit them in with Mom's appearance and what happened at my old house. Too much had occurred too quickly and my mind couldn't absorb it all.

Instead of having my little think fest though, Lobo and I walked a short distance up San Marco. He wanted to get dinner for all of us and take it back to his house. I'm usually ready to eat at any time, but when the guy mentioned food, I couldn't seem to wrap my mind around the idea. I had way too much going on inside my head. Even so, as soon as we walked into Borillo's, and I caught a whiff of pizzas baking, my stomach started rumbling.

After getting our food, a neighbor of Carla's gave us a ride. In no time, we were back at Lobo's place instead of having to walk all that way with our bags and boxes. Speaking of Lobo's place, that house, Carla keeps telling me, is one of the oldest in St. Augustine. It dates back to the second Spanish Colonial Period, well over 200 years ago.

Lobo's home looks old, no doubt about it. The white plaster covering the coquina stone walls of the first floor are all stained, chipped and cracked. And the unpainted boards that make up the top floor look ancient enough to possibly be the original wood from the days of the Spanish. With those display cabinets full of ancient weapons and arrowheads in his living room, Lobo's place always reminds me of a sort of living museum.

As soon as I saw the old guy's dock in front of the house when we got back from our walk though, the memory of Mom appearing out there flooded my brain. While we were in Borillo's and on our way back to the neighborhood, I had been able to tuck the details of her visit away in the back of my mind.

What exactly was she trying to tell me? I asked myself, as I recalled Mom pointing at the dock. The dock? What kind of warning could that be? None of it made any sense.

Just as we were about to walk onto Lobo's front porch, Edgar dive-bombed my head again. This time though, he was able to yank a clump of my hair with his only claw.

"Get out of here, crazy bird!" I yelled as he flew off a short distance. Finally, Lobo opened the door and I quickly escaped right behind him into the hallway that runs the length of his house.

While balancing the pizzas in one hand, I shut the door with the other just as Edgar returned trying to harass me some more. I saw a blurred version of him outside on the porch, flying past all that stained glass.

Stained glass. I tell you what, Lobo's door contains more of it than wood. Carla says it's an authentic work by Louis Comfort Tiffany, old and valuable. I never thought of a door, even one with stained glass, as being a work of art, but that just tells you what I know about such things. Before she mentioned the guy's name, I had never heard of Tiffany.

Anyway, after watching Edgar's fuzzy image finally disappear, I froze, my gaze locked onto one particular part of the door's central scene. It seemed to sort of leap out at me—like it was brand new or something. Of course, it wasn't. I had gone in and out of the same door countless times looking at that same item as well as the others there, but just then, it took on a whole different meaning.

You see, set in a bunch of mostly glass ovals is a picture showing a wolf at night, sitting on top of a cliff, howling at a full moon with the Orion constellation above him. A cliff! As soon as I saw it, Lobo's words slammed back into my mind from the talk we just had—about the danger Carla and I might be in and how what we might be facing, would for us, be "like stepping off a *cliff*.

As I stared at the picture and inhaled the musty smell of Lobo's old house, it almost seemed as if I could actually hear the wolf howling. Howling and mourning the future loss of two teenagers who had gone over the cliff to their deaths. The fact that the word *wolf* in Spanish is *Lobo* didn't help. There were just too many coincidences. Coincidences that Lobo always told us often had hidden meanings.

With a shiver running up and down my spine, I tore my gaze away from the door and saw Carla standing in the arched opening to Lobo's combination dining and living room.

"It's about time, you two." Her eyes were kind of squinty and worried looking. In fact, her entire face looked like a tight mask. Not the usual Carla I know, but at least Spock was glad to see us.

That's when I realized Carla had been there all alone for a long time right after Mom's appearance, not knowing what Lobo and I were talking about. "Sorry we took so much time," I said to her. "We decided to bring dinner back with us as you can see and that's why we're—"

"Salads, drinks, pizzas, and vegetarian lasagna for the particular one in the group," Lobo said as he walked past her and put his food bags on the dining room table. Lobo's table sits in front of a huge picture window that offers a great view of the bay and, yeah, the dock where Mom appeared. As soon as I saw it, I looked away.

"Well, I'm glad you're back," Carla said, softening a little as Lobo left the room.

"You and me both,"

"So, how'd it go? Your traveling chat with Lobo that is."

"Uh, it was another weird time with our local shaman, as you can imagine." I took a quick glance out at the dock before giving her what felt like a weak smile. "I'm not sure how to even begin explaining it to you.

"We were right about one thing though. Lobo says Mom definitely appeared so she could warn me something might happen. He says whatever this event is, it could be dangerous and it also involves you—maybe even other people." I tried not to let her see how deeply my time with Lobo had affected me, but the look on her face said she saw right through my attempted cover-up. Increasingly, we both seemed to be able to read each other's emotions no matter what we said or didn't say.

Carla raised both eyebrows, took my hand and squeezed it. "Ohhh no, not again! I thought we left all that business with your ancestor behind us at the National Cemetery."

"We did but—" Down the hall, a toilet flushed giving me a chance to put that discussion and any concerns Carla had on hold for a while. "Come on, Lobo's on his way so let's set the food out." As I spoke, I pulled loose from her hand, and I hoped, from her concerned gaze.

Instead of responding, Carla walked over to the couch, pulled something out of her purse and came back to me. Seconds later, she held up a small mirror in front of my face, making me look at it. "Don't try to hide from me, Jeff. Take a look at yourself and tell me what you see."

I really didn't want to look, but I did what she asked just to keep her happy. As usual, my blue eyes stared out at me from under the short blond mop that was my hair. What a big square head you have, I said to myself, comparing it to Carla's perfect oval of a face. The contrasts between us tend to startle me at times and that was one of them.

But as I stared at myself, I also saw how I looked like a truck had run over my face. OK, exaggeration. I did look pretty worn down though, by the day's happenings—the whole week of events, actually. Even the blue in my eyes seemed a little washed out, but of course, such a thing wasn't possible—or was it? That's when Lobo walked back into the room.

"You giving Jeff some beauty lessons are you?" Lobo walked over to us and looked at the mirror in my hand.

Without missing a beat, Carla took the mirror from me and offered it to him. "Sure, can I educate you in that department as well?"

"I think I'll pass," he replied. "Besides, Jeff's hungry as usual."

I had to smile at how Carla turned the tables on him. And as I did, Lobo shot me a steely look just before turning and going over to the dining room table.

"OK, gentlemen," Carla said, flashing me a quick grin of triumph and putting her mirror away. "Then let's get at it." In no time, she had Lobo setting the table while she and I opened the rest of the food containers and cut the pizzas some more where the slices still stuck together.

You know, I think Carla is probably the only person in the world who can, on occasion, give Lobo orders and live to tell about it. Within a few minutes, we were all at the table munching away with our host talking in between bites about the incoming weather front. Yeah, old Lobo talked about the weather.

"*Mr.* Lobo, sir." Carla interrupted him, with just a hint of sarcasm. "Could you please cut the meteorology report and one of you two tell me about your little walk?" She fired a quick glance at me and went back to eyeballing Lobo.

I loved it how she emphasized the word Mr., just the way Lobo had addressed me when I first met him—*Mr. Golden.*

His eyes glittering, Lobo crammed half a pizza slice into his mouth instead of responding immediately. Chewing slowly, just to teach her a lesson, I was sure, his gaze never wavered even when he grabbed his bottle of beer and washed down that last bit of food.

Arms crossed in front of her, Carla stared back at him with arched eyebrows, waiting for her answer.

"Patience, young lady, patience," Lobo growled as he wiped his lips with a napkin. At the words, "young lady," Carla's jaw muscles tightened and she fixed him with a smoldering stare of her own. She hates it when adults call her that.

"I'll tell you," I said, also getting tired of Lobo's delaying, lesson-teaching tactics. So for the next fifteen or twenty minutes as we continued to eat, and with Lobo eventually helping, I told her about the walk he and I had taken. So between the two of us, she got it all—Lobo's statement about Mom's visit as a warning, his sense of a coming and possibly dangerous event, the visit to my old house, the dragonflies up on San Marco and lastly, my experience with Frozen Time.

As we finished, she looked at me in disbelief, her eyes wide. "Frozen Time? It was you who did that? On the battlefield back in December?" Her expression seemed to say, "My, my, look at you."

"Jeff's ability to freeze time and your ability to manipulate matter and energy," Lobo told Carla, "might well be needed if indeed this warning by Jeff's mother proves valid."

"Lobo," Carla said. "You keep talking about this warning from Jeff's mom combined with your own perceptions about an event that could occur, but you won't tell us what you know. Come on! The more we understand, the better prepared we'll be."

You go, girl! She was so on target.

Looking at me for a second and then back at Carla, Lobo spoke in his good old schoolteacher-type voice. "No matter what you both think, receiving that advanced information from me could absolutely do more harm than good.

"Besides, the future is never set in stone. Predictions and warnings, whether they come from me, other people, or from the spirit realms, are just educated guesses about the countless possibilities in the vast shifting potentials of existence. And for all of those reasons, I won't tell you. After tonight, you both simply have to go on with your lives in as normal a way as possible."

"Live normally?" I protested. "Are you kidding me?"

"Since when do I kid?" Lobo growled, his stare all icy. I'd heard similar words from him before. Yeah, I knew better than to ask that question. I just didn't like him making something so hard sound so easy. My response to the man shot out of my mouth before I could stop it.

"OK, fine," Carla said. "But can you at least give us some small idea about *when* this event, whatever it is, might occur?"

"Soon, if it is going to happen at all." Lobo's eyes looked almost as if they were spitting sparks. "If, however, nothing occurs by next weekend, it will all have been a false alarm."

6

Seloy

The sun had set and it was rapidly getting dark over Matanzas Bay. Lights on the far shores and on the bridges to our left and right twinkled as the beam from the lighthouse on Anastasia Island flashed over St. Augustine.

When I glanced at that familiar scene through Lobo's picture window from his couch, I wondered how Carla and I could attend school on Monday and go on with our lives as normal, the way Lobo suggested. Life had been anything but normal since my mom died. Just who the hell did he think he was kidding?

Realizing I had lost the thread of the conversation still going on between Carla and Lobo, I tuned back into it. They were sitting in the two recliners on either side of Lobo's coffee table.

"My walk with Jeff," Lobo told her, was an effort to prepare him for all eventualities. In a little while, you and I need to go out on the dock so I can do the same for you. But now, I want to share something with both of you." That's when he pointed towards his picture window where I had been looking just seconds before.

Besides the Matanzas Bay scene I already described, all I could see out there was the tip of Lobo's peninsula and his blue canoe turned upside down next to the dock. Oh, and there were the three rocking chairs that sit on Lobo's porch just on the other side of the window. I couldn't see anything out of the ordinary, but all of a sudden, Spock jumped up and went to the window wagging his tail. And that's when I heard it—a distant meowing.

"Sounds like a—" But before Carla could finish her sentence, a calico cat jumped up on a little white table sitting between two of the rocking chairs out on the porch.

"No way," Carla said, her voice full of disbelief.

The orange, black and white calico sat there staring at us through the window, its tail curling back and forth in the light coming from Lobo's Tiffany lamp hanging above the dining room table. Spock started whining and his tail wagged even more than before.

Slowly, Carla swung her gaze away from the cat and with a startled expression asked Lobo what was just about to come out of my mouth. "Seloy?"

Nodding, Lobo got up from the table and walked out into the hall. He opened his front door, and in came the cat, Seloy, the one who died over two years ago.

One of the many things that happened to me soon after I first met Lobo was seeing the ghost of his long lost cat when Carla couldn't.

At the time, I didn't realize the thing no longer lived as it walked around Carla and laid down on Lobo's couch right next to her. That was my introduction to "seeing into other worlds" as Lobo might say. This time though, Carla and I both saw Seloy.

Looking as solid as anything else in Lobo's house, Seloy bounded into the room only to run into Spock heading full steam to meet her. The two collided, or should I say, came together, in the middle of the hall.

The thing is, Seloy went right through Spock as if he didn't exist. The poor dog came to a screeching halt, not understanding where Seloy had gone.

Before Spock could figure out what happened, the cat jumped up on the back of the couch and down again onto the cushion next to me. There she curled up, and looked all around the room with her bright, yellow eyes. Those actions were almost an exact repeat of what happened the first time I saw Lobo's pet.

By then Spock had tracked Seloy down and gave her such a good sniffing that for some reason it caused him to sneeze. When that happened, poor Spock whacked his chin on Seloy's couch cushion.

When I think about it, that scene was pretty funny. But at the time, Carla and I didn't laugh. Being so startled by the whole thing, and with the atmosphere so serious, we just sat there and gawked at a cat that was no longer alive.

Seloy didn't even flinch when Spock sneezed. And for whatever reason, Spock simply lost interest, went over in the corner, laid down and pulled himself into a tight ball with his back to us. According to Carla, Spock and Seloy enjoyed a great friendship, once upon a time.

"I've invited Seloy here this evening," Lobo said, walking over to the cat, "because you both need some relaxed, yet attention-getting instruction. Instruction that will lessen the startle effect in case you do end up confronting something during this next week—something very few other human beings have ever encountered."

I didn't like the sound of that statement. At all. He was giving us just enough information to scare us some more but without details.

"Look, Lobo," Carla said, not taking her eyes off Seloy. "If Grandma finds out you've been conjuring spirits, there's going to be a big problem."

"Conjuring, by your grandmother's definition," Lobo replied, "means calling the spirits of people, not animals. Even if she did mean animal spirits, which I truly don't believe she meant, the potential for tremendous harm befalling you both far outweighs your grandma's viewpoint. You just leave her to me."

"You had better know what you're talking about."

"Tell me Carla," Lobo replied, ignoring her concern. "Would you like to pet Seloy? You used to love to do that, sitting there in front of the fire." Without waiting for a response, Lobo pulled the coffee table away from the couch and out at an angle between the two recliners to provide easy access to his cat.

"Pet her?" Carla brows arched as high as they would go.

"Yes, go for it."

After a slight hesitation, Carla walked over to the couch and squatted on the floor in front of Seloy. With a slowly waving tail, the cat just sat there next to me, looking at her. Carla slowly reached out her hand but as she did so, her fingers partly disappeared into Seloy's body.

I'm telling you, Carla pulled her hand back faster than I have ever seen her move.

That reaction reminded me of what happens when a person touches something really hot.

Carla wasn't burned but she inspected her fingers in amazement.

"Your turn," Lobo said, looking straight at me even before Carla had time to fully recover from her experience.

Fascinated but now knowing what to expect, I extended my right hand and saw it also disappear into what looked to be a very solid cat. I could feel nothing but the couch cushion under my fingers—the fingers I couldn't see because of Seloy. "That is so cool," I said, pulling my hand away.

"You have both now experienced the insubstantial nature of Seloy's standard spirit body, Lobo said. "Try it again, Carla. My little kitty longs to feel your touch."

"Hi Seloy," Carla said, surprising me with how casual she sounded. "I've missed you." Once again she put her hand out toward the cat. This time though, she definitely made physical contact. When her fingers didn't disappear, she turned to me with a huge grin like a kid with a new toy. "I can feel her," she said with excitement in her voice. "Come on Jeff, try it."

"OK, here goes," I replied as I slid a hand over the top of Carla's until I felt cat hair around the edges. "Wow!" I smiled, moved my fingers away from Carla's and stroked the silky fur of a long-dead cat.

"What you are feeling is not the actual cellular structure of a living being of course," Lobo said. "But it is a temporary and indefinable solidity caused by a different frequency variation in the cat's essence. She has many from which to choose. You are able to touch her for two reasons.

"One is the simple fact that you can see her. The other is because she wishes you to see *and* touch her. Not many people have ever participated in an event such as this one.

Just as Lobo finished speaking, Seloy jumped to her feet, startling both Carla and me. A split second later, she ran right over my lap and launched herself impossibly high in the air. That cat actually sailed right over Lobo's vacant recliner and the dining room table beyond.

With her paws extended in front of her and tail flying, she went right into the glass of the picture window, but didn't break it. And she didn't come out on the other side either. I swear, it looked like the glass just absorbed every bit of her. It reminded me of how another ghostly being did the opposite by trying to emerge from the very same window back in December. But that's a story for another time.

Even with Seloy gone, Carla and I kept staring at where she had hit the glass. Something about Lobo's window sure seemed to attract unusual visitors.

"I won't attempt to give you an explanation of what you just saw." Lobo spoke in a rumbling, loud voice that shook us out of our trance. "Like many such things, it's too complex, and in this case, it simply has no importance."

Carla got up from squatting on the floor and sat next to me on the couch in the middle of what Lobo was saying.

"The true value here lies in the experience itself. For you to witness and accept such an incomprehensible event as valid, without understanding how it occurred, will inoculate your minds even further against the impact of what may yet enter your lives."

Lobo's words seemed to make sense in a vague sort of way, but all I could do was look once more at where a long dead cat I had just petted disappeared into a pane of glass.

"OK, folks," Lobo bellowed, "the show and lecture are all over. Time to wake up." His voice felt like an electric shock, and out of the side of my eye, I saw Carla's body jerk.

"Carla!" He picked up a couple of the empty soda cans from the dining table. "You're with me out on the dock—without Spock. Jeff, you have kitchen duty." Without waiting for a response from either of us, he went into the hall and flipped switches turning on the porch floodlights and the ones on the dock.

Carla looked over at me, exhaled a big puff of air, shrugged her shoulders, and told Spock to stay where he was. Without any further conversation she and Lobo left the house with their Coke cans. I had already seen what Carla could do to soft aluminum so I had a vague idea of what might be going on.

For one of the few times since getting up that morning, I found myself completely alone, except for Spock. It felt really weird after what had happened in such a short time and especially so soon after Mom's funeral the day before. So I just sat there, sort of dazed, and looked through Lobo's picture window. I watched as he and Carla walked out onto the dock in the glare of floodlights—the same dock where we all saw Mom appear, looking so very real and delivering her warning. Spock watched with me and whined, wanting to be with Carla.

"Screw kitchen duty," I said. "I'll do it all later." Shaking my head trying to clear it, I glanced around the room and remembered the day I entered it for the first time.

Lobo's display cases in there held my attention almost as much as they did the first time I saw them—the circular one filled with arrowheads, spearheads and stone knives above the fireplace and the long rectangular ones full of old weapons on each side of it.

Back in December, Lobo had pulled a bayonet out of one of those cases that eventually helped lead me to my ancestor's spirit.

To my left on a small tall table, sat another one of Lobo's stained glass Tiffany lamps, this one looked like blue flowing water with bright green dragonflies along the bowl rim, their heads pointing down at the table. After my experience with green dragonflies that afternoon, I knew I would never look at Lobo's lamp quite the same again.

In front of me stood Lobo's coffee table at an angle where he'd left it after Seloy's visit. In the middle of the table sat his Ball of Realities, as Carla calls the thing. It's about six inches across and made out of Mammoth tusk, one of Lobo's exotic carvings. Wood and ivory carving is what he does for a living.

It's called a Chinese Puzzle Ball, actually, white, with two dragons carved all across its surface. Large holes in the ball lead to increasingly smaller, separate balls below the surface of the original one—twelve balls in all. It's really something.

Lobo flipped that ball to me soon after I met him and used it to help me understand how, below the surface of life as we know it, there are an infinite number of other worlds, other realities—some of them the realms inhabited by the spirits of Seloy, my parents and Carla's folks.

"And now, Mom, what?" I asked her out loud as chills ran up and down my spine recalling her appearance that afternoon. "What is it you saw out there on the dock?"

By then, the possibility of both Carla and me having to face the challenge of some other unknown, described by Lobo as possibly dangerous, was really giving me the creeps, as well as a dull, sick feeling in the pit of my stomach.

Wanting to divert my attention from all that anxiety and wondering what Lobo and Carla were up to, I looked through the picture window once more. They both stood there at the end of the dock under the bright flood lights. Lobo seemed to be saying something to Carla and pointing towards the Coke can in his other hand. A few seconds later, he threw the can up in the air.

Uh-oh, I thought, one more time. Carla once showed me that human beings definitely have abilities beyond the normal. I watched in awe on that day as she lifted an empty Coke can into the air and crushed the thing into a very flat disk using only the power of her mind.

This time as I watched though, I saw the can wobble upward maybe eight feet or so and silently explode in a brilliant flash of white.

It was like watching a very powerful and unusual camera flash. "Damn!" I said as my eyes adjusted. "What has he got her doing now?"

Part Two

Discovery

7

The Living Past

I think the best way for me to explain this next little twist in my story is to fast forward to that next morning, the day after Mom's appearance. Actually, the "twist" I'm going to tell you about isn't little at all, but you'll soon see what I mean.

Carla needed to be at the St. Augustine Historical Society's Research Library by 10:00 AM to work on a project for her AP history class, but she didn't want to walk or bike through the cold and wet. Rain and quite a bit of wind still hung on over north Florida after a storm front moved through the night before, chilling things off enough to at least require wearing jackets or coats. Without her grandmother around to act as chauffeur, Carla talked Lobo into driving her in his rusty old pickup truck.

She intended on doing her research alone, but I decided to join her. After Mom's warning and Lobo's talk of something possibly happening, I wasn't about to let her out of my sight. Going on as normal with our lives in the face of possible danger had its limits as far as I was concerned.

Lobo drove us downtown as promised and let us out on King Street at the plaza next to Potter's Wax Museum.

By the time we got there, the rain had stopped. That left us with just a quick walk down Aviles Street to the library. Like many of the streets in downtown St. Augustine, Aviles is narrow and often clogged with cars as it was on that day. Balconies jutted from the old buildings, many of them decorated with flowers and other kinds of plants.

"I don't know about this," I said to her, looking around as we walked under the coquina and wood street entrance. Even though I volunteered to go with her to the research library, I started getting nervous. "No matter what Lobo says, it seems to me we should just hide out with him for a week instead of being out in public."

"Jeff, I've got to look this information up now. Today is the only Saturday the research library is open until next month and that will be too late. Besides, either you trust Lobo's judgment or you don't. And if you don't, maybe you'll feel safer if you go back to his place."

"Wait, wait just a minute. I'm here because I'm worried about you being out alone, not because I want to come downtown and roam around on a cold, rainy day. Besides, after what we've both experienced with Lobo, you know that just about anything can happen."

"Yes, I do," Carla replied. "And if you'll recall right after Christmas, when we could have died, we were sitting right next to Lobo in the National Cemetery. What good did he do us then? You see my point? He said to try and go on as normal with our lives and that what I'm going to do."

I hate to admit it when she's right, probably because she is right much of the time. But at that moment, I couldn't escape her logic. "Yeah, well, OK, you win—this time." I zipped the dark grey sweater she wore against the March chill tight up to her throat. "At least stay warm, will you?"

"That's a deal," she replied with a satisfied grin. "So tell me, did you get wet after you walked me back to Grandma's place last night?"

"Not too much." On my way back to Lobo's house, it started to sprinkle. And by the time I crawled into bed, thunder and lightning made it difficult to sleep. Wind and heavy rain blasted the window in the storeroom where Lobo had set up a cot for me. I lay there wide-awake for the longest time watching the bright flashes light everything up all around me as I thought about my mom and her warning.

"You gonna tell me now what you and Lobo were doing out there on the dock?" I asked. The night before, she had refused to say anything, putting the blame on tiredness. "I saw what you did to one of the Coke cans Lobo threw up into the air."

That stopped her. I mean she actually stopped walking.

"You weren't supposed to see my little training session." She stared straight ahead. But after a few seconds, she turned to me, sighed and continued in a hesitant kind of voice, very unusual for Carla. "Lobo was, well, trying to train me to … um, disrupt matter at a subatomic level."

"What?" I understood her words, but had no idea what that really meant.

"Sounds weird, huh?" She nodded her head as we continued walking. "Believe me, I hear you."

"Yeah! Like right out of Star Trek or something." Carla and I both love to watch videos of those old TV programs and the Star Trek movies.

"Lobo says it's the next stage in helping me deepen my control over those poltergeist happenings in our house that used to drive grandma and me crazy. From what he said, my continued training might help if your mom's warning turns into reality. How, I don't know. He wouldn't explain."

"Typical Lobo. He'll only tell you just so much and only when he's ready."

"True, Jeff, but what I was doing last night is just way too much power for one person to have. I know Lobo says I'm ready for it, just like he says you're ready for a heightening of your abilities, but I'm not so sure."

"Who's not trusting Lobo now?" I used her own logic to help her out, even though I had similar feelings about my own Frozen Time ability.

"Besides, part of your power, like Lobo's, is a calming, relaxing and healing energy that can benefit people. I felt it from both of you yesterday when my mom's visit shook me up so bad and you both grabbed me. And remember what you did to help my ancestor at the end of last year? Keep all that in mind."

"I don't know. But right now I've got a project to do, and we're already here." Carla jerked a thumb back at a three-story, light grey colored building behind her. "The Segui-Kirby House. It was built in 1764. It's been restored and serves as the research library for the St. Augustine Historical Society."

"OK then, let's do it." We had just left trying to understand the almost overwhelming strangeness of our situation for another time.

"Follow me," Carla said, leading the way through the arched entrance to the building, around a corner and up a wood staircase. The varnished banister slid easily under my hand.

As soon as we got to the second floor, we ran into Millie, a heavyset, elderly lady with white hair. She turned out to be the Senior Research Librarian and one of Carla's many friends.

Millie quickly got us signed in while she and Carla carried on a conversation about a recent discovery in Guatemala and how that would have fascinated Carla's parents if they had lived.

Listening to that conversation made me realize that many of the history loving citizens of St. Augustine might have known Carla's parents. They had been prominent archaeologists at the University of Florida. Both of them died in a plane crash down in the Yucatan several years ago. That's how Carla came to live with her grandmother.

Millie pointed to a large table at the end of a long room, surrounded by other tables, bookcases and file cabinets. On that table, I saw several stacks of files, what looked like oversized maps and a clump of something white.

"There you go, sweetie," she said to Carla. "We've got all you asked for lined up as usual, so just come get me if you want anything else. Whoops, I have one more thing I meant to show you but forgot. I'll bring it out in a few minutes." With a wave, she walked back to her office at the far end of the room.

"So you really want to be my research assistant, huh?" Carla asked as we walked over to the table with all the files and maps on it and sat down.

"Absolutely," I replied. I wasn't particularly interested in the focus of her research that day, but I wanted to help her. "What can I do?"

"Well, like I told you before, I'm looking for information on the nineteenth-century hotels of St. Augustine—even the ones that don't exist anymore. So if you could find the best pictures of each place I have on a list that would be great."

"I can handle that. Where do I start?"

Carla pointed to a stack of labeled file folders and handed me a typed list. "There you go. Just use the list and find pictures to match those names. Oh, and use a pair of white gloves over there next to the files when handling the photos. The library staff doesn't want the oils and dirt from our hands degrading their important holdings."

Once I got those white cotton gloves on, I dove into my assignment with a little more interest than before. It was actually pretty cool to be trusted with all those important old photos.

The thing is though, I didn't get far into the first file before I had to ask Carla a question.

The black and white picture I found was obviously Flagler College under construction, with scaffolds over parts of it but minus the huge towers you can see today from just about anywhere in town. I recognized King and Cordova Streets, but back then they were unpaved. Horses or mules walked through the dirt, pulling wagons along what looked like little railroad tracks.

Written in an old-fashioned type of handwriting at the bottom of the photo were the words, "Creation of the Ponce de Leon Hotel," followed by the date, "1886."

"Hey." I nudged Carla with my elbow and held up the picture for her to see. "This shows Flagler College but says it's the Ponce de Leon Hotel. I don't understand."

"Oh," she replied, "Flagler College started out as the Ponce de Leon Hotel. It opened in 1888. Henry Flagler built it along with the Hotel Alcazar right across the street.

That's where city hall and the Lightner Museum are located now. Old Henry, one of the richest men in America—"

Millie returned before Carla could finish, bringing with her a thick file. "Here's the little prize I kept aside for you," she said handing her the file to Carla. "What you're holding there is part of a fantastic collection of photos that has been sitting in someone's attic for a very long time. It turned out the photographer was a professional from Jacksonville who retired to St. Augustine sometime shortly after 1900.

"Since part of the collection contains pictures of old St. Augustine hotels, I thought you might like to go through it. You'll be two of the first people to set eyes on all these. Enjoy."

"Oh my! Thank you so much!" Carla's eyes were bright with anticipation as she stared at the folder in her hands. It looked like she might drool all over those pictures any minute.

As soon as Millie went back to her other duties, Carla put the folder on the table in front of us, grabbed my arm with both hands and shook me like a little kid who can't wait to open her birthday presents. "Oh, Jeff! Lobo is so right. There are no coincidences. Isn't this great? Come on, we've got to look at this batch together before we do anything else. You have the gloves on so you do the work. I'll just look."

"Yes ma'am!" I opened the folder and began gently lifting each photo from the stack for Carla's inspection. Sometimes she even used a huge magnifying glass Millie had provided.

Oh, sure, I looked at those old photos as well. But most of all, I loved seeing her so happy and excited. And for just a little while there, I forgot about my mom and even old Lobo preparing us for who knew what.

But they say all good things have to come to an end and they sure did, or at least they changed—very quickly. It took one picture from near the bottom of the stack to turn everything completely around. I think both of us figured out what we were seeing at the same time.

"Dear God!" Carla said.

"No freakin' way!" I answered.

Without another word, Carla slid on her own pair of white gloves, grabbed the magnifying glass, gently took the photograph from me and studied it intently.

"It is him." she whispered as she handed the picture back to me to study for myself.

Sure enough, especially under magnification, staring out at us was … Lobo. Yeah, good old Lobo.

He stood next to what looked like three female figures carved into a huge column of wood. And standing close to him was a very distinguished looking man with a mustache and wearing a suit.

"That's … I mean it can't be possible," I whispered back to Carla but knowing with Lobo anything was possible.

"Turn the picture over," Carla said, excitement building in her voice. Sure enough, as usual, she knew what she was doing.

There on the other side of the photo were these words: "Henry Flagler in the rotunda of the Ponce de Leon Hotel previous to its public opening in January 1888. Next to Mr. Flagler is the primary carver of the hotel's exquisite oak caryatids." But nowhere did it mention Lobo's name.

"I've heard two different stories about who carved the caryatids but not this one," Carla said, almost too loudly.

STEPPING OFF A CLIFF 73

"What's a rotunda?" I flipped the picture back over. I thought maybe the picture itself might give me a hint as to what that word meant.

"It's a circular room, usually with a dome over it like they have over at the entrance to Flagler College."

"Oh," I replied, only vaguely interested. Lobo's being in that picture is what had me really stumped. "It can't be real. Somebody's pulling a fast one on the library. They probably digitally enhanced the thing somehow."

"I don't think so, Jeff. Millie said these are part of a photographer's collection from those days. See how old it looks?"

"Yeah but—"

"Turn it over again."

I did as she asked. Stamped on the back, enclosed by a circle were the words, "R. J. Hanson. Photographer. Jacksonville, Florida."

After I set the picture down for a minute, Carla and I looked at the other photographs from the folder. On the back of each one, we found Mr. Hanson's stamp. All those pictures were originals, created long before computers and digital photography.

"He looks … just like he does now," I said, picking up the picture of Lobo and Henry Flagler again. "But the date on this picture would make him—"

"Somewhere close to 200 years old." Carla paused. "Wait a minute! In the 1870s and 1880s the United States used the Castillo as a jail for Native Americans from out west who were still fighting against white invaders. I wonder … " Carla jumped up, found Millie, and in minutes, we had two photo files from the days when the old Spanish fort served as a prison in the late 1800s.

"Did you tell Millie what we found?" I asked. While I was speaking, I remembered looking at the Castillo the day before and for some odd reason, associating it with a jail.

"No, I don't want to say anything to anybody, Jeff," she whispered. "I think this had better stay between us. Now let's forget for a while how impossible the idea is that Lobo might be so old. Instead, let's just see if we can find any additional evidence of him being part of imprisoned Native American groups, OK?"

"Uh, sure." I shrugged, finding it hard to believe we were trying to prove or disprove the possibility of the man's great age.

"Good," she replied, handing one file to me and keeping the other one for herself. "You see, some of those Native Americans imprisoned back in the day were excellent craftsmen and they sold what they made or carved to people in the city or to tourists.

"In the 1870s, the military even allowed some of those men out of the Castillo to work for people in town. If Lobo came from one of those groups, maybe we can find another photo of him in one of these files."

"Good idea," I replied. And without any more discussion, we started reviewing our new photo files of Native American prisoners.

Most of the pictures I saw showed proud men staring into the camera individually and in groups. I don't know, I guess I expected to see discouraged, beaten down guys ready to give up and die but that wasn't the case. Even when photos showed them wearing U.S. military uniforms and short hair, there was still something solid and unbroken in how they looked.

While glancing at the last picture in my file, the words, "He's not here," almost came out of my mouth. Almost, because something caught my eye at the last minute. It was the blurry face of a man standing well behind a group of prisoners and a bearded white soldier.

When I put the magnifying glass on the guy, his slightly fuzzy face stared back at me. Fuzzy or not it was definitely familiar. "Look at that," I whispered excitedly as I handed Carla the magnifying glass and pointed to Lobo.

When Carla saw that second photo with old shaman in it, she turned her head to look at me as if she wanted to say something. Her expression held a mixture of awe and wild excitement, but she still didn't say anything.

At that moment, without a doubt, I knew she and I were thinking the exact same thing. In her hands was even more evidence of an unbelievable and long buried secret.

"We definitely can't tell anybody about this," she whispered after staring in silence at the picture again for a long time.

"No, of course not." My mind was going in ten thousand directions at once. "But, how … how can he possibly be that old?"

Carla shook her head and laid the picture on top of the first one we discovered with Lobo and Henry Flagler. "Good question," she said. "I guess this shouldn't really surprise us though, with all we already know about Lobo and have experienced with him."

"You got that right." Memories of meeting two Lobos at one time in downtown St. Augustine last December flashed through my mind. "Could this discovery of ours be part of the big event he warned us about?"

"The timing with your mom's appearance fits, but finding these pictures sure doesn't seem dangerous."

"Maybe so, but I'll bet old Lobo knew what we were going to find when he dropped us off this morning ."

"I wouldn't put it past him."

"So let's confront the guy with these two photos and see what he says." I couldn't wait for that to happen.

"I not too sure about that." Carla's face turned very serious. "I've known Lobo for a long time and he has a way of wiggling out of things. He's likely to blow us off and say the man in these pictures just happens to look like him."

"Aw come on," I said a little too loudly. "What you're holding there would be enough evidence for a conviction in any courtroom."

"Nowhere is his name written on these things," Carla looked at the backs of the two pictures again. "Henry Flagler's name on one, yes, but not Lobo's anywhere. So, what if we could find another photo of him with his name on it?"

"And where are you going to find that?" I was getting increasingly impatient with her need to find more evidence. Sometimes Carla can be a little too persistent and precise.

Flashing a smile and her voice rising in excitement, she said, "Wait a minute! When Millie gave us the new batch of pictures from the Jacksonville photographer, she said it was only part of the man's collection. What if the rest of those pictures are here in St. Augustine and we could find just one more photo that would box Lobo in so he has to talk to us?"

"Sure, that would be great but—"

"Good." Carla jumped to her feet with both pictures in one hand and ran the length of the library, disappearing into Millie's office. That's all it took, just a few words even sounding like agreement. When she gets her mind set, there's no stopping her.

For five long minutes I waited, getting increasingly agitated thinking about confronting Lobo and trying to understand how anyone could live so long, especially without anybody knowing about it.

When Carla returned, minus her gloves and with photocopies of the two Lobo pictures safely in a file folder, I saw continued excitement in her face and heard it in her voice. With both eyebrows raised, and no longer whispering, she said, "Guess what? The other pictures from that Jax photographer are over in The Treasure Chest at the Lightner Antique Mall."

Seeing my blank stare, she realized I had no idea where the places she mentioned were located. "The Treasure Chest—it's an antique store over there in the back part of the Lighter Museum. Together, the Lighter Museum and City Hall used to be the old Hotel Alcazar. That's the other hotel Henry Flagler built here in town all on his own."

"Oh, OK," I replied, mentally zeroing in on the location. You see how hard it is to keep up with Carla sometimes? She's got all this knowledge about history and especially about St. Augustine that I get lost once in a while. A lot of the time, actually. I swear, she ought to be a tour guide.

"So you definitely want to go there now?" I asked.

"Yup," she replied with iron determination in her voice. "We've got plenty of time before Lobo is supposed to pick us up.

"What about your school project?"

"This," she said, holding up her file containing the two Lobo pictures, "is now my project. I'll do the hotel research later somehow."

8

The Search

Back outside on Aviles Street, it had begun to rain again, a light drizzle, really, but the day's chilly wind made it seem worse.

As I zipped up my old University of Florida jacket, I remembered wearing it when Carla and I got lost in my ancestor's dream world less than three months before. Memories of that terrifying time made me shiver, and I hoped nothing even close to such an experience was in store for us.

"Come on—shortcut," Carla directed, pulling me by the arm around the corner of the library and into what I would call an alley, but she called it Artillery Lane.

For a girl who didn't want to go out in the wet, she had definitely made a complete turnaround.

Cold, but light wind driven rain smacked us in the face and coated our clothes as we silently but quickly walked behind Trinity Episcopal Church and through a parking lot, finally ending up on Cordova Street. Further down on Cordova to our right sat the Lightner Museum and City Hall—the old Hotel Alcazar.

As we crossed the other side of the road, slick with the day's rain, I looked up at the huge building ahead of us and remembered it was once one of Henry Flagler's creations—a famous man from the past who might have known Lobo.

Four floors high and surrounded by brick sidewalks, it looked like it was made of layer after layer of concrete. On top were brick colored tiles and spires. Two huge towers with brick red columns also up there faced King Street. On the other side of King, was Flagler College, the old Ponce de Leon Hotel, with its huge towers and reddish roofing.

Guiding me to a fountain and onto a covered walkway with large concrete arches on either side of it, Carla finally got us out of the wind and rain. Following the walkway to the right actually took us into a part of City Hall and then out into a huge courtyard complete with plants, and a pond.

Right next to the pond sat what looked like a very large tombstone. *Tombstone?*

"That's where Otto Lightner is buried," Carla said, seeing where I was looking. "It's his collection they exhibit here in the part of the building that's the Lightner Museum."

Turned out, Carla wanted to use the restroom before going any further. Someone she knew who worked the front desk of the museum gave her access. I waited outside the front door of the place for a minute but decided there was time to do a little exploring. It seemed to me that was the best way to keep my mind busy and off those warnings from both Mom and Lobo.

To make that happen, I trotted down the sidewalk and around the side of the museum. There I found another large fountain and walkway with arches like what we had just seen on the other side of the building. As I watched the fountain squirt straight up in the air, memories of stop-action photographs I'd seen on TV flooded my mind. And that made me wonder if I could make the spurting water in front of me do the same thing—freeze time—without a camera. Yup, that thought came right out of my experience with Lobo and stopping traffic.

Not being able to resist that little self-challenge, and since no one was around, I sprinted down to the fountain. Its walls were brick, maybe two feet high. Painted light blue, the bottom had maybe six inches of water in it. I watched the single nozzle noisily spray large and small droplets up maybe five feet before they fell back into the blue colored pool.

Remembering Lobo's instructions to me while watching traffic up on San Marco, I looked past each droplet and stared at a central point where the water squirted from the nozzle at the fountain's base and willed the entire flow to stop. Nothing happened.

Frustrated, I closed my eyes, concentrated on my breath for a few seconds in order to relax, and pictured all the drops I'd just seen no longer moving. Instantly, all sound went away except for my own breathing and, believe it or not, I could hear my heart beating. All around me, the air got that familiar thick and syrupy feeling.

Slowly, I opened my eyes to find glistening blobs floating there in place directly in front of me—drops of all sizes. The surging water coming from the base looked sort of like a large but weird shaped icicle—going up instead of hanging down.

Seeing what I'd done shocked me into not breathing, leaving me only the sound of my heartbeat. For the first time since experiencing Frozen Time, I was alone with what I now recognized as my own creation. Unable to resist, I bent over, reached out and touched the closest drop.

What a weird experience. When I tried pushing it, the thing wouldn't move. I mean it was like pressing against a brick wall.

At first, it felt like a hard piece of very cold, smooth glass. But if I touched it for long, I had to pull my fingers away. The cold was just too intense. The sensation reminded me of what it feels like to try and hold dry ice. And as soon as I felt that pain in my fingers, normal time returned. That's when I heard Carla calling me.

"What are you doing down here?" she asked when she got to the fountain.

"Just uh, exploring." I felt guilty for not wanting to tell her about my experience with the fountain, but I wasn't sure I wanted to share that information with her yet.

"Well, you came the right way. We can only get into the Antique Mall from this side of the museum."

From the fountain, we walked down some steps, onto a driveway and then onto a brick sidewalk heading to the very back of the museum along Granada Street. There, the old Hotel Alcazar bulged out into a semi-circle with its own little brick red tile roof, a twin to the bulge I had seen before on the opposite side of the building.

The wind continued to blow, rustling nearby trees and palms, but at least, it had stopped raining, again. Even so, the air still smelled of dampness, and little puddles of water were everywhere reflecting a very dull sky.

Carla pointed out the entrance to the antique shop area just before where the building bulged outward. A short sidewalk led us there between two grassy areas to a wood door painted dark yellow with large glass panels. Above the door hung a blue and white striped awning and above that, a sign said, "Lightner Antique Mall Entrance." Nearby on the sides of the building, four large, rectangular downspouts noisily drained rainwater left over from the previous rain shower.

Inside the entrance was the biggest safe I have ever seen. The thing was huge, and I wondered if the old hotel back in the day used to keep its cash and the valuables of its guests there. Ahead, two life-sized, cutout figures on the wall, a man and a woman, looked like they were about to go swimming, but in real old-fashioned type bathing suits.

"Just so you'll know," Carla said, jutting her chin towards a large photograph on the wall to our left. "Where we're going used to be the indoor swimming pool when this entire place actually had paying guests."

Sure enough, the picture showed what looked to me like the inside of an old Greek or Roman temple, big columns and all, and with a large expanse of water instead of a floor.

"When was this built?" I asked.

"It opened the same year as the Ponce de Leon Hotel, 1888."

"And they had an indoor pool back then?"

"Kind of amazing, isn't it, for the 1800s, especially in Florida." Carla spoke as she led me to the left beyond the pictures and into another, smaller entrance that made me think of a tunnel.

After passing a couple of antique shops, we walked up a small flight of steps to our right and out onto what used to be the bottom of the Hotel Alcazar's swimming pool. The place was freakin' huge and had that same Roman temple look as I had seen in the picture.

The wide-open, green painted cement floor angled slightly downward to its far end where there was a little open-air café. Its tables were empty, probably, I figured because they hadn't opened for lunch yet. Even so, the smell of freshly brewing coffee filled the air.

"Pretty awesome, place, huh?" Carla asked, grinning. "Welcome to the Antique Mall." I could tell she was happy to see me appreciating something historic, but she still had Lobo's pictures on her mind. Of that I was sure.

"This is awesome," I replied, still trying to take in all I was seeing. On either side of the café, old-time street lamps sort of made it look like an outdoor restaurant, blending with other similar lamps hanging from the walls. And set deep into those same walls, antique shops gave the entire floor area the feeling of being a street, instead of an old swimming pool.

At the back of the café, in each of its corners, were two sets of concrete steps with curving banisters that led up to a second floor making the connection to the surrounding museum more than obvious. And behind us in the opposite corners of the building, I realized after turning around, was a duplicate of those stairs and banisters—all four were entrances to the swimming area back in the day, Carla pointed out.

A huge potted plant, sculpted into globes of green, stood a short distance in front of the café on the cement floor. On either side of the plant were two sets of back-to-back, wrought iron and wood benches.

People walked in and out of the shops or just gawked. Following some of their stares, I looked up and saw huge white columns that seemed to hold up the floor above and even another floor above that.

"This place is all part of the Lightner Museum," Carla explained, seeing where I was looking. "The arches up there in front of us belong to the Grand Ballroom from when this whole place had dances for the rich and famous. I'll take you up there one of these days. It's really quite beautiful."

"I'm sure it is," I agreed, looking, no doubt, like a tourist as I scanned everything around us.

When we arrived at the Treasure Chest antique shop, Carla groaned. A "Closed but I'll be back in fifteen minutes" sign hung from a hook on the locked door. I could feel her disappointment.

"Sorry," I told her. "Let's just call Lobo, and we'll use the pictures we have."

"No way." She looked at her watch. "The owner will be back any minute. Come on, let's go grab a seat and wait."

"You are really wanting to get that final piece of evidence, aren't you?" I asked my question as we walked over to one of the benches in front of the café and sat down. Carla set her backpack on the floor in front of her. In it was the file with the pictures of Lobo we had already found.

"Yup," Carla replied firmly, "the more pieces of this puzzle we can confront Lobo with the better. But if we somehow can't find another picture, we'll try rattling his cage with what we've got."

"How much do you really know about the old guy anyway?" I asked. "I've never been able to get much out of him about his background, have you?"

"Me? Ha! Are you kidding? Getting Lobo to talk about himself is alm—" Carla's eyes widened as a vibration rattled the entire Antique Mall. Before either of us could react, a deeper rumbling caused people in the mall to stop walking and look around, startled.

That's when it happened.

The bench where we sat, and the floor beneath us, ceased to exist. Carla and I fell screaming into the darkness below.

9

Gasping for Air

In total darkness, a swirling, thickness pulled me downward to what I just knew had to be my death.

Pressed face first into something cold, soft, twisted and rubbery, I was suffocating. Filled with panic, I pushed against the gunk in front of me with both hands and strained my neck to lift my head as far as possible.

With my mouth and nose finally free, I sucked in a ton of needed air, but that's when I noticed there was nothing behind me except a shrieking, frigid wind. It blasted from somewhere below my feet and up across my entire body. Each breath felt like little knives digging into my lungs. My jacket flapped wildly around my head, and I began to shiver.

G-force. That's why I found it so tough to move—all the rubbery crap and I were spinning downward into the howling darkness at an incredible speed. The word vortex popped into my head, and I swear, it almost felt like someone had flushed a huge, refrigerated toilet and I was going down the drain.

The only thing close to that I had ever experienced was a ride at the fair where they rotate you in a circular cage and then the floor drops away leaving everybody stuck with their backs to the inner wall.

With each passing second, my lungs ached even more and the shivering increased. Freezing to death seemed like a real possibility. A memory of stepping on ice crystals in cold darkness with Carla and Lobo at the St. Augustine National Cemetery shot through my mind, but I pushed it away. I had to concentrate on my present situation in order to survive, if survival was possible at all.

The only thing I could think of was to turn over on my back so my face didn't get pushed back down into the gunk again. It took every bit of my strength and a bunch of time, but I did it—very, very slowly.

Once more, my body sank three or four inches into the squishy cold stuff. This time though, the wind ripped across the front of me. At least I didn't have to worry about suffocating, but trying to breathe in that howling, freezing wind wasn't easy.

I knew Carla had to be in there with me, wherever *there* was. I wanted to find her, help her, do something, but I couldn't even help myself. When I shouted her name, my voice came out so weak I could hardly hear it above that roaring wind.

Just when I thought I would go absolutely crazy with fear for both of us, the circular motion slowed a little. At the same time, the darkness lifted enough for me to look for Carla and figure out where I was. That's when I finally found her, about fifty feet away but stuck upside down. She was plastered against a glistening blackness, her hair whipping across her face. The blackness extended in a curve from both sides of her all the way around to me. It had to be the same stuff I felt beneath my body.

There was nothing between us but open space. And wind. Nasty, roaring wind.

Oh God, it was so good to see her, and as I stared, she lifted a hand very slowly and gave me a tiny wave. I waved back, wanting to be with her, but I knew that sure wasn't going to happen any time soon.

Above us, the inner wall of the vortex snaked its way up into total darkness. That meant the source of light making it possible for us to see had to be coming from somewhere below. To check that out, I tilted my head forwards, again straining my neck muscles against all that G-force.

I'm telling you what, squinting into that blasting, Arctic-like wind really ripped across my eyes, but below my feet, way far away, I saw a pulsating, sparkling, circular glow. Purple in color, whatever it was, kept shifting all around, I guess because the inner walls of the vortex were constantly moving in different directions.

The longer I focused on the glow, the bigger it got and the more it seemed like I was dropping towards a million twinkling, purple stars. Or, maybe all those lights are heading for us, I thought, just as we passed through them. But when we did that, I definitely felt a slight prickly sensation start at my feet that fired all the way through every part of my body.

For a split second, my vision filled with rushing sparkles and then they were gone. I looked up and saw the glittering mass shoot up through the twisting hole above us and out of sight at an unbelievable rate of speed. That's when I knew those lights had definitely passed through both Carla and me instead of the other way around.

Right after that, I got a quick whiff of a sharp smell that I couldn't identify just before I hit some kind of liquid. The impact forced the stuff up my nose, into my mouth and into my eyes. Turned out, it was water—salt water—cool, but not cold. Definitely warmer than the inside of that terrible vortex. And yeah, I did say salt water.

At the same time, a sharp pain ripped its way into the palm of my left hand and up my arm.

Choking and gagging, I tried to swim but found both of my hands stuck in what felt like cool, squishy mud. I had to struggle to pull them loose and when I did, I was able to wildly paddle until my head popped through the surface. Surprisingly, that little swim didn't take long at all.

Gasping for air, I found I was able to stand up in the muck below about four feet of water. The gross stink of tidal mud filled my lungs as Carla popped to the surface right next to me, also coughing like crazy.

Through my blurred vision, I saw marsh grass nearby and blue sky above us. Beyond that? A few old buildings and two men about forty feet away standing on a high bank of sand looking down at us.

One guy's face was shaded by a hat he wore, but the other looked an awful lot like Lobo.

10

Maria Sanchez Creek

The next thing I remember? Sitting once again on that hard wood and metal bench at the Lightner Museum's Antique Mall with Carla next to me—both of us shedding water and mud all over the green floor and coughing.

Carla's backpack sat at her feet looking just as dry as it did when she put it down.

The smell of salt water and tidal mud still pressed its way up into my nose. My hand hurt for some reason, but it didn't seem to matter. I felt like I was drugged or in some kind of weird dream.

A few people nearby stared at us as if we had just arrived from Mars. Now that I think about it, they might have accepted such an explanation instead of the truth. My God, what a sight we must have been.

The next I knew, Lobo was in front of us. The guy seemed to appear out of nowhere. He grabbed Carla's backpack and pulled us to our feet.

Those people who had just been trying to figure out how two kids could suddenly become drenched and muddy no longer moved. Caught in Frozen Time mode, caused by

Lobo I realized, they stared unseeing in complete silence except for the sounds of our coughing and movements.

Lobo walked, dragged and partly lifted Carla and me to the mall's entrance. He got us out onto Granada Street where his truck sat, and there time proceeded normally. As the sounds of the world returned, a cold wind whipped across our wet bodies, and I shivered. Tourists in a full tram rumbled past Lobo's truck and turned their heads to gawk at us.

"Jeff ... you're bleeding," Carla, her face streaked with mud, pointed between coughs. Following her gaze, I saw a lot of red dripping from my left hand.

"Probably an oyster shell cut." Lobo reached to help me. "A deep one." Before he could touch it though, Carla grabbed my hand in both of hers. As soon as she touched me, soothing warmth rushed up my arm, and she quickly let go, startled as if she had felt it too.

I looked at my hand, wiped the blood away but couldn't find a wound anywhere. Still coughing a little, Carla followed my gaze and then stared at both of her hands, now bloodied. On her face was this look that said she couldn't believe what she had just done. I felt the same way.

"Nice work Carla, but you need to save your energy." Lobo pulled down the tailgate of his truck. "Both of you. Get in. Quickly." With his help, we climbed into the truck and sat there still dripping water and mud. "Now lie down on your backs. Leave as much room between each other as you can and don't try to say anything."

As soon as he got us settled, Lobo hopped into the bed of his truck, squeezing his big old body between Carla and me. After a blur of motion, I realized Lobo had his left hand resting on my forehead. Using his right hand, he was doing the same thing to Carla.

"Close your eyes and do your best to relax," he told us. Still fuzzy-headed, I did as he asked. And just a few seconds after shutting my eyes, I felt his energy surge into my body like I had several times before.

Next thing I knew, we had arrived at Carla's house—well, my house too since I was in Grandma's custody—where Lobo helped us out of his truck. Why there instead of at his place I couldn't figure out, but it really didn't seem to matter.

A damp, chill wind off the bay made me shiver again, but I felt a lot better than I did coming out of the old Alcazar. The shivering, I think, was as much about remembering that nasty vortex and its freezing wind as about what I was experiencing that moment. I still couldn't understand what had happened to us and my mind overflowed with questions.

Carla looked about as dazed and cold as I felt. Her hair hung in stringy, wet clumps across her forehead and a smear of mud looked almost like someone had painted it there. I knew I probably had even more mud on my face than that.

"Don't either one of you ask me anything until later," Lobo barked. "Carla, you get a shower, change clothes and meet us back at my place. Bring a toothbrush. You're staying with us tonight. Oh and also bring the copies of those pictures you found today."

By then, I was well beyond being surprised Lobo knew about the photographs.

Looking kind of bewildered, Carla just nodded. She seemed a little unsteady, so I took her backpack and walked her to the door. With each step, I felt and heard the squishiness of wet socks against soaked and muddy sneakers. Neither of us spoke until Carla unlocked and opened the front door.

Spock bounced out to greet us with furious tail wagging and a lot of whining. It didn't take him long though to start sniffing us, probably attracted by the smell of mud and wondering where we had been.

"I must look horrible," Carla mumbled, standing with Spock on the front porch and running a hand through her wet hair.

"Umm, not bad for a half drowned rat." I smiled and pushed some strands of hair she had missed away from her face.

"Oh Jeff, I thought we were both going to die in that horrible place." She wrapped her arms around me and laid her head on my chest,

"Yeah," I hugged her back and shuddered at the memory of what we had been through and wild fantasies of what might have happened. "I felt so helpless. Thank God you're OK."

Trying to make her feel better, I lifted my bloodstained, muddy, but undamaged left hand up for us both to see. "But you know what? You sure know how to patch a guy up."

Carla pulled away and refused to look at my hand. "I'm glad," she said. "But having that much power still scares me."

"Well, lady, I'll tell you something. I didn't find what you did for me one bit scary." The pained expression on her mud-stained face told me my attempt to make her feel better had definitely failed.

"You don't understand." A tear trickled down her face. Without explaining any further, she turned, scooted Spock back into the house, walked through the door and shut it behind her.

When Carla finally arrived at Lobo's place, she seemed to be doing better. Actually, we both were. A hot shower and fresh clothes sure helped me and I'm sure it made a difference for her too.

As soon as she arrived though, old Lobo didn't waste any time. He immediately directed both of us to sit down in his living room. Until that point, he hadn't said much to me except, "Clean yourself up, change clothes and we'll talk when your girlfriend gets here. It will take the three of us to piece this together."

"Now," he said to Carla first, as we all settled into our seats, "tell me everything that happened after I dropped you off at Aviles Street. Then to me, he said, "Jeff, you fill in the blanks as she talks. Add in anything you think she's missed."

Without waiting for a response, he looked back at Carla and said, "Go!"

After taking a deep breath, Carla did a great job of telling our story. I only had to add a few little things and occasionally, Lobo threw in a question or two. But when she got to the part about the pictures of Lobo we found in the research library, she hesitated.

"Keep going, don't stop on my account," he told her. So she did, telling him detail by detail what we experienced right up until he hauled us out of the Antique Mall. When she talked about the photos of him, he didn't say a word or change expression.

"There is one more thing that I guess you didn't notice," I said to Carla because she hadn't mentioned it. All she recalled seeing after we fell into the water was the marsh grass and some buildings. "When I surfaced from the water, I saw Lobo and some other guy standing on some sand above us looking down."

"Lobo?" she said, her eyes wide.

"Well, it sure looked like him," I replied with a shrug.

"Were you there?" Carla asked as we both looked at the old shaman.

"Yes, I was there." The man said nothing else after dropping his little bombshell explanation. His tone and facial expression seemed to say, "So? No big deal."

Of course, Carla and I then started throwing all kinds of questions at him starting with a demand to know all about that vortex and the water where we landed.

"Enough!" He growled, his eyes blazing "You will get your explanations when I'm ready and you will get them in the order I think best. Now, first of all, the water you fell into was Maria Sanchez Creek."

"Maria Sanchez?" Carla repeated. "Impossible. We were nowhere near Maria Sanchez Lake or what's left of the creek."

"On the contrary," Lobo replied. "You fell straight into Maria Sanchez *Creek*, not the lake, exactly at the spot beneath the Lightner museum where that old waterway *used to be*."

Instead of saying anything back, Carla just stared at him with a startled look on her face. Me? I had no idea what either one of them was talking about. But before Carla could figure out what to say, Lobo kept going.

"Consider this question, Carla. How far did the original Maria Sanchez Creek go into downtown St. Augustine *before* Henry Flagler built his hotels?"

Obviously still startled but always thinking, Carla said, "It, uh, went to at least to King Street and maybe a little bit beyond. But ... that would mean—"

"Yes, that would mean you and Jeff fell into the creek in the 1800s. 1885 to be more precise."

1885? Even after seeing pictures of Lobo that far back in the past, I still found it hard to believe his words. There was no way we could have actually been there with him even if he had somehow lived that long.

At first, Carla didn't move. She looked like she had mentally short-circuited and I knew exactly how she felt. 1885? I kept asking myself. With Lobo?

"Snap out of it you two," the man growled. "And Miss Carla, if you would please be so kind as to show me the evidence you have of my advanced age?"

After shooting me a quick look of wide-eyed amazement, Carla unzipped the backpack at her feet, reached in and pulled out the file folder containing the two photocopies. She stared at the folder for a few seconds before sliding it across the coffee table to Lobo where he sat in the other recliner.

"Hmm," he said, first looking at the two pictures and back at us. "I thought the one taken at the Ponce de Leon would never go beyond the photographer's family or possibly the Flagler Museum down in Palm Beach. And as for the picture taken at the Castillo, that's not a very good picture of me is it?"

As he finished speaking, he put the photocopies back into the folder and flipped it onto the coffee table as if the contents were of no importance. On his face though, a tiny smile appeared, a very rare Lobo event.

His response was so open and so completely confirmed his impossible age that Carla and I just sat there in surprise.

"But, how…?" Carla asked, almost stuttering, her eyes wide and eyebrows stretched as far as they would go. "I mean, you? Us? Back then? That … terrifying hole we fell into?" I knew exactly how she felt, but what a rare thing to see Carla fumbling for words.

"Again," Lobo replied, "what I'm saying is that you both definitely fell into Maria Sanchez Creek exactly where the Lightner Museum Antique Mall is located today. I happened to be there at the exact same moment in 1885 with my business partner."

"Business partner?" Carla asked, looking at him like she couldn't have heard what he said accurately. "And you both just 'happened' to be there? At that exact moment?"

"We both saw you two drop into the water from a height of about five feet above the surface, splash around, and then rise to the surface for a few seconds before disappearing, leaving only big ripples in the creek.

"To my partner, it was as if two people had popped briefly into existence. Seconds before he saw you, however, I noticed something he didn't see—a large swirl of distorted air shimmering over the creek."

"Uh," I interrupted, finally finding my voice and trying hard to accept Lobo's story. "Sooo, what did you think had happened … back then?"

"I knew exactly what had occurred, but your arrival scared my companion. In order to not arouse his suspicion, I simply agreed with him that what we saw was indeed one of the strangest things imaginable—sort of like a UFO sighting today. In effect, you both were indeed, Unidentified Flying Objects.

"You knew?" Carla, asked, her voice getting high pitched at the end. "You knew *in 1885* who we were?"

"Yes, but there's no need to get tangled up in that just now," he said, casually, as if Carla's question carried no importance. "I think maybe it's best if I go back to the beginning.

11

Proud Warriors

In 1875," Lobo said, "I was a Shaman to a small group of Cheyenne people in the Black Hills of what today is South Dakota."

When Lobo spoke those words, the whole impossible idea of him being close to 200 years old slammed into my brain full force. Even after seeing the pictures at the research library and our experience at Maria Sanchez Creek, I think a large part of me just wasn't ready until that moment to accept his great age as a fact.

I hadn't even adjusted to the first date he gave us of 1885 when he went even further back in time to 1875. Those two dates kept flickering back and forth in my mind like great big, flashing signs. Without even looking at her, I could feel Carla's reaction to Lobo's actual age mirroring mine as he continued his story.

"By that point," Lobo explained, "the invasion of our lands by the Americans had all but destroyed our way of life and that of the other plains Indians. In order to exert full control over us, the United Sates government rounded up seventy-two Indian leaders and their supporters and jailed them at Fort Sill, Oklahoma—most came from the Cheyenne, Kiowa, and Comanche tribes.

"There were no charges officially brought against these men and therefore no trials. In today's terms, they were considered terrorists and had no rights.

"On midnight of April 28, 1875, the United States army herded all seventy-two prisoners into eight wagons and exiled them in chains to the Castillo here in St. Augustine over 1,000 miles away. I realize you know some of this history Carla," Lobo said, looking right at her, "but Jeff doesn't."

In response, Carla just nodded, but her facial expression and body language told me she had arrived in history heaven. Lobo, the living visitor from a long ago world, was giving her a firsthand account of an event she had only read about in books.

"In addition to the seventy-two men were an Indian woman, her child, a black captive of one warrior and me. All four of us went voluntarily so we never officially had the classification of prisoner. In my case, I went to support the spiritual needs of my Cheyenne brothers. My English name as listed in the historical record? Frowning Wolf."

I couldn't help it. When Lobo said the translation of his Cheyenne name, I started to laugh, and then I tried to stifle it. What came out was a loud snort. "I'm sorry, Lobo, really I am, but you gotta admit that name really fits you."

Looking at me and shaking her head, I saw Carla trying to hide a smile. She felt the same way. I could see that, but she had way more self-control.

Maybe my reaction was just a stupid way of releasing nervous energy built up from trying to absorb all of Lobo's story. I don't know.

"Got yourself under control now do you?" Lobo demanded, his rumbling voice and penetrating eyes nailing me to the couch where I sat.

After I straightened up and said, yes, he continued. "The military commander of our group was Lieutenant Richard Henry Pratt. A good man, really, by the standards of the day. He stayed with us through our entire three-year imprisonment. I'll have to say, Pratt tried to do his best for us even though he didn't understand how damaging those efforts really were to the core of our beings.

"We eventually called Pratt, our 'white chief.' That he was, whether we liked it or not.

"After twenty-four long, hard days of travel by wagon, train and steamboat, we arrived at the Castillo in St. Augustine. They called it Fort Marion back then, after the Spanish left for good, but by whatever name, the place awed us when we saw it for the first time.

We had never seen such a huge structure, no less one built out of stone. In fact, we made ourselves touch the coquina walls, to feel their roughness, before we could believe they were real. That building, especially with all of its cannons, drove home to us the immense and unstoppable power of the white world as nothing ever did before.

"Inside though, we found the place in terrible disrepair. Water leaked into the rooms, green scum covered some of the walls and it stank, horribly. It became our job to clean the place up and make it fit to use. In time, we also built a huge shed on the deck of the fort where we could sleep. With the fresh breezes up there, it was a lot healthier place to live than down below.

"The ocean. Of course, none of us had ever seen an ocean before—endless water and salted no less. Incredible.

And sharks! What odd creatures. We called them, "Water Buffalo."

As the man talked, I kept wanting to ask him his exact age but didn't. Carla had a million questions, I was sure, but somehow, she restrained herself. Actually, she looked sort of hypnotized as she sat there listening. That was probably the reason she didn't say a lot.

"Eventually, the soldiers took off our leg chains, cut our hair, took away our traditional clothing and put us in military uniforms, just like one of your pictures shows. You see, it didn't matter that I wasn't officially a prisoner, I lived exactly as they did. So together we learned to march, speak English, read, write, and do arithmetic. We went to the white man's church, heard about his God, and sang the hymns.

"Eventually, they even trusted us enough to give us rifles and have us guard the fort. A very strange series of events."

"There they were, proud warriors like Bear Shield, Howling Wolf, Biter, Boy Hunting, Bull with Holes in his Ears and Black Horse, all looking and acting like white men. Which is exactly what Pratt and his superiors wanted.

"Sickening, but we all did it because we had no choice. The goal that white America had for our group held here in St. Augustine in those days? Kill the Indian in us and make us white inside.

"Well, it only worked part way. Even though we came from different Indian nations, we merged as a unified group of sorts, almost like one tribe. Beneath the surface, we stayed as true to our traditions as we could.

"Sure, there was some resistance, one big revolt, really, mostly by the Kiowa. Some lost the will to live, sickened and died. Others even took their own lives. In the end, nine didn't make it out alive. Good men like Heap of Birds, Standing Elk, Skywalker and Straightening an Arrow."

Lobo paused, and in his glittering eyes was a sadness, a loss beyond words. Suddenly, I saw him in a very different way, the only survivor of all those people. The thing is, what I had just witnessed was rare—old Lobo showing deep emotion.

Even so, the man didn't blink, and of course, no tears came to his eyes. If there was ever a time I thought the man might blink that was it. Nope, didn't happen. Still, the more he talked, like Carla, the more fascinated I became.

"Believe it or not," he went on, "what really saved us during those days was tourism."

"Tourism?" I had learned over time to accept the tourists who flood our city but to think that back in the old days they helped Lobo and his friends?

"Yup," Lobo replied. "We became a tourist attraction. By 1875, St. Augustine already had a reputation as a place for rich northern whites to escape the cold winters. All those people flowing into the city wanted to see wild Indians. So with Pratt's permission we satisfied that desire and even made money doing it.

"We set up demonstrations for all those tourists, as well as the locals, and charged them to watch. We wore our traditional clothing, sang our old songs, created pretend battles, did war dances, and demonstrated buffalo chases.

"Once, 2,000 people filled the Castillo at night to see us perform. Paying customers! Pretty smart business dealings for a bunch of ignorant savages, huh?" He asked.

What do you say to a question like that? Lobo knew his question put us in a bind no matter how we answered it so he went right on with his story not giving us time to respond.

"All of that acting allowed us to wear our native dress and to at least somewhat be ourselves instead of acting like white men. Without the tourists, such events would have never happened. Besides, we made money doing it and Pratt let us out of the fort to spend it in the city.

"Pretty soon, our White Chief actually gave permission for some of our group to work in town doing odd jobs, like cutting wood in saw mills, tending horses, picking oranges and carrying suitcases for people arriving at the train station. Some of us artistic types even sold our drawings, crafts and carvings to the locals as well as the tourists.

"Lobo," Carla said, shaking her head, "you are blowing my mind." I had to agree.

"Good," he replied. "We can all do with a flushing out of the brain at times. It makes for newer and better perspectives. Now, back to my story.

"In the spring of 1878, three years after we arrived in St. Augustine, the United States government released us. Forty of the original seventy-two prisoners went back out west to the reservations and twenty-three went bravely into the world of the white man to work.

"Through special arrangements made by Pratt, I managed to stay in St. Augustine and make my living as a carver of wood. The day I saw you both fall into Maria Sanchez Creek, Thomas Hastings had just hired me to carve the caryatids for the Ponce de Leon Hotel.

"As one of the two young New York architects Henry Flagler hired to draw up plans for the place, he happened to be in town looking over the city's buildings when he spied some of my work for sale. In fact, the day my partner and I saw you fall into Maria Sanchez Creek, I was showing him where they were soon going to fill it in to make way for Flagler's new hotels.

"It took me two years to complete the caryatids, but old Flagler liked the results so much, we became friends. When he found out I lived on the peninsula here that my business partner owned, he bought it for me." As he said this, Lobo swept his arm around the room but he definitely meant his entire property and not just his house.

"Henry Flagler ... was your *friend?*" Carla asked, her eyes wide and hanging on Lobo's every word. "And bought this place and the peninsula ... for you?"

Without answering her question directly, Lobo said, "Well, in those days, the peninsula was terribly overgrown. No one had lived here for many years. The house needed lots of work. Most people would have just torn it down.

"I saw Flagler for the last time right after the turn of the century—the twentieth century, that is," Henry came out to the house and brought unexpected gifts of appreciation for my efforts with the caryatids.

"I told him at the time he had done enough, but the man insisted. There they are," he said pointing to his three stained glass lamps. "He knew how much I liked stained glass and admired Louis Comfort Tiffany's work with glass panels in the Ponce de Leon. Because of that he commissioned the man to make those lamps and the glass for my front door."

"You told me a rich friend had given you all that Tiffany glass," Carla said, her voice barely above a whisper, "but you didn't tell me how rich."

"And who he was," I added.

Carla later told me how Henry Flagler made his money helping to build the famous Standard Oil Company with John D. Rockefeller. Today he'd be called a billionaire.

Carla also explained to me that after building the Ponce de Leon and the Alcazar Hotels, Flagler created the Florida East Coast Railroad, pushed it all the way to Key West and then built more hotels down in Palm Beach.

Stunned as I was by Lobo's story at the time, I decided to ask a question that had been bothering me. "What's a caryatid?"

"You tell him," he said to Carla.

"Oh, ah, OK," Carla replied, still very focused on Lobo's life history. " A caryatid is just a name for Greek statues of women used as architectural supports. In this case, it's the wood carvings in Flagler College's rotunda. The ones in the picture we found of Lobo and Henry Flagler."

"You actually carved those … back then?" I still couldn't get my mind around not only the man's age, but also his connection to one of St. Augustine's major historical sites.

"I already told you that and you have a photo to prove it," Lobo grumbled as he got up from his chair and opened a door I hadn't noticed before in the wood paneling between two of his book cases.

Reaching inside, he pulled out a three-foot tall version of a Flagler College caryatid that was maybe six inches in diameter. Stained dark brown, four intricately carved female figures in flowing robes looked outward from a central point and reflected the outside light because of a shellac or varnish coating.

I knew Lobo was a great carver but what he held in his hands went way beyond the word "great."

Carla gasped. With her eyes as wide as I have ever seen them she just stared at the model caryatid with her mouth slightly open.

"That was the sample I made for Hastings before starting work on the big ones," Lobo said to Carla, handing it to her. "After Hastings showed it to Flagler, I got the commission."

Looking at the thing as if he had just given her a check for a million dollars, Carla gently took the carving from him.

12

Eruptions

All three of us had shifted location from inside Lobo's place to his porch with its three rocking chairs.

The smell of salt water replaced the mustiness of Lobo's house, but it also brought with it a sharp reminder of falling into what the old guy told us was Maria Sanchez Creek—in 1885.

Carla wanted fresh air, so there we were, even though the wind-chill made it somewhat uncomfortable. I think she was feeling a little claustrophobic after our experience in that nasty vortex. Once out on the porch, I have to admit, I felt better myself.

1885. That impossible date again slithered through my mind. The thing is, on the porch in front of us where I had placed it, stood Lobo's model caryatid—a perfect replica of what I saw in the photo from the research library. Lobo had asked me to bring it with us out onto the porch.

"How can you possibly be so old?" I asked, but Lobo shifted his gaze out over Matanzas Bay instead of answering.

He sat there, bare-armed in the chilly breeze, rocking slowly, making a floorboard squeak each time he tilted forward.

When the man didn't respond to my question, and the silence grew heavy, Carla said, "You going to answer him?" As she spoke, she zipped her jacket up against the March wind blowing in off the water. Spock looked up at her from where he lay curled up at her feet. Carla had left him on the porch when she entered the house.

In mid-rock, the old guy's chair stopped dead and he pointed to his dock where Edgar had just landed. "Back in 1879, the tip of this peninsula stuck further out into the water than it does now. Erosion over time has taken its toll. The tip extended almost to where the end of the dock is now."

"And," I prompted.

"Jeff, you and your friend Carla here would both do well to develop more of the virtue called patience. The impatience of youth is what got you two into deep trouble over on the floor of the old Alcazar's swimming pool."

I started to give Carla a friendly nudge to remind her how this time she had been the more impatient one, but I didn't. Why? Right as I had that thought, I felt this sudden rush of emotion. It seemed to come from outside of myself somehow and felt vaguely like guilt mixed with apology. Really weird.

That's when I saw Carla staring at me. Her face reflected exactly what I was sensing and I knew those feelings of guilt and apology were floating into my head from her mind somehow. She looked so miserable I gave her a little smile and a wink.

I swear, right after that, the word *thanks*, in Carla's voice, swam into my mind but she hadn't actually said anything.

"If you recall, Jeff," Lobo's voice broke into my thoughts about Carla, "when your mother visited here yesterday, she pointed to the end of the dock where you and Carla sat."

"Yeah," I agreed but I wanted to also say, "So what does that have to do with your age?"

"It has everything to do with my age," he replied, turning to look at me, his eyes seeming to blaze a lot more than usual. For some reason that look made me shiver. "Out there where the peninsula used to be, I maintained a fire pit for ceremonial and healing purposes.

"On the night of January 12, 1879, a small earthquake hit St. Augustine just as I was performing a sacred dance around a roaring fire. The quake wasn't severe, but the lighthouse keeper going up the lighthouse steps over on Anastasia Island got bounced around a bit."

"But we don't get earthquakes in Florida," I said.

"We aren't a state that's usually prone to them but we're not immune either. This part of Florida is more susceptible than most others. The first recorded quake in our written history occurred in 1727 and since then, there's been over thirty. Of course they aren't severe like they are in California. Even so, the one in 1879 changed my existence forever.

"During the quake, there was an eruption from deep in the earth below St. Augustine nobody but me could sense, as far as I could ever tell. It wasn't an explosion of lava or gases or anything even remotely physical. Right through my fire and all around it for about five feet came a blast of extraordinarily tiny, glistening particles, white in color. I felt them slice through my body in multiple pulses, but there was no pain.

"Mom!" I said loudly, suddenly seeing the message she had been trying to give me about what might happen to me in the near future.

"Yes," Lobo said. "Her warning was clear if you knew what to look for. She pointed to the exact spot on the dock, now under water, where the eruption occurred. Then in departing, she configured her essence into tiny particles to show you what had happened on that very spot long ago and also what you might encounter."

"So the glowing cloud that passed through us at the Lightner Museum," Carla asked, "was a group of those same kind of particles?"

"They were," Lobo answered simply.

"Wait," I said, "what does that—"

"Don't get ahead of me," Lobo ordered. "It's time to back up and let me finish my story in sequence so you'll get the entire picture.

Lobo has this infuriating way of having to tell a whole lot of details sometimes before getting to the point, but forcing him to change wasn't an option. So I just had to take a deep breath and let the man do his own thing.

"During that eruption, the wind stopped blowing, my fire seemed to solidify, and I found myself surrounded by total silence—my first experience with Frozen Time. The only movement I could see was all those particles quietly shooting up out of the earth and through me. But in that linkage, I realized I was in direct contact with a living being of some sort. All of those particles were part of one huge creature.

When Lobo spoke the words, "living being," and "creature," my body twitched. For a split second, in my mind, I was back in the vortex with particles shooting through me, leaving behind a prickly sensation.

"So what went through us at the Antique Mall was *alive*?" Carla asked. The look of disgust on her face mirrored exactly what I felt.

"Yes, and for some odd reason, the particles you encountered were purple. Why the difference in color from those during my time, I have no idea."

Even as he went on speaking, the word "yes" continued to bounce through my brain. I flat could not get used to the idea that something alive has pierced my body so many times. A quick glance from Carla told me she felt the same.

"But as quickly as those particles arrived, they left me and my little peninsula, exploding off into the night sky like a boiling stream of incredibly tiny white bees. Not for a second though, as my fire once again roared in front of me, did I lose full contact with the creature. It was possible to shut off that connection consciously and not be aware of it, but the link stayed with me.

"Over the coming days, I learned if I wanted to know what the creature was doing, I simply had to think about it and that knowledge somehow entered my brain. To my way of thinking in those days, this Particle Being, as I have since labeled it, was some sort of demon from the spirit world sent to chastise me for past misdeeds.

"So I went on spirit journeys, prayed, sang and danced in order to appease it and make it go away. But nothing worked."

"The particles didn't actually harm you?" Carla asked, leaning forward in her chair and no longer rocking. I really wanted to hear the answer to that question.

"No, not at all," Lobo replied. "Just the opposite. I eventually understood how my contact with the Particle Being had enhanced my shamanic abilities and gave me others such as the power to create Frozen Time.

"Then I noticed how any cuts or bruises I received healed almost immediately. Only years later, after never getting sick and not aging, did I fully comprehend the physical effect the creature had on my body."

"The Particle Being made you what? Immortal?" I asked, knowing that couldn't be true but still trying to get a handle on Lobo's long lifetime.

"I'm sure I would die like anyone else if I got run over by a train," he replied. "The fact is, I simply seem to be disease resistant and I don't age."

After that explanation, Carla and I fired all kinds of questions at him, but the man refused to answer. Instead, he just kept on with his story.

"It took time, but in observing the Particle Being and listening to the limited communications the creature offered, it became clear to me the thing was only curious. It seemed to be fascinated with everything material, and especially, I discovered, human beings and sea life. Looked to me like it might just be observing and collecting information and nothing else.

"So you can see how at first, I wasn't afraid as the creature continued to travel around the city and over the bay in small groups or as an entire unit. One question kept nagging me though. Why, I wondered, had this life form spewed up out of the earth right under me and nowhere else?

"From my contact with it, I knew the Particle Being had targeted me, making it have only one point of entry into our world. The creature never answered any of my queries directly. But what little I sensed in that area gave me the impression the earthquake's energy combined with my shamanic abilities drew it to the surface right here somehow.

"The particles, I also found out, had a movement radius of somewhere between two or three miles, at the most, in any direction from where it erupted. If even a single piece of it went beyond that limit, it would then lose its coherence and simply cease to exist. The thing had become a prisoner of St. Augustine, I guess you might say.

"For a number of years after I first encountered the creature, I simply accepted it as an odd, but harmless part of the spirit world. That all changed, however, in August 31, 1886, the year of the biggest earthquake in St. Augustine's recorded history.

"A product of the Charleston Fault, this new shifting of the earth sent some strong shocks up and down the east coast of Florida and even down into Tampa. In St. Augustine, dishes broke, windows cracked and church bells all over the city rang without anyone touching them. Not a severe quake, true, but with it came another, more massive eruption of what felt like greatly more energized particles.

"And when I use the term particles, I offer it in the sense of what they looked like, not what they actually were. In essence, each tiny glint you see is simply a flash showing the location of an incredibly small concentration of energy."

"A second Particle Being?" I asked.

"Turned out," he replied, "it was all one creature. Each of the two eruptions were just two different portions of the same being with much more still locked within the earth.

The thing used me again as a focal point of entry into our world when I happened to be in the Castillo on that day in 1886. But of course, I was the only one able to see it.

"This second eruption quickly spread throughout the city and merged with the first group of particles, making it one huge creature. When that happened, I also sensed a transfer of information from the first set of particles to the second."

Creature? The term "Living Being" was bad enough but Lobo's constant use of the word "creature" made his story and our experience in the vortex even scarier than before.

"OK, weird stuff, I have to admit, but what does it have to do with Carla and me?" I asked. "I mean, why did *we* meet up with that *thing* today and not *you?*"

"And what was that ... horrible hole we fell into?" Carla wrapped her arms around herself as she spoke. Her face looked all pinched together. The fear created by the vortex experience seemed to radiate from her and merge with my own.

"The rumbling you felt just prior to your encounter at the Antique Mall," Lobo said, "was a slight earthquake. People from Charleston down through Orlando felt it.

"Evidently, like in my experiences, that seismic activity produced energy enough for a linkage to take place. Unlike my experiences though, the creature used you both as its final avenue of escape. Why you and not me this time is a good question. The only answer I can come up with is twofold.

"First, you both were closer to one of the earth's quantum level power points than I was back so long ago— evidently a natural travel route for this nonphysical being.

Those power points spread outward in all directions from the earth's core.

"Second, your association with me has awakened within you, abilities that radiate an energy pattern similar to mine. Such an energy pattern, when combined with one of the earth's power points, establishes a superhighway through which Particle Being segments can escape. In my case, I had enough power reserve to help bring the particles to the earth's surface. Not so for you two.

"You both opened the highway because of your connection to me but then found yourselves sucked into it. The creature didn't want you as such, it just wanted to use your energy to propel it from the earth. When it passed through you, that gave it the needed boost to continue its journey to the surface."

"Uh, OK," I said, not sure I fully understood what the man had just told us. "But how did we end up with you back in 1885?"

"The vortex that pulled you down was a quantum construct, much like the wormholes theorized by today's physicists. Within such a thing, time and space can have infinite configurations.

"In this case however, the closest energy signature similar to your own was mine, but back in the past. This resulted in you being deposited right there with me before almost instantly bouncing back again to the Antique Mall in our present time."

"So we definitely … went back to 1885?" Carla asked, her voice dripping with awe that such a thing might have truly happened to us—a dream come true for someone who loves history and the city of St. Augustine as much as she does. "I thought time travel was just science fiction."

"Your experience with Maria Sanchez Creek in 1885, as witnessed by me, tells you that time travel is indeed possible." Lobo paused after speaking, I'm sure, to let the weight of his words sink into our brains. It worked.

And in that quiet, I somehow sensed a particular question bubbling up inside Carla well before she asked it. In fact, I could hear inside my head the exact words she was going to use. "You told us you knew, at the time, exactly what had happened when you saw us fall into Maria Sanchez Creek, right?"

"My current understanding of what happened then is this. For quite a distance around where the vortex was going to deposit you, a quantum field had built up that extended far beyond the creek itself. And because of my sensitivity to such fields, two things occurred.

"First, I had an immediate flash of understanding that two people would, for whatever reason, pop out of thin air and land in the creek.

For you, that incident, facilitated by the vortex, meant traveling backwards in time.

"Simultaneously for me though, a portion of my consciousness lurched into my immediate future a few seconds. This means I saw you plunge into the water a second or two before the event occurred.

"With the full quantum field still very active while you floundered in the creek, I immediately linked with my future self—the Lobo you know.

"In that linkage, we exchanged just enough information to be useful to each other. I, the future Lobo, saw what was going to happen to you five minutes before it took place. So when you popped back out of the vortex again at the Antique Mall, I knew when and where. The past *me*, from

1885, on the other hand, received enough data about you both so that *he* would be prepared to work with you when you actually showed up in *his future life,* or in *my recent life,* if you prefer.

"What? You knew who Carla and I were *before* you met us?" By then, my head was spinning from trying figure out Lobo's very complex statement.

"Yes, indeed I did."

13

Attracted to Humans

I'm having trouble absorbing everything Lobo is telling us. It's just too much all at once." Carla scanned the bay as if looking for something. "And, of course, he's only giving us what information he thinks we need to know right now."

Lobo had gone into the house a few minutes before while Carla and I continued to talk on the porch.

"Yeah," I agreed, "All those particles have to be some-where, I j—"

Edgar flew into the porch and landed on the little white table sitting between Lobo's rocking chairs next to the cary-atid model. He startled Carla and scared the heck out of me. The last I knew, he was perched on Lobo's dock.

"Get lost, Edgar." I didn't want to deal with him right then.

"Caa," Edgar replied, standing there on his one leg, going nowhere and studying me with his beady little black eyes. *Lobo eyes.* Of course they didn't look exactly the same as Lobo's but had some similarities that I couldn't quite figure out.

Trying my best to ignore the bird, I went back to telling Carla what he had just interrupted. "Lobo really hasn't explained the effect those particles might have on us. I wonder if he even knows."

"Good question," Carla replied. "What if we ended up like him? Would you want to? Live as long as he has, I mean?"

Before I could answer though, Lobo came back out on the porch, sat down in his rocker and continued his incredible story.

"Now, after the second eruption in 1886, as I told you before, both groups of particles merged into one creature that eventually seemed almost addictively attracted to humans and sea life. This development disturbed me greatly, so I started keeping a watch on the thing more closely. But it wasn't until the Loring funeral in March of 1887 that I realized the creature might actually be dangerous."

There it was, the word "dangerous" again, the one I thought might be coming up but also the one I didn't want to hear. Instead of showing the stab of fear I felt, I asked a question.

"Loring?" I looked back and forth from Lobo to Carla. My knowledge of St. Augustine history hardly exists, especially compared to those two.

"You tell him who Loring was," Lobo said to Carla. "The short version."

"You were at the Loring funeral?" Carla asked, like me obviously still adjusting to Lobo's age. When Lobo didn't answer, she just shook her head in amazement and answered my question. "Ah, well, William Wing Loring became one of St. Augustine's best known citizens back in the late 1800s.

"In his early days, he served honorably as an officer in the United States Army. Then during the Civil War he was a Confederate general. And finally, he became a military leader in the Egyptian army. His remains are buried under a monument set up in his honor behind Government House.

"So how was that for a short version?" She asked, looking at Lobo, eyebrows raised with just a hint pride. "It sure was a lot shorter than some of your long, drawn-out stories."

"Your effort was adequate." Lobo admitted like he was having a tooth pulled, never an easy guy to please. "The Loring funeral, Jeff, was a huge event for St. Augustine on that beautifully clear day in March of 1887. Being so well known and respected, the man's burial drew 8,000 visitors. Since the city population at the time only amounted to about 3,000, it turned out to be a very crowded event.

"The General's body lay in state in the plaza at the old market, surrounded by countless flower arrangements. Near the casket sat stacks of rifles and a pyramid of stars made from bayonets. Stores closed, black and white funeral decorations hung everywhere, and flags flew at half-mast in the city as well as on ships in the bay.

"Exactly at noon, the funeral procession began at the plaza with bands playing and rifles firing. It proceeded up King Street, then down St. George Street all the way to the city gate. From there it came down Bay Street, back to King, and out to the Woodlawn Cemetery. The city later moved Loring's remains to the current downtown location Carla mentioned.

"The Bishop of St. Augustine, politicians, judges, the police department, school children, old friends, visitors, and 255 soldiers followed the casket on its journey. People in buildings on either side of the procession filled balconies to overflowing.

"One of the most remarkable things about that procession was a long line of both Union and Confederate veterans from the Civil War marching two-by-two, arm-in-arm, dressed in their old blue and grey uniforms. Quite a sight and one viewed from Fort Marion by another group of Native American prisoners, the Apaches—nearly 500 of them, half of whom were women and children. But that's a different story for another time.

"As important as the Loring Funeral was for St. Augustine, for the creature, the great numbers of people concentrated in such a small area ignited within the thing a great thirst to more directly involve itself with humans and their activities.

"By the time I got to the plaza, right before the procession started, a seething, sparkling mass of particles hung just over the treetops in that area. To me, it looked like a boiling cloud of overexcited, lighting bugs. And from the creature, I sensed its need to connect with people building by the second.

"Up until then, I thought no one else could see those things. In the plaza, however, I noticed very young children pointing up into the sky and laughing. Little people can often see beneath the surface of our reality so much better than adults, but usually the adults ignore such a talent, just like the parents attending the Loring event did.

"As the funeral procession stretched out on its trip around downtown, the Particle Being cloud expanded with it. And by the time the casket arrived back at the plaza and began heading out to the cemetery, the creature's color had darkened slightly with just a hint of purple, like the color of the particles you both encountered today.

"Why or how that coloration occurred, I have no idea, but in light of our current situation, it is interesting.

"Only then did I notice thin, flashing particle strands occasionally dipping from the main portion of the creature down into the crowds. Upon inspection, I watched as those strands pierced people's heads and upper torso areas, apparently though with no ill effect.

"This happened repeatedly, like little harmless lightning strikes, but looking more closely, I watched people jerk ever so slightly with each hit."

"Did it ever strike out at you?" Carla asked, grimacing and wrapping her arms around herself.

After she spoke, I stole a glance out over Matanzas Bay, thinking for some reason I might see the particle cloud we had encountered in the vortex. Thankfully, I didn't, but I still wondered where the thing might be hiding.

"No, it avoided my presence, actually," Lobo replied. "It got a distaste for me initially in both eruptions because of a necklace I wore in those days. It had a large piece of silver on it shaped like an arrowhead that covered my heart—made by one of my fellow prisoners at Fort Marion. That didn't make me fully immune to the creature's probing, but the result ended up nearly the same.

"Silver?" I asked, "like in silver bullets vs. werewolves? No way." Despite all the weirdness I had seen associated with Lobo, any link of the guy's story to pure fiction seemed a bit much.

"Wait just a minute," Carla said before Lobo could answer, fishing in her jeans pocket. Seconds later, she pulled out her key chain with a silver oval attached, identical to the one I had, and dangled it in the air. "You gave one of these to both Jeff and me. Were you trying to protect us in case—"

"In case either of you were ever caught in an eruption?" Lobo said, nodding. "The lines of probability surrounding you both told me there was a chance something like that could occur. And yes, what happened to you today is the initial stage of the danger I mentioned to you before."

Back in December, Lobo had explained to me how he is able to look into the aura around a human body and sometimes see what might happen to the person. Did I fully understand that explanation? No, but then again, I really didn't need to. What counted was that I believed the man had such an ability.

"Whew!" I said, thinking about our key chains and their silver ovals. I didn't want to imagine what damage those particles could have done without that metal protecting us. "Thanks, Lobo."

"Initial stage?" Carla asked, clearly alarmed. In my focus on the protection Lobo's silver had given us, I missed those two little words. Carla was right. That sure sounded ominous.

"Yes, initial stage. Your encounter with all those particles in the vortex was clearly the beginning of the threat Jeff's mom and I both warned you about.

"How do I know this? Because my experience in dealing with the particle cloud at the Loring funeral leads me to such a conclusion. During that event, the creature ignored me, but I still tried tuning into it with the goal of understanding why it was so vigorously penetrating people.

Evidently, the creature interpreted my probing as a question because I received a very clear answer. The reply didn't come in words but in images. Those images that told me the Particle Being wanted to find a way to actually insert particles into humans so it could experience physical existence, regardless of any damage it might cause.

"Damn," I said, without thinking. As much as I want to respect Carla's wishes about cursing, there are times when that is so hard to do. That was one of those times. But surprisingly, she didn't fuss at me. The look on her face told me the impact of Lobo's words had all of her attention.

"I found the idea of the Particle Being possibly accomplishing its goal," Lobo continued, "not only disgusting but also probably very dangerous."

"I can relate to that," Carla said, shuddering and throwing a quick glance in my direction.

"Oh yeah," I replied, remembering those particles in the vortex going right through us. That was bad enough, but the idea of having particles actually stay inside me, like Lobo described, made my skin crawl.

In fact, as soon as he started talking about the particles penetrating people, every science fiction movie I had ever seen with alien creatures invading the bodies of human beings flooded my mind. Only by trying hard to concentrate on the next part of Lobo's story was I able to push those nasty mental pictures away.

"After the Loring funeral, the opening of Henry Flagler's hotels and all that human activity provided ample opportunity for the Particle Being to continue its efforts at an even faster pace. Only then did I truly see how deeply at risk the people of St. Augustine might be. At that point, I decided to rid the city of the threat, if such a thing could be done at all.

"Sad to say, however, it took me all the way from 1887 until 1896 to find a solution. But at least I found it before the Particle Being could accomplish its goal. We don't have time for me to try and explain to you the intricate details of how I did it, but I was finally able to put the creature into a state of suspended animation in Flagler College where it remains today."

"Flagler College?" Carla yelled. "Where in the college and why there?

"Yes, the college. You'll find out where and why later."

"Suspended animation?" I said. "Why didn't you just kill it?"

"I couldn't find a way," Lobo growled.

"Now, listen to me, both of you. It's time to focus on the present and not the past. The latest batch of particles of that creature you both just encountered is massive, probably 100 times the size of the first two eruptions and much more energized this time.

"If it's able to activate those old particles in suspended animation, it will absorb their knowledge, interest in humans and the motivation to experience human life by inserting portions of itself into any people who are in St. Augustine at that time. And with the size and energy of this new infusion of particles, the results could be truly catastrophic."

For a few seconds, Lobo's words hung in the air like a huge iron beam lifted by a crane with the potential for crushing everything below if it fell. Catastrophic was a word I had never heard Lobo use before. But before either of us could react, he said, "Now, I need to stop jabbering with you two, get you out of town and see what I can do to keep this situation from getting out of hand."

"Out of town? What are you talking about?" Carla demanded.

"I'm talking about getting you both away from St. Augustine in case I can't control this possible merger of old and new particles. When I went in the house a while ago, I called a friend down in Crescent City. You'll be staying with her until I get this all under control.

"In fact," he said, getting up from his rocker, "I'm going to go call a cab right now. Get some clothes together and a toothbrush—the both of you."

"A cab?" I said loudly and jumping up from my chair. "Are you kidding me? No freakin' way am I going to run out of here on you when maybe I could help." That's when it hit me. Carla would also want to stay. As anxious as I was about my own safety, I saw hers as way more important and she definitely needed to leave the city.

"Lobo, don't you even think about leaving me out of this," Carla barked, also getting to her feet. There she stood, all five feet four inches of her ready to do battle. Classic Carla. I should have known. "Forget the cab. Neither one of us is—"

"Let me make myself clear, Missy. You are both leaving, like it or not!"

"Missy?" She shouted right back at him, eyes almost bulging, eyebrows arched and pinched close together, hands on hips and jaw jutted out as far as it would go. She then walked up to Lobo with eyes like slits and said, "You and what army is going to put me in that cab and make me stay there?"

Increasingly scared as I was of what we might be facing with the Particle Being, I loved every second of Carla's resistance to old Lobo's control. Beyond a doubt, she is a master at it. As often happens between Carla and Lobo at this point, they glared at each other in silence with Carla waiting for Lobo to give in to her. This time though, it didn't happen. Lobo inhaled deeply, blew the air through his nose like a bull and pursed his lips as if he was really frustrated—a reaction I had never seen in Lobo before.

"There's a problem with you both staying." His reply came in a firm but lowered voice. "Yes, you both had your silver key chains with you when you encountered that huge mass of particles, but they weren't enough to protect you fully."

Oooh no! Lobo's words caused my stomach to knot and an incredible sinking sensation flowed from the top of my head right down into my legs. Almost at the same time, I felt Carla's fear, not just for herself but for me as well.

Slowly, I turned my head and found her already looking at me. Gone from her face was all the angry defiance from before. Our eyes stayed locked for a few seconds even as Lobo continued with his explanation.

"After I pulled you two out of the Antique Mall," he said in a gentler tone of voice, "as you know, I placed my hand on each of your heads. The resulting energy transference helped boost your recovery from that encounter with the Particle Being. But in the process, I sensed a few pieces of it still inside you. When I say, 'a few,' I mean just that. Some are located in your brain, some in your heart and others in your solar plexus."

When I heard those words, a chill ran up and down my spine and my mouth seemed to dry up. That's when Carla, sat back down in her rocking chair, her eyes wide and her mouth partway open.

"I realize this is a shock to both of you," Lobo said. "The good news though is that I was able to neutralize those particles inside you, at least for now. However, and hear me on this, if there is a merger of both the old and new Particle Being eruptions, the massive energy of that combination could easily reactivate what is already within your bodies. And if that happens, those particles could easily draw more to join them.

"If such a thing actually occurs, it could cause incredible damage and might well kill you. In essence, within each of you now a ticking time bomb that could go off at any second."

"If you leave St. Augustine as I have planned," Lobo said to us almost softly, "the particles within you *will* lose their coherence because you will travel beyond their limit of tolerance. It is that simple. Remember, the Particle Being can only go a short distance from the center of the city."

I'm telling you, those were some of the most beautiful words I have ever heard in my life. From the horror of knowing part of a dangerous creature inhabited both Carla and me, Lobo had come up with a solution. We could get rid of the thing's pieces it had left in us. That turnaround was so quick it almost made my head spin. "Cool!" I gushed, smiling. "After that, we can come back and help you!"

"See there," Carla said to Lobo, giving him a hopeful smile.

"You still don't understand," he replied, and my confidence in what I had just said to the man started slipping. "You can't come back. It isn't only the particles themselves. The next problem comes from what happens when they are removed.

"Even if you exit the city and rid yourselves of the particles, that process will leave even stronger traces of them within your tissues. This would make you be twenty to thirty times more susceptible than anyone in St. Augustine to personal invasion if all those particles become connected."

"Oh," was all I could say. Brilliant, huh?

After a few seconds of silence, Carla said to Lobo, "You know what? I see it this way. If Jeff and I stay, we just may tip the balance in favor of keeping this catastrophic event of yours from happening, and if we can, we should.

"Lobo, you've helped us to develop some unusual abilities that we might be able to use in dealing with the Particle Being ourselves. So why leave the city and then come back more even vulnerable than we were before? No way! We just stay here and help you any way we can.

"What do you think, Jeff?" she asked at the end of her little speech. "I don't mean to talk for you."

Besides being brilliant, Carla does have a great way with words. I think she's learned it over the years from Lobo.

As I listened to her, all I could do was admire the girl's sharp logic and incredible bravery. It's not that she didn't have any fear, because she did. I could see the fear written across her face and even feel it somehow, but she needed to help Lobo and protect the people in her beloved city. End of story.

As she looked at me, I knew what she wanted us to do was right on target. "Count me in," I told her but swallowing hard.

"Well then," Lobo said, shrugging his shoulders and frowning, "you've both made you've your choice. I hope you survive it."

Part Three

Exploration

14

It's Back!

I don't see anything so far," Carla said as Lobo steered his pickup truck onto Cathedral Place in downtown St. Augustine. He wanted to scout the city to find the newest concentrations of the Particle Being.

"Me either," I agreed.

"Oh, it's here all right," Lobo corrected, his head and eyes shifting all around. "Evidently your interaction with the vortex gave you both only a temporary ability to see this thing."

"You mean you've found some particles already?" Carla asked from her seat between the two of us.

"Here and there," he replied. Not the answer I wanted. Part of me. I think, hoped that maybe the Particle Being had found a way back into the earth. No such luck.

"Some of it's on statues but mostly I see it on trees, bushes, flowers and grass—living things. Lobo pointed at a white toy poodle on a leash with a teenage girl attached. That dog over there has some clustered on him.

"The good news, however, is that at least I haven't seen any strands probing people as yet."

I stared at the little dog as long as I could until Lobo pulled his truck into an open parking spot right on the street close to Government House. I wondered if the poodle would be OK.

As soon as I got out of the truck though, I started getting nervous. It was one thing driving around talking about the Particle Being but quite another to start walking in the area where Lobo said parts of it were attached to living things—even if they weren't human. I know it had to be my imagination, but my skin started feeling prickly in places, kind of like my whole body felt in the vortex when that thing went through me.

On the damp chilly breeze blowing across us came the distant sound of a police siren. For some reason, it seemed to add more urgency to our mission, if that was possible.

Without waiting for Carla and me, Lobo began walking towards Flagler College just a short distance away. He wanted to check on the two initial Particle Being eruptions he put there in suspended animation back in 1896.

1896! No matter how hard I tried, I still couldn't get over the guy's age, whatever it was exactly. Somewhere around 200? Still close enough to blow my mind.

Lobo was certain it wouldn't take long for the new batch of particles to find the old ones he captured long ago. And once they got together, he said, the new ones would definitely try to reactivate the old ones.

"Hey!" The shout came from behind us and the voice with a lisp sounded vaguely familiar. "Lobo!" When I turned to look, there was Lyle, an old homeless guy I know, running towards us wearing what he calls his "lucky red baseball cap" and a dirty old trench coat.

As he ran, Lyle's long grey beard he pulls together in the middle with a rubber band shook from side to side. "It's back!" He shouted again when he got closer to us, but this time I saw the wide-eyed fear in his eyes, grey like his beard. In seconds, he was in front of Lobo, grabbing his shirt with both hands.

Lyle. The last person I ever expected to find downtown on that day. We aren't friends actually, but we do chat sometimes when I'm in the plaza when we happen to run into each other.

This time though, it startled me to see he knew Lobo. Then when he mentioned *something* was *back,* that really got my attention. Lobo keeps telling Carla and me there are no coincidences and right at that point, I had to agree with him.

"You gotta do something, man!" Lyle screeched at Lobo, his voice cracking badly. You told me you got rid of them all long ago but—"

"Shut up Lyle and calm down," Lobo commanded, yanking the man's hands loose from their grip on his shirt. Lyle is short and skinny so it didn't take much effort. "You get control of yourself right now or you are on your own."

Lobo's tone was like ice and he gave Lyle one of his piercing stares.

After taking a deep, shuddering breath and looking all around him like he might be attacked any second, Lyle swallowed hard, nodded nervously and said, "OK. Right. OK. Sorry."

All that time, he never once looked at Carla or me. Carla on the other hand stared at him as if he just arrived by parachute from a passing circus. I guess the guy's raggedy clothes didn't help any—under his trench coat he wore an old Disney World t-shirt and baggy tan pants with worn out knees. At least his faded red sneakers sort of matched his red hat, I thought.

Gotta say, as usual, Lyle's didn't smell very good either. I saw Carla's face crinkle. I don't think the guy had bathed in months.

"Now you listen to me," Lobo scolded him. "We're working on it. You just get out of town as fast as you can and you'll be fine." Obviously Lyle knew about the Particle Being and it scared him silly. But how did he know?

"We?" Lyle asked, and for the first time he noticed Carla and me standing there. "Oh, Jeff Boy," the man said in recognition with a slight smile showing the hole where his two front teeth should have been. "Who, who's this?" he questioned, looking at Carla in alarm.

Why that reaction, I had no idea, but I figured the guy was so frightened, anything out of the ordinary might set him off.

"Her name is Carla," Lobo said to him, his tone a little softer this time. "She's a friend of ours and she's here to help." Carla kept looking at Lyle, Lobo and me, wondering, I'm sure, how either one of us knew the guy.

"OK, Lyle," Lobo said, reaching in his pocket and pulling out a small wad of money, "let me solve your problem for you. Things might get very nasty around here soon so take this money, grab a bus or a cab and take off. Get out of town as far as you can."

"No!" Lyle shrieked and he actually started shaking, his eyes almost popping out of his head. "I've got to stay with you. That's the only way I can survive." People walking by on either side of the street looked at him and us. I really couldn't blame them.

Breathing a sigh of exasperation, Lobo put the money back into his pocket and then reached out with both hands, firmly grabbing Lyle by the shoulders.

"All right," Lobo agreed, "you're with us. But first of all, you keep your big mouth shut. You are either going to work right alongside us and do as you're told or you are nothing more than dead weight. And *that* we can't afford. Got it? I need to hear the words and see it in your eyes how much you mean it."

"OK, yeah, I got it," Lyle replied with a weak, gap-toothed grin. "And I'll keep my mouth shut. Big time. No problem, Lobo. I'm your man for whatever you want me to do. Just don't send me away." A city garbage truck rumbling by on the street made his words hard to hear.

Both men locked eyes for the longest time until Lobo finally nodded and let the little guy loose. Turning to Carla and me, Lobo said, "Lyle was with me during the first eruption of the Particle Being. It went through him like it did me, but he didn't have any silver to protect him."

What? Somehow I sensed the same surprise in Carla that I felt at hearing this new information.

"But I do now, have silver protection," Lyle said. "And have had it for what seems like forever." When he finished speaking, he dug under the neck of his shirt and pulled out a leather strip with an old silver dollar attached to it. "See?"

"Both of you?" Carla asked. "Back then? In 1879? Together?" She took the words right out of my mouth.

"Yes ma'am, we surely were," Lyle replied in a much calmer voice.

15

Flagler College

"Come on, let's go," Lobo said to all of us right after Lyle's startling revelation about the past. Without waiting a second more, he turned around and again headed down Cathedral Place.

Lyle scooted after him, but Carla and I hesitated. She looked about as confused as I felt. "Are you believing this?" she asked.

"I'm not even used to thinking about *Lobo* being so old," I replied. "And now both of them?"

Ahead of us, the two men with a mysterious joint history were walking fast. That didn't give Carla and me much time to think or talk, which was a probably a good thing. Instead of trying to figure things out, we hurried to catch up and learn what we could.

When we all arrived at the entrance to Flagler College on King Street, we didn't slow down a bit. Nope. Lobo just zipped us past the statue of old Henry Flagler and through a large arched opening with an iron gate of what used to be the Ponce de Leon Hotel back in the day.

The place sort of looked like an old castle in some ways, and according to Carla, it was made of poured concrete just like the Hotel Alcazar. She had been trying to get yours truly in there for months in order to educate me about the beautiful historic buildings in St. Augustine. Well, she was getting her wish, just not in the way she hoped.

As we entered a large courtyard, the wind that had been blowing died down to almost nothing. It was a sheltered place, full of palm trees, bushes and flowers. A sweet scent from all the flowers floated up to us.

The two huge towers on top of the college came into full view and for whatever reason, they looked to me at that moment like giant guardians of some kind. Wishful thinking, I told myself, hoping somebody or something would protect us against the Particle Being. Back in the plaza, church bells announced the time, but I didn't pay any attention.

Just head of Carla and me, Lobo and Lyle started talking. They seemed to be having an argument, but we could only hear parts of the conversation.

That's when Lobo stopped abruptly next to a large, circular fountain squirting water downward from little lion heads on top of a very tall pillar in the middle. Some turtles and a bunch of frogs around the fountain's base spit water back in the opposite direction.

"Now!" Lobo said to Lyle while pointing to a bench not too far away from where we all stood. Lyle looked up at him and hesitated for a few seconds as if he wanted to say something, but in the end, he didn't. Instead, he looked down and shuffled off, heading for the bench Lobo wanted him to use.

"Problems?" Carla asked as we all watched Lyle climb a short set of stairs just beyond the fountain and take a seat.

"Not anymore!" Lobo replied, his tone sharp, like a gunshot. The guy was definitely not in any mood to waste time.

Two college students walking past us turned and looked at him as he spoke, probably because of his shirt as much as the impact of his words. Like Carla and me, one student wore a sweater and the other a jacket, but Lobo stood there in the same denim work shirt with the sleeves cut off. I'm so used to seeing the old guy's resistance to cold, I forget how people react when they see him like that.

Ignoring his no nonsense attitude, Carla tried again. "Come on Lobo, what's with you pushing your friend off to the side?" While she spoke, Edgar showed up and landed in a bush near Lyle.

"Get away from me, Edgar," we heard Lyle say to the bird. "I don't need no babysitter."

Turning his attention away from Lyle and Edgar, Lobo replied to Carla's question. "He wouldn't be able to take what you're probably going to see."

"It's that bad?" I almost shouted, causing more looks from a tour group walking past us. Even as I spoke, my skin started feeling all prickly just like what happened out in the plaza, again reminding me way too much of what happened in the vortex. Not a good memory at all.

"Relax," Lobo replied. "The problem is with Lyle himself. You two have nothing to worry about. Not yet anyway."

Not yet? Oh great! Lobo's words were definitely not helping my nervousness.

"Lyle's unprotected experiences with the Particle Being long ago badly traumatized him. Taking him anywhere near such massive concentrations of particles right now could cause him considerable psychological harm." As soon as he finished his sentence, the man turned around, waved us forward and went up the same steps Lyle had just used. End of discussion. We followed behind him as we did before. As I glanced at Carla, she just shook her head and shrugged.

After going up a second set of stairs, the three of us arrived at a large semicircle shaped area on the front of Flagler College covered with all kinds of figures popping out of it, including little cherubs. Terracotta, Carla calls all that stuff of the same brick red color you see on lots of downtown St. Augustine buildings, especially around doors and windows.

Two large wooden doors stood open right in the middle of all that artwork, showing a darkened interior. Lobo quickly walked through the doors and into the gloom with us trailing behind him like before. To be honest, I hated going in there, but I really had little choice.

Once inside, my eyes slowly adjusted to the lower light enough to see a crowd of people clustered in the middle of a large room. And nothing jumped out at us.

I don't know what I was expecting exactly, but I felt a little better when I wasn't immediately attacked.

In a high-pitched voice, a young woman with an I.D. badge, probably a college student, was telling the crowd about Henry Flagler's first visit to St. Augustine.

Under all those feet, I noticed a mostly light colored mosaic floor with lots of intricate designs. And forming a circle around all those people from floor to ceiling stood Lobo's caryatids—eight wood columns, each with four carved female statues facing outwards in different directions.

Tell you what. Seeing Lobo's small prototype caryatid column back at his house hadn't prepared me for the real ones. I mean those things looked like a band of old-time goddesses. Sure I knew Lobo created and sold beautiful carvings for a living but I never expected to see anything so huge and magnificent.

"I've always loved these wooden ladies," Carla said in a low voice next to me, eyebrows arched high, "but now they … take on a whole new meaning knowing Lobo created them."

"And he made these things in the *eighteen hundreds*," I added in a whisper as I reached up and ran several fingertips across the folds in the robe of the figure closest to me. Hard, smooth and cool. I still found it difficult to accept the reality of Lobo's great age. And now, Lyle's age as well.

"Oooh yeah, he did." Carla replied in a tone of almost religious worship as her eyes slid over the carving in front of us.

Wanting to get a better look at all the caryatids, I walked farther out into the circle they created but found myself startled one more time.

There above me were two more floors, both with their own wood columns and an even higher central dome covered with what looked like gold colored paintings—Flagler College's rotunda. Carla had told me about it on our walk to the Antique Mall, but it's size and beauty still surprised me.

The ceiling between the two floors even had brightly painted murals all over it.

What a place.

As I tried to take in the stunning sight above me, I felt a sharp jab in my side—from Lobo's elbow. When I looked at him in surprise standing next to me, he tilted his head to the left and then slid his fiery dark eyes in that same direction.

That's when I saw Carla walking towards a large, circular window made out of cut glass pieces. Obviously the man wanted me to follow her, so I did.

"What?" I asked when he came over to stand between us near the window.

"You can be a gawking tourist some other time," he replied, his voice at an unusually lower volume. "Listen carefully you two. What I feared the most is starting to happen. I saw signs of it in the plaza and elsewhere on our walk here, but now it's confirmed.

"The particles that passed through you both have already partially detached the previous segments of the Particle Being in here from their suspended animation. There is now an active merger taking place between the new and the old."

"How do you know that?" Carla asked.

"Because the caryatids are where I imprisoned the first two Particle being eruptions. I can see the new particles overlaying the old. The color variations show me the blending has already begun, the white mixing with the purple."

"Oh crap!" I whispered in a panicked voice, scared out of my wits. "I just touched one of your carvings." Carla's eyes widened when I said what I did.

"Not a problem," came Lobo's quick reply, much to my relief. "The silver keychain in your jeans pocket makes you unappealing to the particles. At least for the time being."

"Whew!" I said with an explosive sigh of relief. "I forgot all about the silver thing. Thank *you* Lobo for your protection."

"Don't thank me yet." He fired back. "We've got a long way to go here and you both have reached a turning point in your preparation for what's to come.

"Now, look closely at the nearest caryatid." As Lobo spoke those words, he put one hand on my shoulder and his other hand on Carla's.

16

The Caryatids

As I looked up at the closest caryatid as instructed, I felt Lobo's energy flow through my shoulder and travel all the way across me until it hit my spine. From there it gushed upward into my head where it flooded my brain like a cool mountain stream—very unlike other energy transfers the man had given me before.

That's when I finally saw the particles. But they really didn't look like the tiny, individual *things* I remembered from the vortex. Not exactly, anyway.

Over the entire statue, outward to a distance of ten or twelve inches, was a glistening, bubbling, pulsating, semi-transparent mass, sort of white in color. I say "sort of white" because within the white were what looked like thick veins of purple. That made the whole thing a strange living mixture of both colors.

"Good Lord!" Carla gasped, as Lobo pulled his hands away from our shoulders. The surprise in her voice said everything I was feeling at that moment.

Have a long, hard look at your enemy, you two. It took me a few seconds to realize Lobo hadn't actually spoken. The man's voice was inside my head. Even though his mind-to-mind contact wasn't something new, it still startled me at times. When he looked over at me, I just nodded as if he had spoken those words out loud.

On the other side of Lobo, Carla was sweeping the rest of the room with her eyes, increasing wonder mixed with fear written all across her face. When I followed her gaze, the reason for her reaction became very clear.

All the other caryatids had their own dense, shimmering particle coverings. And from the head of each statue, two thick strands, one white and one purple, rose for about ten feet and then curved inward, forming a huge, glittering jagged edged ball of violet.

From that concentration of particles, thin shafts of the same violet color shot downward rapidly at various times like lasers and just as quickly went back up to their source.

The targets of those particle blasts from above? The heads of people in the crowd listening to the tour guide. Not everyone, maybe three fourths of the group.

It took me until that moment to understand what Lobo must have felt when he first saw the Particle Being firing threads of itself into mourners at the Loring funeral so long ago—horror. My impulse was to run up to that group and scream at them to get out of the building but I didn't. All those people would just think I had lost my mind.

From somewhere came a sharp stink, sort of like a mixture of ozone and burning wires. Ozone. That electrical smell in the air you get during a thunderstorm.

Once again, Lobo's voice rang in my head and I assumed in Carla's as well. The merger of the old and new portions of the Particle Being is proceeding at an even higher rate of speed than I projected. The development of that violet object above us is a clear indicator of such activity.

At least now you both have the permanent ability to sense all particles regardless of which eruption they came from. This includes a special sense of smell. That electrical scent you've just noticed is another way you can always tell particles are somewhere close.

The good news, if you can call it such, is that most of the particle coloration in here is still white. What this indicates is how most of the suspended animation continues even though it is weakened. But if this all turns violet like the ball up there, we shall find ourselves in deep trouble.

"What about all those people?" Carla asked, tilting her head in the direction of the tour group and echoing my own thoughts.

Her shaky voice and the disgusted look on her face seemed to match the newly developed knot in my stomach somehow. I really wanted to get out of there as fast as possible and I had a very strong feeling that Carla agreed.

No one in the crowd is being harmed, yet. Even as Lobo's voice in my head continued, the word, "yet" stuck in my mind. Not good. Not good at all.

True to form, the creature is attracted to the many humans in such close proximity to it. The thing is simply probing those people trying to learn what it can, much like I saw at the Loring funeral. That part of the crowd not being probed are mostly those who are either wearing or carrying silver, or both.

Just as Lobo completed his last point, a thick strand of violet popped out of the jagged core above us, dropped close to the rotunda floor and then shot straight at Lobo. The old guy never twitched a muscle, but Carla and I flinched.

I'm telling you what. That's when the urge to run really hit me—big-time.

But that strand didn't actually touch Lobo. Instead, it stopped about three feet from his nose before stretching out another foot until the end of it came to what looked like a sharpened point. To me, it looked like a nasty, thick needle, getting ready to inject itself.

I wanted to yell at Lobo to move out of the way, but before I could even get that thought together, the needle strand shot back up into the huge jagged ball above us. As usual, Lobo never blinked once during that very scary that event.

"I've been recognized," he said just as if he had met someone on the street he knew. "Bound to happen sooner or later."

"Look," Carla said in a sharp voice that even made some people nearby glance in our direction. She was pointing at the violet mass above us.

Following her gaze and finger, I saw why she wanted us to shift our attention. A piece of that ball, about the size of a person's head, had just about broken loose and was slowly flattening. Within a few seconds it stretched out into a long, violet shaft.

Then without warning, the shaft disappeared into the opposite wall facing the courtyard. It looked like a spear being thrown by an unseen force.

"What the—" Luckily for me, Lobo interrupted me before I could finish my sentence. Carla would not have been happy with the word I was about to say.

It's sending out colonies, Lobo said in continued telepathic mode. His voice inside my head had a definite hardness to it.

My close proximity to that probing strand a short while ago allowed me to pick up information that two dangerously large portions of the creature have already been released. This is in addition to the smaller pieces I already saw evidence of on our way into downtown. One has entered Matanzas Bay where it will continue its investigation of sea life.

"From what I can tell," Lobo then said out loud, "the other large piece is somewhere in the vicinity of the plaza. We need to find it and find it now."

17

A Flower for Henry

How bad is it?" Lyle shouted from his bench just before he ran over to us as we walked out of the college and back out into daylight.

At the same time, Edgar squawked and exploded out of a palm tree before flying away towards the plaza. The first tour group we had seen on our way into the courtyard was still there, but now they all turned and looked at Lyle.

"Are you trying to start a panic?" Lobo said in a low, harsh voice when the little homeless guy joined us.

"I'm sorry, I'm sorry," Lyle whispered loudly, his eyes almost popping out of his head. I could just about taste the man's fear which sure didn't help reduce mine any. A quick glance at Carla told me Lyle might be affecting her the same way.

"No more talk," Lobo ordered, grabbing Lyle by an arm and almost dragging him down the main walkway towards King Street. The tour group eyed all of us, wondering, I was sure, what the heck was happening.

After hesitating for a few seconds, Carla and I followed right behind Lobo and Lyle. But by that point, they were about twenty feet ahead of us. We didn't want to run and arouse any more curiosity so we walked at a normal pace as if we had all the time in the world.

We exited the college grounds in less than a minute, but it seemed to take forever. While Lobo steered Lyle to the left onto the sidewalk alongside King Street and its noisy traffic, Carla and I stopped dead in our tracks as we faced the statue of Henry Flagler. Unlike when we passed by the thing on the way into the college, this time it had a bubbling, glistening, violet colored covering of particles.

That nasty stuff looked almost like a coating of sparkly cotton candy, but you could see through it. Old Henry was still at least partially visible. One more time, the odor of ozone and burning wires raced up my nose and I wondered if the colony around the statue had been there when we walked by it the first time.

"Oh no!" Carla whispered just as I saw a dark-haired woman lift her little girl, a toddler with the same color of hair as her mother, up to put a flower in Henry Flagler's hand.

When the child's fingers got within about a foot from the statue, a dozen or more strands of violet shot outward from its particle covering and then arced inward right at the child. That whole scene made me think of a spider using its legs to close in on something to eat.

It all happened so quickly that Carla and I didn't have time to decide what to do. My instinct was to yell at the mother to pull her daughter away. But before I could even open my mouth, everything changed very quickly.

The strands stopped in midair about a foot from the little girl's head and as they did, she looked around as if she could see them and laughed. And like it was all a big game, she giggled some more while putting her hand right through the particle covering to give Henry his flower.

Instantly, the particles around Henry's hand and wrist went away, taking all those strands with them.

"It's ... the bracelet," Carla said as the mother gently lowered her child to the ground. Only then did I see the band of silver around the child's wrist, helping me to understand what Carla meant.

By then, Lobo and Lyle were long gone down King Street and we had to hustle to catch up with them.

18

A Thin Stream of Drool

As Lobo started talking, I couldn't help but steal another glance at Potter's Wax Museum on the other side of King Street. The figures in the windows over there glowed a soft, rippling violet, matching the covering around a wooden pirate on the sidewalk a few stores to the right and the nearby statue of Ponce de Leon.

It was starting to feel like clumps of the Particle Being had us surrounded and it made my skin crawl.

"Before we can actually do anything," Lobo said, "we have to locate the creature's major colony in this area. What we see around us are just minor concentrations." He had gathered all four of us together under a big oak tree in the plaza just across from Potter's.

"Looks like they're everywhere," Carla said, her eyes flickering back and forth nervously from Ponce de Leon to Lobo.

"Everywhere!" Lyle repeated in an excited voice, his head shifting back and forth while he kept scanning as much of the plaza as he could.

"All we've seen so far," Lobo explained, shaking his head, "are small groups of particles that have attached themselves to some plants, small animals and random human-like forms they happen to encounter. There are two likely places for us to search, places that have a lot of statues and other representations of human beings like large paintings and stained glass.

"Both Potter's Wax Museum and the cathedral fit such a description more than other locations right around the plaza. We can see from here that Potter's already has its share, but the bulk of the particles we're looking for still could be in either location.

"You two take the wax museum and search each exhibit room," Lobo said to Carla and me. "You'll know if you find it and if you do, get out of there fast. This creature is evolving so rapidly I don't want to take any chances even though you both are protected by silver."

Lobo pulled the wad of money out of his pocket he had tried to give Lyle. This time though, he peeled off a twenty-dollar bill and shoved it into Carla's hand. "Ticket money for Potter's."

OK, to tell you the truth, I thought we were all going to be together doing that search of the wax museum and go on as a group to the cathedral. Umm, no. No so much.

You see, up until then, having Lobo around had given me a certain sense of security. Now, the idea of going into the wax museum without him made me think twice, even with a silver key chain in my pocket. I didn't want to show too much fear around Carla so I didn't say anything in protest.

"Uh, you're not going with us?" Carla asked, making me at least not feel alone in my concern.

"No time," he replied. "Lyle, you're with me." Without giving Lyle a chance to react, Lobo grabbed him by the arm again and the two of them headed towards the cathedral on the other side of the plaza.

In silence, Carla and I watched the two men walk away. Finally, she said, "You ready for this?"

"Without Lobo? Not a chance. Besides, I'm not wearing long, silver earrings like you are."

"I can loan you one if you like."

"And leave you partly unprotected? Not a chance."

"Don't go saying I didn't give you the opportunity," Carla replied with a grim smile.

"Yeah, yeah," I replied, taking her hand. "Let's do it."

The sounds of kids somewhere behind me in the plaza, mixed with traffic noises, made everything *seem* so normal. But the slight smell of ozone and burning wires on the wind at that moment told a very different story.

With no more conversation between us, Carla and I walked across King Street hand-in-hand. In the windows at Potter's Wax Museum were wax figures of devils and angels, covered in violet particles. The sign said, "Now Presenting, The Worlds of Good and Evil."

"Talk about appropriate," I whispered to Carla, pointing at the sign just as we walked through the open front door.

"Very synchronistic," she whispered back. When I didn't reply, Carla realized I had no idea what she meant.

"Synchronicity," she said as we walked over to the ticket counter. "A quick definition: purposeful, linked coincidences. It's a term invented long ago by Carl Jung, the famous psychiatrist. I started reading up on all that after hearing Lobo say so often how there are no real coincidences."

"Oh," was all I could say, amazed once again at Carla's razor sharp mind and incredible storehouse of knowledge.

"Hey Carla," said the girl sitting on a stool behind the ticket counter right after taking money from a young couple with two middle school-aged boys.

"Kelsey!" Carla replied, putting a big old smile on her face even though I knew she felt anything but happy. "They've got you on duty today, huh?"

"Yup … my turn … to run the store." Kelsey's words came out of her slowly and a little slurred. On top of that, she had this weird half smile on her face and her eyes didn't seem to be able to focus or something.

At first as we walked up to her, I thought she might be drunk or on drugs until I saw a violet coming out through the bottom part of the wall behind her. It curled around and around until it arched high above the girl and then went down in a straight line to the back of her head.

When she moved, just the slightest bit, the strand from above also moved. It had to be attached to Kelsey's head somehow. Seeing that made the hairs on the back of my neck stand up. A quick, hard squeeze from Carla's hand in mine told me she had seen the same thing.

"Um, two tickets please," Carla said, putting Lobo's twenty dollar bill on the counter.

"No charge today … for friends and locals," Kelsey said. "Just … go on in … enjoy." After speaking, her head angled forward a little and her lower lip hung loose. Over it flowed a thin stream of drool that dripped onto her black Potter's Wax Museum shirt. She didn't seem to notice. Not good. Not good at all.

"Right. Uh, thanks, Kelsey," Carla said as she picked up the money and we both let go of each other's hand.

As fast as possible, we turned around and headed for the entrance to the exhibits we had passed on our way to the ticket counter.

"Did you see that?" Carla whispered when we got to the door marked, "This Way to Good and Evil." The young couple and their two boys had already gone inside.

"Couldn't miss it," I whispered back. "But I thought Lobo said the Particle Being wasn't a real danger to people yet?"

"Looks like his calculations were off. Besides, you heard what he said about that thing evolving quickly. We've got to do something, Jeff. Get Kelsey out of here, now!"

"Uh, hold on a minute," I said, feeling that same urgency but thinking a little differently.

"Why?"

"Well, we don't know what trying to disconnect Kelsey from that thing will do to her or to us. Besides, we still have to find out how big of a Particle Being colony is actually inside. We'll be seeing Lobo soon and we can ask him about Kelsey then, OK?"

Carla stared at me, wild-eyed now and obviously torn about what to do for her friend.

Closing her eyes tight for a few seconds, she took a deep breath, and opened them again. "OK, OK, you're right," she said, after exhaling slowly and reaching for the door handle. "But I hate leaving her here like that."

19

Infested

As soon as Carla opened the door to the exhibits, we knew something was radically wrong. Hot, humid air hit us in the face, carrying with it the now familiar stink of ozone and burning wires. Only this time, it was much worse than we had smelled before.

In front of us stretched a long, wide hall with a very high ceiling that ended where two huge doors stood wide open. In the dimly lighted room beyond, violet colored, lightning-like flashes erupted continuously. Not a good sign at all. Going into that room and turning to the right, was the family who were buying tickets when we entered Potter's. As they disappeared around the corner, their voices drifted away, leaving the hallway totally quiet.

"It's dark and nasty in there," I said to Carla. The only light in the hallway came from that distant room. "It feels like they have the heat turned up high."

"This is crazy," Carla replied. "It makes me think of those haunted houses people set up for Halloween.

"Yeah, but this isn't Halloween and the violet color of those flashes can't be good news. I'll bet all that bursting light and the creepy strand sticking in your friend's head is more than enough evidence of the particle colony Lobo's looking for. Let's just go tell him now and not take any more chances."

"Wait, hold on a minute." Carla stepped into the hall, not in the direction I wanted to go. "As you said, we owe it to Kelsey and Lobo to find out as much as we can. The more information we're able to gather, the better chance we'll have of putting a quick end to all this."

"I was afraid you were going to say something like that." Reluctantly, but knowing she was right, I joined her in the hot, eerie atmosphere. Behind me, the door swung shut with a bang, startling both of us. "OK, OK, let's get this over with and then get our butts out of here, fast."

"I wonder why they left it so dark in this hallway," Carla said as we both walked forward slowly. "There are lights on the ceiling, but they haven't been turned on."

"Or somebody deliberately shut them off for some reason," I corrected, looking for a switch and not finding one.

On each side of the hall, there were three closed doors, spaced evenly apart. Only the dim light and flashes of violet ahead made it possible for us to see our surroundings at all. Attached to each of those doors was a piece of light colored paper.

"Where do they lead?" I asked, pointing to the door closest to us.

"To the new exhibit rooms, I suppose." Carla angled over to the first door on our left and look closely at one of the signs.

"It's a handwritten note and it says, 'Repairs in Progress.' But that can't be right. Potter's just reopened after being closed for so long. I heard they completely redesigned the place so there shouldn't be any need for repairs. Anyway, it looks like somebody scribbled this in a hurry. The other notes probably have the same thing written on them."

"Locked," I said, after joining her and trying the door handle. "And that thing is moist."

"Probably condensation from all the heat and humidity."

"I hope that's all it is," I replied, wiping my hand on my pants while we continued walking. The smell and the heat in that place were really starting to get to me. What a contrast to the cool temperature outside the building.

After only a few steps, we both heard the murmur of distant voices. "Good news, right?" I asked, hopefully. "I mean at least the visitors up there are just talking and not screaming."

"Well, Golden Boy," Carla replied after taking a deep breath, "we're about to find out." Ever once in a while, Carla uses that old nickname I had back in elementary school. Kids called me that because of my last name, Golden, and my blond hair.

By then, the big double doorway loomed about ten feet ahead of us. Inside the room beyond, even in that dimness with its flashing light, I saw what looked like a crowd of people with just a tinge of violet all over them. I hoped all that color we were seeing was just part of the new exhibit, but down deep I knew it wasn't.

"Most, if not all, of the people you see up there are wax and not visitors," Carla said while we moved forward. "I recognize some of them. There's Franklin and Eleanor Roosevelt, Harriett Tubman and Moses. And it looks to me like a large room in there so this must be the Good versus Evil exhibit."

"Can't wait," I groaned, really wishing we could get the hell out of there.

As much as I wanted to avoid it, we finally arrived at the big open doorway. That's when I realized the crowd of permanent Potter's residents ahead of us about another twenty feet was larger than I thought. So I could see more of it and get our little inspection trip over with as quickly as possible, I stepped just inside the room a short distance. Carla came in right behind me.

The place contained not one but two large groups of wax figures separated by a space of maybe thirty feet. In the tall ceiling, out of fifteen or so fluorescent light fixtures, only five or six had bulbs that were working.

Unfortunately, the violet coloring of the group directly in front of us came from a thin veil of particles all over them. That was bad enough, but the second group of wax people to our far right were swimming in a boiling sea of deep violet that silently popped like it contained millions of little ongoing explosions. Above all those figures rose a huge Particle Being cloud about eight feet in the air.

And from that huge cloud, snaked thin, sparking strands that arced upward and then down into the heads of maybe fifteen *real people*, including the family we had just seen enter the room. Apparently, none of them could see the violet infection spread all over the room.

Part of me wanted to grab Carla and run out of there, but to be perfectly honest, I was too fascinated.

"Dear God," Carla whispered, sliding an arm around mine and holding tight. Her words mirrored my feelings. This was not good. Not good at all.

As we watched, a few of the real people moved around inspecting the exhibits as best they could in the dim light from the ceiling. And some of them were talking to each other in low voices. Most of the folks in there though just stood around as if they were in a trance. Those long, slender, glistening pieces of violet kept hitting each of them in head, rapid fire. Obviously, Kelsey wasn't the only one having a problem with the Particle Being.

"Why all that activity around one group of wax figures and not the other?" I whispered back to Carla.

"I guess it's because that's the "Evil" bunch," she replied, holding my arm even tighter. "See, it's led by Lord Voldemort from the Harry Potter series. Right behind him is the monster from the old *Alien* movies, Adolf Hitler and Darth Vader from *Star Wars*."

Harry Potter in Potter's Wax Museum? Talk about coincidences.

Sure enough, a sneering Lord Voldemort, wand in hand, stood in front of his followers of evil, all bathed in explosions of violet.

Facing that group, with much less of a particle covering, was Harry Potter, backed up by Hermione Granger, Ron Weasley, Luke Skywalker, Martin Luther King, Jr. and Abe Lincoln, just to name a few.

"That means this creature likes bad guys?" I asked. But before Carla could answer, a large shaft of sparkling violet twisted straight up out of the particle cloud and came to a sharp point. Slowly, the entire shaft bent in our direction. It was starting to look way too much like what happened to Lobo at Flagler College.

"Run!" I shouted, yanking Carla backwards until we both were able to turn around and take off the way we came. Silver or no silver, I was not about for us to take any more chances.

20

Damaged Forever

Carla and I didn't stop running even when we got to King Street outside of Potter's Wax museum. A break in traffic allowed us to keep going, but people in cars and on the sidewalk looked at us as if we might have just robbed the place. We could have cared less.

In the plaza, Lobo and Lyle waited under the same oak tree as before and they became our destination. Only when we got to them did we dare stop and look behind us. What a relief to see that no strands or shafts of violet had followed us and were about to attack.

"Having fun are you?" Lobo asked when we got to him.

"Uh-oh," Lyle said, "they found it for sure."

Out of breath, neither one of us could say anything, so Carla and I just leaned against the tree and sucked in big gulps of fresh air. I can't begin to tell you how good it felt to be out in the cool openness of the plaza and away from the stifling, closed-in atmosphere at Potter's.

"I'll talk and you listen for a minute," Lobo growled as if we had done something wrong. "We only found more minor colonies in the cathedral but it looks to me like you two must have stirred up a hornet's nest in the wax museum. Now I need to go over there and see for myself.

"While I'm gone, tell Lyle what you found." Without another word, he turned around and followed the exact path we had taken just a short time before. Lyle watched him leave with a frightened, lost puppy look on his face.

Still breathing heavily, I decided to sit down on the grass facing King Street and Potter's. I wasn't about to turn my back on the hiding place of that huge Particle Being concentration.

"Good idea," Carla said, grabbing her own plot of grass next to me. Above us, a squirrel started chattering and competing with the traffic noise, probably unhappy we were near his tree.

Lyle looked down at us. "Don't want to hear anything. I know all I need to know about that damned PB. Old, new or whatever. This time, Lobo's not going to control the thing, No sir! Oh my good God we are truly doomed."

"PB?" I asked, still breathing deeply.

"Short for Particle Being." Lyle shuddered as he said those words.

"Oh, OK," I replied. But the man's deeply negative outlook was definitely not what either Carla or I needed to hear.

To calm him down, even though I wasn't very calm myself, I invited Lyle to sit with us. "Come on, we'll all wait for Lobo together. You can see him coming from here just as good as you can standing up there."

Lyle took a nervous glance at the wax museum, hesitated, and then sat cross-legged on the other side of me but a little too close, actually. The wind kept bringing me, and even Carla, whiffs of his body odor. When I glanced at her, I saw Carla eyes squint and her nose wrinkle.

"What can you tell us about the PB?" Carla asked, once Lyle got settled. Sure, she wanted to know, but I think she also wanted to keep her mind busy and not think about the slight smell of ozone and burning wires still in the air.

"Me?" Lyle replied. He looked startled that anybody would ask him for information. "Oh. Yeah. Bad night, long ago. Real bad night. Those sparkly things just blasted up through me like a knife through butter. They did that to Lobo too.

"And made Swiss Cheese out of my brain you know. Damaged me forever. Wasn't protected like Lobo. Nope, not a bit of silver on me.

"I used to be smart. Good business man too but no more. Lost my business. I ended up working for Lobo for a long time after those particle things got me. Me and Lobo used to be partners—before everything changed.

Partners? That meant, I realized, that Lyle must have been the other person with Lobo when Carla and I fell in Maria Sanchez Creek in 1885. I got a definite feeling Carla had just recognized the same thing.

"Wife up and left me," Lyle had the saddest look on his face. "Took my little boy with her too. Never saw him again. He must have died. Ten years old he was, back in 1879. And here I am still alive."

All of a sudden, the man's eyes filled with tears and they flowed down his cheeks into his beard. "I need a beer. You got a beer, Jeff?"

"Uh, sorry Lyle, I don't drink beer." God, I felt bad for the guy. I couldn't imagine being a parent who not only lost his child but stayed the same age as that child grew old and died.

Carla reached in her jeans pocket, pulled out some tissues, handed them to me to give to Lyle and said, "I'll bet he was cute, your son."

Lyle wiped his face and smiled his gap-toothed smile. "Yes ma'am. A fine looking boy he was.

"I'm an alcoholic you know, but I can quit drinking anytime I want. I just drink beer, wine and such to shut off the pain and the memories. I don't like thinking about all those particles."

"I see," Carla replied. "I don't like thinking about them either. But what makes you feel that Lobo's not going to be able to control the Particle Being?"

"Oh that! Well now, I watched him fight to corral it the first time. Lotta years it took, but now that there's more particles added to the old. Lobo stands no chance at all. No sir! Nary a chance."

Just as if he had switched channels on a TV set, Lyle said to both of us, "You two brought this new PB batch down on us didn't you? Isn't that right? Lobo told me about it while we were walking."

"Well, I guess you could say that," I replied. "But we didn't mean for it to happen and we had no way to control the situation."

"Lotta good that does now." Lyle spit into the grass next to him.

"Is there anything specific we should know about the Particle Being?" Carla asked, obviously trying to change the subject again.

Lyle thought for a minute and said. "There's too many to count. Thing is, my brain won't fire on all cylinders enough for me to recall. Oh, but here's one. I'll bet Lobo didn't tell you about the monster, did he?"

"Monster?" Carla and I said at the same time.

"You mean the Particle Being?" I asked as I noticed Lobo emerge from the wax museum and wait for traffic to thin so he could cross King Street.

"No, the monster part," Lyle replied. "The St. Augustine Monster. Look out, here comes King Lobo, back from his reconnaissance."

"Why call him *King* Lobo?" Carla asked.

"Simple." Lyle replied. "His first name in Rex. In Latin that means King."

"Really? I never knew his first name." Carla shook her head.

"*Rex* Lobo?" I said in wonder as I thought about the man's mailbox that said, "R. Lobo." I wasn't surprised so much about the name as the fact that he actually had a first one. He only wanted to be called Lobo. Then again, *King* Lobo sort of fit the man's personality.

At that point, his majesty arrived at the plaza and walked over to us.

"The main Particle Being colony, besides the one out in Matanzas Bay, is there inside Potter's all right." Lobo kept shifting his fiery old gaze back and forth between all of us as he spoke. "And it has strengthened so much that we need to make a counter move quickly." Then to Carla and me he said, "As you saw for yourselves, its domination of humans has already begun."

"Sure looked that way to me." A chill flashed all over my body as I remembered what Carla and I saw in the main exhibit room at the wax museum.

"Saints preserve us," Lyle whimpered.

"Carla, your friend Kelsey didn't want to let me into the exhibit area. I was able override her link to the colony temporarily but that's all. I couldn't safely sever it. To do so would have killed her, instantly."

When Lobo spoke those words, Carla's head snapped back almost as if he had slapped her. At the same time, I felt a heavy sinking sensation in my stomach. For the two of us, all of Lobo's warnings about danger were increasingly becoming a clear-cut reality.

"And you," Lobo said, turning to Lyle, "definitely talk way too much."

Part Four

Fishing

21

The St. Augustine Monster

Relax," Carla said to me from the bench where she sat on Lobo's dock. Spock lay curled up at her feet as usual. "They'll be out when they're ready. At least it isn't raining." I swear, sometimes that girl has nerves of steel.

After driving all of us back to his place from downtown without saying anything more about the wax museum, Lobo ordered Carla and me to sit on his dock while he and Lyle had a quick conversation in the house. Poor Lyle looked like he would rather die than have that chat with Lobo. We had been waiting for them since then.

"But Carla, this hanging around is driving me crazy!" Not really looking for a response, I continued pacing up and down the dock. "They've been in there for at least fifteen minutes."

In the bay not far from us, a large mullet jumped out of the water and splashed back down again.

"You're going to burn yourself out with curiosity," Carla replied.

"OK, then talk to me," I said, finally sitting down next to her. From our bench, we could keep a watch on Lobo's front door for any activity. "What was all that monster stuff Lyle started talking about back in the plaza?"

"That? I'm not sure exactly what he was trying to say, but he might be referring to one of those weird pieces of St. Augustine history."

"You mean there really was something called the St. Augustine Monster?"

"Yup. It stirred things up for over 100 years. Google it sometime and you'll see the story is still alive and well, even in other parts of the world."

"No way."

"Umm hmm. It all started in 1896 when two boys were riding their bikes over on St. Augustine Beach. They found a huge dead animal washed up on shore, badly decomposed"

"So how big is huge?"

"I think it weighed in at somewhere close to seven tons."

"Tons? Oh, come on now."

"I'm not kidding. It's all documented. The boys got Dr. Webb from the St. Augustine Historical Society to go look at the thing with them. After he did his investigation, he said he thought at one time it had tentacles and was probably a giant octopus. Webb actually measured the main part of the body at around 20 feet long or so.

"That's incredible."

"Yeah, but even though Dr. Webb provided photos and tissue samples, scientists from a lot of universities and the Smithsonian Institution over the years have argued back and forth over the creature's identity. Some agreed with Webb that is was a giant octopus and could have been as wide as 200 feet. But the most recent analysis classifies it as nothing more than a giant chunk of whale blubber."

"Whales? Around here?"

"Sure. The Atlantic Ocean off St. Augustine is the prime breeding ground for Right Whales. Haven't you seen the caution signs for boaters to watch out for them along the edges of Matanzas Bay?"

I didn't want to admit I hadn't seen any such signs so I answered her question with one of my own. "OK, but why would Lobo be upset that Lyle said something to us about the monster, blubber chunk, or whatever you want to call it?"

"Don't ask me, ask him," Carla replied, jutting her chin towards Lobo's front door as it swung open.

22

The Slab

Lyle followed Lobo onto the dock but at quite a distance, like he deliberately didn't want to be very close. Each man carried a cardboard box. *What the hell?*

"Look out," Carla whispered to me. "I think you're about to get more answers than you bargained for."

When he arrived at the table where we sat with its sunken metal fireplace in the middle, Lobo plopped his box down with a thud. "Yours too," he said to Lyle, pointing at the table.

Lyle, who was standing a good six feet away, hesitated, licked his lips and gulped, but did as Lobo directed. As soon as he set his box next to the other one though, he quickly stepped away from the table and stared at it as if it might explode.

That's interesting.

In typical Lobo style, he didn't say a word at first. Instead, he reached into his box and pulled out a large glass jar with a glass stopper in it. When he did that, Lyle flinched and then looked away.

"It's best if you send Spock off the dock," Lobo said to Carla. "For his own good." Carla returned the man's intent gaze for a few seconds and then did as he asked.

The jar in the man's hand looked old, like something out of a doctor's office from a couple of centuries ago. Knowing Lobo came from such a period in time, I wondered if he bought the thing new or was it old even back in those days.

Inside the container, a milky liquid went almost up to the top where tar or black wax sealed the glass stopper in place.

As Lobo placed the jar on the table in front of him, all that liquid sloshed around a little and I saw Lyle wince. On the outside of the jar there was a peeling, discolored label with faded writing I couldn't read.

Again, reaching into his box, Lobo brought out a glass dinner plate, a pair of metal tongs and a large kitchen knife with a wood handle. The plate and tongs he put next to the box, but he used the knife to strip away that tar, or whatever it was, from the top of the jar as it sat on the table.

What is all that for?

"You might want to hold your breath for a little bit," he said, glancing at each of us. "Otherwise the smell could be a little overpowering." Lyle did as he was told, but he also closed his eyes.

What is going on here? I wanted to ask questions and Carla looked like she was about to when Lobo put his hand on the jar top. Obviously, the man was allowing no time for discussion so both of us quickly sucked in some air and held it.

With a little twisting and a squeak of glass on glass, Lobo loosened the top, pulled it off and stepped back a little. As soon as he did that, the white liquid inside started bubbling and making a slight sizzling noise.

Then from the jar's open top flowed a thick white mist. The stuff slowly twisted its way upward several feet until it slowed and began creating what looked like a wispy mushroom cloud. And just as that cloud expanded to about the size of a basketball, a chilly breeze came in off Matanzas Bay and blew it all away.

With a nod from Lobo, we all went back to breathing normally, but wished we hadn't.

A nasty stink still filled the air around us, sort of a mixture of chemicals and something rotten. I started coughing.

"Gross," Carla said, waving her hand in front of her face.

"Gah!" Lyle's eyes were open now, but the expression on his face reminded me of someone who had just taken a mouthful of bad tasting food.

I hated to think what sniffing the air might have been like before that breeze came along. Lobo didn't seem to be bothered by the smell at all.

"It'll pass," he replied to our reactions as he picked up the tongs, plunged the grasping ends into the jar and pulled out what looked like a thick piece of grey colored fish, maybe seven or eight inches long and about three inches wide.

"Yeah, right," I said, still coughing while Lobo dropped the unidentified, dripping chunk onto the glass plate in front of him. More of that terrible smell filled the air. Things were getting stranger by the second.

"What is that thing?" Carla asked, her face all scrunched up.

"All in good time. First, however, both you and Jeff need to hear about the rest of the story with regard to the St.

Augustine Monster." I wasn't really surprised the guy knew Carla had already given me some background information on the subject.

"If you're really going to go through all of this Lobo," Lyle said, staring at the chunk of grey sitting on its plate, "then I need a beer."

"Not now," Lobo growled, and Lyle quietly hung his head.

"Rest of the story?" Carla asked. "Lobo, what *are* you talking about?"

"That slab of tissue on the table, my dear young lady, is the last existing specimen taken from our infamous monster long ago before Dr. Webb sliced his own pieces from the carcass."

"No way!" Carla replied in a loud voice. "You can't be serious."

"Oh but I am. Over the years, the scientific community *conveniently* lost what the good doctor gave them—an excellent way to make the last analysis conducted become the final word—*whale blubber.* They chose not to allow any more investigation into something they didn't understand."

"Did you cut that chunk off the creature yourself?" The words just slid out of my mouth before I had time to think about what I was asking. Why I would think such a thing, I didn't know.

"Oh you bet!" Lyle said. "Chopped it right out of that thing. Back before the twentieth century, for sure."

"You did?" Carla whispered, her eyes shifting back and forth between Lobo and the smelly old specimen. "You actually got to see and touch the monster."

I could almost feel the fascination flowing out of her. Besides having lived through parts of St. Augustine's distant past, with his own hands, Lobo had also preserved an important part of it.

"Stupid scientists," Lobo muttered, picking up the kitchen knife and giving the preserved slab a poke. "None of them realized the source for their specimens was a blending of *both* whale *and* octopus."

"But that's impossible!" Carla fired back at him.

"Not when you're dealing with the Particle Being," Lobo replied forcefully.

Before Carla or I could ask another question, he continued talking. "Besides having a deep interest in humans, the PB, as Lyle calls it, was also deeply curious about sea life. More specifically—whales and octopi, both available to it for study here in the saltwater regions off St. Augustine.

"Through my linkage with the Particle Being, I discovered it had somehow been able to manipulate what we now call DNA from both animals in order to create its own hybrid creature. That's the body of the seven ton monster those two boys and Dr. Webb discovered on St. Augustine Beach."

"They found the lifeless body because Lobo killed the thing, thank God," Lyle said, still not taking his eyes off the specimen.

"Only in a manner speaking," Lobo agreed. "That sea creature didn't exist in the way we think of something being alive. Its animation only came about because the PB inserted a majority of its own particles into the flesh it created in order for it to experience at least a limited type of physical existence. The remainder of its particles continued probing humans within the city of St. Augustine, as I told you before.

"So how could you kill something that wasn't truly alive," Carla asked.

"Simply by removing the particles from it."

"Come on Lobo," I said, "you make that sound so easy."

"The concept was simple but not the process.

"You see, the story I told you before about tricking the PB into hibernation at Flagler College was true as far as it went. A winter storm forced the hybrid sea creature out of Matanzas Bay and into the Atlantic through the St. Augustine Inlet.

"Previous to that time, it had been hiding in one of the deepest parts of the bay. In fact, I never saw the thing until just before it ceased to function. The only reason I got involved with it was because the PB cried out to me in desperation since so many of its particles were close to being destroyed.

"Destroyed?" I asked. "How."

The creature had gotten very close to the distance it could go from downtown St. Augustine without endangering that huge storehouse of particles inside it. Only by using the hybrid's tentacles to hold itself in place on the ocean bottom near the shore had all those particles survived the storm up until then.

"The PB contacted me simply because by that time its creation was so weakened, the outgoing tide would have taken it into deeper water past the danger zone."

"Couldn't the particles just detach themselves from the creature?" Carla asked. That made sense.

"Yes, but much too slowly. For those particles to even begin to extricate themselves would have meant withdrawing physical control over their creation. And if that happened, the creature's tentacles would have stopped holding onto the ocean bottom allowing it to be taken out with the tide before they could have time to escape."

"OK, let me understand this," Carla said, interrupting Lobo's tale. "Half or more of the PB's particles were locked inside the creature and they were going to be destroyed no matter what—unless you did something to save them?"

"Exactly."

"So you decided to just let the creature wash out into the ocean and that killed it along with those particles, right?" I asked.

"Wrong. I could have done that, but in doing so, the city of St. Augustine would have still been in great danger from the *remaining* half of the PB that had not entered the creature.

"Oh." I felt pretty stupid forgetting that part of Lobo's story.

"That's when I took a gamble," Lobo went on as if I hadn't said anything. "I offered the Particle Being a way to survive while still keeping the people of St. Augustine safe. To my surprise, agreement was immediate."

"He made a deal with the devil is what he did," Lyle grumbled, looking out across the bay. "And he forced me to help him do it."

Without looking at Lyle, Lobo nodded and said, "Together on that same night, Lyle and I traveled out to a lonely spot on present day Vilano Beach as directed by the Particle Being.

"There in the moonlight and rough surf left over from the storm sat at the creature, which was at least twice the size of the remains found by Dr. Webb and the two boys. Extremely long tentacles just barely kept the thing attached to the sand in that receding tide.

"Above it, the PB cloud from downtown St. Augustine hovered and sparkled.

"Lyle and I didn't have much time, but we worked quickly, using the ropes and large stakes we carried with us to temporarily anchor the thing against being swept away. In that way, we had plenty of time to accomplish our true task."

"Ho ho, that was fun!" Lyle added in a sarcastic tone of voice."Wrapping thick rope around disgusting tentacles with all those little sucker things, waves smashing into us and the water freezing cold at that time of year. Lucky the tide didn't carry me and Lobo away, no less that octopus and whale combination. And having to hammer those stakes into the sand up on the beach! What a job. What a night! Gave me nightmares for years."

"OK, Lyle," Lobo said to him. "We've heard enough from you for now."

But before Lobo started speaking again, I thought about what Lyle had just said. It made me shiver imaging what it must have been like out there in the freezing water at night with that … thing.

"Our efforts to keep the Particle Being's creation from being pulled out to sea gave us the time needed to transfer all those particles inside it to a silver box I brought with me."

When he said what he did, Lobo's dark eyes sparkled even brighter than usual. I almost got the feeling of humor lurking somewhere within him. He knew his words would startle and confuse us. I felt sure he did it deliberately just to amuse himself.

"Hold on Lobo," Carla said. "Transfer? Silver box? What—"

"The agreement with the PB, Carla," Lobo interrupted, "was this. In order for me to save the particles *within* the sea creature, *all* PB particles would have to compress themselves and enter my silver box—the ones from St. Augustine floating in the air above us on the beach first, and finally, those within the creature itself.

"Knowing how silver affected the PB, I realized it would become a prison of sorts to keep all of it contained, at least temporarily."

"And it worked?" I asked.

"Perfectly. The PB really had no choice. Once all particles were in the box, I went out into the surf and cut that little slab from the creature you see before you now as a souvenir. Lyle and I then pulled out the stakes in the sand, allowing the outgoing tide to drag the ropes and the hybrid out to sea.

"Ocean currents eventually carried the carcass down to St. Augustine Beach, where it was later *discovered* in a rotting condition and became known as the St. Augustine Monster."

"Unbelievable," Carla said, shaking her head, but even so, I knew she was loving the whole idea of being in on the secret of a long debated historical and scientific event. "But what do you mean the silver box was only temporary?"

"The terms of the agreement with the creature was that I would then take the box to the Ponce de Leon Hotel and allow all of its particles to surround and enter the caryatids where they would remain, as I told you previously, in a type of suspended animation. The choice of my wood carvings came about because they were the largest representations of people in St. Augustine—the closest I was willing to allow the PB to get to actual human beings.

"However, in order to make my wooden statues a permanent prison for the PB, I had to strategically insert silver within them previous to that event. As the creator of the caryatids, and with my connections to Henry Flagler, I had no trouble in scheduling *additional touches* to my carvings at night with Lyle as my helper in order to make that happen.

"It took forever to get that job done," Lyle complained, "balancing on ladders when we should have been asleep."

Lobo ignored Lyle and went on with his story. "Within two weeks, we completed preparing the caryatids to safely receive the PB. That following Monday, in the early morning hours, we brought the silver box to the hotel.

"It took almost until dawn for us to release small batches of particles at a time into the caryatids. But in that way I could rest assured none of them had any chance of simply ignoring our bargain and escape. Those two initial eruptions of the Particle Being have remained there ever since, as you saw in our visit to Flagler College."

"You could have just been done with it and killed those things by taking the box outside the city limits a few miles," Lyle grumbled. "But no—"

"That's enough," Lobo barked at him. "We settled that long ago so let it be."

"Maybe you two settled that question," I said, "but I'm surprised you didn't kill it too. Why? Why take the chance it could get loose again like we're worried about now?"

"Would you have killed it?" Lobo fired back. "A highly intelligent creature that had not actually done harm to anyone in the city except accidentally to Lyle? A creature I made a bargain with in good faith?"

The man's questions hung heavy in the air as a big water bird flew past us making loud noises like it was fussing at the whole world.

"He's got a point, Jeff," Carla said before I had a chance figure out whether I would have done things Lobo's way back in 1896 or not.

"And now, after all those years and work," Lyle complained, eying Carla and me, "you two upset everything by bringing more of those horrible particles into the city."

"It's not their fault." Lobo's voice was strangely subdued. "They have residual particles within them just like you do. Exactly like you, they're more susceptible to attack by the Particle Being than anyone else in St. Augustine besides you. So just back off."

"Oh," Lyle replied, lowering his eyes. "Didn't know. Sorry. But still—"

"No buts." This time Lobo's voice was firmer. Still though, for some reason he wasn't sounding like the tough old guy I had come to know. "Besides, we need Jeff and Carla if we're going to get this situation under control again. With my help, each of them has developed certain *abilities* that are going to be crucial very soon now so thank your stars they're here."

"Abilities?" Lyle asked, suddenly interested. "You mean like—"

"Exactly."

"Well then," Lyle nodded, "guess that'll be OK."

23

Bait

If we're lucky, we'll end this tonight." Lobo spoke while looking over the new items spread across the table on the dock. He had just finished emptying the box Lyle brought with him from the house.

"What is all that stuff?" I had to ask.

"Fishing equipment," Lobo replied.

"Not like any I've ever seen." Carla shook her head, clearly not believing him. I agreed, sure he had to be kidding.

"Oh, he's serious, now," Lyle said. "But I told Lobo this is dangerous business."

Before us lay a stack of old silver dollars, some paper grocery bags, four rolls of duct tape, a ball of string, four small glass boxes with fitted tops, a cordless drill, a pair of pliers, a box of sandwich bags, and a cutting board.

Makes sense, doesn't it? I mean why Carla and I were a little confused?

"Listen up you two," Lobo said, pointing to the slab of preserved hybrid sea creature. "That's our bait. There is a very high chance that specimen will attract both former and new versions of the Particle Being like flies and ants to a picnic lunch, if we use it properly. It is after all, a PB creation, even though it's old and smelly.

"And in that potential attraction, the particles will actually enter into our bait to investigate. If this happens, as I think it will, we have a good chance to capture most, if not all of the Particle Being similar to how I did it back in 1896."

"Uh huh," Carla said. "But it's the words you just used like, 'high chance' and 'might be able to,' that make me a little jittery."

You tell him. She spoke my thoughts as clearly as if I was saying them.

"Look, Carla," Lobo replied, raising his voice, "the Spanish Night Watch Parade starts at 7: 00 PM, remember? All of that activity and human energy will no doubt stir any particles in the city to action. In fact, that event could bring the old and new particles together at Flagler College into a critical mass, finally welding them into the extremely dangerous PB version you and Jeff found in the wax museum—only hundreds of times larger."

That got Carla's full attention and mine too. "The parade!" she said, closing her eyes and hitting herself in the head with the palm of her hand. "How could I forget about that? It'll be like the Loring funeral only—"

"Worse," Lobo finished for her. "Much, much worse. At that point, there will be nothing between the combined Particle Being and the people in this city. And it will attack unless we stop it."

"You got that right," Lyle said, his eyes wide, obviously scared out of his wits.

Lobo went right on talking as if Lyle hadn't spoken. "What I sensed when I entered Potter's Wax Museum today is a rapidly building appetite to experience human existence *at any cost*. That means merging with people and dominating them. The full consequences of such an event are almost unimaginable. So forgive me for not being able to give any of you 100 percent guarantees, but such a thing just isn't possible. We simply have to give it the best shot we can.

"Now, what we have here on the table, are tools that will give us the best chance of getting this situation under control." The more Lobo had talked, the more poor Lyle seemed to shrivel into himself. I thought the guy might collapse at any minute.

Silence greeted the end of Lobo's little speech. I guess none of us knew what to say after all that and for me, his quick and powerful description of what might happen unless we acted as he wanted was pretty overwhelming.

Carla threw me a quick glance that said she didn't think we had much choice. I nodded but hated having to agree. "OK," Carla said, "one question though. Are you still in contact with all the original particles you imprisoned from 1896?"

"No. Once they went into suspended animation, I lost that link. Even with their partial revival now by the newly arrived particles, the old connection hasn't been reestablished. I can *sense* all particles in the city but nothing more. The only direct connection I've had is when the combined aspects of the PB recognized me at Flagler College.

"Uh, so how are we going to do this?" I asked.

Lobo answered as if he was reading off a checklist.

"*We* are going to cut up our slab of bait and place those pieces in the glass boxes over there.

"*We* are going to drill holes in six silver dollars and make two necklaces out of them for each one of us.

"*We* are going to divide up the remaining silver dollars equally into four sandwich bags.

"*We* are going to open up four of those paper bags, and in them, *we* are going to place a sandwich bag full of silver dollars, one glass box with enclosed piece of bait, and one roll of duct tape.

"*We* will put on our silver dollar necklaces, one with the silver on our chests and one with the silver on our backs.

"All of us will then have a quick bite of dinner where I will explain how we will conduct our fishing expedition before embarking upon it. That will be the time to ask any further questions. Got it?"

Oh yeah, we got it all right.

24

Setting Traps

We didn't take Lobo's truck into downtown St. Augustine after dinner. With traffic building from people going to the Spanish Night Watch Parade, the quickest way was to walk. So walk we did, but almost at a run. With the sun already down, our late start meant we had little time to waste.

Each of us wore two silver dollar necklaces and carried a grocery bag containing equal portions of Lobo's "fishing equipment." Before dinner, I was the one assigned to cut that smelly slab of sea creature into four equal parts and put one each into the glass boxes with the tongs—our special *bait*.

Since our neighborhood sits right near the old Spanish fort, we were able to travel across the grassy areas surrounding it right to Avenida Menendez. Noisy, bumper-to-bumper, stop and go traffic on that road in both directions showed that a big event in the old city was about to get underway.

Horns honked and church bells rang in the distance. The glow of headlights, taillights and streetlights in the approaching darkness increasingly reminded me we were about to face all those sparkling, nasty particles. And the closer we got to downtown, the more I couldn't get out of my mind the fact that Carla, Lyle and I still had PB pieces inside us.

Inside! I think that's what really got to me. Memories of watching movies in biology class about how parasites could infest people and do nasty things to them kept flashing through my mind. And of course every alien creature Sci Fi movie I had ever seen kept running through my head. You know the kind, where baby aliens burst out of peoples' bodies after growing inside them somehow.

Lobo's explanation about how the particles within us could attract more of them   made me feel like I was wearing a sign saying, "Calling the PB. Free lunch! Come Join Those Little Pieces of You That Have Already Arrived." Sure I wore two silver dollar necklaces in addition to my key chain. But was I confident of full protection no matter what? No, and Lobo certainly didn't guarantee it.

A light flashed on my left out in Matanzas Bay, startling me.

Normally I wouldn't have reacted in such a way, but on that evening, things were very different. Silly, I know, to let the beam from the St. Augustine Lighthouse scare me like that. But for just a split second, I thought the PB was attacking. In my imagination, I saw myself covered with particles like millions of stinging insects burrowing into my body. Nervous? Me? Naw, not a bit.

There were more flashing lights as we got to the Bridge of Lions. But this time they came from police cars blocking King Street and Cathedral Place running alongside the city's crowded central plaza on our right.

A cop stopped traffic allowing us and a lot of other people to cross the street.

In no time, we were all huddled in front of Potter's Wax Museum. Lobo had assigned Potter's to me as the location I would guard. A quick glance around the plaza from there showed it as being free of particles. Where the ones from that afternoon had gone I didn't know and didn't want to ask about.

Potter's was dark and had a "Closed" sign on the outside of the front door. We couldn't see anyone inside. I didn't even want to think about what was going on with poor Kelsey and all those people trapped by the PB not very far away in the back of the wax museum.

"They never used to shut down this early during a big event," Carla said, pointing out that someone had also removed all the wax figures in the display windows.

"As I told all of you before," Lobo replied, "things are moving very quickly and we need to be complete our task exactly as planned."

At dinner, Lobo had assigned a particular location for each of us, including himself, to guard in downtown St. Augustine. Besides me at Potter's, he had Flagler College, Carla got the bandstand in the plaza and Lyle was to go the south end of Government House, which is between the college and the plaza.

Lobo told us ahead of time not to question who went where, but what he did say was this: "Because Flagler College and Potter's contain the vast majority of particles, those locations will be our first line of defense. When the parade arrives at the plaza, things will begin to happen in both of those locations.

"The attractiveness of so much human activity in such close proximity will definitely cause a final fusion of both the old and new particles at Flagler College and stimulate the already merged Potter's group to expand its attack on nearby humans. Eventually, all particles will come together as one massive, and possibly unstoppable creature—unless our plan works.

Turning to Carla and Lyle, he said, "I've got you two stationed at government house and the plaza as backup in case Jeff and I can't contain our two portions of the Particle Being."

I knew Lobo took Flagler college because the place had so many more particles than Potter's. If anything went wrong there, he would know what do. But *me,* at Potter's? The place where the old and new particles had already merged and were clearly the most dangerous? What Lobo's reasons were to assign me there, I couldn't imagine but I sure didn't want Carla there in my place.

It was interesting though, that Carla actually protested my assignment to the wax museum. She told Lobo her ability to manipulate energy at subatomic levels made her more qualified than me to handle whatever might happen. She was just trying to protect me, I thought, something she didn't like when I wanted to protect her.

Lobo dismissed her logic and said there were going to be no changes in his plan. And as people walked around us at Potter's, he instructed me to put my shopping bag on the sidewalk against the low brick wall behind us under one of the empty display windows."You ready?" He asked.

"Not really, but I know what to do, if that's what you mean." It was as honest a reply as I could give him.

"I've placed you here, Jeff, for a very good reason that will become apparent," he replied. And to Carla, he said, "Any questions?"

"Several thousand, but none you would answer." Her response made me smile even with the seriousness of the moment.

"I'll take that as a no." After speaking, Lobo pointed to the bandstand where Carla was to take her grocery bag. "Time to take your position."

"I'm going to stay with Jeff for just a minute," she said in a firm voice. "It will take you a little while to put Lyle in place and get over to the college."

Lobo stared at her for a few seconds and then to both of us he said, "Follow my instructions exactly as I gave them to you." Without waiting for a reply, he pulled Lyle by an arm and both of them walked up King Street towards Government House along with a lot of other people.

As we watched them rush away, I said, "And good luck to you too, Lobo."

Carla snorted as she took my hand. "You didn't really expect for him to be like a normal person and give us good wishes in this time of crisis did you?"

"I can always hope," I replied with a grim laugh. It was easier thinking about what a jerk Lobo could be at times instead of what we were about to face.

"Now listen," Carla said, stepping closer while reaching up and stroking my check, "You take care of yourself and don't take any chances, OK?"

"Yeah, sure," I replied. "You too. I'll do my best here." And if my best wasn't good enough, I knew, Carla's life was definitely on the line—the scariest thought of all.

That's when I noticed the fear in her eyes, not for herself but for me.

"I'll be fine," I told her, not really sure if I meant what I said or not. And in that moment, I saw how deeply in love I had fallen with the beautiful, wonderful girl in front of me.

That did it. On an impulse, I threw my arms around her waist, pulled her to me and kissed her long and hard. As I did that, both her arms went around my neck and she kissed me back in a way I had only imagined in my daydreams. Unbelievable.

"I love you *too*, you know," she said as she finally pulled away, her eyes full of tears. I hadn't actually spoken the L-word, but somehow she had picked up on my innermost thoughts without even realizing it. Up until that point, we had never openly talked about how far our feelings for each other went.

Without saying anything else, Carla quickly turned and walked towards her assigned spot in Lobo's plan to defend the city.

25

Spanish Night Watch

I watched Carla until I lost sight of her in the crowds of people in the plaza.

Not being able to find her after that passionate kiss and what she said to my unspoken thoughts was like losing a part of myself. I couldn't get over it. The girl really did love me.

People nearby probably figured I had to be crazy or on drugs because I just stood there for the longest time doing nothing but staring into the plaza with my mind going in a million different directions.

But then reality slid back into my brain and threw ice water on my vivid memory of kissing Carla. Behind me, in Potter's Wax Museum, a huge bunch of very nasty particles were soon going to roar outward into all those unsuspecting people unless I did my job right.

The rumble of drums in the distance snapped me out of my tangled thoughts. The parade was coming down St. George Street right on schedule. Those drums were the signal, Lobo told us, to prepare our traps.

Following his instructions exactly, I turned around and took the glass box containing the bait out of the grocery bag. For just a few seconds, I looked at my sliver of the hybrid sea monster through its transparent container and then set the whole thing down on the sidewalk up against the front of Potter's, near the front door.

The top stayed on the box, held there by a little piece of duct tape on each side of it. Over that, I laid a silver dollar as directed by Lobo. Next, I made sure the grocery bag remained open and sitting next to the box. Once all that was done, I turned around to face the crowds of people with my body shielding the PB trap from being seen.

By that time, the drums had gotten louder and people were lining King Street to watch the parade. Directly in front of me, a mother held her baby while the father hoisted a small giggling boy onto his shoulders. A chill shot through my body as I thought about those people being infected by the PB if things didn't go well.

Cheers and applause came from the crowd across the plaza at a diagonal to my left. The parade had emerged into the open on St. George Street, but too little light, too much distance and too many people in the way prevented me from seeing much of anything.

From what Carla told me at dinner though, I knew that a troop of reenactors, dressed in blue uniforms of Colonial Spain, were marching with muskets on their shoulders to Government House at the far end of the plaza. Behind them, she said, would be citizens of St. Augustine dressed in costumes of the 1700's and behind them, hundreds of visitors to the city wanting to join in the fun.

"An attraction irresistible to the Particle Being," Lobo explained to us at dinner. I was beginning to see what he meant.

The thing is, nothing happened. With all those particles in Potter's behind me, I expected them to explode out of the building by now. Not that I was disappointed, you understand, just pleasantly surprised. I began to wonder if maybe Lobo had gotten it wrong somehow.

But before I could get too wrapped up in that hope, the drums abruptly stopped and I heard distant commands being shouted in Spanish. According to Carla, this was when the soldiers would rest the butt of their muskets on the street near their feet while holding the barrels with one hand. Then they would listen to a speech by someone dressed as the Colonial Governor of St. Augustine.

It all happened as she said, although I could barely hear the speech. After that, more commands, followed by the pop, pop, pop of those muskets firing in the air, the flashes easily visible to anyone looking over in that direction from anywhere in the plaza.

Again, the crowd cheered and clapped. But those musket flashes and the sounds reminded me of when Carla and I faced similar weapons in a fight for our lives during an exact dreamworld replica of an important battle in Florida's Second Seminole War. For just a few seconds, I felt like I was actually on that horrible battlefield again, bleeding and sure both of us were going to die.

The smell of ozone and burning wires. That's what snapped my mind back to the present. The PB! I couldn't see it anywhere around me, but I knew it had to be close.

By that point, those drums had started again. The troop of Spanish soldiers and their followers were coming down King Street in my direction. Ahead of them marched the uniformed drummers. And in front of them were three soldiers, one in the middle carrying the flag of Spain and one on each side of him, holding a flaming torch.

People all up and down the street cheered and clapped as the others had before them. I could understand their appreciation. It was quite a sight.

At first, the slight violet glow gently rippling across the crowd all around me and out into King Street didn't look odd or out of place in all the festivities. But when it got brighter, my overloaded brain finally figured out that it might somehow be coming from the Particle Being.

Frantically, I looked on both sides of me, but there were no particles anywhere. I even turned and tried looking through the window of Potter's again, but with no luck. The wax museum was still dark.

The only place I hadn't looked was up. So I did. And there they were—a hundred or more glistening strands of closely packed, violet particles, each about an inch wide, slowly waving all around far above my head and extending outward over King Street.

The PB inside Potter's had gone through the roof of the museum, risen about six feet more and then extended itself out over the crowd in front of me. And the head of the parade would be in that exact spot in a very short time. At that point, the drums were so loud I could even feel the vibrations in my body.

But from what I was able to tell, nobody but me could see all those particle strands.

Knowing I had to act, but still dazzled by the incredible sight above me, I watched in horror as several PB threads fired downward into the heads of people below.

That did it. As fast as I could, I turned, snatched the silver dollar off the top of the glass box and stepped back exactly as Lobo had instructed us. That left the bait open and free of any interference by silver.

Like magic, all those PB strands overhead instantly stopped moving.

Seconds later, they all merged in a blur of motion. The result was a single, massive, glowing PB column coming out of Potter's roof and arcing out over King Street. The end of that huge thing tapered off to a sharp point, and aimed at the road below it—just ahead of the oncoming parade.

Obviously I had gotten the PBs attention, but would it turn and go for the bait or would it go for the large crowd of people in the parade heading its way? Seconds seemed to stretch into minutes as I stared at the column, not daring to breathe.

While I watched, that sharp tip of the thick PB shaft slowly turned away from aiming at King Street and curled back around so it then pointed at the front of the wax museum.

Whether it was looking for me, or the bait, I wasn't sure, but a split second later, I found out. Almost like what happened to Lobo in Flagler College, the PB shaft fired directly at me and came to a stop about a foot short of my chest—stopped only, I was sure, by the silver dollar hanging there from my neck.

My reaction was to jerk backward a step, but I couldn't go far. The PB trap and the Potter's building were right behind me. My breath caught in my throat as I looked down at that thing and I could feel myself tense up and begin to shake all over. Talk about scared?

Just then, the stink of burning wires and ozone increased—a lot. That made the inside of my nose start burn and my throat felt gritty, like I had swallowed sand or something. I wanted to cough and turn away both at the same time, but I didn't dare make any kind of move.

I felt like a mouse staring at a huge snake ready to strike. Still, trying to stifle my cough sure didn't help any. Sweat poured down my sides and my stomach knotted up into a painful, tight ball.

You know what to do, Lobo's voice said somewhere deep inside my brain.

What? I screamed at him mentally and as I did, the answer popped into my consciousness. Lobo's guidance about my ability to stop time in its tracks suddenly made perfect sense.

Right as that thought flashed through my mind, the air around me thickened as all movement and sound stopped dead. The drum sounds and vibrations ceased so quickly their absence actually felt like a shock to my body.

And as I had seen happen several other times during Frozen Time situations, no one and nothing moved. The huge, pointed PB column not twelve inches from my heart almost looked like it was a solid thing that you could partially see through. In it, millions and millions of particles glistened at steady but varying rates of intensity. The only sound coming into my ears was that of my ragged breathing and beating heart.

I almost didn't believe I had done it, stopped time for a nonphysical creature. That made no logical sense, but the evidence was there right in front of me.

By then though, my need to cough overwhelmed all fears and caution. I couldn't keep it in anymore so I stepped to the side of the PB's pointed end and hacked my lungs out. All that time, the PB didn't move or sparkle. Thank God!

After coughing as much as I needed to, all I could think of doing was getting as far away from that PB column as I could, so that's what I did. Tell you what. I doubt you've ever seen anybody move as fast as I did right then. I mean I ran like hell while trying to avoid people who couldn't see me and weren't able to move out of the way.

In a very short time, I found myself in the middle of King Street, almost at the east end of the plaza and opposite the oncoming parade. I stood there panting like crazy but also staring in wonder at all of those people in downtown St. Augustine who were frozen in total silence. Logically, I knew I had caused it, but down deep, I found it almost impossible to believe.

As I looked around, I noticed the three Spanish soldiers leading the parade were not more than fifty feet from me. The flames from the torches two of them carried looked beautifully solid, like carefully sculpted works of art—things that you could go up to and touch if you wished. I wondered if they would feel super cold like the fountain drops did over near the Antique Mall or would they be painfully hot.

Still in awe of the scene all around me, but with renewed confidence, I focused on the PB column. It continued to point to the spot where I had been standing. Finally realizing Lobo had assigned me to Potter's because of my ability to stop time, I trotted back over there. But once I arrived, I still kept what I hoped might be a safe distance from that vicious looking extension of the larger particle mass inside the wax museum.

The second I stopped walking though, life returned to normal in downtown St. Augustine.

Sound and movement reappeared as if it had never left, and instead of attacking the parade that was just arriving at Potter's with its bone rattling drums, the PB column jerked from side-to-side as if was looking for me.

Finding nothing in the spot where I had been, the thing slowly twisted its pointed nose downward until it seemed to be touching the glass box. *Yes, go for it!* And it did.

The sharp point of the PB penetrated the top of the glass box. Right after that, that entire column became a fast moving, glittering stream of violet for a short time. What happened was, it fired itself through the box's glass top and rapidly squeezed every single particle inside that little container in less than ten seconds. Boom! Gone. What an amazing transition.

"It worked," I whispered to myself excitedly as I rushed to the grocery bag and pulled out the role of duct tape and my bag of silver dollars. Nobody noticed what I was doing because all eyes were still glued to the passing parade.

Again, following Lobo's instructions to the letter, I quickly tore six strips of tape off the roll and used each strip to attach a silver dollar to every side of the glass box. When I finished, I set the trap back down on the sidewalk and against Potter's front wall.

Lobo told us our efforts stood a sixty percent chance of working, but it was the best chance we had. Surrounded by silver, he said, the PB would most likely go into a state of suspended animation. Even if by some chance he and I couldn't contain the thing at first, he explained to all of us, we could at least weaken it enough to allow Carla and Lyle to imprison the PB forever.

26

The Swarm

Five minutes went by and nothing happened. Nothing bad, that is. I timed it with my watch to make sure.

"If your portion of the Particle Being isn't able to get loose after five minutes," Lobo told us during dinner, "then there is an extremely high probability you've got it under control."

Yes! I had actually captured my part of the PB and so far, it hadn't been able to escape its silver prison. From a few places where there was no duct tape on the glass box though, brilliant shafts of purple light fired outward like lasers.

They seemed harmless enough. I mean people walked right through them with no problem.

Of course, nobody else could see that light but me. Oh, and one very small boy who walked by Potter's with his parents. Cute little guy. "Pretty," he said, grinning and pointing at the box, but his dad just shrugged, grabbed the kid's hand and pulled him away.

A quick look up King Street towards Flagler College told me Lobo must have had the same kind of success. There were no strands or huge columns of particles anywhere up in that direction at all. In fact, there were no particles anywhere except that big batch concentrated in my glass box. The sweet look of victory! And smell too. No more burning wires and ozone in the air.

The parade had gone well past me by then and was on its way up Avenida Menendez, heading to the fort—the Castillo they call it in Spanish around St. Augustine—the Castle. The sound of the drums continued to fade with each passing minute.

Finally, I could breathe easily and just watch everything return to normal. Traffic flowed once more on King Street and Cathedral Place. People walked back and forth in front of me, all of them never realizing how close they came to disaster.

Soon I knew, Lobo, carrying his own PB filled trap, would be checking on both Lyle and Carla before they all ended up back at Potter's with me.

That was our plan if everything went well. But what Lobo would do with the two batches of captured Particle Being, he chose not to share with us. "You'll find out when it's important for you to know." Typical Lobo.

Thinking of Carla, I decided to look for her again over in the plaza at the bandstand. I eventually found her in the bandstand itself with a crowd around her, waving at me.

After waving back, I clasped my hands high over my head, our agreed upon signal of definite victory over the PB. As soon as I did that, she started bouncing up and down and pumping the air with her fist. Next, she did a little victory dance. She looked as happy as I felt.

Watching her made me laugh, but people around her probably thought she had gone crazy.

Unfortunately, that's when things changed.

Out of the corner of my eye, I noticed someone standing there just outside the nearby door to the wax museum, staring at me. When I turned to look, I saw that it was Carla's friend, Kelsey, the girl from Potter's.

But that wasn't all I saw. Trailing behind her, and right through the closed door to the museum, was a thick strand of compressed particles. My heart sank as I realized some part of the original PB was still in Potter's. A slight stink of ozone and burning wires once again drifted my way.

Oh crap!

Kelsey looked at me with a chilling fierceness. At the time, I thought if she had a weapon of some kind in her hands, she would have used it on me. A small trickle of blood ran from her nose down over her lips and chin. As scared as I was right then, I felt so sorry for her. It could have just as easily been Carla or me in her place.

Tell you what though, I just froze and stared back at the girl, not knowing what to do.

Seconds later, Kelsey turned, looked down at the PB prison and pointed at it. From the tip of her finger came a PB strand maybe a half inch in diameter that hit the glass box. I swear, I thought I was watching a Harry Potter movie, but with fictional magic somehow coming dangerously to life.

OK, so obviously what I saw wasn't magic. Poor Kelsey served right then as nothing more than a human transmitter for the remaining PB in the wax museum. But even so, I watched as dozens more strands popped out of her finger, arc up a little, and then zip down alongside the main particle shaft until they all hit the glass box.

This is not good. I felt sure I knew what was coming.

Slowly, the air about a foot around the PB trap began filling with a brilliant white light that got so bright I had to look away. Just as I did, I saw all those strands retract back into Kelsey's finger.

Once more, she looked at me, but this time she had this little smile on her lips that I definitely did not like. Still, she said nothing. Instead, she licked the blood off her lips, turned around and walked back into Potter's, trailing that big, thick PB strand stuck in the back of her head.

When I looked back at the trap, all the duct tape was burning. And as I watched in horror, both the glass box and silver dollars started melting. If the PB through Kelsey could do that, I realized, it could have done the same to me but didn't. I had no idea why. What I did know was I needed to get away from there as quick as I could.

But before I could move, a thick, violet stream of particles silently burst out of the collapsing PB trap and rocketed straight up into the darkness. It was as if someone had ripped off the top of a fire hydrant—a very weird one.

That's when the ozone and burning wires smell really got strong. But of course, nobody nearby smelled or saw any of this but me. Lucky me.

And from the roof of the wax museum, a second, very large stream of violet particles joined the first one high overhead. They came together creating one huge, glittering river of light that twisted in on itself over and over again. It only took a few seconds for the trapped particles and those left over in the wax museum to escape into the night air. But when it finally happened, the entire knotted mass shot off to my left above the buildings and sidewalk so quickly I wasn't actually sure I saw it move.

Seconds later, a soundless explosion of blinding white light to my left told me that the wax museum PB had probably made contact with all the Flagler College particles.

When my vision fully cleared, I started worrying about Lobo and his attempt to capture all of the PB in his own silver prison.

As I stood there in front of Potter's staring up King Street towards the college, people walked by, glancing at me and probably wondering what kind of problem I had. But that didn't matter at all. What mattered was whether or not Lobo captured all the particles even though it looked like the old and new versions might have successfully merged.

When after about two minutes passed and I still didn't have an answer, I glanced over at the bandstand only to find Carla looking back at me. She shrugged and put her hands out with palms up to say she had no idea what was happening. She and Lyle were the last lines of our defense if Lobo failed.

And just as I was about to call Carla on my cell, violet balls of light sprang up into the sky over Flagler College. As soon as I saw them, I pointed so that Carla would turn around and look.

Judging by the distance I was from the college, each of those balls had to be at least the size of a medium sized car. They slowly lifted into the dark air like huge, sparkly weather balloons, hundreds and then thousands of them, I would guess. I'm telling you, they just kept rising and spreading out in the sky, high over downtown St. Augustine.

That scene reminded me of a National Geographic program I had recently seen. In the documentary, a diver filmed a huge jellyfish swarm from beneath it, looking up as sunlight made all those countless bodies glow. At the time,

I thought how alien all those jellyfish looked, like creatures from another world. And now, we had our own alien invasion looking very much the same.

My heart sank. Obviously, Lobo hadn't been able to prevent the massive amounts of old and new particles in Flagler College from combining to create a stronger and more dangerous version of the Particle Being.

Their continuous eruption into the air meant, I was sure, that Carla and Lyle would not get their chance to control the Particle Being.

But had Lobo survived? That was the final question. All I knew for sure was that anyone even close to downtown St. Augustine was in extreme danger.

27

Downpour

Snap out of it, all of you!

It was Lobo's voice inside my head and I realized he was also talking to Carla and Lyle, as well as to me.

Carla and Lyle. Your mission is aborted. Both old and new particle eruptions have fully merged and you have no chance of containing any of it.

We all need to get out of downtown immediately.

Carla, for right now, you stay put.

Jeff and Lyle. Leave your fishing equipment where it is and run to Carla's location. I'll meet you there.

Move!

I didn't need to be told twice. Lobo was alive and he could help keep Carla safe. That's all I needed to know to get my legs moving under me. In seconds, I found myself rushing across King Street, forcing two cars into screeching stops.

Up onto the sidewalk and sliding between groups of people everywhere in the plaza, I arrived at the bandstand and found Lobo already there with Carla. How he got there so fast, I had no idea, but it really didn't matter.

When I arrived, all out of breath, Carla threw her arms around me. "Thank God you're OK," she said. "You had me so scared. I saw what happened when Kelsey came out the door."

But before I could answer, Lyle staggered up to us even more out of breath than I was. His eyes were wide and glassy with panic.

"Time to go, folks," Lobo barked, stealing a quick glance up at the PB globes that now filled the night sky over the central part of downtown St. Augustine. Above us, a high ceiling of glistening, violet particles had completely replaced the darkness. I couldn't tell where one globe started and another ended.

Lobo's instructions to us were very simple, but the continuing urgency in his voice underlined every word. "We are going to get out of here as a group, so stay close together. Walk fast, but don't run. Lyle, you're with me. Jeff and Carla, you follow us and I mean stay close."

As soon as he finished speaking, Lobo grabbed Lyle by an arm just as he had been doing all afternoon and started walking rapidly towards the Bridge of Lions. Carla and I fell in step right behind them.

Everything went well until we got near the statue of Ponce de Leon just past the end of the plaza. At that point though, it was as if a bolt of lightning had struck somewhere near us. Violet lightning. Soundless but blindingly brilliant. And then it started. A downpour of particles.

Those globes overhead were opening up and letting loose their contents exactly like a summer thundershower.

Instantly, downtown St. Augustine was drenched in particles. They were everywhere, thick clouds of them making it hard to see anything else. And in that moment, I knew they were looking for people, people to enter in preparation for enslavement.

The stink of ozone and burning wires became overwhelming and made breathing very difficult. God how I hated that smell.

Instead of actually falling to the ground like rain though, all those particles hung in the air just above ground level, up to about eight feet high—like sparkly fog, invisible except to the four of us. Anyone walking through them would definitely become infected and never know what happened. And since the particles were nonphysical, I figured they probably went right through the tops of buildings and cars as well.

When the downpour hit, I saw how they stayed far away from Lobo, Carla, Lyle and me—at first. It was like we were in a large cocoon of open space, caused, I figured by the silver we carried. But seconds later, Lyle screamed and fell backward to the ground right in front of me as particles began firing right at him from all directions.

Some of the particles seemed to go right into him and disappear while others stuck to his skin, beard and clothes. Then as quickly as it started, the attack stopped and the particles covering him went away. Once again, he was in a cocoon of open, protected space.

The man wore silver like the rest of us so I didn't understand how the PB could get to him. And why it left him alone after the start of a successful attack made no sense at all.

When I reached down to try and help him up, that little mystery deepened even more. Why? Because, my hand hit something solid—solid but invisible, about six to eight inches from Lyle's body. I felt all around until it became clear to me that whatever it was covered Lyle completely.

A split second later, two things happened, one on top of the other. Time stopped, freezing everyone and everything in place outside of the four of us. I knew it had to be Lobo's doing, because it sure wasn't me.

Next came bright waves of red that continually swept the area right around us causing thousands of very tiny explosions. And when I looked for the source of those waves, I finally found it in Carla. Yes, Carla. Those waves were radiating outward from her head wherever she looked, clearing particles away as she turned in slow, little circles.

"Lyle!" Lobo shouted, leaning down and knocking on that hard, invisible shell surrounding the little guy. "You're OK."

From his fetal position, with his hands over his face, Lyle peeked at Lobo from between his fingers. "You sure?" He sobbed, his voice all muffled.

"Yes, but you've got to get up and get out of here with us, now!" Lobo barked.

Lyle slowly struggled to a sitting position. "But I don't think I can walk," he moaned from behind his weird shield. "I'm too shaky and my legs are too wobbly."

"Your dimensional field is weighing you down," Lobo yelled at him. "Concentrate and turn it off." *Dimensional field?* Obviously Lobo knew all about Lyle's hard shell. It sounded like something right out of a science fiction movie.

"I can't focus, Lobo, I can't." By then the poor guy was crying his eyes out.

"Come on Jeff," Lobo said to me, "let's see if we can carry him. I only have so much energy to spare when I'm projecting this time freeze and Carla needs to keep clearing a path for us. With this many particles, our silver will only fully protect us for another couple of minutes so we really have to get Lyle moving."

Way too much was happening all at once that I didn't understand, so I just had to shut it off in my head and do what needed to be done. Lobo had taught me well and it worked.

With him on one side of Lyle and me on the other, we bent down and grabbed him under his arms. But his shield, dimensional field, or whatever, made him much too bulky and slippery.

We were having so much trouble getting him up that I said, "I wish I had two of me."

And that's exactly what happened—but even more so. Right as I finished saying those words, I felt this weird tugging all up and down the right and left sides of my body, and suddenly two more Jeffs appeared, one on either side of me, dressed as I was dressed.

Even though I had seen my body from distances before, and even run into another Jeff, when those two Jeffs came out of my body, it still blew me away.

"Well done," Lobo said, giving me one of his rare and very small smiles.

"Are we going to do this or what?" The Jeff on my right said, whacking me on the arm, hard. That hurt, but it also startled me out of my surprise at seeing those duplicates of myself.

"Uh, right," I replied, not sure how to use the extra help effectively.

"We each take an arm or a leg in both hands," Lobo barked to me and the other Jeffs. "We lift him up and carry him across the street to safety. The particle cloud stops in the middle of Avenida Menendez."

Then to Carla, he said, "You'll need to walk ahead of us, clearing away the particles as we move forward. We'll be moving in a diagonal direction to the other side of the street towards the left side of the Bridge of Lions."

"Got it," Carla replied and she positioned herself in front of where Lobo stood.

Finally, with Lobo's help, the other two Jeffs and I picked Lyle up just as directed. "Now, Carla!" Lobo ordered, and she stepped off the curb wiping out particles in countless bursts of red as she moved. The four of us carrying Lyle followed along behind her, all zigzagging our way between cars and trucks frozen in place by Lobo.

About half way across the street, we exited the farthest point of the particle rain and Carla's job came to an end. In twenty seconds or less, we had all arrived on the other side of Avenida Menendez. On top of a nearby street light, a one-legged crow bobbed up and down. Somehow, Edgar had joined the party.

As we got Lyle into a standing position, and held him upright, time resumed its natural flow and the little homeless guy's shell went away. Once that happened, both of the other Jeff's just seemed to evaporate as sound flooded my ears and the chilly breeze from the bay again blew across us. Only later did I wonder if anybody had been watching as the two Jeffs disappeared.

In the distance, the drums from the parade still beat, but now the sound came from near the Castillo.

We could see the old fort bathed in yellow light just a short walk up the street. It was there that all the people following the parade had gathered for the firing of the cannons—the signal for the end of the night's festivities.

But it wasn't the Castillo or the parade that held our attention. Instead it was the fog of particles that continued to cover the central part of downtown St. Augustine.

Then as if watching that disgusting sight wasn't depressing enough, a large PB shaft fired high up into the air out of all that mess, arced over Avenida Menendez to the Castillo and descended as another shower of particles on the unsuspecting parade crowd below. I had really hoped all those people might escape infection but no such luck.

Suddenly, I felt an overwhelming sense of guilt. I should have been able to figure out a way to stop Kelsey from releasing all those particles from Potter's, I told myself.

But as soon as I had that thought, I felt Carla's hand slip into mine. "Don't," she said to me. "There was nothing you could have done."

Not surprised she had sensed what was going through my mind, I wanted to protest her logic, but before I could do that, another and even larger PB shaft erupted from the plaza area, raced high over the Castillo and came down somewhere far out in Matanzas Bay before disappearing.

Why that happened, I had no idea and I really didn't care. The only thing I could think about was all those poor people who were now saturated with deadly particles—or soon would be.

Part Five

Information

28

Blue Glow

Just as we got to the Castillo's parking lot, two cannons on top of the old fort facing Matanzas Bay boomed, one after the other, peeling back the night.

Those explosions and brilliant flashes of light startled the heck out of me. Carla flinched, and ahead of us, I watched as Lyle dropped to his knees while covering his ears with his hands. After our encounter with that PB storm, it didn't take much to spook all of us except Lobo.

Speaking of Lobo. He just stood there with his arms folded, waiting for us until we recovered from our shock and for us to start moving again.

But once that happened, nobody said anything as we walked onto the grass surrounding the Castillo and past the crowds. Almost at the same time, the Spanish soldiers fired their muskets again, followed by more beating of the drums.

And by flickering torch light, soldiers and observers started their march back downtown. A downtown, that for us, still had a slight violet glow to it. glow to it.

But the good thing was that we couldn't see any more particles anywhere around the Castillo. Of course, we knew where most, if not all them ended up when they showered everybody at the old fort.

By then, Lobo and Lyle had walked quite a ways ahead of Carla and me. We could just barely hear them talking, only catching a word or two here and there. We seemed to have been following those two guys all day.

Every once in a while, we saw Lobo reach out and keep his old friend from falling. Obviously, Lyle still hadn't fully recovered from the PB attack. Why it went after him and not any of the rest of us, I still couldn't understand.

Carla and I didn't speak on that walk back to Lobo's place. There would be time for discussion later. Just being together and alive was enough.

I did keep my arm around her all the way there though. It wasn't the boy-girl thing, at least not in the usual way. After what had happened with the PB, I guess I just felt sort of protective. Silly, I guess, because after what I saw during that time, I knew Carla could take care of herself and more. Oh boy, could she!

Instead of taking us all into his house when we got there, Lobo made us all hop into his truck without any explanation. Not unusual for Lobo, that's for sure. "You'll find out in time," was the man's often standard reply to our questions about why the nighttime road trip.

The next thing I know, we're traveling out on a dark part of Highway A1A north of downtown and onto the bridge that goes high over the Tolomato River to Vilano Beach. Carla sat between Lobo and me as usual while Lyle stretched out behind us in the open truck bed using a block of wood as a pillow.

Over the bridge we went and just barely into Vilano Beach when Lobo took a sharp U-turn, taking his truck and all of us back the way we had just come. I heard Lyle hit the side of the truck above the bed as he rolled and yelled in anger behind us. "That hurt, you crazy Indian! What are you trying to do, kill me?"

"He, uh, didn't phrase it very well Lobo," Carla said, "but what are you doing?"

Silent as ever when he didn't want to respond, Lobo drove back to the crest of the bridge and parked. By then, Lyle was at the back window banging on it and cursing. Poor Carla, she really got an earful of some very explicit language.

"There's a wider emergency lane on this side of the bridge." Lobo's response to Carla came just before he got out of the truck and slammed the door behind him. As logical as his answer seemed, it really said nothing about why we were there.

Outside, we heard Lyle fussing at Lobo about his driving skills and parking decision. "The police are going to get you for parking here with no reason, Lobo," he babbled. Actually the word "police" came out of him sounding more like "pole-lease." Lyle and the "pole-lease" didn't get along very well. Usually, he just called them "cops."

"I guess we're supposed to join them, huh?" I asked as Lobo quieted Lyle down. I wondered if I looked as tired as Carla did. I know I sure felt it.

She didn't say anything at first. Instead, she turned her head away from me to look at the twinkling lights of St. Augustine in the distance far below the bridge. "What's happening to our beautiful city, Jeff?" Her voice was tight, as if it was tough for her to get the words out. "All those people down there and they don't know they're being infected. People we know like Kelsey."

I had no answer for her. Hell, I was so overwhelmed myself that I still had trouble believing what I had seen that evening. Kelsey's face bubbled up in my mind with blood dripping from her nose.

When Carla turned her head to look at me in the silence, I saw tears glistening in her eyes. She can be a pretty tough chick, but her love for St. Augustine and her compassion are bottomless.

"As usual," I said, holding her close, "we've got to trust in old Lobo. And like he says, we've got to stay focused on the present moment. We can't afford to get all caught up in what's already happened and everything that could happen if we don't get the PB under control, right?"

"You're sounding more like Lobo very day," Carla replied with a chuckle as she wiped her eyes with her fingertips.

"Oh no!" I said in mock horror. "I'm becoming Lobo! Somebody save me, please!"

That's when Carla laughed and I knew she was going to be OK. "Come on Lobo number two," she replied, giving me at least a partial smile. "Let's get out there and see what's going on."

But before we could move, we saw the old shaman and Lyle quickly walk to the opposite side of the bridge during a small break in traffic. Lyle kept a hand on top of his head, holding onto his "lucky baseball cap."

"Looks like we're late to class," I said, undoing my seatbelt and opening the truck door.

As soon as we got outside though, a cold wind, smelling slightly of salt water, smacked into us. Cars and trucks rushed by, going both directions in the yellow-orange glow from huge streetlights all up and down the bridge to the right of the truck.

That's when I noticed a high pitched sound I couldn't identify. It seemed to be coming from everywhere. I heard it as soon as I got out of the truck. "What is that noise?"

"It's the wind rushing against the slender upper parts of all these aluminum streetlights up here," Carla replied, trying to keep her hair from whipping around her head too much.

"No way," I replied, looking up at a huge light pole towering above Lobo's truck.

"Go put your hands on it," she urged.

So that's exactly what I did, after climbing over the concrete wall separating the street from the pedestrian walkway going over the bridge. As soon as I touched the base of the streetlight, I felt a deep vibration that blended with the sound I was hearing. It almost felt like a very mild electric shock. *How cool!*

"If you're done playing, Jeff," Lobo shouted at me from the other side of the bridge, "you and Carla have important business over here." He stood there in the cold wind without a jacket, as usual. It made me shiver just to look at him.

"Coming!" I shouted and climbed back over the wall. When I got to Carla, I thanked her for my little side journey. And when traffic cleared a bit, we ran across the road to join the two old guys who were born over two centuries before. I still couldn't get over their ages and all they must have seen in their lifetimes.

Anyway, once we got to Lobo and Lyle, we found them both leaning forward a little with their hands on the concrete railing as they scanned the dark scene in front of them. I had to admit, the view from there was spectacular. We could see all the lights from Vilano Beach, Anastasia Island and downtown St. Augustine. The deep darkness in the middle of all that evidence of human life was water. Most of it was Matanzas Bay plus the outlet to the Atlantic and some rivers. Across the entire scene below us slid the beam from the St. Augustine Lighthouse on its way out to sea.

"It's started again, hasn't it?" Lyle asked, in a small, defeated sounding voice. What he meant, I had no idea.

After a brief pause, Lobo inhaled deeply and said, "Yes. Yes it has." It wasn't often Lobo paused like that, no less taking a deep breath before speaking.

"You all want to share what you're talking about?" Carla asked as we held hands, her voice carrying across me to Lobo who was on my left.

In reply, Lobo said, pointing, "Look out over the bay to where you see the lighted channel markers.

"OK, so what about them?" I asked, finding them easily.

"I can feel it, but I can't see it," Lyle said before Lobo could speak again. He too stared into the darkness still holding his baseball cap to keep the wind from blowing it off. "It's there. It has to be."

"Look closely at the water between the last two lighted channel markers," Lobo replied, still pointing out into the bay.

"Oooohhh no!" Lyle moaned after a short pause. "That's it all right. I told you I felt it. I told you so."

"The light blue glow?" Carla asked in a tense voice.

As soon as she finished speaking, my stomach fluttered in a weird way that almost made me nauseous. "Is that where the PB shaft from downtown landed just before we came up here?" I wasn't really sure I wanted to hear a reply from either Lobo or Lyle, but I needed to ask.

"It can't be part of the Particle Being," Carla said. "It's the wrong color."

"You would think so, wouldn't you?" Lobo's question lay heavy in the air, filled with its own answer. "But it's the right color when the Particle Being goes underwater. That's what our eyes see. Our eyes. No one else's. It's too complex to explain beyond that."

"And so what we're seeing is a mass of particles from downtown at the bottom of the bay?" Carla's voice was cool and calm, a lot cooler and calmer than I felt.

"Yes and no, girlie!" Lyle yelled, almost hysterical. "Another monster is in the making too! Dear God in Heaven."

"What?" I yelled over the traffic and wind noise, looking at Lobo instead of Lyle. "There hasn't been enough time, right?" Later I wondered why Carla didn't go after Lyle for calling her "girlie." She probably felt sorry for him, and besides, there was too much else happening.

"There's been more time than you think. Don't forget that when those two colonies of merged particles left Flagler College today, one went to Potter's, but the other went out into the bay.

That means it has indeed had time, *on a quantum or subatomic level*, to create another hybrid sea creature. Remember, the PB is a nonphysical entity allowing it to operate outside of the laws of nature as we understand them. And the additional particles we saw fire off into the bay tonight have probably just sped up the process even more."

"Why?" Carla asked. "I mean why would the PB create another one of those *things* like it did back in 1896?"

"Doing so is most likely even more important now than it was then. The Particle Being currently spread out all over a large part of St. Augustine, and also stored within peoples' bodies, desperately needs such a huge creature in order to effectively interact with and control all humans in the city.

"In essence, a giant brain is nearing completion out there, one modeled after those of two very intelligent species, whale and octopus. A giant brain which will act like a transformer of the PB's power and intentions. Unless we are able to stop it somehow."

"Uh, so this creature, this brain, "Carla asked, "will sort of act like a booster to allow the PB to do to everybody in the city what it has already done to my friend Kelsey at Potter's Wax Museum?"

"Yes," Lobo replied.

29

The Creature Down Deep

Motion detectors made flood lights pop to life all over the little peninsula as soon as Lobo drove up to the back of his house.

"Now, this is what we're going to do," he said as soon as we got out of the truck. "Jeff, you're with me. You and I are going to take my canoe out into the bay."

"What?" Carla said loudly. Exactly my reaction, but she was quicker at expressing it.

"Are you out of your ever lovin' mind, Lobo?" Lyle croaked, looking at him wide-eyed and trembling.

"Just go into the house and have a beer," Lobo told him firmly. "I need to talk to Carla and Jeff. Alone."

"But—"

"Now."

"Uh, yeah, OK," Lyle said, looking down. As he turned around and shuffled off towards the house, he mumbled, "A beer is just what I need, that's for sure."

"You treat him like a child and then give him beer?" Carla asked once Lyle rounded the corner at the front of Lobo's house.

"Years of alcohol and drug abuse," Lobo replied, "on top of the damage done to his mind by the Particle Being, long ago have made him childlike."

"All the more reason not to give him beer," Carla replied. "He's probably an alcoholic. He even admitted it."

"That he is, Carla, but especially after the PB attack, he will drive himself and us crazy with his worry unless it's managed properly. We don't have the time to try and help him with his addiction issues right now. Besides, having Lyle go into even the initial stages of alcohol withdrawal will benefit no one. The beer will calm him down. A temporary solution and one I want *you* to monitor."

"*Monitor? Me?* You want me to do *what?* be his *bartender?*

"In a way, yes. He'll respond better to you in his agitated state of mind than he will Jeff. It's the male-female thing and since you are the only one of us who fits the female description, you are elected.

"No matter what, somebody has to stay with him. So like a good bartender, just keep him supplied with beer, listen to him and assure him everything is going to be OK. And make certain he wears his silver necklaces."

"While you and Jeff are doing what on the bay?

"Collecting information."

Whew! I thought maybe he wanted the two of us to try and find a way to kill that thing out there. "And how are we going to collect this information?" I asked, breathing a little easier but not a lot.

"I'll tell you later." After replying to my question, he spoke to Carla. "Now go. Go be with Lyle. I'll watch out for your boyfriend here. You needn't worry."

"Uh huh," she said in return. "You had better take care of him. I sure hope you know what you're doing."

"Let's get back to Lyle for a minute," I said, interrupting. "Why did the PB attack him?"

"Because he forgot to wear his silver dollar necklaces," Lobo replied.

"But I saw him put them over his head as soon as we made them," I protested.

"So did I," Carla agreed.

"Yes, but I found out he took them *off* to shower before dinner and left them in the bathroom. I got that out of him while we walked back from downtown."

"Oh," Carla and I said almost at the same time. But I had one more question. "Uh, so what was that hard shell around him during the PB attack? What did you call it? A dimensional field or something?"

"That's just the name I gave to what Lyle does when he feels overwhelmingly threatened. It's a residual effect left over from his first terrible interaction with the Particle Being back in 1879.

"Somehow his connection from back then produced within him the ability to solidify his natural human aura as a protective force. It prevents penetration from anything in the physical world except air. But unfortunately, Lyle's shield didn't go up in time tonight to fully protect him. He undoubtedly has countless new particles inside him now that he didn't have before.

Sitting in the stern, Lobo maneuvered his fiberglass canoe around the little islands that separated his property from Matanzas Bay. Even with the quarter moon that had just risen, the stars glistened brightly overhead. I never realized before how getting away from the light pollution of downtown St. Augustine made them pop out of the darkness.

As I sat in the bow shining a large flashlight up ahead for Lobo to see, I thought about poor Lyle being attacked by groups of particles twice in his life. Twice! And so what that he had lived longer than most people? A lot of good it did him, ending up disabled and still haunted by the Particle Being like he was.

It didn't take long though for the slight humming of Lobo's electric motor and the lapping of small waves against the hull to shift my attention back to our mission. A sea creature full of particles rested on the bottom of the bay out there ahead of us somewhere.

Let me tell you, I was definitely not looking forward to finding that thing even if we were just going to be, "gathering information." As the seconds slid by, my imagination started working overtime making me jump when some nesting birds on a large island to our left fluttered and squawked loudly.

"Don't let your mind wander like that," Lobo shouted from behind me. "The more you do, the more frightened you'll get and the more mistakes you'll make. Concentrate. This isn't going to get any easier so you might as well start now."

"Got it working," I shouted over my shoulder and waved, right as we hit the open water of Matanzas Bay. There, the breeze was stiffer, colder and it created higher waves. Lobo's canoe bounced around a lot more in the choppiness coming at us, but we kept moving forward at a fairly good speed, at least for using an electric motor.

How Lobo didn't freeze his butt off out there with his bare arms, I couldn't imagine. Just thinking about him in the wind and cold like that made me zip my jacket up all the way.

You can turn off the light now. The words weren't my thoughts. They were Lobo's, flowing through my mind.

I almost laughed at how easily I now accepted that fact after how strongly I resisted the old guy and all things paranormal when I first met him. Once that split second reaction passed, I did exactly as he asked, plunging us into darkness. Well, semidarkness, I guess I should say, because of the quarter moon and the stars as well as the lights onshore all around us.

It took me a while, but I finally caught sight of a light blue glow radiating up into sea mist. Like before, when we saw it from the bridge, the glow was coming from an area between those two lighted channel markers.

Lobo had the canoe pointed in that general direction when a larger wave than usual caused water to splash on me. Good God that was cold! In the Florida summer, the temperature in the bay averaged somewhere in the eighties, but we were out there in mid-March after a very cold winter.

Correcting his angle of approach, so we didn't catch any more bad waves, Lobo brought us into the channel well past the glow and to the east of it. That let him use the incoming tide from the Atlantic to carry the canoe back directly towards where the creature lay hidden. With me in the bow, that meant I would get there before him. Not a very comforting idea.

Slowly, but surely, the murky water all around us grew increasingly light blue, even reflecting off the channel markers. The actual size of the glowing area we had entered was huge, maybe a couple of hundred feet in diameter.

Deep under the water ahead of us at the center of all that brightness, but barely visible, was a large, light colored lump. And from that lump, going out in all directions, were extremely long, extensions that I knew must be tentacles. Tentacles! They were thick at their bases and tapered at the tips. I swear, each one was probably close to a hundred feet long. Maybe even more, but that's just my best guess. A hundred feet!

Oh man. That's when Carla's description of Dr. Webb's giant octopus carcass from 1896 flooded my mind and all I wanted to do was to get out of there, fast.

"OK, Jeff, ignore what you're seeing down there and get the anchor ready," Lobo yelled from the stern, startling me. Before we even got to the dock, he told me I had only one assignment besides lighting part of the way with a flashlight. That job was to drop the anchor that now sat on the canoe bottom right in front of my feet with a coil of rope attached to it.

Nervous as I was though, I picked up that cold, wet piece of heavy metal in both hands. "Uh, OK, ready," I yelled back. *I think. I hope!*

"Now!" Lobo roared and cut off his electric engine when I was about thirty or forty feet from the creature.

Just as I'd been told to do, I pitched the anchor overboard, making a small splash. Immediately, that coil of rope started rapidly unwinding and whizzing out through an aluminum ring attached to the very end of the bow. In seconds, it pulled taught.

When that happened, the current in the channel rotated the canoe around until Lobo's end floated almost directly over the creature. We were now in a stationary position, held by the anchor.

Moving quickly, the old guy took off his boots and socks and then stripped down to his under shorts. Boxers. I never in my life thought I would see a sight like that, especially in such a weird blue light—old Lobo almost naked. Gotta admit though, he had the body of much younger man and with the muscles of an athlete. Pretty good for a man over a couple of hundred years old.

"You're going in such cold water with that *thing*?" I couldn't believe that was his plan. It was no wonder he didn't tell any of us his exact plan ahead of time.

"Look Jeff, what I'm about to attempt is the surest way to link with the developing brain portion of the Particle Being. If it works, I might be able to figure out at least some of its intentions."

While saying all that, he opened a large yard bag at his feet and dumped its contents out on the canoe bottom making dull thumping sounds.

I watched in stunned silence as he fastened a weighted dive belt around his waist that had a great big old sheathed Bowie knife attached to it. Next, he pulled a dive mask over his face and attached flippers to his feet. "If I don't resurface within five minutes, this is what you do, so listen carefully."

Oh no, I thought. No freakin' way am I going to seriously consider the possibility of Lobo not surviving what he's about to do. Knowing something could happen is a lot different than planning in detail how you will deal with it if it does. But Lobo fired off his final orders before I could protest.

"Use your jackknife and cut the line to the anchor. Then you crawl back here, get this motor running and return to the house as fast as you can. You've run the motor before, so there shouldn't be any problem with you handling the canoe.

"When you get there, you pile Carla and Lyle into my truck and you waste no time doing it. Then drive to Jacksonville and don't ever return to St. Augustine. Find Carla's grandmother. Tell her all of what's happened.

"After that, all of you go to the Coast Guard and explain to them what's going on here. They won't believe you at first but after a few weeks, when things start changing in this city, they probably will. I doubt if anyone will be able to do anything about this situation, but it will be worth a try. Got it?"

Talk about chillingly negative words. I thought I knew how serious that entire PB situation was, but in hearing Lobo's orders in the event he died took that understanding to a new and terrifying level.

"Yes, sure I've got it but—" Lobo didn't interrupt me. No, he didn't even wait for me to finish my response. Instead, he jumped into the water with a huge splash.

I just knew the canoe was going to capsize, but somehow it didn't. As the thing wobbled back and forth, I watched as he swam downwards towards that great big lump. It made me shiver to see what he was doing—especially when I lost sight of him.

And that's when it happened. Something long erupted from the water not more than three feet from me on the left side of the canoe.

When I turned to look, I realize with horror it was a glowing, violet colored tentacle sticking up into the air about ten feet high. The base of it, about a foot wide, stayed steady, but the skinnier end near the top whipped around like crazy. Those suckers all over part of it made the thing even more terrifying. I didn't want to imagine how thick the actual base of those arms were where they connected to the creature down below.

Tell you what though, I acted on pure instinct. I grabbed one of the paddles Lobo and I brought with us in case the motor failed. As soon as I had it in my hands, I swung it with all my strength as best I could from my seated position in the canoe.

The impact with that tentacle jarred the hell out me, hurt my hands and arms something fierce and shattered the business end of the paddle. But at least as soon as I hit the thing, it retracted back into the water and disappeared, leaving me sitting there shaking.

My breath came in jagged gulps as I grabbed the remaining paddle and snapped my head all around looking for more tentacles that might pop up. And when I stared into the water at that big, grey lump far below, I saw something coming up at me. In batting position again, I got ready to strike as soon as it came out of the water.

When it did surface, I was about to swing when it said, "Back off. It's me." *Lobo.*

Talk about being relieved! I just about collapsed. What a welcome sight. The old guy never looked so good.

30

Glittery Snakes

After climbing back into the canoe, and almost capsizing it again, Lobo said nothing and dressed quickly. No amount of questioning or prodding on my part would get him to tell me what happened underwater with that sea creature.

But finally, after pulling on his socks and boots, he said, "Things are about to go from bad to worse. We have to get back to my place as soon as we can."

As soon as that last word came out of his mouth, the glow all around us started dimming.

"OK, what's going on?" I asked.

"It's shifting location," Lobo replied, starting the electric motor. "Pull up the anchor—fast! We'll talk in a minute."

I didn't need to be told twice. In less than a minute, I had the anchor back in the canoe and Lobo was steering us back the way we came. By then, we were back in semi-darkness and I watched as a bright patch of light blue water far to my left moved across the bay towards downtown St. Augustine.

"Here's what happened," Lobo shouted from behind me. "When I got to the creature, I plunged my knife into it. I did so in order to hold on and be able to touch its body for an extended period of time without getting swept away by the current.

"The central core of that thing is more like brain tissue than anything which means that part of it doesn't feel pain. But when you hit its sensitive appendage, the entire creature reacted violently. I think it felt true discomfort for the first time."

"So I made it move away like that?" I shouted over my shoulder, worried I had done something wrong, but wondering even more why we needed to get back to shore so fast. Was Carla in more danger now because of me?

"The creature began moving *when* it did because both of us took action almost simultaneously," Lobo shouted back in the darkness, his loud voice cutting easily through the wind, the slight whine of the engine and the slapping of water against the canoe.

"It felt what you did with the paddle and sensed me as I touched it with my hand right about the same time. Too much at once—a danger signal that then merged with plans it already had."

"Plans? You know what its plans are just from touching it for a short time? Is Carla—?"

"Details later," he replied, "but Carla is fine." Lobo said nothing more until we spotted his dock up ahead of us. With all those floodlights turned on, it looked like a huge beacon in the surrounding darkness helping to guide us home. For that reason, Lobo found he didn't need for me to help him see by using the flashlight.

When we got to the dock, Carla stood there waiting for us. Arms folded, she had a worried look on her face. Spock sat at her feet but no Lyle. Carla and Lye should definitely have been together. Not good. Not good at all.

We're too late, Lobo's voice in my head whispered as he guided the canoe alongside the dock. *Lyle's in trouble.*

I hated to hear that, but at least it wasn't Carla. "You OK?" I asked her.

"Yes," she replied, but her voice sounded strained and her eyes held a squinty tenseness that I didn't see in her very often. "But something's happened to Lyle." Old Lobo was on target as usual.

"Tell us," Lobo rumbled once we exited the canoe, tied it up to the dock and stood there talking to Carla. Spock whined and wagged his tail so much at seeing us, Carla had to hush him.

"By his second beer," she explained, "Lyle wanted to come out here on the dock and wait for you both. That went O.K. for a while. We talked and he petted Spock, but about fifteen minutes ago, everything changed.

"He chugged the rest of his beer, threw the can in the water and then started walking up and down the dock and mumbling things I couldn't hear.

"When I spoke to him, it seemed like he didn't even realize I was there. The next thing I know, the poor man screamed, 'No! Not again!' and he ran off the dock and into your workshop, Lobo. He locked the door behind him and closed the blinds. Nothing I said would get him to come out. He's there now in the dark, moaning and crying."

"Understood," Lobo said as he pulled his silver key-chain out of his pocket and jangling it in front of us. "We'll get him out of there. Let's go."

Flashlight. The word burst into my mind just as we all started walking off the dock. It was as clear as if Lobo actually said the word aloud, and I knew without a doubt that he wanted me to grab the flashlight out the canoe where I had left it. Almost without thinking, I turned around, did as he asked, and rejoined him and Carla just as they reached the end of the dock.

In less than a minute, all three of us stood in the glare of a security floodlight pointed at the front door of the workshop.

"There is definitely a strong concentration of particles in there," Lobo said, making my blood freeze. "Shouldn't be, but it's there for some reason. Luckily, this batch isn't as strong as what you both faced at Potter's so none of us is in immediate danger. The silver we're all carrying will offer the needed protection.

Then taking the flashlight from me, he said, "When we enter, do just as I do, but do *not* talk. Carla, you're second and Jeff, you're last—you get to close the door as quietly as you can. Do you both understand?"

"Yes," we both said, while inside the little building, Lyle whimpered and mumbled.

After making sure we knew what to do, Lobo unlocked the door and slowly opened it all the way. The security flood lit up only a small part of the floor, showing some wood shavings and a few carvings, but not much more. Lobo turned on the flashlight and waved for us to join him.

In seconds, all three of us were inside with the door closed. Along the outer edge of the flashlight's beam, Lyle sat there in the middle of the floor cross-legged. His eyes were closed, and he held his hands over his ears. The air smelled of wood, paint, stain and PB.

As he cried and moaned, Lyle kept bobbing forward and back at the waist. He didn't seem able to hear us even with our feet crunching wood shavings beneath them. I thought at least the flashlight might startle him, but Lobo avoided shining it directly in the man's face.

The good thing? I didn't see any particles. But the nasty scent of ozone and burning wires told me they were definitely there just like Lobo said.

Slowly, Lobo walked over in front of Lyle and sat on the floor about five feet from him. Once he got settled in the crunchy debris, he motioned for Carla and me to sit on either side of him, which we did, all three of us facing Lyle.

God that made me squirm, seeing the poor guy in such bad shape. The more I looked at him, the sorrier I felt and the more frightened I got—for all of us. And when I stole a glance at Carla, I saw the glint of tears in her eyes, even in that low light.

"Lyle," Lobo said finally after a few seconds but in a very loud voice.

The little guy instantly reacted almost like he had been hit by a grenade or something. His eyes flashed wide open, his head snapped back knocking off his lucky red baseball cap, showing a perfectly bald head. I had no idea he didn't have any hair.

That's when his mouth flew open as if he was about to scream, but that never happened. Unfortunately, it got worse, a lot worse.

From deep inside him came this gurgling sound as if someone was strangling him and his tongue stuck straight out of his mouth. And his eyes, my God, his eyes. They looked as if they were going to pop out of his head or explode.

I swear he looked like something straight out of a horror movie making both Carla and me start to scramble and get the hell out of there but Lobo stopped us.

All it took was a hand on each of our shoulders to calm us down, at least enough so we didn't leave.

Just as Carla and I stopped trying to escape, bright violet PB strands slowly slid out of Lyle's mouth in all directions until his head and body were mostly covered by them. They looked like glittery snakes slithering all around, constantly moving. Horrible. I wanted to back away but Lobo's hand on me kept that from happening. I'm telling you, if Lobo wasn't there helping me keep my reactions under control, I would have jumped up, grabbed Carla and been out of there at the first sign of particles or the color violet.

But no, I didn't do that. Instead, I sat there staring at poor Lyle with a strange mixture of terror, fascination and deep concern for the poor guy. A quick glance over at Carla told me she had similar feelings.

Seconds later, still covered in sparkling violet strands, Lyle seemed to relax. No more nasty noises came from him. His eyes and tongue went back to normal, his head came back level with his body, and he took a deep breath.

Smiling with a very confident look on his face, Lyle spoke to Lobo. "Ahhh, at last. So that's what it's like being human, eh, shaman? Extraordinary! How very much we look forward to expanding this experience."

The voice wasn't Lyle's. It sounded almost like glass breaking over and over again. Maybe that doesn't make any sense to you, but those are the only words that come to mind to describe what I heard.

Just as Lyle finished speaking, Lobo flipped his silver key chain at him. It hit the poor guy right in the forehead and then dropped into his lap.

In that next instant, all those strands around Lyle's body shot back into his mouth. There was no more violet anywhere and the Lyle we knew looked at all of us as if wondering what we were all doing sitting on the floor of Lobo's workshop at night. With a flashlight.

Seconds later, Lyle's eyes rolled up in his head and he collapsed in convulsions.

Rapidly jumping to his feet, Lobo scooped the shaking man up into his arms, and to Carla and me he said, "In the house, quickly!"

31

Lobo's World

"OK, you two, time to wake up." It was Lobo's voice and I didn't want to hear it.

Instead, I just wanted to keep sleeping, but at that moment, I felt something move all along my right side. *What?*

Startled awake, I saw Carla snuggled up next to me rubbing her eyes. I had my arms around her and we were in a corner of Lobo's couch. How and when we got there I had no idea.

Lobo sat in the recliner to our right, staring at us intently in his usual way. Stretched out almost flat with a blanket over him in the other recliner on our left was Lyle, snoring softly. And for some reason a dark brown sheet covered Lobo's picture window.

"Caa," Edgar squawked from the mantle over Lobo's fireplace where he stood on his only leg. That whole scene made no sense to me at all. Especially Edgar. He rarely came into Lobo's house. And I didn't see Spock anywhere.

"What is going on?" Carla asked, sitting up and looking about as confused as I felt.

The last thing I remembered, Lobo had Lyle in his arms. When that memory seeped into my half-asleep brain another one followed—one of Lyle and the PB over in Lobo's workshop, and I shuddered.

From somewhere way in the distance came a rushing, almost thundering sound that I couldn't identify. Daylight peeked around the edges of the sheet covering Lobo's window—the only source of light in the room. It was definitely not nighttime. *A sheet?*

"You both need some orienting," Lobo said in his matter of fact way of expressing things, even during the weirdest of circumstances.

"You can say that again," I whispered, stretching and putting one arm back around Carla. No matter what, I really liked the idea of waking up with her beside me.

"No need to whisper," Lobo said. "Right now, Lyle could sleep through a war. He's exhausted, but he'll be OK."

"How long have we been asleep?" Carla asked.

"About an hour and a half," Lobo replied, his dark eyes flashing in that dim light.

"No way!" I said. "It wasn't even midnight when we caught up with Lyle in the workshop."

"He's right," Carla agreed. "It should still be dark outside after an hour and a half. And why do you have a sheet up in front of the window?"

"That's where the orientation comes in." As he spoke, Lobo got up out of the recliner, went over to the fireplace and stroked Edgar's neck with one finger.

Then turning back to look at us he said, "You both are missing part of your memories because an hour and a half ago, you expended a tremendous amount of energy in helping me to save Lyle's life. That effort literally burned away your memory surrounding it.

"When we all arrived here in the house after that nasty encounter with a segment of the Particle Being, Lyle was near death. It took the three of us, but especially you, Carla, to revive him."

"Me?" Clearly, Carla didn't believe him and I didn't understand what part I could have played in what happened. Carla and Lobo, sure, but not me. Not a chance.

"Yes you, Carla," he said to her. "Your ability to manipulate matter and energy in relation to the human body now exceeds mine." Now that was saying something!

"You can't be serious," she replied, shaking her head.

Just as if she hadn't spoken, Lobo kept on talking. "And your friend Jeff there was able to support both of our efforts by channeling to us the energy he uses to create doubles of himself and stop time in its tracks."

"Oh yeah, right." Lobo didn't lie and he didn't joke, but I still found what he said hard to believe.

"Just because you both didn't retain those memories doesn't mean that what I told you isn't true. Under the tremendous pressure of the moment, and with my guidance, each of you came through with flying colors.

"There is one thing though, Carla, that you must understand. What happened to Lyle was not your fault in any way. You made sure he put his silver necklaces back on. I know because I checked. He's wearing them. But they obviously weren't enough to protect him because of his weakened condition and all those extra particles inside him."

"Oh, thank God," she replied. "I thought I missed something." Underneath those words, I somehow sensed that she was finally relaxing. Actually, it was like I felt it *inside me* somehow.

That's when Lobo gave her the details about the canoe trip out on the bay. When he finished the story, he continued telling her information I didn't know.

"After I made that short contact with the sea creature, I found I could sense its basic intentions but no more. There simply wasn't time.

"But what little I know now is this. The sea creature has moved just outside of the St. Augustine Marina. That's close enough for it to make a very limited connection underground with a much larger and greatly enhanced PB concentration that is now at the wax museum. All of the remaining particles are collected in that location—and there's a lot of them.

"This bolstering of the power and reach of the wax museum particles allowed them to sniff Lyle out underground and penetrate him. They were successful in their efforts mainly because Lyle had absorbed so many particles in the previous attack in the plaza.

"The thing is, another more successful assault on Lyle would have no doubt happened soon after we revived him even with his protection by his silver. And if I hadn't immediately moved him, he might now either be dead or, in terms you can easily understand, converted into a zombie-like being under full PB control."

"Oh, poor Lyle," Carla said.

"Caa." Edgar, like me, seemed to agree.

"So why did moving Lyle into your house protect him?" I asked. "Can't the PB slide up from underground here exactly like it did at the workshop and get him?"

Lobo nodded. "That would be true if I hadn't moved the deep essence of who Lyle is far away from my house."

"Uh, you lost me," Carla interrupted. "You mean Lyle's deep essence, his soul, spirit or whatever isn't in his body over there, right in front of us? You ... moved it to safekeeping somewhere else?"

"This is where it gets difficult for you and Jeff to comprehend, so pay close attention.

"What I'm saying is, I moved the essence of *each one of us* to safekeeping while also giving Lyle enough time to strengthen his defenses and rid him of those excess particles he acquired in the plaza.

"We are protected as well but, all of our time here is limited.

"This house and everything you see in this room, including your own bodies, is a temporary reproduction of the reality you know. Back in St. Augustine, in my actual physical house, we are all lying there in coma-like states. Since people in comas don't interest the PB, our true bodies are protected there as well.

"Edgar is with us and not Spock because Edgar enjoys little adventures like this."

When Lobo's explanation ended, I felt my mind go blank. Our *essences*? And when I glanced at Carla, I saw her mouth open as if to say something, but no words came out. Like me, I could feel her struggling to understand what Lobo had just told us.

"Let me try again," Lobo said, obviously seeing we didn't understand.

"What you are experiencing is similar to what you both encountered right after Christmas when you entered your ancestors' combined dream worlds and seemed to live in a very real reproduction of the Dade Battle firsthand.

"Remember, at that time, your actual physical bodies remained with me in the St. Augustine National Cemetery. And if you recall, those circumstances seemed as real as the life you left behind."

"Uh … our bodies now are temporary reproductions?" I asked, stroking Carla's hair. Lobo was right. We had experienced something like that before. But as I studied Carla carefully, I found it hard to believe she wasn't actually *the* physical Carla.

"Yes," Lobo said.

"Um, OK, I guess," Carla replied, looking around the room. "So this, all of it, is sort of a what? a virtual world?"

"Yes and no." Lobo's answer didn't really seem to help. "What you see and feel has aspects of an actual reality that *may or may not exist* somewhere. It doesn't really matter either way, but what you are doing now is a version of what shamans have done for thousands of years—spirit traveling."

I understood the man's words and I remembered in detail the experiences Carla and I had in such a place before. But looking at Lobo, Carla and Lyle still made my mind want to rebel. The reality of what I was seeing was so clear and so identical to what I knew, that it made Lobo's explanation seem impossible.

"Jeff!" Lobo barked. "Snap out of it. Don't fight what is. Accept it and move on. We don't have time for you to sort it all out right now. I need your full attention."

"Uh, sure," I replied, working on turning those little switches in my head that I knew had to be flipped in order for me to adjust to my new situation. Lobo had taught me well that I had such control, but it wasn't always easy for me to do."

"Good start," he replied, eying me intently. "Keep it up. There are a lot more surprises on the way so listen carefully.

"After my initial interaction with the original Particle Being back in the nineteenth century, I found that my shamanic spirit traveling abilities had been greatly enhanced. This is just one of the many locations I found in my expanded journeying back then. I find it a place of great relaxation even though I can't seem to stay here more than a couple of hours."

"Spirit traveling," I repeated as if saying the words would help me understand and accept the man's explanation a little faster. "To some location that might be real or it might not."

Continuing that line of thought, Carla said, "So because the reality outside this house is something that's totally different from what we know you put that sheet up to block our view out the window. To make sure so we don't freak out, right?"

"Correct. But before you take a look, I want to remind you both that this place, this world we inhabit right now, may be a figment of my imagination, another planet, or we could now be even be in a different dimension or universe. Take your pick, but, as I said before, it simply doesn't matter. What does matter is that it's offering Lyle the rest and temporary protection he needs.

"I'll give it another hour just to be sure and then return us to our usual reality."

"How about you let us see what's outside the window," I said, ready for whatever was to come and tired of all the talk.

"By all means," Lobo replied, walking out of the room and into the hall." But let's take it a step further. Come with me."

When we joined him in the hall, we saw he had put a sheet over his recreated stained glass door as well. "Double precaution," he explained as he opened the door to an astounding sight.

Slowly, hand-in-hand, Carla and I walked onto Lobo's porch and then out onto a large outcrop of flat rock, light red in color, overlooking a wide, volcanic cone far below. I couldn't believe it. We were actually standing on a cliff. After Lobo's warning about Carla and me "stepping off a cliff," the *coincidence* was really startling.

Beyond the volcano below was, a vast ocean of deep green stretched out to the horizon with lots of islands receding into the distance. And from that direction, a warm breeze blew over us that smelled of salt and something else I didn't recognize.

Carla gasped.

"Holy crap," I said, staring at the sight in front of us.

Here and there, great big, puffy, white clouds with grey bottoms moved against a dark blue sky. Almost directly over the nearest island to our left, a thunderstorm sent showers downward at a slant along with an occasional lightning strike.

Grey in color, with some kind of blue green vegetation all around its base, the nearby volcano seemed to be part of land that helped to create a huge bay to the right of it. On the bay, long series of waves eventually broke on a curving beach of light red sand.

From the land and the water to the right of the volcano, giant shafts, knife-like rock, brick red in color, poked steeply upward at an angle going from left to right.

As if we had planned it, Carla and I turned around at exactly the same time. Behind us, and behind Lobo's house, were even bigger shafts of red rock that gradually got larger, taller and more numerous until they merged into a huge mountain range.

And from a small cliff high up to our left, flowed a tremendous waterfall. That thing fell all the way down to hit rocks at our elevation probably less than a mile from Lobo's house. There it created a very short river before plunging out of sight. I had found the source of the noise I heard when I first woke up in this strange place.

In the sky above the mountains in front of us, a cloud parted, revealing not just one sun, but two.

"Welcome to my home away from home," Lobo said.

32

Life Forms

"Come on, I want to take you both down to the bay while Lyle recuperates."

I heard the man speak but all I could do was to keep physically turning around in little circles, trying to take in everything around me while Carla did the same thing.

I tell you what, being in that incredibly beautiful place, yet knowing our bodies were still physically back in St. Augustine, still made my mind a jumble of confusion. And then to see Lobo's house, or at least his shamanic recreation of it, sitting there in the middle of all that, sure didn't help any.

"Are you believing this?" Carla asked as I slid my hand into hers.

"I'm having a tough time absorbing it all," I replied, still shifting my gaze all around like crazy. "How about you?"

"I'm absolutely astounded. But it does make me think about us being stuck in that virtual battle your ancestor pulled us into."

"Oh yeah! Very true, but at least this time we're escaping danger instead of walking into it."

"If you two are quite done being flabbergasted," Lobo interrupted while waving us to follow him, "we'll get on with the task at hand."

Still mentally stuck in our sudden arrival at such a strange place, Carla and I watched the old guy walk around the right side of his house and slowly disappear between some large, bluish-green ferns and down into a ditch, gully—a low place of some sort.

We couldn't quite tell exactly where Lobo had gone, but we figured we should run and catch up with the guy. When we finally got to where we last saw him, we found ourselves looking down on him. He stood there waiting for us in what looked like a wide, sandy, boulder and fern-lined trail that angled lower and lower, until it went out of sight.

Actually, it seemed to end right at a huge stadium-sized chunk of rock a deeper color of red than the sand leading up to it. The top of the rock curved gently so it almost looked like a dome.

"The waterfall you see up in the mountains," Lobo said, pointing towards the giant, knife-like rocks behind his house, "used to flow directly through here and then down into the bay. Evidently, if this is indeed a physical place, over the eons, it cut through solid rock to get there. You'll soon see what I mean by that.

"Watch your step and don't stray from the riverbed. There are no dangerous life forms here that I've discovered, but I can't guarantee your safety if you go wandering around very far. We don't want to put the reality of this place to such a test."

That last comment from Lobo came over his shoulder just before he started walking down the old riverbed towards the bay. It seemed to be such an easy thing for him to say, but Carla and I exchanged worried glances as we scooted after him.

The sand beneath our feet crunched loudly, a lot more it seemed than the beach sand back home. Why, I'm still not sure. We didn't have time to do any investigating.

Lobo moved too fast for us to catch up with him right away. I think he just didn't want to answer all the questions we had, especially about what types of creatures lurked in this strange world of his. Even so, we got a partial answer seconds later when something moved under my left foot and hissed loudly.

Startled, I yelled and jumped out of the way just as that something, about the size of a dinner plate, scuttled off into a big patch of nearby ferns.

I didn't see it at first because the little creature blended perfectly with the light red sand all around us. Only when it moved could we see the thing because at that point it quickly turned a deep shade of blue. It looked like a weird cross between a scorpion and a rat, or a squirrel maybe, with spindly little legs. Scared us both to death, but at least it seemed scared of us as well.

By the time we recovered from our little encounter with the local wildlife, Lobo had disappeared again. We wanted to run after him but didn't, worried we might stomp on some more of the camouflaged, unknown "critters" as Carla calls all kinds of animals.

After about five minutes of walking and watching where we stepped, the riverbed led us down to a huge, brightly lighted cave in that huge dome-like rock. As we stood in front of the entrance, a cool, damp breeze blew out of it, smelling strongly of saltwater and other things neither one of us could identify.

We didn't fully realize how big that cave was until we got in there. I swear, it looked like long ago, water had hollowed out almost the entire rock.

Ahead of us maybe 200 feet, a big ray of sunlight from a very large hole in the high ceiling of the place lit up the interior and pooled on a wide expanse of reddish sand—all around Lobo. He stood there with his hands on his hips, like someone about to perform under a giant spotlight, obviously waiting for our arrival.

A hundred feet or so beyond him, there was another opening, one leading directly to the bay. Between Lobo and us, the old riverbed merged with the cave's almost circular, sandy floor. The place almost looked like a covered stadium. Yeah, it was that big in there.

"Come on, let's go!" Lobo shouted. The man's deep, bigger than life voice seemed louder than usual. Even though the rock walls and ceiling were far away, I figured they must be acting like an amplifier somehow. Yup, I thought, Lobo was onstage with his built-in spotlight and microphone, raising hell because his audience hadn't arrived.

Minutes later, all three of us walked through the opening directly opposite where we had entered the cave and out onto the beach surrounding the bay. And as we did, rays from those dual suns beat down on our backs and reflected brilliantly off the red sand.

The volcano in front of us towered high above our heads, as did some of those knife-like shafts of rock slanting towards our right everywhere, even out into the bay.

Judging by one of those shafts closest to us, they all had to be at least forty feet tall. On each of those big chunks of rock in the bay as far out as I could see were high tide marks—a lighter color of red below than above.

Small, clear waves broke onto the beach in front of us and all up and down the curved bay, sending thin sheets of water onto mostly dry sand. It looked to me like the tide was coming in. I wondered about the coincidence of a bay being almost right outside Lobo's door on this world, very much like Matanzas Bay being close to his house back on Earth. Very interesting.

All along that shoreline, far back from the water, was a thick line of darker material, stuff left over from earlier high tides just like any beach on earth. *On earth.* Those words still get to me today when I think about them because we were definitely somewhere else at that time, even if was in Lobo's shamanic imagination.

On the wind coming from the bay and ocean was a partially familiar smell. It reminded me of a mix of fish, shrimp and squid that had been in the sun too long.

Anyway, Lobo led us across the nearest batch of that dark material which really crunched and popped beneath our feet. And as I looked closer, I saw it contained a tangle of old seaweed, pieces of driftwood and what looked like sea shells. Almost at the same time, both Carla and I bent over and picked up some of those shells.

Some of the ones I found looked like three, cream-colored corkscrews linked together at a joint opening. Another made me think of a four-leaf clover, four light green clam-like shells evenly spaced around a common base.

"Join me over here," Lobo called from where he now stood next to one of those knife-like rocks. It had broken off at some point in time and was lying flat but partially buried in the sand. The far tip of it was actually under water. Incoming waves traveled part way up its surface and then receded again.

When we got to Lobo, he told us to ditch our shells and have a seat on the rock. He needed to talk to us.

I shrugged and dropped mine but not Carla. "Why throw them away?" she asked. "These are beautiful and unique. I want to take them home."

While she spoke, I glanced out at the islands and the ocean beyond the bay. On the horizon, against the deep blue sky and puffy white clouds, I noticed a line of darkness that seemed to ripple, as if maybe it had moving parts or something. It took me until then to recognize what I was seeing must be a big flock of birds. *But what kind?* I wasn't sure I wanted to find out.

"You can't take them home," Lobo replied to Carla's question. "We're in spirit bodies and you won't be able to transport anything from this world. It's something like knowing you're in a dream when you try to bring an object back into the real world. It just doesn't work."

Not wanting to give up her shells, Carla said, "But when Jeff and I left his ancestor's spirit world we brought back blood, dirt and pine needles. Remember? So explain how we could do it in that situation but we can't do it now?"

"That previous situation, Carla, was an anomaly. Something I have no way of explaining except to say it probably had something to do with Jeff's direct connection to his long lost relative. There is no such linkage here, but if you insist, take some with you and see what happens later."

"Fine," Carla replied, discarding all her shells except for a few small ones which she stuffed into her jeans' pocket. "You never know for sure until you try."

"Have a seat," Lobo directed, pointing at the flat rock that stuck up out of the sand about three feet.

Both of us did as he asked, sitting next to each other. But Lobo kept standing. Slowly, he turned to face the bay's outlet to the ocean, exactly where I had been looking just moments before.

While the man stood that way for a few minutes without saying a word, Edgar showed up. I didn't think Lobo let him out of his house, but there he was hopping around on the rock next to Carla on his one leg. *A spirit traveling crow?*

After another thirty seconds of silence from Lobo, I turned to Carla with a questioning look. She just rolled her eyes, made a weird face and shook her head. I had to agree. Trying to figure Lobo out was an impossible game to play. "Caa," Edgar said. I decided to think Edgar meant that he agreed with us.

As the ocean breeze ruffled her hair, Carla gave me one of her dazzling smiles. My God, she looked so good I couldn't resist staring. And for a moment on that alien world, I escaped all my confusion and fear for the future. Instead, I allowed my mind to fill with admiration, appreciation and, yeah, love for the beautiful girl sitting next to me.

Unfortunately, all those delicious thoughts and feelings didn't last long.

"Here they come!" Lobo said as he pointed towards the sky over the bay.

"They who?" I asked, but then I realized he was pointing towards the dark line on the horizon I had noticed just a short time before. The birds.

Now though, the line looked more like a massive, rolling storm front of deep orange and black several miles across. And it seemed to be heading our way—fast. Fascinated, I stared while the bay darkened and it became clear that what we were watching had nothing to do with weather.

The water out there was getting dark because sunlight couldn't get through the living mass flying over it. When I looked above the boiling orange and black, I could see thousands and thousands of little dots against the sky.

"Birds?" Carla asked, echoing my observation from before.

"Watch and learn," Lobo replied, but his answer told me they probably weren't birds.

"There's got to be millions of them out there," I said, gawking at the mass of living things speeding in our direction. The scene in front of us reminded me of rain showers sweeping across Matanzas Bay at home. But this was definitely not a bunch of slowly moving clouds dropping a wall of water.

"Friends of yours? I hope." Carla spoke to the same concern I had.

"More than friends," Lobo said calmly just as the first batch of the creatures ahead of the main mass arrived in a dry rustle of wings. They moved so quickly as they circled around all three of us and Edgar that it was hard to see exactly what they looked like. Immediately though, my mind labeled them as giant dragonflies—giant as in yard long with black wings and orange bodies.

Lobo's calmness told us we had nothing to fear, but when the rest of that swarm showed up seconds later they blotted out the sun, I mean suns. We could still see, but it was like the time after the sun goes down and just before it gets really dark.

In the increasing darkness, Carla and I wrapped our arms around each other. And as we did that, the rustle of wings grew to a roar. And instead of the warm ocean breeze from before, we were whipped by cool disturbed air that smelled something like vinegar.

Lobo deliberately caused this somehow, I thought as I remembered another dragonfly swarm in St. Augustine on San Marco Avenue just before I learned to consciously stop time. *He knew back then this might happen and he was preparing me for the possibility.*

As soon as I realized the connection between the St. Augustine experience and what was happening right at that moment, I could sense some kind of change occurring. It took me a few seconds to figure out that dozens of huge openings were appearing in the swarm on all sides of us allowing daylight to appear once again. And as that happened, the thundering sounds of wings beating air slowly lessened.

And within less than two minutes, there wasn't one of those dragonfly-type creatures flying anywhere. They had all settled somewhere, on plants, rocks, the beach, the volcano—everywhere. I mean they covered *everything* but the water in a carpet of black and orange as far as I could see—everything except for a circle around the three of us and Edgar about ten feet in diameter.

"Get ready," Lobo said into the quiet, "you're about to receive some very important information."

Exactly as the man finished speaking, one of those dragonfly things out on the beach shot straight up into the air about eight feet high with wings shaking noisily. It hovered there for a few seconds before flying right at Carla and me, making us flinch and jerk backward. It actually ended up at eyelevel, about five feet away.

"Relax," Lobo said, "this is about communications and education, not hostility."

"If you say so," Carla replied, eyeing the living thing in front of us warily.

Close up, the creature looked a lot like a yard long, bug-eyed lizard with dragonfly-type wings and a stubby tail. Black like its wings, those two eyes showed a splash of orange in the middle just like its body color. Four very skinny legs hung from both of its sides. Every leg had what looked like three long, jointed toes, each ending in a single, sharp looking claw.

While our visitor fanned us with its huge, rustling wings, the smell of vinegar got a lot stronger.

Seconds later, Lobo said, "OK, you two, you're about to be linked with all of the beings you see all around us, each and every one. But to do that, I need for you both to slowly reach out toward the creature now in front of you and intertwine your fingers. "There's nothing to fear in what is about to happen."

Connecting with each and every one of those things? The impossibility of the man's statement made me hesitate even as Carla extended her hand as directed. I wanted to ask questions but decided to follow Carla's lead instead by sliding a hand along her arm and grasping her fingers.

Now don't move. It was Lobo's voice inside my head. *Don't even blink.*

A split second later the dragonfly-like creature slowly flew towards us until its legs made contact with our hands.

Those sharp little nails actually tickled at first as they danced across my fingers—that is until they dug in with a bite.

I remember wanting to pull away when everything changed. In that next instant though, I found myself with countless others like me flying over a vast ocean a short distance above the water—water the color of gold. There was no sound even though our dark wings beat rapidly.

Below us swam a huge school of little, brown, fish-like things that constantly broke the surface, making it easy for us to catch them with our claws. After taking one small bite of each captive, I gently released it back into ocean—an extremely enjoyable snack. Sort of like quick a mouthful of candy, ice cream and cookies all mixed together. But one bite from each fish-like thing and no more.

If I grabbed one with a bite already taken from it, I tossed the thing back into the water. And as soon as my fellow creatures around me and I had eaten our fill, we shot up into the clear, cloudless, pale pink sky to join others of us hovering in a dense, dark cloud. When we got there, we inserted our bodies into the group to await the arrival of the next feeding pack from below.

There it is, the basic story. For that short time, I fully experienced life as a dragonfly-type creature—as did Carla. We eventually compared our versions of what happened to us and they were almost identical. Weird and fascinating as it was though, there's another, deeper version, one Carla and I find a lot harder to explain, but I'll try.

You see, when I was part of the swarm, even though there were millions of us in it, I somehow knew exactly what each of the others were experiencing. It was like I had two brains, one little one for doing my tiny job as part of the group and another great big one where I could see and feel everything going on with all the other creatures at the same time.

Together we functioned as one giant, living being. And together we were stronger, more intelligent and more creative than we were as individuals. Hold on, because it gets even stranger.

This part has to do with those brown fish-like things we liked to use for bite-sized snacks. Those little guys were our favorite meal actually, one we could never get enough of but we continually searched for across the many shallow areas of that world's seas.

Now you might think it had to do with taste, texture and smell of what we were eating but you'd mostly be wrong. Yes, those bites were delicious food for us but here's where it gets tricky.

The reason we greedily made mini meals out of those little creatures was that the more we ate, the more we could experience their existence down on the ocean bottom where they usually lived. As flying beings, we could never hope to actually travel underwater and we were fascinated by the strange and unusual lives the fishy guys lived.

Yes, I said, *experience their existence.* Don't ask me how it worked because I don't know.

What I do know is that by taking those bites, the dragonfly types somehow became each of the fishy guys as separate parts of their consciousnesses. For them it was sort of like taking little vacations in a strange country, being actors in weird movies and taking college courses all at the same time. Great fun and educational as well. Simple as that. Sort of. Or as simple as I can make it.

Each nibble meant a wider variety of experience, but the effect only lasted a certain period of time. That's why the dragonfly types were always on the lookout for the little brown ocean creatures. And if you're worried about those fishy types, don't be. The dragonfly guys knew exactly how to take a nibble without badly hurting them permanently.

That experience of existing as another life form is the last thing I remember on Lobo's strange world.

33

Particle People

I found myself staring at Lobo, vaguely wondering when I had arrived and why I was sitting there with both him and Carla on his porch. It almost felt like we had all been in deep conversation, but somehow I couldn't remember the topic.

"He's coming around," Lobo said to Carla.

Coming around?

All three of us sat facing Matanzas Bay in Lobo's rocking chairs on his porch with Carla in the middle. It was dark out there and chilly. Both Carla and I wore our jackets but as usual, Lobo didn't. Light from somewhere made it possible for me to see him and Carla.

"Let me talk first," Carla said. In response, Lobo nodded.

"We're back," she said to me. Her voice was soft and low, almost a whisper.

Back? Back from what? The word "back" made no sense, but more and more I felt like I was waking up from a dream—something about dragonflies, it seemed.

Slowly my groggy mind cleared and I knew exactly what she meant. A very brilliant and clear picture of flying over a golden ocean with a pale pink sky overhead flooded my awareness. "How—?"

"Lobo brought us back," Carla interrupted gently as if speaking to a scared child. "We were spirit traveling with him to that other planet, reality or whatever, remember?"

Taking a deep breath, I glanced to my left. The tip of Lobo's peninsula including his dock stood out in the glare of floodlights against the darkness of the bay. In the distance, the bridge to Vilano Beach sat there as usual at night, bathed in its orange and yellow glow from its huge streetlights that sing in the wind.

"Right," I said after a few seconds, but still trying to adjust to the incredibly rapid transition from one world to another. "OK," I replied, "I know where I've been and where I am."

Actually, I wanted to ask Carla how we got to Lobo's porch from his special world, but then I realized it just didn't matter.

"Good," Lobo said, "because there isn't much time. Jeff, it took you longer for your normal awareness to return than it did Carla. Unlike her, you became much too involved with those flying creatures I introduced you to and your mind had trouble letting it all go."

From his focus on me only, Lobo switched to include Carla. "Now listen carefully, both of you.

"I arranged that linkage with the alien life forms in order for you to have direct experience with a group consciousness derived from millions upon millions of individuals. Your all-consuming, firsthand connection with such swarming creatures has now given you better insight into effectively dealing with the Particle Being. Believe me, you are going to need it.

"Be aware that Lyle's visit to my special spirit traveling world has indeed eradicated the infestation of new particles in his body as I hoped. I can't explain the process, so you are simply going to have to trust me when I say it worked.

"He's asleep in the living room where we left him after his encounter with the PB in my workshop. I've placed silver over and under his body at strategic points, but I need to stay near him as an added layer of protection from another attack. And just in case you're wondering, Lyle was, and still is, the only one of us susceptible to a long range, subterranean probing by the Particle Being—but considerably less so than before.

Well, that's something positive in all this, I thought as Lobo continued talking.

"Now, since I have to stay with him, this means I need to use you both as my eyes and ears to see what's currently happening downtown where a huge part of the Particle Being still resides at the wax museum. And of course the hybrid sea creature is lurking nearby somewhere in the Matanzas River close to the marina.

"Such proximity of the two PB portions means things will be coming to a head relatively soon."

"Downtown?" I asked, my brain was still trying to adjust to such a rapid return to our normal reality. "Without you?" I couldn't believe the man was telling the two of us to go back into that danger zone—without him.

"You both can handle it as you've so ably demonstrated in multiple ways."

"So you want us to go back into Potter's?" Carla asked, with a look on her face that said, "Are you out of your mind?"

"Nothing of the kind," Lobo replied. "In fact, make sure you don't get within fifty feet of that place.

"Your job is simply to go to the plaza, sit there across from the wax museum for a while and observe. If after fifteen or twenty minutes you notice nothing out of the ordinary, you return. Simple as that.

"Oh and take my truck. They'll be plenty of parking by now and driving will be a lot faster."

"But all we have are our learners' permits," Carla protested. Lobo had taken us out on some dirt roads to practice our driving skills using his truck, but never in the city. And certainly not without him. This was definitely a major change and it startled both of us.

"We don't have time for rules and regulations," Lobo growled. "Just drive carefully, act confident, and nobody will question you.

"You want me to drive back when we leave?" I asked my question as we continued to sit on a bench in the plaza much further than fifty feet from Potter's Wax Museum. "I mean you did a great job and all, but it's only fair that we divide it up."

We had been sitting there in the chilly air for a good ten minutes not seeing any particles or anything out of the ordinary. In fact, it was very quiet. What a change, I thought, from earlier in the evening during that nasty particle storm. I had just asked Carla about me driving back to Lobo's because she lost the coin toss deciding who would drive into town.

"Umm, sure," she said while she continued to stare at Potter's with a slight squint. " It's all yours. But if you were a true gentleman, you would have gallantly volunteered to do it in the … first … place." Carla's part in the conversation trailed off into actual silence as she squinted again, like she was trying to focus on something in the distance.

She seemed to be seeing something, but when I glanced at the wax museum, it looked the same as before—dark with a few people walking by it occasionally on the sidewalk and a little bit of traffic on King Street. The closed sign was still on the front door.

The plaza itself was almost deserted. The only sounds came from the occasional cars passing by and country music coming from somewhere way in the distance.

"What?" I asked, starting to get a little nervous. "What are you seeing?"

"I'm not sure, really. It's just that when cars go past Potter's, I think I see something in their headlights. Then again, maybe not."

Instead of responding, I stared intently, waiting for the next car to go by. And when it did, I saw *them*.

"There!" both of us said almost at the same time.

"What in God's name are they?" Carla asked, grabbing my arm.

"I don't know, but it looked to me like six long, glistening, whitish blobs."

That's what I saw too," Carla whispered while she watched another car pass right through whatever it was that we were seeing.

The thing is, after that second car went by, those white blobs started turning into human-shaped forms that were coming our way—arms, legs, and heads increasingly visible. Trailing behind each figure was a pulsating strand of violet particles maybe a foot wide that led back through the closed door of Potter's.

"Particle people?" Carla asked, trying to put a label on what we were seeing.

"Uh-oh, not good," I said, "not good at all. I think we had better get out of here."

"You got that right," Carla replied, standing up and pulling me with her.

Unfortunately, we didn't move fast enough. Before we could turn around and run for the truck, all six figures shifted towards us so quickly I barely saw them move. In less than a second, they had formed a semicircle around us. Startled, we instinctively tried backing up, but the bench stopped us.

Being cornered like that caused a memory to flash through my mind of Lyle sitting on another bench at night in the plaza and turning into the bloody ghost of my ancestor. Panic shot through me. My chest tightened, my breath came in short little gasps and my heart slammed ferociously against my ribcage.

Breathe, I told myself. And focus on your breath. A few seconds of slow, deep breathing and concentrating on each breath like Lobo taught me, and I found myself calming down, at least a little.

Just then, two young couples strolled past us chatting loudly. All four people walked through those the particle strands attached to the glistening white figures that had us trapped without noticing anything out of the ordinary.

Again, so fast I couldn't follow the action, those human-like forms shifted and came together as one. Now standing before us was a single being somewhere between Carla's height and mine.

Across its, *body*, I guess you would say, colorful, moving pictures flashed so rapidly I couldn't see what they were in detail, but I could tell they were scenes showing people and places. It looked like somebody was projecting those pictures on the figure like a movie, completely covering the whiteness.

Second-by-second, the pictures slowed down enough for me to see that they were all showing my mother as she looked at various points in my life. Nothing unusual, just every day, regular things like washing the dishes or sitting in her chair at home and watching TV.

Fascinated, I stared at each scene as it zipped by until the entire being standing before me just … well, turned into my mother. She looked exactly as she did when Carla, Lobo and I saw her on the dock the day before except she wore jeans, a jacket and sneakers.

Instantly, fascination turned to stunned amazement. Seeing Mom appear, looking very solid, was incredible enough, but seeing her a second time took my breath away. And this time she appeared so close to me—not more than seven or eight feet away. All thoughts of the PB immediately left my brain.

"This can't be real." Carla cautioned, but I ignored her.

"Jeff," Mom said, her voice was just as I remembered it. "Help me, please." On her face I saw a look of total desperation, her eyes wide and shifting back and forth. "This Particle Being as you call it was able to dip into human afterlife and capture my soul. You're the only one who—"

Before she could finish her sentence, Mom screamed, her eyes rolled back into her head, and she shot backwards straight across King Street before going through the now open door of Potter's.

I didn't think. Instead, I just reacted by trying to untangle myself from Carla, but she wouldn't let go. The PB had captured my mom, or at least her spirit, and I needed to go help her. It was a gut reaction and an irresistible one. "Let go!" I shouted at Carla, yanking my arm away from her grip.

"Wait!" she yelled back at me, grabbing me by both arms this time. "It's a trap. The PB is imitating your mother, don't you see? Besides, Lobo told us to definitely not go in there."

For a few seconds, the urgency I felt to help Mom loosened its hold on me just enough for a little logical thinking to seep into my brain. Carla could be right, I realized, but then again if she wasn't, and I didn't try to help my mother, I could never live with myself.

"I don't have any real choice here," I told Carla firmly, peeling her fingers off my arms. "If I'm not back in five minutes, drive back to Lobo and tell him what happened."

Without waiting for a response, I turned around and ran towards Potter's.

34

She's Waiting for You.

After closing the door to the wax museum behind me, I looked back through the glass and saw Carla about to run across the street in my direction.

"No way," I whispered to myself, still breathing hard from my run across the plaza. I quickly felt around in the darkness until I found a deadbolt. Putting myself in danger was one thing but sharing it with Carla was another.

Jeff! Carla shouted deep in my mind as the slight smell of ozone and burning wires pushed its way up my nose and into my lungs. Her voice came through loud and clear just as Lobo's did when he used his mind-to-mind contact. She startled me at first, but I chose to ignore her.

With a turn of my wrist, I snapped the lock shut and quickly stepped backward, deeper into the gloom. Right at that moment, Carla arrived at the sidewalk outside the museum. And so did a police car.

Cops! Oh crap. Did they see me come in here? The police. That was the last thing either one of us needed. And when I say the cop car stopped, I mean it actually pulled over to the curb directly behind Carla.

"She's waiting for you." The voice caused me to whirl around. It was Kelsey, Carla's friend, but I couldn't see a thing in the darkness back there. Kelsey sounded stronger now, and much more assertive. *Oh great!* After what that girl did to my silver trap, I did not want to make her unhappy. So I froze and said nothing.

"You'll find her in the large exhibit hall." As Kelsey spoke again, I caught a quick glimpse of a violet PB strand shimmering to my right and then it was gone. Concentrating on where I saw the strand, I was slowly able to see the silhouette of what had to be Kelsey standing either in front of, or behind, the museum's ticket counter.

"She doesn't have much time." The girl sounded very insistent. "Take the door you used this afternoon."

I looked in the direction where I thought the entrance should be located. And as my eyes adjusted better to the darkness, I saw a slight violet glow stretching in a thin straight line where the far wall of the place met the floor opposite the front door. Light from the PB concentration in the exhibit hall area was bleeding between the floor and the door above it.

But as I started walking cautiously towards the glow, I remembered Carla and the police. A vision of cops shining flashlights on me through the windows of Potter's flashed through my mind. But when I turned my head to look, I saw Carla standing next to the police car and talking to an officer through the open passenger side window.

If they had seen me enter the museum, I decided with a sigh of relief, they would have already come to the door but they obviously hadn't. *Whew!*

"Go!" Kelsey said. It was an order and not a request. She almost sounded like Lobo does at times.

Hesitating at first, I continued walking towards the violet glow on the floor where I knew the door had to be. When I got there, I felt around in the darkness until I found the handle. In seconds, I was in the same long hallway from that afternoon. Hot, humid air wrapped itself around me in the quiet like a big wet blanket, much worse than before.

This time the increased stink of ozone and burning wires had some other nasty smell mix with it. I didn't even want to think about what that could be. Up ahead the open double doorway leading to the large exhibit room glowed violet, the only light I could see anywhere.

For just an instant, I wished Carla was with me, but then I pushed that selfish thought into the back of my mind.

"Mom?" I yelled, forcing myself to do what needed to be done. "Mom, are you in there?" The only answer I got was what seemed like a deepening of the silence all around me.

"In here." The voice that came from the room at the other end of the hall was faint, but it definitely belonged to my mother. I didn't even think. It was like my body reacted instead of my brain because the next thing I knew, I was running full blast towards that open doorway ahead.

When I got to the exhibit room, that's when I saw them. People. Tons of people bathed in a violet glow, and I'm not talking about wax figures here. In fact, I couldn't see any wax figures at first for some reason, but all those people came in a close second. Why? Because they looked sort of like mannequins in a department store.

Maybe that doesn't make sense to you, but it was my first reaction since none of them moved—at all.

No, they just stood there in the absolute silence, hands hanging straight down and unblinking eyes wide open. Wide open and staring right at me with horribly blank expressions on their faces. I swear, there must have been at least 100 people crammed in there—men, women, kids—all ages and races.

Across the entire high ceiling in that room, and down about halfway to the crowd, was a dense particle cloud. And from that cloud hung glistening PB strands, one attached to the head of each person in that place.

Freaky doesn't begin to describe the scene in front of me. It was as if I had stepped into the making of a zombie movie or something. I'm telling you, it looked like everything that made those people human no longer existed—sucked right out of their bodies and minds.

Even so, they were definitely alive. How could I tell? Because they were sweating. I couldn't see them breathing, but sweat ran down their faces, arms and hands.

And that's the other thing. Walking in there was like entering ten gross locker rooms all at once. Locker rooms where somebody had set the heat on ninety degrees, turned on all the showers using only super hot water with the sewers backing up through all the toilets.

Gross, you say? You bet. Really nasty. On top of all that, of course, was the very strong acidy scent of ozone and burning wires. The atmosphere in there made me want to gag.

It made sense how so many sweating bodies concentrated together without air conditioning raised the room temperature and humidity as well as using up all the oxygen. But I couldn't figure out the source of that overwhelming sewer smell until the obvious answer hit me in the head.

Some of those people must have been in there a long time and if they needed to go to the bathroom…Well, you get the picture.

So what did I do when faced with that really bizarre situation? Once again, I froze. Well, that and I tried to breathe only through my mouth while staring back at all those eyes looking at me. I had run into a lot of weird stuff since meeting Lobo, but to see all those people caught by the PB was more than overwhelming.

"OK, Jeff, enough gawking." Mom's voice, a strong voice this time, shattered the thick silence and made me jump.

Without having time to think, I just watched as all the people in that room suddenly shifted around by shuffling their feet but otherwise not moving their arms, hands, heads, or eyes in any way. A very, very weird dance, especially when all those particle strands moved with them.

What that did in about ten seconds was to create an opening in the crowd leading directly to my mother. She stood there in her jeans and jacket, smiling with her arms folded as she stared at me intently—without a particle strand sticking in her head. On the floor where the crowd had moved away were dark stains in the carpet that I didn't remember from my visit there before. The smell in the room told me how they might have gotten there, but I really didn't want to think about that anymore.

Behind Mom were all the wax figures from the evil side of the exhibit completely covered by the transparent particle cloud. That whole area of the room looked like a boiling, bubbling stew of pure nastiness.

"No hug now that I've come back to life?" Something was definitely not right. Even drunk, Mom never requested a hug.

"Mom?" I asked walking towards her but scared out of my wits. With each step though, I began to feel less and less sure that the person in front of me was actually my mother. Carla's words of warning about the PB just minutes before kept running through my brain.

Behind me I could hear shuffling which meant all those people were filling in the path they had created. Not a good thing. I was now surrounded.

By the time I got to Mom, I somehow definitely knew she wasn't real. I had come face-to-face with a very solid appearing Mom look-alike created by the PB.

"No hug, Jeff my boy?" the fake Mom said, now with a smirk twisting her face. "That tells me you've seen through my little disguise."

I stopped, not knowing what to say or do. *This can't be happening.* My heart pounded so hard I thought it was going to pop out of my chest. My mouth got very dry making it hard to swallow. Sweat poured down my left side.

This is a creation of the PB, like Carla said, I kept telling myself. That's not Mom. But oh God, it was so hard looking at such a perfect reproduction of her.

"Aw," Mom's look-alike said as she took a step closer. "Afraid? Of little ol' me?" By then, the smirk had turned into something more like a sneer. "Aren't you impressed with my handiwork all around you?"

As I tried desperately to think of a reply, the fake mom quickly lashed out with her right arm and hit me hard in the chest with the flat of her hand.

Totally surprised I staggered backward. I think I expected just about anything but getting physically smacked. That little attack really hurt because the mom look-alike had hit the silver dollar on my chest smashing it into me.

"That felt so good!" PB Mom said with a bright smile, looking at her fake but very solid hand. "True human physical existence is so much fun! And obviously, short-term contact with silver isn't a problem for me. How interesting."

"Now, dearest Jeff, that little love tap I just gave you was for trying to put me back into a silver prison earlier this evening. Such a naughty boy. Didn't your mother ever teach you not to hang out with bad people such as your repulsive Indian friend? What's his name? Lobo, isn't it?"

"What do you want?" I asked after focusing on my breathing to calm down. Besides, by then I figured I didn't have much to lose by speaking out, so why not?

"Ooohh, so little Jeffy wants to get right down to business, eh?" Instead of waiting for an answer though, PB Mom slowly turned around, walked back to the *evil* wax figures behind her. There she entered that horrible particle fog and draped herself over Adolph Hitler and said, "Don't you just love Hitler?"

"Uh, not really," I replied, wondering why the PB focused so much on all the bad guys. "He started World War II and killed millions of innocent people." I still couldn't wrap my mind around the fact that I was talking to a highly compacted form of nothing more than a bunch of particles.

"Exactly!" PB Mom replied, her eyes wide and lips pulled back in a cold smile. "The raw power Hitler exhibited excites me no end. What fun he must have had."

Fun? Power?

"Oh, poor Jeff," the Mom look-alike said, staring at me with a pout. "You're so confused. Is all this moving too fast for you? Well, dear, let me clear things up the best I can."

I didn't really want anything cleared up. I just badly wanted to get out of there.

But seconds after PB Mom finished speaking, her entire body turned into a deep violet silhouette. It bubbled and glittered brightly, and from that dazzling display came Adolph Hitler himself. Or at least what *appeared to be* a living Hitler with the clipped little mustache, uniform and swastika armband, just like the wax figure next to him.

At that moment, the intense stink of the dense, super-hot air surrounding me felt like it was pressing against my body, hard. My legs were going wobbly on me and I realized I was drenched in sweat, exactly like all the rest of those people in there with me. I felt like I was one of them, a prisoner captured by the PB forever with its incredible power to shape shift in seconds.

"Does my talk of having fun with raw power offend you?" Hitler shouted at me in a harsh male voice with a German accent as he stepped out of the particle cloud in my direction.

After speaking, he walked to where I stood with an arrogant look on his face. "Poor baby. But you ain't seen nothing yet so you had better get onboard before it's too late. I could have had Kelsey take your life out there on the street, but I have bigger plans for you. Much bigger."

Hitler's use of the words "baby" and "ain't" just didn't fit. They were more like things my mom would have said. "Onboard what?" I asked, ignoring the odd vocabulary.

"You only get this one chance," Hitler replied, in Carla's voice now, "so listen carefully."

Carla? Why her voice?

But before speaking again, Hitler disappeared in a blinding flash of violet, only to be replaced by an exact Carla look-alike wearing her fish hunting uniform. That did it. I had to close my eyes. No way did I want to see the PB forming itself into Carla.

Breathe, Jeff, I told myself as I knew Lobo would have. It's nothing more than a passing image like Lobo showed you with that crazy traffic parade up on San Marco. Immediately as I focused on my breath, I could feel myself relax just enough to open my eyes again.

Dressed exactly as the real Carla had been when we were fishing on Lobo's dock the day before, the PB version of her said, "That Lobo person has taught you well. Nice recovery. And your shaman friend has brought your energy levels up to an impressive degree. Very nice work indeed."

"What... energy levels?" I asked, at least feeling a little more confident in my ability to not overreact.

"You have no need to understand those details, but it is important for you to know this," PB Carla said, stepping closer and looking up at me intently. "No matter what you and your friends do to try and stop me, silver or no silver, by midday tomorrow I will be in control of all the people located in the city of St. Augustine.

"Rest assured, if you and your friends oppose me, I will take special pleasure in slowly tearing lovely Carla into little, tiny pieces right before I kill Lyle, Lobo and then *you*."

As she finished speaking, PB Carla tilted her head slightly and smiled a perfect Carla smile. That's when I felt as if I had turned into a block of ice. Why? Because I knew that without a doubt the PB could definitely carry out such a threat.

"You can, however, save your friends and yourself from such a grisly death by simply following instructions. And the instructions are these. All you have to do is to come back here well before 11:00 AM tomorrow, alone and ready to freely share your energy with me. You will also come without a shred of silver on you."

"I don't—"

"No questions!" The PB Carla shouted, her form shifting for a few seconds into that of angry Hitler who stamped his feet. "You will follow orders or suffer the consequences."

In another rapid shifting of form, Hitler disappeared, leaving in his place, a beautiful young woman with long blond hair, green eyes and wearing only enough clothing to cover the most important parts of her, ah, very curvaceous body.

I guess I must have gasped because the blond laughed and said, "So this form is much more pleasing to you than old Hitler, eh Jeff?" Her voice was soft and soothing.

"I know you like your women a darker shade from top to bottom, but this body might prove an interesting contrast. Besides, we fair-haired types need to stick together.

"Now, wouldn't a continuous and *close* association with such a pleasing female representative of the human race be to your liking? No need to answer that. I could tell the answer would be yes by your initial reaction to my appearance.

"The option I've given you," PB Blondie said, flipping her hair and flashing me a sexy smile, "is the only good one open to you. The stakes are high, Jeff, so choose carefully. Remember, before 11:00 AM tomorrow. Now, go back to your little dark girlfriend."

Behind me, feet began shuffling and I knew without a doubt an exit route had opened up. Believe me, I took it at full speed.

Part Six

Decisions

35

What Went on in There?

Carla was waiting for me when I burst through the wax museum's front door back out onto the sidewalk like a crazy person.

The cops were gone, thank God. Turned out they were people Carla knew who just pulled over to say hello. But as soon as they left, she frantically called Lobo on her cell. He told her to stay put and wait a few more minutes.

The cool, clean, night air outside of Potter's felt and smelled so good—such an incredibly huge contrast to the atmosphere inside the house of horrors behind me. And Carla never looked so good, the very person the PB had threatened to pull apart.

"Jeff what—"

"Not now!" I gasped. "To the truck. Quick. We have to get out of downtown." I didn't trust the PB or Kelsey to not suddenly pop out of the wax museum and attack us.

By the time we ran to the parking lot on the other side of St. George Street, I was so exhausted and shaky that Carla wouldn't let me drive. "Not a chance," she said. "I drove here and I'll drive back. In your condition, you would either have a wreck or end up getting arrested."

"OK, OK," I agreed, "but get us out of here. You're in deep danger."

Carla's eyebrows shot up high, but instead of asking questions, she pulled the truck keys out of her pocket, unlocked the doors and did just as I asked. In less than thirty seconds, we were on the road heading back to Lobo's place.

It really was a good thing Carla drove. All I could see in my mind were the eyes of all those poor people trapped in Potter's. And the PB's threats seemed to ring in my ears as if they were being said over and over again. Carla was right, I probably would have caused an accident if she had let me drive.

"You going to make it?" Carla reached over with one hand and stroked the back of my head.

Soothing electric warmth slid from her fingers and into my head. And from there it radiated downward into all areas of my body feeling almost like a gentle electric current. Her touch was a continuous river of calm and healing. It helped to squeeze the impact of what I had just experienced into something smaller, more nonthreatening. How, I didn't know, but in seconds, my breathing slowed and the shaking stopped.

"Lobo's right," I said to her, sighing deeply and covering her hand with my own. "Your healing abilities definitely go way beyond his."

"I'm glad it helped." Carla gently pulled her hand away to steer the truck as she turned left on Avenida Menendez. "OK, so talk to me," she said, her voice full of tension this time. "What went on in there?"

Even though Carla had been able to calm me down a lot, my mind was a jumble. For just a second, an image float-ed through my brain of an open garbage can full of smelly and toxic stuff spilling out all over the street. Those were my memories of being in Potter's, I realized, a bunch of mixed-up, dangerous trash that I didn't want to look at just then.

"It was bad," I said to her, "really bad. But I tell you what. We'll be at Lobo's place soon so I think I would rather wait until we get there. Then I can tell everybody at one time and not have to repeat the details all over again. Besides, I need a couple of minutes to let the whole mess sink into my head before I can make it clear to anyone. OK?"

Carla sighed, but she agreed with what I wanted to do. I knew she was disappointed at not hearing about what happened at Potter's from me first, but she wasn't going to push it.

When we got back to Lobo's and walked up to the house, we found both him and Lyle out on the end of the dock drinking beer and roasting hotdogs over a low fire in the metal fireplace. *Hot dogs?* They were using long, wooden handled forks. Torches fluttered around them in the cold breeze coming in off the moonlit bay barely giving off enough light to see.

According to Lobo, while we were gone, Lyle woke up from his long sleep of recovery craving some of Oscar Mayer's finest and a lot of beer. He looked and sounded like the old Lyle I knew, sitting there in his old trench coat and lucky red baseball cap. What a difference from when I saw him in Lobo's workshop.

Carla and I refused his offer to share the hot dogs. They smelled good, but neither one of us was hungry. After what I experienced at Potter's, I had no appetite. A very rare event for me. But we did accept the cans of Coke that Lobo had ready for us.

In the semidarkness as we sat down, Lobo studied me intently from across the table. "You had to go in there, didn't you?" he said, raising his bare arms and putting his hands behind his head. The man's eyes glittered even more than usual, reflecting the low flames of the dying fire between us.

Carla sat opposite Lyle. Out on Matanzas Bay, a jumping fish splashed back into the water. Small waves lapped at the dock pilings and the shore between Lobo's house and us.

Even though I knew Lobo had asked me a specific and simple question, I guess I was still partly in shock after what happened at the wax museum. Resting my arms on the table in front of me, I tried to get my churning thoughts organized enough to make sense before they came out of my mouth.

Seeing my difficulty, Carla jumped in and explained about the appearance of the particle people in the plaza and how they combined to create the fake image of my mom. She then looked at me as if to ask, "You want to take it from here?"

At first, I hesitated. And as I did, Lyle shot me a nervous glance while taking an enormous bite of his hot dog and washing it down with beer. "The boy's too spooked to talk," he said, his voiced muffled and partly distorted by some of the food still in his mouth.

"No, not really," I said, closing my eyes and taking a deep breath before opening them again and zipping up my jacket all the way against the wind.

"The bottom line is this," I said turning to face Carla and putting a hand on her shoulder. "You've got to get out of the city. Tonight! Maybe you can go stay with your grandma in Jacksonville. Please, you've got to do it. The PB—"

"I'm not going anywhere," she replied with an even stronger tone than I used as she squinted at me like I just asked her to rob a bank or something. "I don't know what went on in Potter's that has got you so shook up, but me leaving St. Augustine isn't an option. I'm not about let the three of you to fight this battle alone."

"Let's back up here, Jeff," Lobo said, "and start from the beginning. Just lay it out for us in detail from the start until the end. And in the process, we'll be able to understand this danger to Carla you're talking about."

Unlike many times in the past, when correcting me or giving instructions, Lobo's tone sounded more like a reasonable request instead of an order—almost like one adult talking to another. That was a shocker.

I looked at him in surprise, thought about his request for a few seconds, and then proceeded to tell my story in all of its terrifying detail. That took about ten minutes or so and while I spoke, nobody interrupted me—extremely unusual for all three of them.

While I talked, Lyle sat there stroking his beard, his eyes all round and darting as if the PB was going to show up again at any minute.

Lobo? As usual I couldn't see any evidence of a reaction in him at all.

From time-to-time, Carla's eyebrows shot up pretty high, especially when I repeated the PB's exact threat on her life. At that point, she even stole a quick glance at Lobo as if wondering what his reaction might be. Of course the old guy gave away nothing about the innermost workings of his mind.

Oh, on interruptions. There was one, actually.

It happened when I got to the part about the PB changing into a blond babe and how I gasped as that happened. Just as I said the word "gasped" the Coke can I had in my hand imploded all by itself with a single, metal crackling sound that made all of us except Lobo jump.

Of course, most of the Coke inside shot out of the can top with a fizzing whoosh. It sprayed all over me, I mean in my face, my hair, everywhere. Some of it came down in the fireplace making the coals hiss, but nobody else got hit.

Lobo and I immediately looked at Carla.

"Did she do that?" Lyle asked.

"Me? I certainly did not." But Carla hardly got those words out of her mouth when I could see the truth dawn on her.

"You're jealous," I said, laughing and trying to wipe Coke off me the best I could with my hand. "Jealous of the stupid PB."

It felt good to laugh, a welcome break from the super seriousness of the situation. And to be honest, I loved the idea of Carla not wanting me to be attracted to another female even if she wasn't real. It might have been subconscious, but Carla's reaction to my description of that PB situation had popped right out into the physical world before she knew what happened.

"Here," she said, flinging a roll of paper towels to me and then looking down. "Clean yourself off and go on with what happened next." She wasn't at all amused.

Her lack of a denial about being jealous just proved my point, but her deep discomfort was so clear that I felt bad for laughing. She wouldn't look at any of us. Carla doesn't embarrass easily, but obviously, she couldn't help it.

"I'm sorry," I said, using the paper towels to get the Coke drops off me. "I shouldn't have said what I did. I mean especially in front of Lobo and Lyle."

When that didn't make her look up, I reached over, took her hand and squeezed it. I just flat didn't care what Lobo and Lyle thought or had to say. "I'm honored you were jealous and I would be too if our roles were reversed, OK?"

"Really?" She replied, lifting her eyes but not her head. The scowl that was on her face just seconds before had already disappeared.

"Yeah, really."

When she returned the hand squeeze, I knew she was going to be all right. And *we* were going to be all right as well.

Up came her head and the old Carla was back. Instead of continuing to hold my hand, she pulled it away, grabbed the paper towel roll from me and wiped Coke out of my hair. "At least I have good aim, huh?" she asked with a sheepish grin.

"If you two lovebirds are quite done," Lobo growled, "we need to get on with the rest of the wax museum saga."

And that's what happened. I finished telling the story, and as soon as I did, all three of my listeners peppered me with questions. After about another fifteen minutes of clarifying every little detail, we were finally done.

"Sweet Jesus!" Lyle said as he chugged half of his third beer. Carla shot him a quick glance of disapproval, but she didn't say anything.

"Now you can see," I said to Carla, "how much danger you're in and why you've got to get out of here."

As soon as I finished speaking, Lobo started to say something, but Carla cut him off as if he wasn't even there.

"Now you listen to me, Jeff. I told you when we started this fight against the PB that I was in it to the finish just like I did when we faced your ancestor's world.

"Am I scared? You betcha I'm scared, but so what? Aren't you? We all are except for Mr. No Fear over there." When she said that last sentence, she pointed at Lobo. I tried unsuccessfully to stifle a laugh while Lyle choked on a mouthful of beer and started coughing.

Even with Lyle making so much noise, Carla kept going like he wasn't there either. She had put him in the same place in her mind where she put Lobo—temporarily out of the picture. "You're trying to pull that old male protecting the female garbage just like you did back in December. It didn't work then and it's not going to work now.

"Maybe I can get embarrassed, Jeff, but I'm at least as tough as you and probably a lot tougher. So get used to it! As I said, I'm not leaving no matter what any of you *good ol' boys* has to say about it or how much I'm threatened."

Before I could even collect my thoughts after that explosive lecture, Lobo jumped back into the conversation—if I can call it that.

"It's settled," he said, looking all three of us in the eye. "She stays. Now it's nitty-gritty time."

36

Strategy

As Lobo threw some more wood on the fire, I thought of arguing with him about supporting Carla's decision to stay and fight but decided against it. Scared as I was for her, I knew she had to make her own choice. Even so, the PB humanoid's threat kept recycling through my brain making it difficult to concentrate.

"Wait a minute, Lobo." Lyle said, stroking his beard, his eyes darting everywhere. "Maybe we should, uh, rethink trying to do battle with that particle thing. You heard the boy.

"Look what it's been able to do in so short a time."

Smoke from the new piece of wood on the fire drifted over me and I waved it away. A train horn in the distance seemed almost like a warning, supporting Lyle's words.

"How about this," Lobo replied to Lyle, his voice sounding calm and his words oddly reasonable—for Lobo, that is. "I'm now going to tell you, Carla and Jeff how I see this situation in general. Then, I'm going to explain what we'll have to do tomorrow to prevent it from happening. And when I get finished, *anyone*, or *all of you*, can take my truck and go wherever you like if you don't want to go along with my plan. How about that?"

After speaking, Lobo shifted his gaze from Lyle to Carla and then to me. That's when the fresh wood he had just put on the fire burst into flame, brightening our little conference area with dancing light.

"Uh, well, yes sir," Lyle replied, "that's, uh, very fair indeed."

Carla and I didn't respond to his offer.

After chugging some beer, Lobo put the bottle down in front of him, put his hands on the table, shook his head and stared directly at me. "First, let me make something perfectly clear." His voice had a sharp yet heavy quality to it, like pieces of thick steel slamming together. "When I tell you not to do something, I do it for a purpose. You got that?"

"I know," I said quickly, realizing he was talking about me going into the wax museum against his instructions. "I'm sorry, but that PB reproduction of Mom was all too real."

"You're sorry?" He roared, making Lyle jump. "You just might have gotten yourself trapped in that place as a Particle Being slave and by going in there you have put Carla even more at risk than she was before!"

"Me? I did not!"

"Of course you did. By being in such direct communications with that humanoid PB all alone, you first *allowed* it to scare you to death, and then you *let* it make a direct threat against Carla. And the result? You're even more frightened than you were before, and your attention is badly diverted.

"It's the additional fear combined with a split focus that weakens you in opposing the PB, Jeff. And if you're weakened, you're *less able* to protect Carla."

STEPPING OFF A CLIFF   297

"Oh," I replied, seeing exactly what he meant. Much too late, I remembered how Lobo had taught me not to let fear paralyze my mind.

"And in your fear for yourself, Carla and the people of St. Augustine, what else did you forget?"

All I could do was look at the man with a blank stare for what seemed like forever until it hit me. "Oh man, I just …"

"Let this be a lesson to each of you," Lobo said, shifting his intent gaze to Lyle and then to Carla. "Never forget how even under the most difficult of circumstances, each of you has developed special abilities that can protect you and others.

"In Jeff's case, he probably could have escaped from Potter's if he hadn't let fear blind him to that fact. The Particle Being would have had a much more difficult time keeping him there if he had used his talent of stopping time."

"OK, OK," I said, "don't make me feel any dumber than I already do."

"We all get the point," Carla said, tilting her head to the side. She was pulling on an earlobe the way she does when she's about to ask about something that has really been bothering her. "But as long as you're talking about our … abilities, I'm really starting to feel like I'm living in some sort of super odd, paranormal action movie or something.

"I mean, you told both Jeff and me it's through our connection with you as a shaman that we can do these things. But in my research on the subject, I've never seen even a hint that shamans anytime in history have ever claimed some of the abilities we all have—like Lyle's hard shell. How do you explain that?"

"Caa!" Edgar fluttered his wings in the flickering fire-light as he landed on a dock piling to my right. Lobo looked at him for a few seconds and in that time I got the strangest feeling they were communicating somehow.

"You're right," Lobo replied, shifting his eyes back to Carla and answering her question. "Some of the abilities you've seen demonstrated, like stopping time, are not the usual shamanic talents. I've hinted at this in my conversations with all of you, but let me now be specific. Some of those more unusual skills come from the Particle Being in a way."

"What?" Carla and I both said almost at the same time. Lyle just stared at Lobo with his mouth open.

Lobo waited a few seconds before speaking again. "When I first encountered the PB, as you know, my silver necklace protected me from harm. And my body retained no particles, even though they passed through me like they did with all three of you.

"What that contact did, however, Carla, was to increase the strength of my usual shamanic abilities and it gave me additional talents like the ones we are now discussing. And as far as the three of you are concerned, contact with the Particle Being opened you up to a deeper connection with me and therefore to the development of a multitude of skills no shaman except me has ever developed."

"Yeah but that particle thing also beat up on my brain and nervous system something terrible." Lyle's eyes looked haunted, reminding me way too much of all those eyes staring at me in the wax museum.

"Now," Lobo said, ignoring Lyle's comment, "let's get back to the fascination the creature has with Adolph Hitler and the dark side of humanity. That new development makes this situation even more dangerous than I thought.

"The Particle Being has probed the memories of all those unfortunate people held captive and is stimulated by the worst aspects of human history it can detect. Evidently, in that process, it perceived how Hitler's evil deeds stand out in the minds of those it has inspected and found that all very attractive."

"OK, that makes some kind of sense, but what do we do about it?" I asked. "Actually, what do *I* do? I mean the humanoid PB says I have to be back at the wax museum by myself before 11:00 AM without any silver for protection. It wants me to help it take over the city or it will kill Carla, you and Lyle!" As interesting as all of Lobo's background information was, it still didn't solve the PB problem and I needed some answers.

"Jeff," Lobo said, "listen to me carefully. The Particle Being colony at Potter's will only be able to carry out its threats if we allow it to fully combine with the other PB colony locked in the hybrid sea creature—the physical brain that will make such a thing possible. But to make all that happen, it needs your energy and the energy of another concentration of people like it had tonight at the Spanish Night Watch Parade.

"Of course!" Carla said. "Now I see. The Blessing of the Fleet!"

I had no idea what she was talking about.

"Exactly," Lobo replied but still looking at me. "Tomorrow is Palm Sunday and at a little after noon tomorrow, the Bishop of St. Augustine will walk from the cathedral to the city marina. There he will bless boats and ships of all kinds as they pass by the outer ends of the docks.

"And make no mistake about it, the particle saturated sea creature will be somewhere out there under water in the Matanzas River.

"Hundreds of people will witness the blessing out on those docks and the event itself will occur not very far away from Potter's Wax Museum where the other largest particle concentration lurks.

"Such a big crowd will provide more than enough human energy needed by both PB halves to merge—a perfect prescription for disaster.

"Uh, OK but why does the Potter's PB need me?" I asked.

"By getting you to *not* use your abilities against it, the PB would gain a great advantage.

That will weaken whatever Carla, Lyle and I do to stop the thing. If you then joined forces with it out of fear for Carla's safety, the PB would make use of your talents and it would win no matter what."

"That's just great," I replied. "So again, what do I do? Come on, I'm still looking for answers here."

"One thing's for sure," Carla said, "you can't go unprotected into Potter's tomorrow and help the PB in any way."

"Not quite true." Lobo's disagreement with Carla's statement surprised all of us.

"Lobo!" Carla shouted. "You can't be serious."

"Oh, but I am." The man shifted his attention from Carla back to me. "If you go into Potter's tomorrow and are able to convince the humanoid PB to leave the museum, then we might have a chance of sending all of the particles that exist in the city back where they came from."

"You want to use the boy as bait, don't you?" Lyle asked.

"Indeed I do."

"You mean lure it just outside the door of Potter's?" I wasn't feeling too comfortable with the idea of being bait. My failed effort of trying to trap the PB at the wax museum earlier that evening by using *bait* slithered through my mind. I didn't like the idea of being a slab of meat dangling in front of such a dangerous creature.

"No, not just outside Potter's" Lobo corrected. "I'm saying you lure it all the way over to the Antique Mall behind City Hall. There Carla, Lyle and I will be waiting for you and together we will all try to force it back down into the earth at the exact spot where you fell into the vortex."

37

Quiet Before the Storm

I had just turned out the lights in Lobo's living room when Carla came back in wearing her robe. As soon as she got there, she started whispering to me intently. Whispering, because Lyle was sleeping under a comforter in one of the recliners. Intently, because, I knew, she was deeply afraid for me.

"Come here," I whispered back, taking her by the hand and getting her to sit next to me on the couch. The fireplace in front of us, with its nice small blaze gave the only light in the room and helped take some of the chill out of the air. That direct heat worked for me because I sat there in my pajamas. I didn't own a robe.

Being so close to Carla on the couch made me thankful I had taken a shower right after we all came into the house from being on the dock. It felt really good to be certain no leftover stink from Potter's clung to my body. My clothes? Those I sealed up in a heavy yard bag for me to wash sometime later.

"We're messing up your bed." Carla was referring to the sheets and blanket underneath us on the couch. Lobo had given her my cot in the storeroom.

"Don't worry about my bed." I put my arm around her as I spoke. "And put your worry about me on hold, please. We already settled this out on the dock."

"Well, I'm bringing it up again." She was protesting me following Lobo's directions and going back into the wax museum alone and unprotected by silver the next day.

"What choice do I have?"

"You always have a choice."

"Sure, if you have a better idea." Ever since Lobo suggested I try to coax the humanoid PB to leave the wax museum on Sunday, Carla had been trying to talk both Lobo and me out of it. "And remember how irate you got tonight," I reminded her, "when I wanted to protect you? You see, it works both ways, doesn't it?"

Instead of coming up with answers to my questions, she nuzzled my chest. There *was* no other choice and she knew that, logically. She just didn't like it.

Instead of continuing the discussion, I kissed the top of her head. Her hair smelled sweet, like flowers of some kind. She had just come out of the shower herself. *If only we could stay like this foreve*r.

Carla looked up at me and said, "I agree. But do you realize you didn't actually say those words out loud?"

"Really?" I could have sworn those words came out of my mouth, but when I thought about it, I wasn't so sure anymore.

"Interesting, isn't it?" Carla stroked the hair on the side of my head. "I mean what we've both learned to understand and do since meeting Lobo. Our mind-to-mind connections are really getting frequent.

"Oh yeah," I said. "Remember what a tough time you and Lobo had trying to convince me the paranormal wasn't just something written about in novels or created by film makers?"

"Remember? I can hear Lobo now," Carla replied, laughing .'There are worlds-within-worlds-within-worlds, *Mr.* Golden!'"

When she spoke those words, forgetting to whisper, she deepened her voice, making it sound amazingly like Lobo. Her imitation was so good, I had to laugh too and not very softly either. Lyle stirred but didn't wake up.

Carla smiled and then got real serious-looking all of a sudden. In the silence that followed, the fire snapped and crackled. The light from it allowed me to see half her face while darkness hid the other side.

"What?" I asked.

She sighed and said, "I know I'm being a continuing pain about this, but these abilities we have, as cool as they are, they still worry me. In fact they worry me even more now, since we know they're also connected to the PB through Lobo. The Particle Being, Jeff! A horrible, destructive creature that adores Adolf Hitler!

"Who's to say that because of our interaction with that thing, you, me or Lyle won't start misusing those powers someday—if we survive all this. What we're living here isn't some Marvel comic superhero plot. It's very real. Maybe Lobo has the wisdom to use all those 'talents' as he calls them, but I'm not so sure the rest of us do."

"Wisdom?" I asked. "What do you mean, wisdom? We're going to be mighty glad we have those *talents* no matter where they came from when we have to face the PB tomorrow. That's all I care about—all of us in St. Augustine surviving and getting rid of every single particle.

"I'll use any weapon I've got to make sure that happens. You didn't see or smell those people in the wax museum like I did or you wouldn't be worrying about our abilities!"

My words were a lot more forceful than I meant them to be.

"I'm sorry," I said when Carla didn't respond right away. My heart pounding hard in my chest showed me how upset I had gotten without meaning for it to happen. "What I said came out wrong."

"You went through a lot tonight," Carla said. "I don't even want to imagine what it must have been like. And I know you're right about tomorrow. It's just that so much power in the hands of a couple of teenagers doesn't seem right, somehow—for the future, I mean."

When she said it that way, I had to admit, she had a point. And it wasn't like I hadn't already had similar thoughts. "Tell you what," I replied. "If, as you say, we survive dealing with the PB tomorrow, you and I can have a long talk with Lobo about it. How about that?" *If we survive.* Carla had just used almost those same words. Neither one of us, it seemed, could avoid the cold, hard truth of our situation.

"Uh, yeah, OK," she replied, squinting with a questioning look on her face. "But about tomorrow. I'm not too sure about you hanging out with a sexy blond even if it's a weird creation of the PB. You might just 'gasp' yourself into unconsciousness or something."

I knew she wasn't completely serious, but part of her still wasn't happy with how I reacted when I first saw PB Blondie.

"Oh, not this again." I shook my head and groaned. "Come on, Carla, give me a break, will you? It's Lobo who thinks the male-female thing might work with the PB to get it out of Potter's and over to the Antique Mall. I'll just be play acting. Like Lobo said, that thing *might* actually think I'm attracted and it will become attracted in return. If that happens, it will be natural to invite the thing to join me for an early lunch over in the Antique Mall."

Even as I said what I did, it still sounded extremely weird, but I was just repeating what Lobo thought I should do. *Lunch?* Unbelievable but it was Lobo's plan, not mine.

"*Might* think you are attracted?" Carla said, poking me in the ribs, hard. "You're the one who admitted gasping when you saw the blond babe. The PB *knows* you were attracted. It probably fished some visuals out of your memories of looking at *Playboy* foldouts to create that slutty thing."

"Who said I ever looked at *Playboy* magazine anyway?"

"Oh please! Nobody had to. All teenage boys do that. I'm sure you're no exception."

"Welllll, maybe in the very distant past, but now the only beautiful, sexy image I want to see is you."

Whoops. Those words just fired out of my mouth before I realized I had definitely said them. Never before had I told Carla she was sexy, but also linking how I saw her with our conversation about *Playboy* was not the thing to say to her. Sometimes a little too much honesty isn't such a good thing. I wanted to kick myself. *Stupid!*

"Really?" she asked giving me one of her delicious smiles.

That great reaction told me maybe I *hadn't* said too much, for once. *Whew!*

"So you actually think I'm beautiful *and* sexy?"

"Ooohh, yeah!" Again, more words came zipping out of my mouth before I had time to think about my reaction.

"Why Mr. Golden," she said with a syrupy southern accent. "I do declare, sir. I am flattered and I think the same thing about you."

That did it. I reached for her with both hands and she was in my arms in no time. I think we kind of met in the middle of the distance between us. And that kiss ... well, it turned out even better than the one in the plaza—until it got interrupted.

"The more you two play kissy face, the less sleep you get and the more danger you put all of us in tomorrow." *Lobo.* Good old Lobo. Just what we needed right then, him and his booming voice.

Both Carla and I jumped and Lyle sat up in the recliner like he had been shot out of a cannon. "What?" He yelled, his beard shaking back and forth and his bald head shining in the firelight. He had knocked his lucky baseball cap off when he jerked awake. He seemed terrified, his eyes wide, searching the partial darkness of the room for particles. At least that's how it looked to me.

"It's OK, Lyle," Lobo said to him gently, "Carla was just saying goodnight to everyone."

"Oh, OK," he mumbled, squinting into the gloom. "G'night Carla."

"Goodnight, Lyle," Carla said, standing up and laughing. "And goodnight to you too, sir." She waved at Lobo. But before getting up from the couch, she turned to me one last time, wrapped both arms around my neck and gave me another huge kiss. What a wonderful, delightful way to help her get the last word in on old Lobo.

"Oh, Jeff," she said, reaching into the pocket of her robe and pulling out a plastic sandwich bag as she stood. "I meant to show you this before. Look what I found in my pants pocket."

In the bag were several odd-looking, but familiar sea-shells—the ones she had kept from Lobo's strange world even though he told her at the time she wouldn't be able to bring them back into our reality.

That night after Carla and Lobo went back to bed, I couldn't sleep. Not at all. Lyle's snoring didn't help either. Around 5:00 AM, I finally sat up and turned on Lobo's stained glass Tiffany lamp. Lyle didn't stir.

I still thought of that kind of old fashioned type of lighting as looking like an upside-down bowl. The familiar green-winged dragonflies with their fiery red eyes seemed to swim right out of the lamp's deep blue, water-like sections towards its base. A lamp given to Lobo by old Henry Flagler himself.

Lobo and Lyle. I couldn't get over the idea they both were born well before the Civil War—and the fact that they were alive because of their connection with the Particle Being so long ago.

Of course, that made me think about how Carla and I had traveled through the Antique Mall's insane vortex to 1885 right after having our first encounter with the PB. And naturally, the lamp dragonflies forced me to remember every little detail of our incredible journey to Lobo's weird planet.

Before I knew it though, deep in my mind, I was reliving every horrible second of my experience in the wax museum, trapped by the PB and all of its zombie-type slaves. I'm telling you, I could feel the heat, just like I felt it back at Potter's.

My stomach turned over as the memory of the smell from that horrible place seemed as if it filled Lobo's house.

And all I could think about was going back into Potter's in not too many hours—alone, unprotected and everybody depending on me to trick the PB humanoid into leaving the place.

I held my hand in front of the lamp and watched as it shook. By that time, my pajamas were drenched in sweat—not caused by the fire in the fireplace.

Particles. By then that word had become the one in my vocabulary I hated the most. It was bad enough having to deal with the PB as a creature, a living being. But with Carla, Lyle and me actually having particles inside us, the word held a very personal meaning. *Inside us!*

How Lyle had lived that way all those years with such knowledge gave me a new respect for the guy.

I mean the three of us were just one step away from ending up like those people who surrounded me not very long ago at the wax museum. Or worse! Maybe even Lobo too.

"Ripped apart," were the words used by the PB humanoid in its threat against Carla. Even thinking about that conversation felt like a knife slicing through me every time I let it happen. Horrible nasty images floated through my mind.

And just as my brain really started getting all twisted up in a knot, Lobo walked into the room and sat down on the coffee table opposite me. It didn't really surprise me he knew I couldn't sleep, but I hadn't heard him come down the stairs again—bare feet. This time he wore pajamas. "So you can't sleep either," I whispered to him. Of course, I knew better, but yeah, no doubt about it, I'm a smart ass sometimes. But generally, I try not to be around Lobo.

"*My sleep* isn't the problem here," he replied in a lowered voice that for Lobo passed as a whisper. Lyle just kept on snoring. "If you don't at least get a little rest, you could make some serious mistakes when dealing with the Particle Being not very many hours from now."

"I've been trying, but my head is so full of what's been going on and what might happen. I feel like I'm going to explode." Outside, an owl hooted loudly, close to the house. It reminded me of the owls I heard when dealing with my ancestor back when I first met Lobo.

"You know better. We just talked about this."

I stared at him, looking into those eyes that seemed like tunnels with tiny bright lights shining at the end of each one. He was right, of course, and I knew it. "OK, but—"

"Stop making excuses. You're *allowing* yourself to be overwhelmed. Remember," he said, picking up his carved Chinese Puzzle Ball off the coffee table and shaking it so I could hear all of those other separate balls inside it rattle. "There are infinite numbers of realities, but you also create your own.

"Those little switches in your head that you discovered a while back are still there. Constantly keep in mind how they are connected to your reactions and how you have the ability to flip them one-by-one to control how you feel. The more you do that, the more your subconscious will relax and the easier it will be to sleep even under pressure.

"Now lie down and close your eyes," he ordered, putting the puzzle ball back on its stand.

I did as he directed.

"Focus on your breath instead of what has happened in the past and what could happen in the future," he said, as he placed a big old hand on my forehead. Slowly, his incredible energy seeped into my weary brain and then throughout my body, helping me to sleep.

38

No Long Goodbyes

That next morning, Lobo decided to drive his truck past the wax museum so we could scope things out before I went in there.

The day was bright and warm, no need for jackets, except for Lyle who wore his trench coat. We had the windows open, letting in the fresh air.

Lyle sat in the truck bed, as he did on our trip the night before, looking like he might jump out of his skin at any minute. To be perfectly honest, I had been feeling that same way ever since I woke up. At least Lobo let me sleep until the last possible minute, giving me every chance to have a clear head for my upcoming mission. I barely had time to wake up and brush my teeth though, before he rushed us out the door on our way to the plaza.

Quietly sitting near the passenger side door holding my hand, Carla had worry written all over her face.

The closer we got to the wax museum, the more I didn't want to even look at the place. Memories of what I had seen in the main exhibit hall mixed with thoughts about what I was soon going to face. Leaving all my silver back at Lobo's place didn't help my confidence much either.

As my stomach started twisting itself into even worse knots than before, I was thankful that Lobo didn't let me have any breakfast. He said eating even a small amount wouldn't be a good idea. I was allowed to have a little water but nothing more. Now I could see why.

Lobo refused to give me any actual guidance in how to talk the PB humanoid into going to lunch. He just kept saying I would figure out the right words to use. And when Carla, Lyle and I all wanted him to tell us what to do once I got Blondie to the Antique Mall, he blew us off. "We'll work on that at the time," was the only response we could get out of the man.

"The 'closed' sign is still on the door," Carla said, looking through the open passenger side window as Lobo slowly drive past Potter's.

"There's too much reflection in the glass to really see inside," I added. "But the lights are out just like they were last night.

"That's not right," Carla replied. "We're not looking at an ordinary reflection. I can't see in there at all. It looks to me like someone painted all the windows black from the inside."

"What?" Adding a new mystery to an already weird, nasty and dangerous situation was not what I needed.

Lobo's response to our observations was one of his typical grunts as he pulled his truck to a stop at the stoplight just a short distance away from the wax museum. Ahead of us, traffic flowed easily across the Bridge of Lions as the water from the Matanzas Bay sparkled in the sun. A few high clouds stretched across a pale blue sky. Quite a contrast to the weather we had the day before. It all looked so normal and peaceful.

So it's really out there, huh? Carla's voice said inside my head. I saw her looking towards the marina to our right and knew that she meant the hybrid sea creature, tentacles and all.

That's what the man says, I replied in the same way, still startled by how easy our ability to connect mentally was becoming. I wondered if Lobo could tune in on our conversations.

The traffic light changed and the old guy turned left. Soon, he turned left again onto Cathedral Place. He had made a loop around the end of the plaza and was looking for a parking spot. Tourists were out and about with locals scattered here and there.

In a little over an hour, Carla said as we neared the St Augustine Cathedral, *the Bishop and a whole lot of people will be coming out of there with church bells ringing.* It was her church, and she probably knew just about everyone inside on that Sunday morning. Normally, she and her grandma would have been in there on Palm Sunday.

Yeah. And they'll be walking right into a buzz saw if we don't succeed. As soon as I sent that thought to her, a picture I had once seen flashed into my mind. It was of Hiroshima at the end of the Second World War, taken shortly after the atomic bomb blasted the entire heart of the city away, people and all.

The situation we were facing wasn't the same, but I guess it was the loss of life in Hiroshima was why my brain made that comparison.

And the more I thought about it, the more it dawned on me how everyone who lived and worked there must have been going about their daily business seconds before the bomb hit—just as the people in St. Augustine were doing right at that moment.

None of them in that doomed Japanese city, I realized, had any idea the world as they knew it was about to end horribly. And as I looked at all those people in the plaza, I couldn't help but wonder if their world and ours might also end soon but in a different and maybe even nastier way.

Lobo pulled into the bank parking lot soon after crossing St. George Street. He slid his truck into the one remaining space and turned off the engine.

"Everybody out," he barked, as if he needed to tell us. Even so, to me his words sounded like somebody telling me to jump out of an airplane without a parachute. The time for me to deal with the humanoid PB all by myself again had arrived, and I was anything but ready.

Once we all exited the truck, Lobo gathered us around him under the shade of a large oak tree. He stood there in one of his sleeveless denim work shirts with his hands on his hips."Now listen up and listen carefully. We don't have much time."

Right at that point, a big crow landed on the tree branch directly above our heads.

"Never mind Edgar," Lobo said, bringing our attention back to what he was about to say. "Like you three, anyone who was in downtown St. Augustine last night, and is still here in the city, continues to be infected with particles. Everyone but me.

"That means if we allow all of the particles in the city to successfully come together with the sea creature acting as its brain during the Blessing of the Fleet, we will have lost the war. And all of us will be at the mercy of an incredibly more powerful and dangerous Particle Being. St. Augustine will become a city of unimaginable pain, terror and death.

"The good news, however, is that together we have the knowledge and power to prevent such a thing from happening—if we manage it properly."

Yeah, if, I said to myself thinking how I could soon blow our whole plan to hell and back by making just one mistake like I had done the night before.

As that fear popped into my head, Lobo looked directly at me, his weird eyes blazing. He then reached over with both hands, grabbed me by the shoulders and pulled me right up to him.

Seconds later, he relaxed his iron grip but didn't actually let me go. That's when I felt a deep tingling in my shoulders that quickly spread to all parts of my body, making my ears buzz. At the same time, much of the fear that had built up inside me and all those terrible memories of my most recent visit to the wax museum reduced their hold on my mind. They didn't go away, but they definitely shrank into something I was better able to handle.

That's when Lobo finally released his grip on me.

"Jeff." he said, as if my name was a statement all by itself. "I just gave you a jolt of the strongest protective energy I have to offer another person. If I had done that when we first met, you would have died. What this shows is how far you've come in your ability to gain control of yourself and how strong you will be when facing the humanoid Particle Being. All I did was to reinforce what you have already created within yourself."

"Uh, wow. Thanks." I said, not knowing what else to say. Yeah, pretty lame, but that's all I could come up with under the circumstances.

There you go. Credit given where credit is due, Carla said, sliding her thoughts into my head, *You're going to do just fine.* She followed that up by nodding her head, smiling and giving me one of her sexy winks. But even so, the worry never left her eyes.

"The plan for after you enter Potter's," Lobo said to me, "as we have already discussed, is simple, whether you believe that or not. Just like when your entered your ancestor's after death dream world late last year, you will know the exact words to use. And when you lure the PB humanoid to the Antique Mall, your only remaining task will be to maneuver the creature to the bench where you and Carla fell into the vortex.

"We'll be waiting in one of the shops and will join you as soon as possible. Then together, we will rid St. Augustine of that thing."

"Uh, OK, but—"

"And don't worry about the PB being able to read your mind. I found out long ago that it can only scan your memories—memories at least a day or two old." Lobo answered the question I was just about to ask.

For just a few seconds, I had this weird feeling that Lobo might be even more powerful than all the PB eruptions since 1879. That's when he turned me around and pointed me in the direction of the wax museum. "No long goodbyes, Jeff, and no more questions." That's when he gave me a solid shove forward.

Part Seven

War

39

Lunch Date

Be reeeealllly careful in there. Please.

Carla's voice inside my head as I walked across Cathedral Place to the plaza felt so good.

I say "felt" because that type of communication didn't involve sound, of course. It was more like actually having part of Carla deep within my mind. Whatever she *said* seemed to glow with shades of meaning way beyond the words.

Oh, you better believe I will. As I replied, I wondered if my mental words I sent had the same kind of impact on her.

Good. One more thing, Jeff.

OK, what?

If the humanoid PB turns into that sexy blond again, try not to get too involved.

Even as tense as things were, I had to laugh. That startled a few people around me.

In Carla's *voice,* I could hear her own grim laughter and I knew she was trying to help me relax. But in her actual words, I also noticed the seriousness and still, a tiny bit of jealously.

Thank you ma'am, I said to her in return, for the impartial advice. I'll keep it in mind.

Make sure you do, and remember how much I love you.

That, I will never forget no matter what happens. But even as I sent those words to her, my focus had already started changing back to my mission at Potter's. Arriving at King Street on the other side of the plaza is what did it. In front of me, the wax museum loomed like some kind of wood and glass monster.

Gotta go, Carla. I'm just about there.

I know. We're in front of the cathedral, watching.

When I took a quick glance behind me, I saw them. Hesitating for a few seconds, I waved, and then sprinted across King Street between oncoming cars.

When I got to the sidewalk in front of Potter's, I stood there and stared at the place, wishing I at least had my silver key chain on me. Memories of what I experienced inside the wax museum the night before kept popping up into my mind. I really did not want to go any further, but I had to move my feet forward. Had to.

What if it's locked? I wondered, staring at the "Closed" sign hung on the door not five feet away from me. Even though I knew better, that small distance looked like a mile.

You're stalling and letting your mind work overtime, I said to myself. Taking a deep breath, I finally walked up to the door. Once there, I tried peeking through its darkened glass and the display windows. No luck. Carla was right. It looked like someone had painted all that glass black on the inside like she said. Couldn't see anything except my own reflection.

"Just do it," I said, forcing myself to try the door handle. It was unlocked, but I only opened the door about six inches or so before very warm air and the strong scent of ozone and burning wires hit me in the face. At least, I thought, it's not that nasty sweat and sewer stink like I smelled last night.

"Come in," a gruff, accented male voice ordered from somewhere deep inside the place—a familiar voice. I hesitated at first but decided to do as I was told. The voice was Hitler's.

"OK," I whispered, "this is it." With a quick shove, I opened the door just enough for me to walk through. There, standing in front of the ticket counter was Adolf Hitler in his Nazi uniform. Even though I had seen him, *it*, before, I blinked rapidly several times, as if that would help make the entire scene in front of me go away. Didn't happen, of course.

A series of floodlights on stands to his right and left bathed Hitler in a high watt glow. It looked like he was about to go on TV or something. That's when I saw Carla's friend Kelsey and some older guy working with a large camera of some sort. There were other pieces of equipment spread all over the place.

Both Kelsey and her companion had multiple PB strands stuck in their heads. Those sparkling, violet connections curled high in the air and then ended at the wall near the entrance to the exhibit rooms. Neither one of those people even looked in my direction. That whole scene was so bizarre that part of me kept thinking I must be dreaming.

No one, I knew, except Carla, Lobo and Lyle, would believe me if I ever tried to describe and explain what I was seeing—if I survived. I mean, that whole situation was so surreal that if I had seen a movie on TV where a high school kid encountered a Particle Being created Hitler in this St. Augustine setting with its enslaved humans, I would have laughed and turned it off. But I wasn't laughing then. Not at all.

"Shut that door and lock it behind you." Hitler glared at me with piercing eyes strangely like Lobo's. But unlike Lobo, those eyes glittered with an intensity that I can only describe as pure evil, making my stomach contract, like it was being squeezed by a giant fist. His stare made me want to run away from there, but I didn't.

Swallowing hard, and trying desperately to focus on my breath to stay calm, I did what he told me to do. Because my legs felt like rubber though, I moved a little slow at first. Right after closing the door, I turned back around, right in front of it, but didn't go any further into the room. I was ready to try and freeze time if I needed to, and get out of there.

"Good boy," Hitler said, placing his hands behind his back while walking out of all that bright light until he got to me. "No silver. Excellent." He then looked me up and down. A tight little smile played along the edges of his lips, but it didn't carry up into his very cold looking blue eyes. I never knew Hitler had eyes that color.

"You'll forgive the confusion around here," he said, his words again sounded more like an order instead of an apology. "This will be my temporary television station by tonight, from which I will broadcast to the people of St. Augustine when it so pleases me."

Broadcast?

"Uh, are all those people still in the exhibit hall," I asked, surprising myself that I even spoke at all, especially with how dry my mouth felt. I still couldn't get all those staring eyes from the night before out of my mind.

"Oh, them," Hitler replied with a wave of his hand as if they didn't matter. I sent all those idiots home soon after you left to clean themselves up and get ready for today's festivities.

Festivities?

"By now, many of them have already gathered at the marina awaiting my arrival." But as soon as he finished speaking, the entire left side of Hitler's body stretched far to the left until he, *it*, completely … separated into … two people—Hitler *and* the blond babe from the night before. Talk about startling.

"Nice trick, huh?" PB Blondie said, stepping closer to me, her black stiletto heels clicking on the tile floor. Actually, she got much too close. That's when I saw she had green eyes. I couldn't tell the night before in the darkened exhibit room. A blue-eyed Hitler and a green-eyed blond. What a combination.

Wearing a very short, low-cut, sleeveless, black dress, she, it, went on talking. "I wanted you to see what happens to you and Lobo when you create doubles of yourselves. And like me, you both normally do it much quicker than the human eye can follow. Now maybe you'll fully understand that any abilities you have developed since meeting Lobo have come from me and not that idiotic shaman.

"That means you owe *me* and not him, in case you missed my point" As she spoke, Blondie's green eyes flashed, reminding me of the lightning over the green ocean in Lobo's weird world.

"Hmm," she said, squinting and smirking. "This body holds much more appeal for you than my uniformed friend here. "I can tell by your increased heart rate and the dilation of your blood vessels how much you like what you see. And so, I'll get rid of Hitler for a while since he doesn't really appeal to you. He can come out and play later on."

As soon as she finished speaking, Hitler just … disappeared. He was replaced by a dense cloud of particles that then quickly fired into Blondie's mouth in a long, thick stream until they were all gone.

Oh boy, I said to myself. You are in for it now. When I walked into that place, I figured things couldn't get any stranger, but was I ever wrong.

"So we have a bargain, right?" I asked, realizing I had to do or say something. "You and me? We join forces and you leave Carla alone." Inside, I was shaking but not nearly as much as I thought I would.

"Why of course we have an agreement, sweetheart," Blondie replied, putting a hand on my chest. At first, I noticed her long fingernails were the same deep red as her lips. The next thing I realized was the intense cold coming from her hand. Uncomfortably cold.

"Our relationship is going to be so much better," she said, "without all that silver getting in the way. And together with Hitler's help, we'll sweep aside anything Lobo has to throw at us. St. Augustine will be ours for the taking as soon as I make full contact with my other particles right near that nice big crowd now building at the marina.

"You see, that's what I need you for, dearest Jeff. Your energy configuration will allow me to fully penetrate all of those people at the Blessing of the Fleet in the most, umm, effective way—after I reconnect with all my particles locked within my marvelous sea creature out in the Matanzas River, that is." Lobo hadn't explained it exactly the same way, but it was close enough for me.

"Right," I replied, trying not to show how the cold from Blondie's hand was starting to hurt my chest. "But there's just one thing I want to do before that happens."

"Oh, really?" Blondie pulled her hand away and stepped back with a wary look on her face. By then, my chest felt numb, but at least it didn't hurt anymore.

While putting a great big old fake smile on my face, I said, "I would like to take you to lunch." No, honestly, those were my exact words. Too blunt and simple, I know, and it even sounded stupid to me when I heard myself say it. But the question was exactly what Lobo's plan called for, even though I could have done a lot better job of asking it.

"Lunch?" PB Blondie asked.

"A quick lunch," I answered. "You have time before the Blessing of the Fleet. There's this nice little café behind City Hall where I would love to take you. Uh, to celebrate our partnership and to, well, show you off to people."

All those words ripped out of my mouth like someone firing off a machine gun. A little flattery, a few half-truths and some fast-talking seemed to work pretty well in my dealing with adults in the past. So I figured it was worth trying, even in this, the weirdest of all situations.

But when I said what I did, I spoke way too fast and thought for sure I must have blown it.

PB Blondie continued to squint at me while folding her arms."This café. Would it be the one in the Antique Mall?"

Uh- oh.

"Uh, yup, that's the one. A cozy little place. Great food. You haven't tried food yet, I'll bet, but you couldn't do any better than starting right there. They serve wine and a lot of times they have—"

"The Antique Mall," Blondie said again, tapping the red nails of her right hand on her bare upper left arm. "That's where we met for the first time, wasn't it, Jeffy boy? In the vortex?"

"Uh … "

"And then the second time we met was last night as I recall." As she spoke, Blondie's voice had a hard edge to it. "Yes, last night," she screamed, her green eyes wild with anger. "Last night, when you and your friends tried to capture me in your silver covered boxes, like Lobo did once before."

"Well, you see—"

"Oh I see very clearly that you and your pals have planned yet another ambush." This time, Blondie's voice sounded almost as low and cold sounding. "And you, stupid creature, think I will fall for such a transparent trap?"

Right then and there, I knew I had just failed in the assignment Lobo gave me. Potter's humanoid PB wasn't about to go anywhere with me. "You've got it all wrong," I protested knowing it wouldn't do any good. But I had to try.

"Oh no, Jeff. Actually I have it all right and … I love it!" At that point, PB Blondie smiled broadly and as if I had just given her a wonderful gift. She almost sang those words as if what I said made her incredibly happy.

What? She loves it? I wasn't sure if I heard her right or understood the meaning of her words.

"So Lobo wants to do battle with me and use you, Carla and that Lyle person as his frontline soldiers. Wonderful! What fun. Yes, let's go to lunch and have a war.

"Hmm. I think I'll have a nice juicy hamburger while I kill Lyle, and then sip some Champagne while I do the same to Lobo. But Carla? I'll save her for last—to destroy while I eat a nice rich dessert. After that, you will still have a choice of joining me *or* joining your friends. See how reasonable I can be?"

40

The Fight

The walk from Potter's Wax museum over to the mall with the PB human look-alike, seemed like it would never end. Blondie talked nonstop during the entire five-minute journey about the changes she was soon going to make in the city after she took over.

Being next to her and listening to that one-way conversation reminded me of old mad scientist films where the newly created Frankenstein-type monster had suddenly gotten loose.

All that time I felt like I was lost in a weird, waking dream, especially when people openly stared at the sexy young woman by my side.

At first, I was astounded anybody could really see her, it. Part of me kept thinking because no one had been able to see PB particles, they might not be able to see the human-like creature itself. Wrong. Two college-aged guys actually bumped into each other trying to walk and ogle at the same time.

As we went past people, I heard them say, "What's that *smell*?" Little did they know they were getting a whiff of Blondie's natural perfume—ozone and burning wires.

Their reactions surprised me. I thought Lobo, Carla, Lyle and me were the only ones who were lucky enough to have that pleasure.

The only change in Blondie came when we got to the entrance leading into the Antique Mall. That's when she abruptly stopped talking and seemed to go on high alert, looking, I was sure, for any traps put in place by Lobo.

"So where are they?" she asked, once we walked into the mall itself. As she spoke, Blondie was frowning and scanning the shops to our right and left. Her tone was sharp and demanding as she turned those flashing green eyes back on me.

My stomach did little flip-flops and my knees felt shaky as I looked back at her and shrugged. There was so much cruel power there, masquerading as a human being, it made me feel like a fly she could swat out of existence at any time. "Oh, they'll be here any minute now, I'm sure," I replied to her question.

Quite a few people were strolling around the mall, and it seemed like every one of them noticed Blondie. If you only knew what you're actually looking at and what it did at Potter's yesterday, I kept thinking all that time.

Directly ahead of us at the far end of what had once been the floor of the old Hotel Alcazar's swimming pool sat the mall's café. A couple of servers busily waited on customers.

The smell of fresh made coffee filled the air as it did when Carla and I first visited the place together. The good thing about that was it helped reduce the stink of being so close to PB Blondie. Being around so much of that ozone and burning wires smell made my eyes burn as well as my nose, throat and lungs. Every once in a while, I had to cough.

I was about to suggest to Blondie that we head to the café so we would have to walk right by the bench where Carla and I fell into the vortex, but she spoke first.

"And just where does Lobo plan for ground zero to be?" Blondie demanded, her lips twisting as if she was tasting something nasty.

"Ground zero?"

"Don't play dumb, boy. Where is it you all have agreed to ambush me?"

"Oh, uh, that," I replied, surprising myself with my calm response. She wants to know and that's where we want her to go, I told myself. "Over there," I said after a short pause, pointing towards the bench I had been eying just moments before.

"I might have known," Blondie replied, grabbing me by the arm with a cold hand and jerking me with her as she began walking again."Come on, Jeff, baby, let's go see."

Her heels clicked loudly on the cement floor as we walked the seventy-five feet or so to our destination. As soon as we got there, Blondie released my arm and slowly turned around, scanning the entire mall once more before she started speaking again.

"So your friend Lobo wants to put the genie back in the bottle where it most recently popped out, eh? He thinks he can stuff me back into the bowels of the earth, does he? Ha! Fat chance!"

As her words echoed inside my head, both Blondie and I saw Lobo, Carla and Lyle come out of an antique shop on our left at the same time.

"Well, well, well," the human look-alike said loudly so anyone in the mall could hear her as she smiled broadly. "Mr. Lobo and company have arrived to do battle."

At that exact moment, I felt Lobo deep inside my head telling me what to do—not in words but in a way I can't quite explain. All I knew was I had to back away from Blondie until it seemed safe to stop. As I did that, Blondie didn't say anything to me. She was too focused on Lobo, Lyle and Carla as they also took up positions around her.

I had very quickly become part of a human circle surrounding a very nonhuman creature. Each of us was about fifteen feet away from it—Lobo on my left, Lyle on my right and Carla on the opposite side of the thing. In setting that all up, Lobo had also stopped time dead in its tracks for everyone in the mall except for him, Carla, Lyle and me.

Lyle. I couldn't believe he actually showed up. The little guy possessed more courage than I gave him credit for. He looked like he might run away any minute, but I guess he felt safer with Lobo than anywhere else.

In the thickened air and in deep silence of Frozen Time, I saw PB Blondie moving her arms but very, very slowly. Somehow, Lobo's Frozen Time was having an effect on her but only partially. It was like watching a video in slow motion.

She stared at her hands with a confused, yet wild look in her eyes as if she couldn't believe how things had changed. Her mouth kept opening and closing, like she wanted to form words but couldn't. Unfortunately, that didn't last very long. The next thing I knew, Blondie turned into a furious looking Hitler in full uniform who opened his mouth, and from it, came a bright explosion of violet particles that fired directly at Lobo.

Carla screamed, but the particles moved so slowly, Lobo easy dodged them and another blast that Hitler sent his way.

Before Hitler could try one more time, I felt a slight tug all over my body. And as that sensation continued, the heavy air all around us started crackling, snapping and popping as if it was full of static electricity. It looked like tiny lightning bolts that kept coming out of Carla, Lyle and me and then flowed directly into Lobo.

This is his doing, I realized, looking at the old shaman. He's tapping into the energy of Carla's abilities, Lyle's and mine, all at the same time.

The guy was acting as a gatherer of power to be used against the PB humanoid. That's when it became clear to me why Lobo hadn't given us any instruction as to what to do in this final confrontation. Like Carla and Lyle, I had no role right then other than to be there and to serve as an energy source.

Even before I completed that thought though, the electrical charges materializing in the air and flowing into Lobo seemed to double. The skin all over my body started tingling. And as it did, the green painted concrete floor all around Hitler began to ripple and swirl. It had turned liquid in a perfect circle, stopping just a foot or so from where Lobo, Carla, Lyle and I stood.

PB Hitler immediately looked down at his feet and howled just as they disappeared beneath the flowing green. It was a horrible sound, like a cross between a blaring police siren and the full-throated roar of a huge animal.

In fascination, I watched as Hitler screamed Lobo's name when he tried to keep standing against the force of all that heavy liquid sloshing against his legs. Behind him, the benches where Carla and I had sat the day before, and that huge potted plant, all broke free from where they were bolted to the floor. They floated freely in the liquid cement, and ever so slowly, began to sink.

At that point, I had to laugh as the Hitler look-alike tried pulling his right foot out of the muck. Doing so only made him sink deeper and tilt to the left. He looked awkward and powerless, so different from before.

We were going to win, that was clear. How it could be so easy, I didn't understand, nor did I care. I had expected a huge, titanic battle with all of us somehow using our individual abilities against the PB, but that's not the way it turned out.

One thing I knew for sure though and that was Lobo's incredible power had merged with Carla's, Lyle's and mine to put an end to the PB forever.

As those electrical charges in the air multiplied and got even brighter, a dark hole about three feet in diameter opened up in the rippling concrete not far from PB Hitler. And when it did, air blasted past all of us from every direction and into that hole, taking with it dust, grit and pieces of trash. Some of that stuff really hurt as it fired across the back of my body, but I didn't care because it told me the PB would soon be next.

The sound of all that wind whipping past us started out as a low howl and then built into a huge roar the faster it got. In fact, the air pressure on me was so strong it got very hard to stay standing and not get dragged into the liquid green. Lyle kept one hand on his head to protect his red baseball cap and I saw Carla tie her long, blowing hair into a ponytail.

Crouch close to the floor! It was Lobo's voice shouting inside my skull, not just to me, but Carla and Lyle as well. *Now!*

And that's what all four of us did at *exactly* the same time. Our actions were so perfectly coordinated, it was as if we had practiced them for hours. Seconds later, the wind became a shrill scream as it ripped over us and down into that nasty looking hole. But our crouching positions kept us from joining Hitler in the muck, and I found that by holding my hands around my eyes and squinting, I was able to still see directly in front of me.

Battered by the incredible hurricane-like wind, Hitler stumbled and fell forward onto both of his hands. They sank up to his elbows as his legs also disappeared into the rippling green from his thighs down. His head was now very close to that horrible, sucking hole.

You wanted to be human, I said to him in my mind, so enjoy.

Just as I had that thought, the softened floor started a slow rotation to the right, pulling Hitler, the benches and that big old potted plan with it. Second-by-second, the rate of rotation caused the liquid cement near the center to actually start sliding out of sight and into the opening.

Lobo had created a swirling, green vortex with Hitler right near its edge. And the more he struggled, the deeper into the cement he sank. Fascinated, I watched as the whirlpool brought its PB humanoid cargo around in front of me, shoulder deep in green.

His eyes wild with fear and anger, Hitler somehow managed to pull one arm out of the liquid cement, really surprising me. For whatever reason, no cement clung to it, and as I looked at him, he lifted his hand in my direction as if asking for help. The expression on his face was one of pure terror. And then, he changed form and instantly became my mom, terrified, fighting for her life and holding out her hand for me to help her.

That's all it took for the energy flow I was giving Lobo to instantly dry up. I felt it as soon as it happened and in that moment, knew that I could do nothing to repair the damage in time. Oh, it only took a second or two of hesitation on my part, but it was enough time to open myself to attack by the PB.

Right at the last second before PB Mom was about to get sucked into the vortex along with the screaming air and liquid cement, the hand she was lifting in my direction transformed into a long, thick, violet tentacle. I'm telling you, that thing shot outward so quickly I barely saw it move.

The next thing I knew, it had me by the leg.

Carla screamed as I found myself jerked into the air. Helplessly dangling upside down, I watched below as PB mom disappeared into the hole of that liquid cement whirlpool while pulling me right in there with it.

41

Butt First

I couldn't see, I couldn't breathe and I couldn't move.

My lungs felt like they were being ripped out of my chest as something icy cold pressed hard on every inch of me.

It was if I had somehow materialized inside a container of freezing liquid metal. The place seemed to have no up or down and no actual movement of any kind, but I could feel and hear a deep humming vibration that penetrated me to the core.

I didn't know if my eyes were open or not because I wasn't able to blink. The cold made them hurt so much I wanted to scream but couldn't.

Filled with pain and panic, the best I could hope for right then was to die or at least lose consciousness.

Oh, I knew somehow I had landed in the vortex Lobo created for the PB, but that knowledge didn't sure make my situation any better. And the PB, I was vaguely aware, had to be somewhere in there with me. I was just too miserable to care.

It seemed like I had been in that terrible place forever when I felt a tremendous increase in pressure on my head, neck, shoulders and chest. With less pressure on the rest of my body, I began moving somewhere feet first—and fast.

In my tortured mind, I saw myself getting squeezed out of a huge tube of toothpaste by a giant. Right as that thought barely fired through my oxygen-starved brain, the extreme pressure on me just went away. And as it did, a brilliant light blinded my half frozen eyeballs for a split second before I plunged butt first into water a lot warmer than where I had just come from.

It didn't take me long to realize I had once again fallen into Maria Sanchez Creek. This time though, I wasn't with Carla.

On my way into the creek, I automatically started breathing again but way too late. I ended up inhaling some water as well as air. As soon as I could get my feet under me in the mud bottom, I burst to the surface gagging and coughing like crazy. As thankful as I was to be alive, I couldn't believe I was repeating what had happened to me the day before.

Through my blurred vision, I saw a small boat loom out of the brightness right in front of me. Two people were inside it but with the bright sun behind them, I couldn't see their faces.

As I wiped my eyes, the person on my right reached out, grabbed my wrist and then my belt.

The next thing I knew, both people were hauling me on board their boat.

Seconds later, I found myself with my stomach over a wood seat, my head and arms on one side of it, and my butt and legs on the other. I did nothing but lay there, coughing and coughing as the boat tilted from side-to-side. During that time, I watched as the rough wood bottom of the boat in front of my eyes got wetter and wetter as water drained off me.

For some reason, the warm air I was trying to breathe seemed just a little too dense. Slowly it dawned on me that I still had to be in a Frozen Time situation somehow.

"Is he all right?" A familiar voice behind me said. I couldn't remember who the person was but I knew I should.

"He'll live." Lobo. Right in front of me. I don't know when I was so glad to hear gruff words coming out of that old guy's mouth. The only other sound? The gentle lapping of water against the sides of the boat.

Still coughing and shivering, I pushed on the boat bottom with my hands, raised my head and looked up at him. He was sitting on the floor of the boat but in bare feet with his legs crossed. He wore his steel grey hair loose around his shoulders as he did out on his dock the day of my mom's funeral.

The sharp features of his face were half in bright sun and half in deep shadow. His sleeveless, grey shirt and dirty tan pants were partially wet, I figured, from dragging me onboard.

As glad as I was to see him, I knew we all had to be in danger. "The PB!" I blurted, sort of a half question and half statement. That's when I smelled the familiar nasty stink of Particle Being.

"We did all the work while you were fooling around getting here." As he spoke, Lobo jerked a thumb behind him and moved aside so I could see.

There in the back of the boat was a huge cloth bag with something moving around inside it. And on the surface of the bag, were silver dollars. Lots of them, glistening in the sun. It looked like someone had drilled a hole through the tops and bottoms of all those coins and used little pieces of wire to attach them to the material.

"Your PB *friend*," Lobo said, "came through the vortex first. In that human form, the water disoriented it enough for us to easily make the capture with our new and improved PB prison."

"You caught it?" I asked that with a big grin, finally able to get words out without coughing. I knew exactly what the man had said, but I needed to be sure.

"Of course. What do you think is in that bag we worked so hard to make? Out of burlap, yet." The answer I wanted to hear didn't come from Lobo, but it was still strangely familiar. When I pushed myself up on my knees and turned around, I found myself facing another Jeff Golden.

"Don't look so surprised," the other Jeff said with my identical crooked smile. Under his shaggy blond hair, he squinted as he looked at me with his blue eyes. Up until that moment, I had only seen doubles of myself very briefly.

He wore a long sleeved brown and white checkered shirt and charcoal colored pants held up with a thick, dark belt. No shoes. A definite contrast to my dark green T-shirt and light blue Levi's. Every one of my doubles up until that day wore the same clothes I did. Why the difference, I had no idea.

Set in a pale blue sky, the sun peeked between two billowing, white clouds, hitting the other Jeff full in the eyes. I wanted to say something, but my mind went blank.

"We don't have time for this chatter, even one way as it is," Lobo growled behind me right as I felt the boat start to move.

Ripples went out into the perfectly still water of Maria Sanchez Creek around the boat for about six feet and then stopped. It was like some kind of barrier existed out there but it didn't prevent the boat from moving forward. When I glanced back at Lobo, I saw he was using both hands to push on a long pole he had stuck in the water.

A hollow thump from the front of the boat made me face forward once more where I saw the other Jeff also using a long pole like Lobo's.

The creek, a couple of hundred feet wide or so, ended just ahead of us where there were three large buildings. Two of them looked like churches. Instead of moving in that general direction though, we headed towards a long dirt and sand road built up several feet higher than the water and running alongside it to our right.

On that street, stood a white horse hitched to a small, weird-looking wagon. It had only two very large wheels, each about five feet tall. A bench, or seat of some kind, sat between the wheels. The horse didn't move and neither did the three people I saw up there on other parts of the road, all caught in Lobo's Frozen Time.

The only sounds came from those two poles Lobo and the other Jeff were using—either splashing in and out of the water or occasionally bumping into the side of the boat.

A quick glance around showed me all kinds of other wood buildings but nothing I recognized.

"Welcome back to 1885," Lobo said, just as our boat pushed through a bunch of marsh grass and stopped.

My mind wanted to rebel against the idea of actually being in the past, but Lobo had more to say. "You've been here before so don't fight the problem and just accept that fact."

As the other Jeff hopped out onto the surrounding sand, Lobo ordered me to do the same thing. Seconds later, he joined us, and together, all three of us pulled the boat up onto the shore. Water and mud squished in my soaked shoes just like after the first time I fell into the creek.

"Show him the handles," Lobo said to the other Jeff as he jumped back into the middle of the boat.

Jeff Two, I'll call him, nudged me and pointed at two leather handles stitched solidly about three feet apart into the end of the bag nearest us in the back of the boat.

"One is yours and the other is mine," he said. "We each lift when Lobo does so we can get this thing out of here. He has his own handles at the top of the bag."

And that's exactly what we all did, lifted the bag out of the boat and onto the sandy shore with Jeff Two and me on one end and Lobo on the other.

The leather handle I used felt very smooth compared to the roughness of the bag itself. When I touched the bag accidentally, I snatched my hand away, not sure if the PB inside could do something to me through the material.

Nothing happened, but Jeff Two smiled when he saw what I did. His reaction made me wonder what he knew that I didn't. I couldn't figure out why he was there. I sure hadn't consciously produced him. But together with Lobo, we hoisted the PB filled bag out of the boat and laid it on the ground.

Tell you what though, that thing weighed a ton. PB plus lots of silver dollars equaled heavy. But strangely, the contents only moved slightly and no sound came from it.

"The silver has our captive temporarily stunned," Lobo explained just before climbing up the embankment leading to the road where the horse and wagon waited.

When he got there, he gently stroked the horse's neck with one hand until it tossed its head, nickered and then pawed the dirt with one hoof.

"Here," Jeff Two said handing me a large coil of rope as he held one of its loose ends. "Throw that up to Lobo." I did as he asked but found that taking orders from my double definitely felt weird.

Lobo took the rope and tied his end to an iron bar going across the back of the small wagon. At the same time, Jeff Two threaded his part of the rope through the handles at the top of the bag and tied it in a solid knot.

"Obviously," I said to Jeff Two, "you guys had this all planned out, but how did you know the PB and I would even be here at all?"

As Lobo got into the wagon and steered the horse out into the dirt street at an angle, Jeff Two glanced at me and then looked away. "Yeah, he knew you were both coming. How? Beats me. You know him. He never tells you much."

Our conversation was cut short as the rope tightened and the silver dollar covered PB bag started moving quickly. Lobo and his horse drawn wagon were pulling it up the embankment and onto the road way before Jeff Two and I could even begin to scramble up after it.

When we finally got to the wagon, Lobo brought it to a stop and motioned for us to climb up there with him. There was just barely enough room for Jeff Two and me to sit on either side of the old guy but we did it.

As soon as we got seated, Lobo flicked the reins hard across the horse's back, while making a sharp clicking sound with his tongue. The horse started moving again, and with more urging from Lobo when he used the leather reins, it jumped into a soft sounding trot on the dirt road.

As I looked back at the rope attached to the iron bar, I watched while it pulled tight, dragging the PB bag and leaving a trail in the unpaved road behind us.

"Where are we going?" I asked as the wagon creaked and rumbled.

"You'll find out very soon," Lobo replied, but by then my attention had turned to the people I saw on the street with us—the ones I had seen while I was down on the creek bank. None of them moved because of Lobo's Frozen Time, but they all looked like they were *about* to do something.

On our right, a tall man dressed in a dark coat and wearing a soft, flat cap had a pipe stuck in his teeth. A white cloud of smoke hung motionless around his head as if he had just exhaled a puff. With his tanned face and white beard, I thought he might be a sea captain or something.

As we moved swiftly past the man, I looked back at him and saw how his eyes glistened in the sun—a living person from 1885, even if I didn't see him move.

Directly ahead, there was a cross street. And on that corner to our left, a young white woman with her brown hair swept up high on her head was about to step off a wooden sidewalk into the dirt and sand. But that was as far as she got before being caught in Frozen Time.

She had pulled up her long purple dress just to her ankles, I guess so she wouldn't get it dirty, when she began to step down. Her shoes were shiny black and laced way up high. In her other hand, she carried a white parasol.

That's when I noticed all the tracks in the dirt road. There were lots of them—human, horse and long lines I figured must be from the wheels of other wagons.

On the opposite side of the street, and to the left of where the woman stood, was a very large two-story building, painted grey with white trim. It had a single tower that went up two more floors. A white wood fence surrounded the place and a sign identified it as the "Sunnyside Hotel."

When he got to the other road, Lobo steered the horse to the right. As the wagon came out of the turn, the glint of sunlight on water in the distance told me I must be looking at Matanzas Bay and the Matanzas River in the distance.

And on our left, I saw the first building I recognized. It didn't look exactly the same as in my time when I knew it as Government House, but it was close. A sign pointing in that direction said, "Post Office and Library."

Government House. That meant we were on King Street and the hotel we just passed had to be where Flagler College was in my time. In the near future, Henry Flagler would build his hotels in that area of town and include Lobo's beautiful caryatid carvings in one of them.

42

The Traveling Bag

There were quite a few people scattered here and there up and down King Street but frozen in the acts of walking, shopping, riding horses, and riding in both carriages and wagons.

The sight just blew me away. My mind raced in a thousand different directions at once as I tried to make sense of how I could actually be in the distant past. *1885?*

No matter how hard I tried to get control of my thoughts, I couldn't do it. The scene in front of me was way too much. Well, that and the eerie quite, except for the soft thudding of our horse's hooves in the dirt, the creaking of the wagon and the dragging sound of the bag.

But there I was, with Lobo and another version of myself in a wagon being pulled by a white horse through St. Augustine, Florida that hadn't existed for a very long time. As impossible as it seemed, it was all too real.

Ahead was another dirt cross street that had to be St. George. And on the left was the city's central plaza. It had grass, bushes, trees, walkways, monuments and the old market building at the far end, looking almost like the plaza

I knew. But most of the trees were small, not like the huge oaks I remembered.

And all around the plaza, were two fences with low bushes behind them. A gate at the corner of King and St. George seemed to be the only way in there.

There were little telephone poles with two wires strung between each, all up and down the plaza side of King Street. I say telephone but at the time, I wondered if maybe there were telegraph poles instead.

The St. Augustine Cathedral stood to the left of the plaza, looking very much like it did in my time, but it had no bell tower. *What?* Then I remembered Carla explaining to me once how the cathedral burned down in 1887 and had to be rebuilt. "That's when it got a bell tower," she said at the time. Of course, I said to myself, this is two years before that fire happens.

Oh Carla, I said to her in my mind, *wouldn't you love to be here now to see all this.* Good thing I wasn't expecting her to reply, because she didn't. Even so, it just felt good to talk to her.

The bell tower. As our wagon got even with the cathedral, the idea that I knew the bell tower *would be there* in two years really hit me.

In the St. Augustine I was observing, coming from the future, I realized I could predict some of what would happen in the city up until my own present time, back where Carla existed. Every bit of history about St. Augustine and the world that I had learned in my life would now be accurate predictions *if* I could actually talk to someone in St. Augustine in that distant past and tell them what I knew.

Where Carla existed? In this world, she wouldn't be born for a very long time and neither would I.

The more I let my mind run with that time travel thinking, the more my brain twisted itself into deep confusion. So instead of continuing to figure out all of those weird angles of my situation, I turned my attention back to just observing what was around me.

To the right of the cathedral, a huge, four story, wood building took up the rest of that entire block, or what I could see of it. That had to be the St. Augustine Hotel Carla told me about where, she said, the fire of 1887 started and spread to other parts of the city including the cathedral.

It dawned on me then how I was so involved in studying the plaza and the buildings on the far side of it, that I had been ignoring everything on my right. When I shifted my gaze over there, to the right-hand side of King Street, I found myself looking at a whole bunch of old-fashioned looking stores and some other buildings that might be offices.

Gold lettering on a plate glass window we passed said, "Sanchez & Son, Grocer." A sign over the door of another building identified the place as "Pinkham Bros." Of course, there was no Potter's Wax Museum where I remembered it in my time, but for some odd reason, I expected to see it.

By then, we were approaching the waterfront. Now that area looked like it had to be from another city. There was a seawall, some seagulls frozen in mid-flight and lots of big wooden docks but no Bridge of Lions. In fact, there was no bridge at all going over to Anastasia Island. Out on the island, I could see no buildings anywhere except for the lighthouse far in the distance.

And where the entrance to the Bridge of Lions would be in my time was something that appeared to be a huge, rectangular swimming pool sort of thing, set into the street in front of the Matanzas River.

An opening on the far side of that pool-like area led to the river. All sides of the rectangle looked like the rest of the nearby stone seawall. A sign identified the place as the "Boat Basin" and there were actually boats in it—tied up to those stone walls somehow.

In front of the Boat Basin, a small crowd had gathered. They were looking at a huge, dead alligator. Someone had stretched it out on top of a bunch of wood boxes with a stick propping its mouth open.

In Frozen Time, three little black boys, probably about ten years old, and with great big smiles, were having their picture taken next to the gator. The photographer stared at his big, old-time camera as he scratched his head, looking as if he couldn't figure out some sort of problem.

Abruptly, Lobo steered his trotting horse to the right of the Boast Basin and right again onto the road running along the seawall.

Seconds later, he pulled on the reins and brought the horse to a stop where two long, wooden docks jutted out into the river—the exact place where the St. Augustine Marina would someday go.

"Out!" He ordered. The PB bag lay in the dirt street, maybe ten or fifteen feet behind us.

As Lobo spoke, I noticed a sailing ship with two masts tied to a dock to the left of the Boat Basin. *A sailing ship!*

And beyond the ship and its dock, the seawall gently curved past a very different St. Augustine than I knew until it ended at the Castillo de San Marcos way in the distance. Just on the other side of the Castillo was where our neighborhood would someday be and I wondered what it looked like in that year of 1885.

After all three of us got off the wagon, Lobo began untying the rope connecting the bag to the wagon's iron bar. That silver covered bag moved only a little, still showing something was inside, but still, no sounds came through the rough cloth.

The contrast of the silent, captured PB to what I faced at Potter's and in the Antique Mall was incredible. I still couldn't believe how easily Lobo defeated the thing in the end.

"It isn't defeated yet," he said to my thoughts as he took the rope end he had just untied from the wagon back towards the bag. "You're getting ahead of yourself as usual."

"Yeah, Jeff," Jeff Two said to me with a grin. "Straighten up why don't you."

"You should talk," Lobo said to him over his shoulder.

I couldn't believe it. There we were in 1885 and Lobo was fussing at two Jeffs.

After tying his end of the rope to both leather handles at the front of the PB bag, Lobo held the rope up to show us he had made a loop. Then he told us to join him.

"This is going to be a very simple operation," he said. "I am going to be the horse and use the rope to pull the bag behind me. You two are going to use the handles at the other end to lift enough to reduce friction and also to make sure the bag doesn't slide off into the water too soon.

"The water?" I asked. "Too soon for what?"

Lobo didn't answer, but Jeff Two did. "We're going to *drag* your PB humanoid, or whatever it is now, out onto the end of that first dock directly ahead of us and dump it into the river."

"The river? Why?"

"Because," Lobo interrupted gruffly as he stepped inside the loop he had made with the rope, "that's where the PB's hybrid sea creature is in your time. Remember?

"If we do our jobs right, the coming together of both PB halves with silver involved will thoroughly disrupt all the particles anywhere in the city during your time and hurl them all back deep into the earth. But that's not going to happen if you keep asking questions."

His answer made no real sense to me, but knowing I had to trust him, I kept my mouth shut.

Good, a voice said inside my head. Jeff Two nudged me and winked as we both walked to the far end of the PB bag where we each grabbed a handle. *You and I will never understand the details,* he said again in my mind, *but the results will be very clear if it works and it should.*

The idea of mind-to-mind communications with my other self made that wildly weird visit to old St. Augustine even stranger.

Lobo stepped into the loop he had made in the rope, grabbed it with both hands and lifted it to his chest. "Now," he shouted and then began pulling, the muscles in his bare arms bulging.

Following orders, Jeff Two and I lifted and pulled. Together, the three of us slid the bag off the street, over the seawall and eventually out onto the end of the dock.

When we got there, my double and I collapsed dripping sweat, but Lobo just stood there not even breathing hard and shaking his head. "You two are so out of shape," he said as he untied the ropes from the bag.

As I sat there panting, I noticed how the waters of Matanzas Bay and the river weren't *actually* sparkling. They looked like they were from a distance, but up close, I saw there was no actual movement of the water out there or of the reflected sunlight.

All that *sparkled*, I finally understood, was a six-foot ring of the river around the dock where we sat. There, the water rippled normally. It was all Lobo's Frozen Time in action—and non-action.

"Come on you two," he said, motioning us to get up, "let's make this happen. I'll take my end while each of you takes one handle. Next we all lift in unison, swing back and forth three times and then let it loose towards the river. Got it?"

The end of the dock was an L shape that gave us plenty of room to accomplish our task.

"Yeah, we got it," Jeff Two and I said at the exact same time in the exact same voice. We laughed, stood up and grabbed our handles just as Edgar flew up in front of us and landed on a piling. I didn't even want to think how he got there so I definitely didn't ask.

"Ready?" Lobo asked. When Jeff Two and I said yes, we lifted the bag, swung it back and forth as Lobo had directed and heaved it towards the river as far as we could. It went up about even with our heads and out maybe eight feet. And as it began the downward arc of its journey, all those silver dollars glittered brightly in the sun.

43

Blessing of the Fleet

I had no memory of the PB bag ever hitting the water.

The next thing I knew, after we flung it out towards the water, was being back in my own time in the Antique Mall. The vortex had vanished and I found myself sitting dazed and alone in the boat Lobo and Jeff Two used to pull the PB and me out of Maria Sanchez Creek.

Present day Lobo, along with Carla and Lyle, ran to the boat and practically dragged me out of it. As soon as I stepped onto the green cement floor, Carla wrapped her arms around me and started sobbing.

"Good God, boy," Lyle said, patting me on the shoulder, "we thought for sure you were gone forever."

"I'm OK," I told Carla, hugging her back. And as I did, I noticed that for about ten feet all around us, the green cement was solid again, but all wet and sort of wavy and rippled.

And another thing. The wrought iron benches and the large potted plant were not where they should be. Partially submerged in that very solid but slick cement floor, they stuck out of it at odd angles. The cement, when it was liquid, had hardened all around those things.

That's when I also noticed the people in the mall were still locked in Frozen Time, just as they were when the PB pulled me into the vortex with its tentacle.

It took Lobo to calm Carla down but once he did, the man quickly gave her and Lyle a quick rundown on what happened to me after I disappeared. Carla's eyes got very wide as she realized I got to actually see the city as it looked back in 1885.

"The past and the present, he said, finishing his explanation, are about to meet in the river at the marina and we need to be there to make sure the PB leaves this world.

"*If* what we have already set in motion in the past works, like it is supposed to, all we should see is a quick flash of light and maybe a slight boil of water coming up from the river bottom right in front of the marina's main dock.

"No one should notice the light but us and any slight disturbance in the water will be viewed as just an eruption of gases under the mud."

"The best vantage point for us to observe is near the highest spot on the Bridge of Lions. And we need to go there *now*." Not allowing any questions or discussion, he hurried us all out of the mall with him and Lyle in the lead.

For me, that rapid walk through downtown was a blur of images and sounds as Carla and I held hands. I was sure she wanted to ask me all kinds of questions, but didn't. I think she sensed correctly that part of my mind was still stuck in 1885.

On King Street, I kept seeing flashes of a dirt road, horses and people dressed in ways you only see on TV or in books and films. When I glanced at the cathedral, I saw in my mind how it had looked *without* its bell tower. And ahead in the distance, for just an instant, the Bridge of Lions disappeared, replaced by open water, wooden docks and a sailing ship.

It took until we approached Avenida Menendez with Lobo and Lyle waiting for us there before I could shake my experiences in the past off enough to feel like talking. The burning question in my mind that I needed to ask Carla was a simple one, "How did I get back into the Antique Mall after getting sucked into the vortex?"

She squeezed my hand and looked at me with this very pained expression. "I thought I had lost you," she said over the traffic noise, her voice shaking and with tears in her eyes again. "It was horrible watching you get pulled into the cement whirlpool by that … thing.

"But right as you disappeared, the vortex widened and you popped right back up in your boat. A second or two later, the vortex went away and the floor solidified."

What, I wondered after that brief explanation, did all those people in the Antique Mall think after we left and time went back to normal. I mean, suddenly they faced that big old rowboat and saltwater that weren't there seconds before. And for them to see those benches impossibly sunk in a rippled floor?

"Hurry!" Lobo shouted over his shoulder to Carla and me as he and Lyle started to cross Avenida Menendez.

We followed at a run, all of us heading for the Bridge of Lions in front of us. The sound of a woman singing "Amazing Grace" blared from speakers at the marina across the street on our right. And from behind us, bells from the cathedral rang loudly.

Together, both of those sounds combined to remind anyone downtown that the Blessing of the Fleet by the Bishop of St. Augustine was about to begin.

As we got to the walkway going across the Bridge of Lions, I saw tons of people standing on the docks of the St. Augustine Marina to our right. Out on the river in front of the docks, a long line of boats and small ships stretched all the way over to Anastasia Island and then south for what looked like a mile or more. There were motor boats, yachts, fishing boats, sailboats and even people paddling kayaks.

Herding all that water traffic like sheepdogs, were small police boats, their blue lights flashing. Assisting them were boats from the U.S. Coast Guard and the Florida Fish and Wildlife Commission.

Some people, like us, were starting to crowd onto the Bridge of Lions for a better view.

Most of them clustered in areas closest to the marina, but Lobo led us to a wide-open spot just in front of one of the towers that mark the four corners of the drawbridge. From there we were able to look back at the marina while watching the river in front of the docks.

When we arrived, Carla, Lyle and I leaned on the concrete railing with our hands, panting from our quick trip from the Antique Mall. Not Lobo. Nope. The old guy stood there with his hands on his hips, breathing normally as he scanned the marina and the river. Lobo, the man of infinite surprises and mysteries.

The view from the bridge was spectacular. I had never walked on it before, even though Carla tried to get me to do it a million times. "You'll love it," she kept saying but I always ended up changing the subject. That day she finally got her wish.

The Matanzas River flowed beneath us and sparkled in the sunlight, making me think of how it looked in 1885, or at least how part of it looked during Frozen Time back then. From up there, we were able to see far into the distance where the river eventually curved to the right and under the next bridge.

The sun beat down on top of my head and I felt its left over heat in the roughness of the concrete railing beneath my hands. It was a gorgeous day. Large, thick clouds had moved in from the west and lazily drifted overhead, their bottoms colored light gray. The breeze was warm, but it still felt cool blowing across my body. Being there actually reminded me of standing on that cliff in Lobo's strange world, looking down on a volcano.

On the air, I smelled just a hint of salt water and mud. The tide was out, exposing oyster beds on both sides of the river. As interesting as that all was, I could only think about what lay beneath the surface of the water in front of the marina. Well, that and what Lobo, Jeff Two and I had done there in the distant past.

Trying to change my focus, I again looked at all those boats in the river stretching in a long line to our left next to Anastasia Island.

The night before, Carla had explained to me how each boat would take its turn during the ceremony, cross the water right in front of the bridge below us, and then make a sharp curve to the left towards the marina. At that point, it would aim straight alongside the main dock. There the Bishop of St. Augustine would bless the boat and send out a generous dose of holy water as it slid past.

I estimated the number of people observing at 500, but Carla put the figure at closer to 700. Right in the middle of that crowd, at the edge of a long dock, stood the bishop. Carla pointed him out to me, but it I could see it obviously had to be the guy wearing the long yellow robe blowing in the breeze .

Young and old, black, white and brown, all those people down there were waiting for the event to begin. One group of them on the dock with the bishop came dressed in clothing showing how people looked in colonial Spanish St. Augustine. I thought I recognize quite few of those costumes from the Spanish Night Watch Parade, but from that distance, it was hard to tell for sure.

Some people carried palm fronds and a lot of the boats were decorated with them as well. Never having been a church person, I didn't realize how important Palm Sunday was to some people.

"I don't like it," Lobo said, staring in the direction of the marina.

"Don't like what? Why?" Lyle asked, his eyes darting everywhere.

"The gulls," Lobo replied, jutting his jaw towards all the birds below us. "They're everywhere and agitated in a way I've never seen before."

He was right. There were a lot of gulls and they sure were noisy.

The number had to be in the hundreds, at least half of them in the air. Screeching loudly, they flew back and forth over the river and the docks. Big batches of them almost covered the roof of the marina and the nearby Santa Maria Restaurant. Individual gulls or small groups took up space wherever they could on the docks, empty boats, the tops of pilings, and even on nearby mudflats.

"I've never seen so many of them together in this area," Carla said. "And they seem to be louder than usual."

Just as Carla finished speaking, Edgar landed on an open part of the railing next to Carla. "Where did you come from?" She asked.

"Caa, caa, caa," Edgar replied, balancing on his single leg and bobbing his head as if to answer her question somehow.

I looked at that crazy crow and wondered if I really did see him back in 1885 or if I had seen a different bird. If it was Edgar, I realized, he must be nearly as old as Lobo and Lyle.

As ridiculous as that possibility seemed, it wasn't any crazier than me traveling into the past.

"Not good, not good at all," Lobo said, now looking straight up into the sky.

That wasn't what I wanted to hear—another negative from the man who always seemed to have the answer. His plan had worked so far, but he was starting to sound as if things might be falling apart.

Along with Carla and Lyle, I looked up into the sky, trying to find why Lobo was concerned.

At first I couldn't see anything different or unusual until I noticed that the clouds directly above the bridge, the river, the marina and the central part of downtown St. Augustine had stopped moving. Other, more distant clouds were still drifting along, but not the ones overhead. And as I watched, I saw how they were also quickly getting darker, the way things look when it's about to rain.

That's when Edgar decided to fly away.

Almost as if his leaving was a signal, the seagulls that weren't flying rose into the air and joined the others already there. And once they were together in a giant flock, all those birds flew directly over the center of the Bridge of Lions.

They came so close to us that all the wing fluttering and screeches blended into the most eerie sound I've ever heard. To me it was a shrill screaming of pure panic and a warning to every other living thing.

It took less than a minute for all of those gulls to cross the bridge and continue flying in a huge mass out across into the bay. And the further they went, the more that sound of panic and warning slowly decreased in volume until I couldn't hear it anymore.

Meanwhile, those nasty looking clouds above us had expanded and thickened enough to blot out the sun. In fact, it got so dark that the streetlights on the Bridge of Lions automatically popped to life. And to confirm the probability of a coming storm, the wind picked up tremendously, bringing with it a quick drop in temperature.

All those rapid changes, of course, meant the end of the fleet blessing even before the bishop got to sprinkle holy water on the first boat.

Over the public address system at the marina came a nervous male voice saying, "Due to the approaching bad weather, we are cutting short today's, uh, festivities. Everyone out on the docks, please return to shore. There is plenty of time so don't rush. This is just a precaution."

But even as people began moving as directed, the dark clouds above us began swirling and boiling. And as the four of us stared at the chaos overhead, a gray colored funnel cloud popped out of it. Not large at first, the thing twisted back and forth, like a snake trying to find something to eat.

When that happened, the person making announcements at the marina changed from sounding nervous to being downright terrified. "Get off the docks now. Now! All boats near the marina and the bridge head towards the bay."

The people on the docks didn't need to be told twice. They immediately started running for shore. In the crush of all those bodies though, there were bottlenecks followed by splashes as the unfortunate ones fell into the river.

Sirens from the police boats out on the river wailed and using their own loud speakers, the officers onboard repeated the directions already given to the boaters from the marina. As the wind increased, whipping our hair and clothes, cop cars with blue lights flashing blocked any flow of traffic onto the bridge.

"We better get outta here," Lyle shouted at Lobo over the sound of the rushing wind. Other people on the bridge were already doing as Lyle suggested.

But before Lobo could answer, the twister above us got a lot thicker and lowered rapidly until the end of it was almost even with the bridge. It was still several hundred feet away from us but much too close for comfort. A second or two later, after causing the wind to violently increase, it looped over towards the marina's docks and plunged directly into the river.

The funnel cloud had become a waterspout. But as I watched that water tornado, it somehow started churning and twisting the river itself at the point of contact. As a result, the waterspout turned black and plunged directly into the mouth of a huge whirlpool it had created.

Luckily, there were no boats in that area, but I swear, the whirlpool in the river reminded me of the liquid cement vortex in the Antique Mall. At that point, I hoped I would never see any kind of spiraling air or liquid again. *Vortex*. A word I wanted to delete from my vocabulary along with the word *particles*.

As if we didn't have enough trouble already, out of the clouds all around the water spout's base, huge bolts of brilliant lightning erupted, one after the other. They zigzagged downward, firing directly into the whirlpool and bringing with them pounding thunder that shattered the air—the kind you can feel in the pit of your stomach.

The strangest thing though, was that it didn't rain, not even a few drops. But the smell of ozone filled the air. Pure ozone without that stink of burning wires for a change.

"Down!" Lobo bellowed as the roaring wind and explosion of sound made even his huge voice hard to hear. "Keep your head below the railing." Lobo led the way by squatting and we all followed his example.

Carla and I clung to each other as we peeked through an open spot in the concrete railing just as the whirlpool erupted in a huge explosion even louder than all that continuing thunder.

Brilliant violet light made me squint as water blew upward in a gigantic geyser and then exploded again a couple of football fields of distance in the air.

And when that happened, we were showered with tons of water and what I found out later were small chunks of the PB's hybrid sea creature mixed up with tiny slivers of silver. This time, the smell of ozone also contained just the slightest hint of burning wires.

The first explosion created a huge wave that washed over the docks at the marina and sent boats crashing into each other. Luckily, most of the people who were out there got away safely before that happened, but not all. Unfortunately, there was a large group who didn't move for whatever reason. They just stayed where they were, staring out at the river.

We watched in horror as the wave caught them before it smashed into the sea wall.

Over the marina a giant cloud of glistening, violet particles appeared and just hung there—particles only Lobo, Carla, Lyle and I could see. At the center of that cloud, the waterspout somehow still twisted and turned with blinding lightning continuing to fire from the clouds directly into the river.

I thought that explosion must have destroyed the whirlpool but amazingly, it too kept going, looking like it would suck the river dry if it didn't stop.

Then slowly at first, the PB cloud began to rotate in the same direction as the waterspout. That's when continuous streams of other particles from across the city joined the cloud, making it brighter and brighter, and rotate faster and faster.

At the same time, the wind lessened and the thunder and lightning stopped abruptly. When that happened, Lobo stood, obviously believing it was a safe thing to do and also wanting to get a better view of everything going on in front of us.

But when Carla, Lyle and I joined him. I felt a prickly sensation in my head, chest and upper stomach area. Scared at first, I noticed Carla and Lyle seemed to be feeling something too.

The next thing I knew, all three of us convulsed once, right at the same time. And as that happened, I watched in amazement as particles rocketed outwards from all three of our bodies towards the marina. It was over in less than a couple of seconds.

When we looked at Lobo for an explanation, he just nodded and said loudly over the dying wind, "You all are now particle free and so is the city." As if we had planned it, Carla, Lyle and I let our whoops of joy.

Calm down and don't draw any more attention, Lobo cautioned in my mind. I had no doubt that Carla and Lyle also received the same message.

Luckily, there were no people left anywhere near us on the bridge.

When I looked back towards the river and marina, I saw the PB cloud moving so fast it had become a dazzling blur of partly transparent movement. But still, the waterspout continued to rotate at the cloud's center. In the next few seconds though, the spinning PB cloud rapidly contracted and actually merged with the waterspout.

And at that moment, the entire water tornado radiated a brilliant, almost blinding violet color before being entirely swallowed by the whirlpool.

I mean that glowing waterspout just detached itself from the clouds above and fired directly downward into the water, causing both waterspout and whirlpool to disappear.

In the river, a large circular boil of water rushed upward a few feet and then flattened out as if nothing had happened.

Epilogue

St. Augustine, Florida
May 15

Right after the hybrid sea creature blew up out in the middle of Matanzas River during that incredible storm, all hell broke loose. It wasn't just those two things that caused so much disruption in town though. No, it was also the pieces of unknown tissue and slivers of silver that people found all over town.

Of course, it didn't help that in the Lightner Museum's Antique Mall they discovered Lobo's boat from 1885 and those benches sunk at wild angles in the messed up, but very solid green cement.

I'm sure you probably saw it on TV, but the authorities went crazy. They didn't know if they had some kind of super weird terrorist attack on their hands, a dangerous biological hazard, or a new kind of environmental threat.

And because they couldn't figure out which one, they reacted as if all three had happened and put the city in a lockdown that you wouldn't believe.

No, not just a lockdown. To my way of thinking, it was definitely martial law, but they didn't officially call it that.

Just for starters, no one could get in and out of the city. They closed U.S. 1 and Highway A1A, shut down the airport, stopped trains from going through the city and halted all boat traffic anywhere near St. Augustine. And when I say closed, I mean armed guards type closed.

The governor sent in soldiers from the National Guard. The U.S. Navy stationed ships from their Mayport base in Jacksonville to guard the St. Augustine and Matanzas Inlets.

Oh, and the Coast Guard patrolled the entire Intracoastal Waterway from Jacksonville all the way down to Crescent Beach. Unbelievable!

At first, people were scared to death but then as time went on, they got pissed because they were living in a huge prison camp.

We had helicopters and airplanes constantly overhead and you couldn't get anywhere near downtown without being stopped by the FBI, Homeland Security and all kinds of other law enforcement people. I'll bet the CIA was here as well, even though their involvement never became public.

Believe it or not, the authorities even cut all phone and computer communications with the outside world for two weeks.

I really didn't blame them for taking a lot of precautions, but they went way too far.

Even now, you can't go anywhere near the marina, Potter's Wax Museum or the Lightner Museum's Antique Mall because they have all those areas fenced off and guarded. Right after the PB explosion, you could see people walking around near those areas in hazmat suites.

Out on the Matanzas River, huge barges with giant cranes still scoop things out of the water. The Army Corps of Engineers are in charge of all that activity. We can even see some of it from Lobo's dock.

Now for the really bad news. Right after the explosion, they found thirty-three people dead around the area of the marina. Yeah, thirty-three.

Lobo had to do a lot fast-talking to help Carla, Lyle and me to stop feeling guilty about what happened. The way we looked at it at first was that by our actions, we helped to kill those poor folks. Eventually though, Lobo helped us to accept the fact that the entire city would have been doomed if we had done nothing.

Of course, at first, everyone thought the explosions caused all those deaths. The explosions and that huge wave. Then they did autopsies and found only two people had died of causes they could identify—one from drowning and the other from being slammed into the sea wall.

The other thirty-one killed? They still haven't come up with what caused the deaths of those people.

Unfortunately, one of those unexplained deaths turned out to be Carla's friend, Kelsey.

That really hit Carla hard. She blamed herself for not finding a way to save Kelsey, but Lobo kept reminding her that nothing any of us did could have made a difference. His words helped, but even now, it depresses her to think about what happened.

Lobo told us that investigators never will come up with an explanation for all those mystery deaths because he's certain the bodies were people from Potter's Wax Museum—some of the ones the PB humanoid had already taken over. His exact explanation? "They were already dead, but walking corpses animated by the Particle Being. When the PB vanished, those bodies simply collapsed. There is simply no evidence left for them to make a conclusion."

Walking corpses? I shuddered when he used that term because it reminded me how I reached almost the same conclusion when I saw those people under the PB's control at the wax museum. Zombies. That was the one-word description that came to mind once again at the time when Lobo said what he did.

You know, up until that night at Potter's, I used to love zombie movies. Not anymore. The real life versions I saw took all the spooky fun out of that type of horror film for me.

Over time, the tests investigators ran on all those pieces of the hybrid sea creature showed there was no danger to humans or animals. That eliminated the threat of a biological hazard and seemed to rule out terrorist involvement.

As soldiers and law enforcement types were replaced by more and more scientists, and lots of media people, the city started getting somewhat back to normal—if you can call it that.

Tell you what though. There are still TV news trucks parked all around the plaza with their big, old antennas sticking up in the air. I think they're here permanently. Carla and I avoid the plaza because those reporters are always looking to interview locals who were in town when the explosion occurred.

So far, all those scientists haven't been able to clearly determine what kind of creature exploded out there in the river or how it actually died. Not surprisingly, extended analyses from multiple laboratories said that what lived out in the river was an impossible mix of whale and octopus tissues. If they only knew.

Of course, as soon as that information became public, people dug up the story about the original St. Augustine Monster from 1896 and the media hasn't stopped making comparisons between the two creatures ever since.

The other thing investigators found were all those pieces of silver, a lot of them in the river. In fact, they even found some whole silver dollars, dated from the 1870's and 1880's with two holes drilled through each one of them. When he heard about that news report, Lobo cracked one of his rare smiles and said people would puzzle over such a delicious little mystery for a very long time.

The authorities created a rule that said you weren't allowed to keep, or even touch, sea creature remains, or any pieces of silver. It stated that anyone finding such things were to report them to the police, even after they found no danger in those things. Even so, pieces of both started appearing on Ebay as soon as martial law was lifted.

Of course, investigators interviewed everybody they could find who was anywhere near the marina that day back in March. The idea of being interrogated scared Carla, Lyle and me almost as much as facing the PB had.

Oh, we knew they would never believe us even if we told the exact truth. Lobo told us as much. But we also knew we would look and sound super guilty simply because we truly did know what had happened.

Carla, Lyle and I had visions of being jailed for months while authorities tried to figure out who we really were and what we knew. Besides, we were sure somebody would remember seeing Lobo near the PB explosion and track him down. He's the kind of person who is a little hard to miss. But that hasn't happened, so far anyway.

When Carla mentioned to him at the time how many TV cameras were at all the multiple downtown locations where we had been, here's what Lobo said. "When they look at all those tapes, they're going to find them blank."

Yeah, *blank*. His word, not mine. He wouldn't elaborate on that explanation. I have to assume that his statement is true, but if it is, Lobo caused it somehow. How? Beats me.

I have to wonder if seeing all those blank tapes might make authorities consider that maybe a conspiracy actually did take place. And it did, really, when you think about it. The actual conspiracy though was one that saved the city.

But the more we worried about things like that, the more Lobo urged us to relax. He seemed like he could care less about any possibly of one or more of our little group having to deal with the cops and government types crawling all over town. "Just stay out of downtown as much as you can until all this blows over," he told us when we questioned him about it.

Well, let me tell you something. About two weeks after the explosion, Lobo, Carla and I actually ran into two FBI agents right outside the gate to Lobo's property. Yeah, that's what I said, FBI. Not downtown. Close to home.

The three of us were in Lobo's truck coming back from a trip to Home Depot and there they were—a man and a woman dressed in dark suits standing by a car parked on Water Street next to the entrance to Lobo's place.

As clear as could be, I heard Lobo's voice in my head saying those three little letters I did not want to hear, sense or however you want to put it—*FBI*. Carla received the same message because I heard her whisper, "Oh, God," as she grabbed my hand.

Calm as anything, old Lobo pulled up to his gate, turned off the engine and told us to stay put.

Then he got out of the truck and walked over to our two visitors. When he got there, they showed him their badges and a conversation began that we couldn't quite hear, even though the windows to the truck were open. Frustrated that I didn't know what was happening, I started imagining the worst.

Sensing my thoughts, Carla looked over at me and said, "Lobo will never let that happen. Especially now, after all we've been through."

"I hope you're right," I replied, but as I did, the air thickened, just slightly, but it definitely thickened. Without having to ask, I knew Carla sensed the same thing. Everywhere outside the truck there was absolutely no movement and that included Lobo and the two agents.

We watched the scene of Frozen Time in fascination as Lobo finally moved. And when he did, he laid a big hand on the head of each of those FBI people like he was giving them a blessing or something. As soon as he finished touching them, the thickened air vanished and time returned to normal.

There was more muffled conversation between Lobo and the agents, and the next thing we know, they are both shaking hands with the old guy. After that, Lobo stood there, calm as could be as the two investigators got back into their car and drove off.

"Never underestimate Lobo," Carla said with a smile in her voice. Instead of saying anything, I just watched the man in awe as he unlocked his gate and then got back into the truck.

His only words as he drove us onto his property were, "They'll be writing up a report giving each of us a complete security clearance." I swear, that's all the man said. And did I believe him? You bet.

Our encounter with the FBI though, stirred up a question about Lobo that I'd had on my mind ever since Carla and I found out how long the guy had lived in St. Augustine. I wondered how people, especially neighbors, hadn't figured out the man wasn't aging. Well, after Lobo's little demonstration with the FBI agents, I didn't have to wonder any more.

On top of the invasion of St. Augustine by the full force of local, state and federal governments, Carla, Lyle and I still struggled for the longest time to believe that the Particle Being was truly gone.

I mean, for weeks they kept finding pieces of the sea creature as well as silver. Hearing about those discoveries always stirred up our fears that just maybe some particles escaped the explosion somehow.

Lobo kept assuring us that there were no particles left in the city. The explosion, he said, had blasted them back where they came from. He also assured us he could sense no particles anywhere except far down in the earth where they belonged.

Yeah, well, maybe. I mean we recognized that Lobo's experience, knowledge and abilities should have proved to us that everything was OK and there's nothing more to fear.

Then again, none of us could fully accept the truth of his words. I don't know, I think it was a gut level, maybe subconscious fear, that no matter what, *anything* could happen. And Lobo's knowledge about the PB wasn't complete.

Far from it. We saw evidence of that during the days before that huge explosion.

To be honest, it took me about six weeks before I stopped looking at myself in the mirror, and also at other people in town, and wondering if tiny PB particles still lurked deep inside, just waiting for a chance to take over.

It took Carla a little less time, most likely because she didn't have as much firsthand connection with the PB humanoid as I did. Lyle? Lyle couldn't take it.

For him, I don't think it was as much about possible leftover PB particles as it was about the PB left deep in the earth.

When Lobo couldn't promise Lyle an even bigger piece of the Particle Being wouldn't erupt again if there was another earthquake, Lyle kind of folded up into himself. The poor guy had lived with that fear ever since 1879. And he had seen the PB enter St. Augustine again in 1886 and once more back in March. As brave as he was in the battle against the PB humanoid, all of the fight seemed to drain right out of him.

After the explosion, Lyle stayed drunk a lot of the time, so much so that Lobo finally put him into one of the best alcohol and drug rehab centers in the country. Lyle finished his residential treatment last week, but then went directly into a half-way house out in New Mexico. I wonder if he'll come back. I kind of miss him. I really do.

Does it worry me that there's a tiny chance the rest of the PB could come charging up through the earth during another quake? Sure, of course it does.

Carla and I talk about it from time to time, but Lobo is right about one thing. Florida isn't a very earthquake prone state, so the possibility of another one big enough to release any more particles in the near future is pretty remote.

I sure hope he's right.

Oh, Carla's Grandma. I forgot to tell you about her.

As soon as communications between St. Augustine and the outside world were restored, Grandma called, worried to death. We calmed her down and told her everything was fine. And as soon as her sister started doing better, and after St. Augustine opened back up to the world, Grandma came back.

When she saw us for the first time, Grandma could see how we were still struggling with our experiences, even if she didn't know all the terrible details. So we just let her think our emotional reactions were because we were right near the marina at the time of the explosion. That's all she knows and all she ever needs to know.

But when I think back to what Lobo said to me right after Mom appeared about maybe having experiences that would be like, "stepping off a cliff," I had no real idea of just how seriously he meant it. In fact, the man's prediction was quite an understatement. Not in a million years could I have guessed what was about to happen soon after he spoke those words.

Even now, when I look at that wolf howling on a cliff in Lobo's stained glass door, it definitely brings back a lot of PB memories. For me, I guess, a cliff will always have a very special, but unusually negative, meaning.

Before the PB event, I thought because of all the unbelievably weird stuff I went through when I first met Lobo, that I was prepared for anything. Yeah, right.

Now that I've had time to stop and think about it, I'm really grateful to my mom. After all the problems between us for so many years, she came back to warn me about the coming of the PB. And by warning me, she helped save the whole city!

I think about that sometimes at night before I go to sleep. Why? Well, because there were so many times in my life when it seemed to me she just didn't care. As tough as her murder was for me to accept, her ghostly visit was an incredible gift and it will be with me forever.

OK, enough. I can only take talking about my mom so much. Life goes on, right?

Things tend to balance out sometimes and even though I've lost my mom, I've gained Carla 100 percent.

What do I mean by those words? I guess you've figured out by now that I'm *hopelessly* in love with that girl. I sort of felt it after we both survived being sucked into my ancestor's self-created world of endless battle back in December, but I didn't fully admit it to myself. And to find out that she really loves me in return was the most wonderful thing to come out of our nasty PB experience.

But there's something Carla and I both still wonder about. It's the initial contact we had with the PB in the vortex. Will that experience result in the same effect on our bodies as it had on Lobo and Lyle so long ago? Lobo says he just doesn't know and not to worry about it for now. Easy for him to say.

When I first thought about not getting old and having a much longer lifetime than most people, the idea sounded pretty cool. But as Carla and I explored that possibility, we realized if it actually happened, we would have to watch everybody we knew and loved get old and die—everybody but each other—and Lobo and Lyle of course.

In thinking about Lobo and Lyle, we wondered what good all those extra years did for them. Really. Think about it.

Lyle is an alcoholic who can't face the world as it is and Lobo, for all of his knowledge and power, is a grumpy old guy who has to stay hidden so he makes absolutely sure nobody will ever find out his incredible age and abilities.

And another PB eruption could happen someday, no matter how remote the chance.

There are bound to be more earthquakes, even though Florida doesn't get many, and they could shake loose some more particles. Wouldn't Lobo and Lyle need our help then, like they did this time? And did that mean no matter how long we lived, Carla and I would have to stay in St. Augustine to back them up with our energy?

Look, I don't think of Carla, Lobo, Lyle and myself as heroes or anything. But when I see people walking around St. Augustine now who would be dead, or at least enslaved, if we hadn't fought together as a team, I know we did a really good thing.

So what would have happened if Carla and I hadn't been around and Lobo and Lyle lost the battle with the Particle Being?

I think you can see how confusing things are for us even today. My thoughts get so tangled up at times I have to keep reminding myself of all I've learned from Lobo about not letting my mind run out of control. So I focus on my breath a lot and work on flipping the little switches in my head so that I can let things go.

Yeah, in Lobo's words I'm really trying not to "fight the problem" but it's hard. Really, really hard.

No matter what though, I have Carla. That's the main thing.

In the meantime, the future is just going to have to take care of itself.

Author's Notes

1. The St. Augustine Monster:
This creature actually did exist, brought to the attention of the world by Dr. DeWitt Webb of St. Augustine in 1896. Studied and speculated about ever since, scientists over the years have described it as a giant octopus on more than one occasion and then also as whale blubber. The photo below is one of many made by Dr. Webb back in 1886 and it appears here courtesy of the St. Augustine Historical Society.

2. The Caryatids:

Just inside the main entrance to Flagler College in St. Augustine, Florida is a beautiful eighty-foot rotunda. When the building opened in 1887 as one of Henry Flagler's world-class hotels, the Ponce de Leon, that entrance was created to impress.

In a circle at the base of the rotunda are eight columns, each with four hand-carved female statues. Known as the art and architectural form called caryatids, they are supporting as well as decorative structures. No exact records exist as to who carved these statues, one of which is pictured below.

3. Native American Prison:

The Castillo de San Marcos in St. Augustine, Florida has served as a prison for Native Americans on three different occasions since the United States received Florida from Spain in 1821:

The Seminoles: 1837 during the Second Seminole War. Among those jailed was the famous Seminole War Leader, Osceola.

The Plains Indians: In 1875, 72 Native Americans of the Kiowa, Cheyenne, Arapaho, Comanche and Caddo nations arrived at the Castillo. Mostly men, they stayed there until 1878.

The Apaches: From 1886 to 1887, 491 Apache people were incarcerated in the Castillo. Only 82 of them were men. The rest were women and children, including Geronimo's wife.

4. **The graphic used on the cover page of each book section:**

This is one of many pen and ink drawings done by Mr. Ernest Myers. He drew it from a photo he took at the Castillo de San Marcos in 1875 when the Plains Indians were imprisoned there. It shows a white man speaking with a Native American guard who is dressed as a solider of the United States Army.

5. The Spanish Night Watch Parade:
Instead of the Spanish Night Watch Parade, the city of St. Augustine now has a nighttime event titled the British Night Watch and Grand Illumination that occurs during the Christmas holiday season. Very similar to the parade described in this book, it features red coated, colonial British reenactors who celebrate the control of Florida by the English from 1763 through 1783.

6. The Blessing of the Fleet:
The Blessing of the Fleet ceremony as described in this book takes place every year on Palm Sunday.

7. St. Augustine in 1885:
Jeff's descriptions of the city from his two visits there during 1885 come directly from multiple sources found in the St. Augustine Historical Society's Research Library.

Acknowledgments

To:

My wife Barbara,
without whose love and constant support, this book could
never have been written.

My daughter Nicole and her husband Marcelo,
for their appreciation of my work and
their wonderful encouragement.

My son Greg,
http://www.gregsgallery.net/
whose professional photography of the keys on the cover of
this book perfectly captures a vital plot element.

My son Fred and his wife Heidi,
for their great interest in the book and support.

Novelist Chuck Dowling,
http://www.chuckdowling.com/author.htm
for his friendship and initial editing of this book that set
me on a solid footing.

Mary Ann de Stefano,
http://madaboutwords.com/
for her expert content editing and literary guidance.

Kitty White,
for ridding this book as much as possible of typographical errors and correcting my terrible punctuation.

Charles Tingley,
Senior Research Librarian, at the St. Augustine Historical Society Research Library
http://www.staugustinehistoricalsociety.org/library.html
for his unending patience and helping me to get my historical facts right.

Gary Stehli,
old friend, extraordinaire,
who allowed me to take up residence in his St. Augustine home more than once for weeks on end to write parts of this book. I also owe Gary for permitting me to use his likeness as the character Lyle, the homeless guy, in the trailer for this book.

Rob and Amy Siders,
the book formatting team,
https://52novels.com/
who have made the various versions of this book so its contents are attractive and read with great ease.

Michael Lynch,
Senior Faculty Member, The Art Institute of California–San Diego,
http://www.bookcoverdesign.com/
whose expertise in creating the cover for this book makes it a true work of art.

Julia Hendrix,
my social media marketing assistant in Oklahoma,
http://asyouwishreviews.blogspot.com/
who kept prodding me to complete this book so she could
continue effectively spreading the world about
The St. Augustine Trilogy.

Cheree Crump,
from South Carolina,
who brought the characters and plot for this book to vivid
life by creating a fantastic trailer.

About the Author

Doug Dillon writes for both young people and adults. He has written a number of articles for Boy's Life magazine in the fields of history, science and entertainment. For many years, he worked directly with troubled teens and their parents in a variety of public school settings. In his long career as an educator, he also taught history and geography at both the middle and high school levels. Doug lives in Central Florida with his wife Barbara. Together, they wrote a nonfiction book about their own paranormal experiences titled, *An Explosion of Being: An American Family's Journey into the Psychic.*

Doug invites you to visit him on his website at
www.dougdillon.com

CPSIA information can be obtained at www.ICGtesting.com
Printed in the USA
LVOW11s1559301113

363343LV00001B/2/P